I0646527

ENDURING YOUR LOVE

A RIVER FLATS SERIES

—————— BOOK 2 ——————

Sheryl M.

Enduring Your Love
A River Flats Series Book 2

First published in Australia by Sheryl M 2025
www.sherylm-author.com

Copyright © Sheryl M 2025
All Rights Reserved

A catalogue record for this
book is available from the
National Library of Australia

ISBN: 978-1-7643038-0-4 (pbk)
ISBN: 978-1-7643038-1-1 (ebk)

Typesetting and design by Publicious Book Publishing
Published in collaboration with Publicious Book Publishing
www.publicious.com.au

All characters and events in this publication are fictitious, any resemblance
to real persons, living or dead, or any events past or present are purely
coincidental.

No part of this book may be reproduced in any form, by photocopying or
by any electronic or mechanical means, including information storage or
retrieval systems, without permission in writing from both the copyright
owner and the publisher of this book.

'Endings are hard my dear,
but oh, how the future shines.

Chapter 1

'Come on, Beth. You know you want to.' The whine in Jess's voice made Beth Kennedy's back teeth grind together. Their argument had been persisting for the last half hour, and the conversation was starting to grate on every one of Beth's usually patient nerves. Jess had been following her around the café trying everything, from bribing and blackmailing to now begging and whining to get her to go and help out the rowing team.

It wasn't that Beth didn't want to go and have a fun afternoon at the town's annual river festival, it was just that she had planned to stay back after the café closed early—on this one and only day of the year that Kathryn closed early—to practise some of her culinary skills before she left at the end of the summer.

That was only four months away. Even that small amount of time was not enough to ensure her skills were up with what she had guessed the other students'—who had also been accepted into the prestigious course—skill levels were most likely at. She had to enter the class knowing as much as possible. They would be already looking down at her once they discovered she was the one who had received the only ever scholarship given by the school. Beth knew the phone call from her boss, Kathryn Harrison, had helped greatly alongside her skills, but she was also aware that it added extra pressure to be as ready as ever, and motivate herself to know as much as possible. She not only had to do herself and her parents proud, but now also Kathryn.

Kathryn had met the head chef and teacher of the school at a charity ball she had been attending alongside her husband,

Drake, many years back, and Kathryn and the head chef had become fast friends. Beth had even met him once before when he came to visit Kathryn and Drake and stayed for the river festival last year. It had been his beautiful compliment about her food, and his encouragement for her to follow her dream and apply for the school, that had set her dreams into a flood of excitement. This too influenced her to study harder and watch shows to improve her skills. Being accepted into the school had surprised her parents and brought her to tears; however, Kathryn had not been surprised at all. Her boss had just cuddled and congratulated her, shouting everyone a round of drinks at Willy's pub to celebrate. So going to the festival this afternoon was not an option.

Picking up the last of the glasses and cups off the table and placing them on her tray, Beth turned and faced Jess. Taking a very slow, deep breath, so she didn't snap at her friend, she replied very sternly, 'No' and then walked off towards the kitchen.

Jess continued to follow her like a blue heeler on the back of a herd of cattle, just waiting to nip at the one heifer who decided to get out of line and not do as it was told. In fact, Jess was so close behind her, whining and complaining about her refusal to go, that when Beth stopped at the bin to empty the contents of a bowl, Jess bumped into her, causing her to drop the bowl and its contents into the bin. The large, black, plastic tub was filled with food scraps and napkins from the lunchtime rush, and smelt sour as the contents inside were disturbed by the heaviness of the plain white bowl.

'Oh Jess,' Beth snapped at her friend. Taking a deep breath and closing her eyes, Beth's shoulders dropped in resignation of understanding. If she didn't agree to go to the festival and help the girls out, Jess's dog-like, natural instincts would just intensify and she would run the risk of getting 'bitten'. And confrontation was something Beth hated and would run from if she could.

2

Jess, on the other hand, seemed to revel and succeed in it. It was a gift that had served her friend well over the years since Beth had moved to this little town in the middle of nowhere and they had met on her first day of school. When put to good use, Jess's tactics were very effective, which was why Beth could feel her reserve weakening with each second that ticked by.

'You know Beth ...' It was Kathryn who spoke. '... it is your last river festival and summer here for a while, especially if you get to go to Paris with Antione for Christmas next year. He only ever takes the top two students for the three months with him. You want to make sure you're in that top two, but you also need have to have some fun with your friends while you still can this summer.'

'That's why, instead of going to the festival, I should be here practising and honing my skill set. Not helping the girls ...' Beth turned and squeezed Jess's bicep to prove her point. '... and their muscles to pull the boy's team off the pier and into the water. See?' She squeezed Jess's arm again. 'They don't need me. They have all the muscle they need.'

Placing the dirty dishes into the sink, she walked back out of the kitchen. 'Besides ...' she called back over her shoulder, '... Drake will step in when you report back to him that I have said no.'

Drake Harrison was Kathryn's doting husband—and the team's coach. He had been their biggest supporter and drill sergeant since they were about fourteen years old. That man had endured being pestered by his twin daughters and their friends to help them become the best rowers they could be. The girls had all been at the Harrison house for Montana and Adelaide's birthday party sleepover and they had all been watching the Olympics when they had their brilliant idea.

After much sweet talking though, everyone knew when it came to his girls—Kathryn included—Drake was as protective as a fierce pappa bear but would never say no to them either, especially once they got set on something. He had convinced the community to support the team and provide all the equipment they needed—and they had trained hard. By the time the girls were sixteen years old, the team had reached the state championships. Over the past four years, since reaching states, they had made the national finals, finally winning the championships this year. Their last year as a team.

On returning home, the team had been welcomed with the main street blocked off with family and friends and the community all flying and shaking streamers and signs of congratulations at them. Today, it was expected the team would win in the river festival's most fiercely competitive tournament of the weekend—the cross-river tug of war.

The competition was set across the narrowest part of the river, and two wooden jetties had been constructed across from one another. Each team consisted of four members, and they would try to pull the other team into the water. The non-wet team would win. It had been a sudden death progress throughout the heats of the competition. Yesterday, the girls had won convincingly against the other teams who were local businesses and other sporting teams from the town. And today was the grand final—the main attraction of the afternoon for the river festival before the evening entertainment started. Saturday afternoon and night was always the biggest part of the festival. The crowds this year had already broken the previous year's records by a few hundred more tourists coming to the event, so the whole community was excited about the girls being in the grand final.

'You know he wouldn't do that, Beth,' came Kathryn's motherly voice. 'Drake wouldn't take away the chance for you girls to shine. You know he thinks of you all as part of the family and given Kate can't make it this afternoon because of work, if you don't go in her place, then the team will have to forfeit.'

'And ...' Jess added, '... we will never live it down if we let those SBs win.'

Oh, the SBs. Snobby Bastards. It was the name most of the kids who Beth went to school with, gave the kids who went to boarding school in the city. They were the kids of the rich farmers in the areas. The ones who grew and sold multi-million-dollar crops and looked down at the poor, simple folk of the town. They were the ones in hundred-thousand-dollar cars and utes. Their snobby wives and daughters wore pearls and chunky chains, with flowery dresses that looked like the fashion from the 1950s. They had power over the town.

However, if it wasn't for them, a lot of the 'normal' people in town wouldn't have a job. A lot of the services in town wouldn't be there either. Beth's own family's success and livelihood depended on those farmers and their businesses. She couldn't really get into hating them, but she understood the separation that her friends felt from the SBs.

Kathryn's café was an example. Their customers were mostly the 'normal' people of town. Usually, if one of the rich farmers or their wives came into the café, it was to seek out Drake or to ask Kathryn to cater for one of their functions, otherwise they wouldn't be caught dead in there. They liked to be seen and the only place for that was at the other café in the centre of town. The little place had opened ten years earlier and was only thriving because of its location and the fact that the only people who could afford the exorbitant prices, were the SBs.

Beth could understand the undercurrent from some of the people in the community, but she never said anything. Her parents had taught her to treat others the way she wanted to be treated, and if they were going to keep a roof over their heads and the banks away, she and her parents needed to be nice and friendly to the SBs. Jess, on the other hand, wanted to beat them at everything and anything—and today's grand final was no exception.

'Come on. Pleeease!' The whine made Beth's teeth grind. Could she really let her friend or team down now? Jess had played her hand well and Kathryn had not been any real help either. Picking up a chair and placing it upside down on the table so she could sweep and mop the entire floor of the café, Beth knew when she had been beaten.

Rolling her eyes and looking skywards, she sighed, 'Ok, fine. I will do it.' Placing another chair on the table, she turned to Jess, who was jumping up and down, clapping her hands. 'On one condition ...' Beth said to her friend. '... you have to mop the floor and finish helping me. Drake won't be happy if Kathryn misses out on seeing our great win.' Beth saw Kathryn's little smile of satisfaction before the woman turned away and back into the kitchen. She had been on Jess's side the entire time.

Jess stopped jumping and before running off to get the mop and bucket, she hugged Beth tight. 'Oh, and by the way ...' Jess said before continuing with, 'You're at the front, so hopefully you won't go in.'

'What? No!! I am the coxswain of our team. The boss. The leader. I am the one who yells at you all. I should be at the back yelling ...' But it was too late—Jess had already left. 'Just great. Just bloody great. I am going to end up in that bloody water, freezing my butt off while everyone is laughing at me. Just great. Bloody great,' she muttered to herself as she finished stacking the chairs with a little more force than before. 'How do I get myself into these things?'

Tom O'Loughlin finally found a parking spot he was happy with at the very end of the long row of cars. The last time he had been to the festival was five years ago. He had been fifteen years old, and had decided to come with his mum and sister for an afternoon of fun and games to support the community. His mother was a very strong believer in supporting the local community of River Flats, and giving back and helping where you could. So, that afternoon, so long ago, he and Megan had done as they were told and came with their mum.

What had been a single-day festival back then, had now grown to a three-day event. There was a town parade, starting and leading from the centre of town, out along the highway to the river flats of the river that flowed around the town, giving life to the community with its seemingly never-ending water supply. This parade marked the official start of the festivities.

There were show rides and river displays, water fun and contests, a formal ball the night before to crown the Miss River of the festival, markets and stalls, a live music concert from some big-name country artists, a triathlon, farewell breakfast, and luxury riverside picnics. The festival had become the main tourist event for the town, and drew in many tourists. Everyone in the town now looked forward to the weekend of celebration. It was like the opening of summer before the harvest session began.

Tom's long anticipated and dreaded homecoming late yesterday afternoon had been anything but a celebration. He had not set foot on his family's home property for nearly three years, and his strained relationship with his father only made the return home harder.

After finally succumbing to his father's constant screaming demands and threats—that his one and only son stop playing around and return home to learn the family business—Tom had receded and gave in to his father's wishes. The family business was important, and it was a business that had made them one of the most influential families in the area—and then some. Though Tom would rather just be like everyone else.

His great-great-grandfather had purchased a large amount of land after World War I, building onto the large amount he had already acquired from his father after his family settled the land. And as each son took over the running of the family business, each O'Loughlin heir had purchased more land—some in other states and territories—diversifying in different farming enterprises and businesses. This in turn increased the family's financial profits and power to a point where Tom's father now had eyes on a very prominent and prestigious political career. This all meant Tom was now forced to come home and continue the family tradition.

It was never a question of *if* he had wanted to do it—it was just expected. And 'no' was not an option. Maybe if Megan had been a boy, then he could've chosen and had more say, but she was a girl and they both knew she would never inherit the company. It just wasn't the 'done' thing in his family. The male heir always took over for the next generation without question.

It was a pity though. Megan was a brilliant and talented, secret CEO behind the scenes—not that his father would ever breathe a word of that to another soul. Megan was the one who did all the paperwork, the legalities, meeting set ups, and she mostly spoke with all the other managers who ran the vastness of the O'Loughlin's other properties. This included their real estate manager and accountant in the city. She did this for their father, but basically acted as their father, even sending emails with his signature on the bottom. Megan had even taken over the full payroll and financial affairs for the entire O'Loughlin company when their payroll officer quit after getting yelled at one too many times. That led to others in the financial division leaving too. Megan was also the one ordering all the equipment, booking the contractors for harvest, and having the road trains ready to roll when cattle from the stations were ready for market.

Having no idea how his sister did it all, Tom was expected to learn it all from her this summer. In truth, his father was really all show and if it wasn't for Megan—and when she was still alive, their mother—Mathew O'Loughlin would have failed and lost the entire company. But failure was something that wasn't allowed in the O'Loughlin household.

Tom had been pushed to be the best at everything. He had been the captain of the rugby and swim team at boarding school, and had been awarded dux of the school in his final year. He had been a very popular student and had many friends, never once caring where or what the other boys' backgrounds were. He just treated everyone the same. His father, however, had not been happy about his attitude towards others and had tried to tell Tom, 'It isn't what you know in this world, but who you know. Hanging out with nobodies from nowhere won't help my ambitions or yours later in life when you follow my footsteps into politics.' Tom had just nodded his head and ignored the man he had to call his father. At the time, Mathew O'Loughlin lived a sixteen-hour drive away, and what his father didn't know didn't matter.

'Tom!! Tom!!' one of Megan's friends called out as he made his way towards the large, chainwire fenced area of the festival. She was with a group of girls who were now ogling at him as he crossed the dirt road to the entrance gates. Desperately trying to remember which one she was, Tom politely smiled at her. All of Megan's friends always wore the same clothing, and as if to prove his thoughts right, a number of other girls all hurried over to the first girl, all wearing the same thing: boots, tight jeans, flowery shirts with the collar turned up, large dangly earrings, and caked-on makeup, which created a look like they had all either turned slightly jaundiced or had never seen a day in the sun.

Never understanding the fashion the girls wore, Tom inwardly shook his head at them all. Megan had at least learned to apply her makeup with a less-is-more approach, but even seeing her before she left the homestead a few hours ago, she had been wearing similar clothing to these girls. And her makeup was still very heavy.

Paying his entrance fee with a genuine smile at the elderly man sitting behind the makeshift desk in the hot tin shed that acted as the entrance to the river festival, Tom nodded at the girls who were clearly now waiting for him to walk over to them. Shoving his wallet into the back pocket of his jeans and sucking down the sick feeling he got when he knew what was coming, he remembered her name.

'Ashleigh. Girls.' He smiled tightly at each of them. They all giggled a little and blushed. Ever since he was a teenager, Megan's friends had done the exact same thing when he acknowledged them—giggled and blushed as they battered their eyes at him. At the age of eighteen, surely they would have grown out of it by now, but it appeared they still had not.

He was under no misunderstanding or illusion about what these girls were after. Their fathers had been drumming into them from birth how they must marry into another wealthy family to help their own. It was such an old custom and should have died out a century ago. Women should be allowed to choose who and what they do with their own lives and not have their fathers decide. But he knew personally, unfortunately for Megan, that it was not going to die fast enough for them both.

His family having both money and power, made Tom O'Loughlin a father's dream. Having girls act this way, was a regular occurrence. Once a girl realised who he was, they would work extra hard to get his attention. Most he was just polite to, but others he had to be a little firmer with, sometimes having to forcefully remove them or stop their hands from wandering all over his body, making him very uncomfortable with their bold actions. Others would try to get to him through Megan, which was what was happening now. Reflecting on his previous thought—life and finding someone to share that life with—Tom figured it really should be more about finding the one person in the world that you fall in love with and want to marry, and then spending the rest of your life together in love and happiness. Not this fake, who-could-do-a-better-deal type of life his father had planned for him and his sister.

His mother had told him many times over when he was young, just how important it was to have that feeling and to know what true love is, so when you met that one person—the one you just know is yours and yours alone, you would never let her go. Your heart would feel the truth of the other person's, and only then would you know what true soul-stirring love really was.

Jane O'Loughlin had been a true romantic. She had loved his father, Mathew, from the moment she had met him. Meeting in their early twenties, even though their marriage had been talked about between their fathers; Jane's father had been an old school friend of his grandfather's. But it had been luck and the divine— as his mother had called it—how she and Mathew had fallen in love with each other straight away. Both had done their families proud. His mother had been an only child from another wealthy farming family, and her father wanted the farm to go to a family who knew what they were doing. This not only related to the land, but also in a business sense for future generations to have the land passed down to them. And of course, to provide for his beautiful daughter.

Their marriage was not perfect, and his father had cheated on his mother many times; however, she had loved him until her dying breath. She told Tom how it was just what Mathew did— how most men cheated on their wives, and it was just accepted, but Tom had seen the hurt and pain behind his mothers' words when he had laid beside her as her breathing became more and more laboured. His father had been in the city, networking and building up his reputation for his political career ambitions, and most likely, Tom had guessed, seeing his latest lover.

Mathew O'Loughlin had missed his wife's last breaths. Jane had whispered his name as her tears slipped from the corners of her eyes for the man she loved but had abandoned her when she needed him the most. Her eyes were on Tom's as they closed for the very last time, her hand holding Megan's as she tried to remain strong for her children. Mathew had not returned home until the following day.

'Are you staying for the entertainment tonight, Tom? We could have a drink to celebrate your homecoming,'

Ashleigh asked. Tom's mind slammed closed the door he had unconsciously opened in his memories, and he swallowed the lump of pain in his throat as he stared at her, hoping his face was still plastered with his fake smile. Her smile reflecting back, spoke of her true intentions—to be seen having a drink together would send a message he didn't want to be sending with her or anyone else even remotely like her.

'We will see,' he replied dismissively cold before looking around them, hoping to give them the clear hint of now being bored of the conversation. Before jogging away towards a group of old friends he had just seen.

'Trust you to be surrounded by all the girls the minute you get back.' Tom was slapped on the back by Jack. Most of the boys here had been to the same boarding school he had. Three of them even went to the same university. But because he had stayed for another year to finish his other studies, they had come home to work on their family farms sooner than he had.

'Just make sure you leave some for us.' Tom turned to the other boy on his left and gave him one of his fake smiles. 'And not too broken hearted that we can't have some fun with 'em.' Trent laughed out loudly at his own joke as he looked to the others for praise and admiration of his thoughts. He was someone Tom had never fully liked but he was part of the boy's gang. Trent just had this way about him that got under Tom's skin, and his constant bad jokes and sexist comments were just embarrassing and cruel.

'Trust me, mate. They're all yours,' Tom replied cooly.

'Geeze man. You're too rigid. You need to dip your gear— and soon.' Tom just rolled his eyes and continued walking with the group through the crowd of young teens and children, all laughing and screaming. He ducked and weaved between the mass of people parading up and down the side show, some racing off to get to the rides, trying to beat their mates there before each other.

'You're filth, Trent,' said Noah, coming up behind Tom and squeezing both of his shoulders playfully. 'Don't worry about him, Tom,' Noah stated and pushed in between Trent and Tom with a quirk of a smile at him, completely ignoring the glare Trent shot him. 'Come on, we need you for the cross-river tug of war.' Noah strode confidently, but a little cocky beside him. 'Jeff is probably off chasing Kate. Trent doesn't want to get his new boots wet, and Dallas is just plain scared. We need a fourth. You up for it?'

'Do I have a choice?' Tom replied with a ruthful smiled, the competitor in him raising its head. 'Who are we up against?'

'Oh, that's the best part. It's the girls rowing team. They are gonna get all wet.' All the boys laughed as Noah rubbed his hands together, a big goofy smile on his lips, like a little kid in a candy store, not sure what to do with himself. 'We can check out what those sexy titties look like underneath without lifting a thing—if you get my drift.' He squeezed Tom's shoulder again.

'Well, maybe something will be lifting,' said Trent. Tom and the other boys just groaned and rolled their eyes at him. Some things were just not meant to be said out loud. Continuing towards the main entertaining area for the afternoon, Tom passed many people he knew or who knew of him, but he didn't stop and talk. He used the group of boys around him as a shield to get himself to where he wanted to go. He stayed cocooned in their sheltered group. It was comforting without the need to fake who he really was.

Hearing the announcer calling out their event, the boys pushed through the large crowd on their side of the river, from where the girls had won the coin toss, and elected to stay on the festival side. They declared loudly as they reached the official, that they were 'here and ready for their place in the final of the cross-river tug of war event'.

Chapter 2

When the girls' team was announced, the noise from the local crowd was near deafening, and Beth couldn't help but smile and wave at them. She blushed a little when she heard their loud cheers and wolf whistles mixing with the celebration of their arrival. The community support had grown each year—as had the girls' skills. People respected and supported them.

Jess had even been offered a job she had previously been declined, the boss seeing her dedication to rowing and the team's success at the national titles as something that may transfer into her new position. It had, and her friend had proven herself so valuable to the company, she had been given a promotion and offered more money within six months of starting. With Jess's dreams for the future now looking like they were becoming a reality, her boss had invited one of the top managers of the company to come up this weekend from the city, especially to meet Jess and enjoy the festival.

Some of the companies in the area saw the weekend as a lazy way to network and build team spirit within their employees. The business teams were some of the most fearsome in the cross-river tug of war, especially when pitted against each other—dealership against dealership, contractors against contractors. Jess's boss had believed if the big boys from the city could see Jess's competitiveness and talk to her in person, then maybe she would be able to climb higher in the company to keep growing her career. So far, it had been a success for her. Last night, after seeing her in action with Kate, Montana and Adelaide, pulling team after team into the water, the manager and his wife had asked Jess to come to the city the following week to talk more. And they even asked her to stay with them when she did.

Looking back over to her friend now, Jess was waving madly, and jumping up and down on the small timber jetty as she encouraged the crowd to cheer even louder. She was determined to show her bosses and the community what her dedication and hard work could achieve.

Seeing Jess's excitement and enthusiasm, Beth laughed and allowed the energy of the crowd to pump the adrenaline faster through her body. She wasn't as strong as the other girls, but what she lacked in physical strength, she believed she made up for in rallying her troops for battle and keeping them pushing harder.

Drake was waiting for them at the end of the jetty. He wasn't in his normal boots, jeans and hat today. Instead, he was in bright orange board shorts with palm trees all over them, and the team's bright pink shirt with the sponsors' names written all over the back. Beth had never seen him out of jeans, and never here in town with the team's shirt on. He had only worn the hot pink shirt at their race days. It was definitely a shock to her and others around them as she could hear him copping a ribbing from a few of his mates standing beside him. Her father and Kate's dad were the worst, but they laughed alongside their mate.

Leading the girls to him, once Adelaide and Montana stepped up onto the deck, Beth took off her sunnies and gave Drake the once-over look with a raised eyebrow and a smirk. 'Wow, Drake. You're looking very colourful today.'

Jess jumped up onto her back and burst out laughing when she saw what Drake was wearing, instantly landing back to the hard timber boards under their feet. She was killing herself laughing at him. 'Jesus, Drake. Can you turn down the ultrabright white light coming from your legs. It's blinding me.' Giggling when he looked down at his legs, he kicked out one and looked at it like he had only just realised the poor thing had probably never seen the light of day before. A wicked smile crept across his face as he joked backed at her and tilted his head to the group of young men walking up to take their spot opposite the girls on the other side of the river.

'It's not to blind you; it's to help distract the boys on the other side.' The girls all followed his nodded direction. Each one of those young men had a beer can in their hands. They cracked them open, foam spraying everywhere while they laughed and joked between themselves, slapping each other on the back. Smiling to herself as she took in the scene before her, Beth quickly turned to her team, huddling into a private circle, coach Drake included. They all smiled widely at each other, the noise of the crowd now fading into the distance as they talked strategy.

'So how are we going to do this? A massive, quick jerk and pull straight away, or do we want to put on a show and make them think they have a chance?' Jess asked, looking around at Montana, Adelaide, Drake, and then finally to Beth. Everyone was suddenly looking at her and waiting.

'I think we need to give the crowd a show. It is, after all, the grand final. And we can't make it look too easy otherwise some might say its rigged.' Beth winked at Drake, and he gave her a smile of knowing. He knew she had seen what he had, and because of that little bit of ego and thought, Beth knew the girls would win. If those boys didn't come prepared, then so be it for them to lose.

'Our big sponsors will like that, and it might help get them onboard next year for the girls who want to go to state and nationals.' It was the first year the other girls' team in the community had decided to really put the effort into their training, and with Drake's help, they too were hoping to get to the state finals. They just needed to ensure the sponsors were still willing to hand out the cash and support them.

'So, it's a "let them think they can win" plan and then, when I give the call, we will pull them all in with a massive jerk and pull. They all need to go in.' Beth turned for a quick glance back at the boys before looking back to her team, making sure they all understood. Each one nodded, and with their hands on top of her outreached hand, they cried, '**Go Swans**!' The cry went out over the crowd, and it made the mass of bodies all cheer louder and call it back to the girls.

Tom wasn't sure how it had been decided he was to be at the front, but he didn't like it. If they lost, he would be the first one to hit the water, and that river water looked awfully cold today, even in this early summer heatwave they were having. This local, young farmer team he had been thrown into at the last second because Trent was scared and Jeff couldn't be found, seemed to be the underdogs. And when they were announced, there were even some boos among the crowd's cheers. Never a good sign, though he had to admit, being the underdog was new but it also made his blood pump for a win.

Putting down their beers for safekeeping at the end of the jetty, Tom asked the boys seriously if they had a plan. Laughing at him, they replied, 'Hell no. Just get these girls all wet. They don't have a chance against our muscles and good looks.' Jack laughed and puffed out his chest, and just to prove their point to him, they all held up their arms in a strong-man pose.

'We're doomed,' Tom joked backed and laughed as he took another sip of his beer. He then studied the competition across the water before setting his drink down like the others had done. The girls were in a huddle, and he had to hold in a giggle when he saw the large, white-legged man standing in with them. Drake took that second to look over and give Tom a wink. He knew that look and, in that moment, he knew the boys had got it wrong. These girls were more than up to the task of taking them on—and possibly winning. Tom's stomach dropped a little and he glanced down at the murky, muddied water before rising his gaze again and seeing Drake's smile widen. Nodding back at the man across the river, Tom returned to the now shirtless boys.

'What the …?'

'It's to distract them with our sexiness and sculptured muscles,' Noah said boastfully with a grin, clearly proud of himself for coming up with the idea. Braydon and Jack were doing their best iron man poses for the crowd of girls standing beside the jetty giggling and blushing.

'Come on. Get yours off.' Noah reached for Tom's shirt and tried to pull it out of his jeans as Tom jumped back.

'Hell no. You idiots can get rope burn on those things you're trying to call muscles, but I'm not.'

'Righto. Be the chicken then,' Noah mockingly sulked. 'It's not like you need any help getting the girls anyway.'

'Yeah, yeah, yeah, whatever you reckon,' Tom replied with a smile. The boys thought it was so easy for him to get the girls, and it was, but not the right one for him.

'Ladies and gentlemen, boys and girls. Are you ready to watch the biggest battle of the year? Our national rowing champions taking on this year's young farmer team. Both have been fast and furious in every round, leading up to today's battle of the sexes, neither giving an inch of ground—or wood as it happens to be,' the announcer said excitedly over the loudspeaker. 'So, tell me ladies and gentlemen, who is going for our young farming men?' The crowd roared and booed, and some girls screamed with excitement as the boys slapped each other and jumped around, spurring themselves, ready for battle. Finally picking up the heavy manila fibre rope and setting themselves in a line, Tom took a steadying breath as his body pumped, ready to put on a show.

'Who is going for our national champions?' came the voice over the speaker. This time the crowd roared so loud, the sound vibrated in Beth's chest and made her heart race with excitement and anticipation. Drake stepped off the jetty, making sure he was close enough to the team to give guidance, but also where he could see the boys and help Beth to know when to give her signal. He was setting himself up for a big battle.

Looking across the water, Beth watched as the leader of the boys' team—the only one with his shirt on—took his slack of the rope and tested it in his hands. The two behind him had taken their stance, and the one at the back had wrapped the rope around his naked top half. Beth smiled again and took her time to take the measure of the young man opposite her. They still had not picked up on their vital mistake and she was not about to yell across the water to inform them.

Taking the slack from the water and waiting for the girls to do the same, Beth watched him. His eyes finding hers, he stared across at her. His smile semi-confident, he winked at her, but she remained straight-faced and took a steadying breath. The crowd started to grow silent with tension, rippling like a wave until the entire event seemed to be waiting with bated breath for the competition to start. The boy behind the leader took the quietening of the crowd to yell over to them.

'Hope you girls are ready to get all hot and wet.' Before Beth could reply to the sexist comment, Jess yelled back, 'When you're all cold and wet, you can go and comfort your little shrivelled thing yourselves, while we celebrate kicking your butts.' The crowd rumbled with laugher as Jess was given the 'bring-it-on' signal by him. The battle lines were now drawn and set. Focused on the rope and the person in front of them, the teams went into full competitive mode.

'The rules are simple ladies and gentlemen. The first team to pull the other into the water—even just the leader—will win and take home our grand trophy and prizes.' The judges took their spots on either side of the river and signalled to each other they were ready as the announcer read out the major sponsors for the event. The crowd grew silent as the teams were instructed to tighten the last of the slack.

Beth took a calming breath as she rubbed the sole of her shoe hard against the solid timber hardboards under her feet and locked her legs into place. Her sneakers locked in against the smallest of ridges in the wood. The little kotch was the reason why Drake had been so adamant about them getting this side of the river, every round. No one seemed to know it was there, and with their shoes, they had better grip than their opponents.

Smiling with satisfaction, her heart beating a strong, steady rhythm, Beth felt the girls take the weight of the rope. Montana, the heavier of the group, locked her legs in and leaned right back, the excess rope to her side to ensure it didn't get wrapped around her or tangled in her feet. A cool determination settled deep in Beth's stomach. Closing her eyes, she breathed deeply and calmly, slowly waiting for the games to begin.

Tom, with a sinking feeling in his stomach, watched the girls take their stance. These girls were strong and fit—and here to win. Montana, one of Drake's twin girls, had taken a completely different stance to the one Braydon had taken. Even though Braydon was the biggest of the boys in both height and weight, he had not taken the same amount of rope as Montana had. None of the boys had. Tom was the one holding most of the slack. The feeling turned to a rock, sinking fast into the depths of his guts. He tried not to let the emotion unsettle him.

Watching the leader, he studied her as she positioned her legs and arms. Her blonde hair was tied back into a messy ponytail, and she shifted her loose-fitting shirt, tucking it into the back of her shorts, so it was pulled tight against her breasts. The shirt now outlined the curves of her body, and Tom found himself fully distracted by her, not focusing on what he was meant to be doing. She twisted her foot into the timber at her feet and looked up, directly into his eyes. Tom's heart skipped a beat and then thumped so solidly in his chest; he felt all the air leave his lungs. With a little smile, she closed her eyes, and Tom took every millisecond of it into his memory.

'GO!!!!'

The rope pulled his arms, and he was nearly thrown off balance instantly. Braydon's weight was the only thing that caught them as Noah and Jack were lurched forward. It was then Tom felt his boots under his feet start to slip on the timber surface.

'Shit!' he thought. They had not thought about the grip on their boots. The girls had though, and it was the reason they were all wearing sneakers and building friction just before they started. They had planned well for this battle. The boys had just thought victory was going to be easy. Easy it was now not.

He could hear the boys grunting behind him, swearing under their breaths at the shear strength and pulling power these girls had. They too, were also only now realising their boots were sliding across the timber, and each time they needed to adjust their stance, the girls pulled harder and gained a few more precious inches of rope.

The pain was even worse than being dragged by a horse. Tom's hands and arms were burning. His entire body was locked tight, fighting to gain even a millimetre of rope back from these girls. But with the pain he was in, even that meagre amount of rope seemed impossible. Braydon was crying out in pain from the rope wrapped around his body. It rubbed his bare skin raw. The need to impress the girls and take an easy victory was now completely gone. They all had to fight hard and concentrate if they were going to win.

'COME ON. PULL!' Tom yelled. He was sweating and trying not to look at the water as centimetre by centimetre, it got closer. 'If I go in, you bastards are coming with me! NOW BLOODY PULL!'

Sweat was building under his cap and in his burning hands. He could hear Drake yelling instructions to the girls. The big man was watching him while instructing the girls on what was going on. This let the leader give instructions to her team and keep her focus on herself. Were they working as hard as the boys? With a split-second look, it didn't appear so.

They were holding their ground as they fought to gain rope from the girls. Gritting his teeth and pulling forth every ounce of strength and determination he had within his body and soul, Tom lectured himself about not going into the water without a fight. The leader, and competitiveness deep within, started to really bite like it had the day he led his school rugby team to victory in their grand final. Coming back from an impossible loss, they had won with a winning try scored by Tom himself. He was not going in today. Summoning all his strength, Tom planted his boots as hard as he could to the timber beneath him and, leaning right back into his thigh and butt muscles, he pulled, even managing to gather some rope from the girls.

'Come on, girls!!! You've got 'em!!!!' Drake was yelling at them. 'I think Tommy boy has realised that those fancy boots they're all wearing are not good on smooth timber. He's knuckling down, Beth. Don't let him get a taste of victory or he will put it over you and win.'

Beth was not going to let 'Tommy boy' get the best of her and win. The boys' egos were going to get the cool down they deserved. She could hear the one who had wrapped the rope around himself, cry out as it cut into his skin. They had not come prepared for her team. They thought it would be an easy victory and they now knew the truth; her team was the best, and she knew it, which fuelled her on more. They had to win.

'HOLD IT, GIRLS!!! HOLD IT. WE'VE GOT THEM, JUST KEEP HOLDING IT!' Beth kept repeating those words loudly through her gritted teeth, to the girls over her shoulder, hoping they could hear her over the roaring of the crowd. Everyone was going wild, screaming and cheering loudly while jumping around and wanting more. Beth's shoulders were burning and felt like they were being pulled from their sockets. Her body, pulsating with pain, began to quiver and shake as the strain against her body, that these boys were inflicting, tore at her flesh and muscles. However, her feet remained locked in place, and her balance had not wavered—thank goodness.

They were holding their ground and were even gaining, little by little, some rope back. But for how long? The boys were fighting hard and somehow, unhuman like, they seemed to be getting stronger. The rope was now pulled straight and taut across the river. It truly was an epic battle, not only of strength and power, but of grit and determination, ego and pride. These boys were not going to let a group of girls show them up, especially girls they had felt were beneath them. The battle lines had been drawn today in more ways than one and now it was up to Beth to ensure that the girls walked away victorious. They had to prove that no matter what, they were equal to the boys.

Drake was yelling that the boys had found their groove, and Braydon, the one at the back with the rope around his waist, was trying to lock in his stance. 'You can't let him get in that position, Montana!' he called. 'He will overpower you, the brute of a thing he is.' Drake stated slightly more quietly, so as only the girls would hear, 'Now, come on, girls. Dig deep.'

He kept his encouragement up. Even when Montana was grunting back at him how Braydon could kiss her ass if he thought he was going to get the best of her. 'If you can talk, Montana, you still have strength enough to beat him, so pull my girl, PULL!' Drake winked at her. The proud father he was.

His girls had grown up not only physically strong but also with a very strong and proud mentality. Tell a Harrison girl 'no' and watch out. If they wanted something badly enough, nothing usually got in Montana or Adelaide's way.

Jess was starting to lose her grip. Beth could feel it. 'Jess. If I go in this water, I'm taking you with me, God dammit. You got me into this and promised I wouldn't go in. YOU will *not* let me go in! Do you hear me?' Beth's hands were on fire and her legs were shaking. She could hear the boys yelling and struggling. They were starting to gain more rope with each passing second. The crowd was still going crazy and were so loud in their enthusiasm, she almost missed Drake's code word. It was time. Gathering up all her strength, she roared over her shoulder, '1,2,3 ... NOW!'

They were winning. Tom wasn't going to go in the water. 'We've got them now, boys. Pull!' Slowly, one hand over the other, they were gaining, and they were about to see all those girls fall into the water. A surge of more adrenaline and excitement went through him. This was about to end. The pain and torture would be over. They only had to give an almighty pull and end it. Tom drew a deep breath, ready to summon the boys to give one last pull.

He felt the rope give a little, a microsecond before his brain registered the move. His hands, automatic and without thought—along with the other boys—moved to gather more rope. The rope was slightly loose in their hands and their bodies weren't locked with the weight and strain of the girls pulling. Tom gripped the rope with both hands as he pulled it in, but he was suddenly jerked with such force, completely surprising him. The rope, and his grip on it, propelled him forward. Stumbling forwards, he managed to quickly catch himself on the edge. He balanced and rocked on the tips of his boots. But it was too late. The momentum of the rope being pulled so fast, and with shear strength, had propelled the boys behind him too. Noah and Jack slammed into Tom's back, and he went headfirst into the water. His body had corrected the others' balance and stopped them from falling in behind him. As he hit the cold murky river water, he cursed and spluttered at them through a mouth full of water.

Chapter 3

The rope went slack as they gave a heaven almighty pull. Stumbling back, they fell one on top of the other, Montana on the bottom taking all their weight. They had won. The crowd was laughing and cheering so loud as the girls laughed and lounged there together in a pile of legs and arms, sweat and pain, in their own private and exhausted celebration. It wasn't graceful at all. Everything hurt and their breathing was heavy. Only when Montana started to complain she couldn't breathe, did they all roll off of each other and struggle to their feet, Drake helping each victor to stand. Within the circle of his strong arms, he gave them all a congratulatory hug, his smile part that of a proud father and part one of a gloating coach.

Finding strength, Beth didn't know how, Jess was leaping and jumping around, now screaming with excitement as she moved to the edge of the jetty to tease the boys. However, they were too busy asking their leader, 'Tommy boy', how the water was and if he had brought any spare clothes. His reply was to splash them with water, obviously not impressed that he had been the only one to go in and not them.

Drake walked to the edge near where Jess was still trying to get their attention, and called out to them. 'Tommy, me boy. You had better get that wet and sorry ass of yours over here and congratulate these girls for whipping your butt.' He nodded to the others. 'You too, boys.'

Nobody disobeyed Drake Harrison. He was a large man and always followed through with his promises. He had known all these boys since they were toddlers causing trouble at swimming lessons and Pony Club, all of which, he was president and/or coach of. If Drake Harrison said he was going to dish out a punishment if you kept disobeying him, he dealt out the punishment he had threatened.

Never had Beth seen or heard a parent try to stop him or get upset with him over his actions. They all knew that was just him. If they didn't like it, they either had to leave or shut up. He was a strict man who always demanded the boys treat girls respectfully, and at the end of any competition, no matter the outcome or what had occurred during a tournament, everyone shook hands and congratulated the winners.

He was a very well-liked and respected member of the community. He even did a lot of public speaking for charities at local formal functions and in the city. He spoke about his work with abused and neglected horses and how he was an advocate for children from domestic violence environments. People often sought him out for his advice and support. So, if Drake ordered the boys to get over there—and now—then that was what those boys were doing. Tom decided to swim. He was halfway across anyway. Turning back, Drake followed Jess back to where Montana and Adelaide were still celebrating with the crowd.

'How about I help you out of there—captain to captain?' Her sweet voice floated over him as he did the last stroke to reach the ladder. Looking up at her, he found himself gazing into the most beautiful sky-blue eyes he had ever seen, her triumphant, gloating smile lighting up her beautiful face. Tom's heart gave an odd little squeeze. 'I bet the water feels nice and cool for your wounded ego. A calming and soothing balm for its embarrassment,' she teased him.

So, she just couldn't help but jest about his predicament hey? Well, she wasn't going to get away with it that easily. Smiling and taking a step up onto the ladder, Tom took her offered, outstretched hand, a tingle of electricity sparking between them. He could see she had felt the sensation too but was not going to acknowledge it.

'Yes, well it is nice down here. Maybe you should join me.' Before she could pull away, Tom pulled her from her squatted position at the edge of the jetty, into the water. Her surprised scream was quickly taken up by the sound of her landing headfirst, not gracefully, but all arms and legs, into the water.

The coldness of the water and the shock of his quick movement forcing her into the water, stole Beth's breath away. Choking and spluttering, Beth turned in the depth of the water and tried to come up for air. She was confused at which way was up and where the ladder was located. The mud from the bottom of the river, and its water, had been stirred up and was now mirky from the two days of events. Spinning and trying not to panic, Beth broke through the water's surface and took a much-needed breath. She found herself right up next to the ladder and the idiot who had pulled her into the cold water. She gasped again, trying to calm her breathing as she reached out her hand for the part of the ladder that was submerged and close to her, without touching him. With her leg, she tried to find the first rung on the slime-covered timber, but he was still standing on it.

'Refreshing isn't it?' he smirked as he looked down at her, watching her still trying to find the rung.

'Very,' she replied through gritted teeth as she wiped the water from her eyes. His brown eyes, filled with laughter, clearly told her he found her displeasure very funny. That he had shocked her, made him even prouder of himself for some stupid reason. An instant irritation burned through her body, and she clamped her jaw tightly closed.

'If you would get out of my way, I would like to get out of this water and enjoy my victory of kicking your ass with my friends.'

Without waiting for him to move, Beth reached in front of him and stepped on his foot to climb out of the water.

Wrong thing to do.

Her shoes, once grippy, now slipped on his wet boots he had gone onto the water wearing, and she slipped off, nearly slamming her face into the wooden ladder rungs. Tom's quick thinking stopped her, and instead of falling forward into the ladder, she fell forward into him, his arm going around her waist to steady her and stop her slipping back under the water. He easily supported her weight and held her to him. Chest to chest, she could feel his heart pounding into her breast and his corded muscles through his wet shirt contract and lock as he gripped her safely to him.

The sensation stirred something deep within her and sent a tingling all over her body until a little tremble caused her body to quiver in his arms. His eyes were locked with hers and for a moment, as she floated there in his arms, Beth lost all thought of where she was, and her surroundings. He saw her little shiver and she felt his arms tighten ever so slightly around her, pressing her even more tightly to his body as she leaned in towards him.

'Ahem. Are you pair ever going to get out of the water?' Drake's voice drifted down to them. The world swelled and reality washed over them. The crowd was still cheering and clapping, celebrating the girls win. Somehow, in all the noise and in the safety of the mostly covered area of the ladder, away from the majority of the crowd, Beth had allowed herself to get lost in the feel of this boy's eyes and muscled body. Heat rushing to her cheeks, she pushed him back and away from her.

Looking up at Drake and feeling her push at his chest, Tom swung away and let her up the ladder first. He had been so lost in the feel of her pressed to him, he had forgotten that everyone was around, that the festival was on the banks of the river they were in, just metres away. Letting her go first, he needed time to let his body's reaction to her settle before he climbed out into full view of all the town and tourists watching and waiting for them to emerge from the water. Her wet clothes clung to her and from his view, watching her ascend the ladder, he thought, *I am going to need to spend the rest of the day in here.*

The roar of the crowd was deafening as Beth reached the top of the ladder and stood. Jess, Adelaide and Montana had already been presented with the trophy and were still celebrating. 'Thanks for helping me,' Beth said as she stood beside them, dripping wet, her clothes clinging to her as water ran down her body. She must have looked like a drowned rat, rather than a winner.

'Oh, you looked like you were just fine,' Adelaide said to her as the crowd still cheered. 'Besides ...' Adelaide turned back to the front and smiled as the local newspaper reporter called for them to all smile and hold up the trophy. '... we all look great for the paper,' she jested to her closest friend.

Montana and Adelaide had been Beth's very first friends when her and her family had moved out here with little more than the car they had and the clothes on their backs. The girls had been there through everything a teen girl goes through and now this was the last year they were to be together.

They were all moving to different cities to study. Beth food, Adelaide dance, and Montana nursing. All three spread across different cities and states. They had promised to stay in touch but after this summer, they wouldn't see each other for a long time. Beth smiled and hugged one of her best friends to her. 'Aargh, you're all wet,' Adelaide squealed and laughed as the reporter snapped more photos of them.

'You just stay down there while my girls get their photos taken.' Drake stood guard at the top of the ladder so Tom couldn't get out. It was fine by him; he needed to stay there as long as possible. It should be impossible in this cold water for things to be obvious, but he could feel his body's response to her still evident against his jeans.

'Still a proud pappa then, I see,' Tom jested back when Drake turned and held out his hand for Tom to take it. Nearly pulling him straight out of the water and up the ladder in one fluid motion, Drake subtly reminded Tom just how strong of a man he truly was. Tom always thought of himself as a well-muscled young man, even though he wasn't as tall as most men, but beside Drake, Tom always felt puny and small. Not that Drake ever made him feel that way, it was just that Drake was pure muscle and solidly built. What some people would call 'built like the preverbal brick shit house'.

'You bet.' Drake's proud smile was clear for all to see. 'Good to see you finally back here at home too, me boy.' Drake shook Tom's hand and grabbed his shoulder in a friendly manner. The man had become somewhat of a father figure to him since his own father had not approved of Tom's decision to study and stay longer at university. Tom was only meant to study what his father had approved of, but with Drake's help and encouragement, Tom had found a real passion. Drake and Kathryn had been the only ones Tom had officially invited to his graduation. His father was there of course. He was all show like normal, but it was Drake and his beautiful wife, Kathryn's, presence there that day, that had made Tom's celebration all the more special and meaningful.

'Well, I would like to say it's been good so far, but you know what the old man's like.' Tom looked over Drake's shoulder as the girls walked off the jetty and disappeared into the crowd. Their leader, dripping wet, was the last to step off the jetty. Drake followed his line of sight with a small knowing smile and with a firm hand on his back, he steered him towards the end of the jetty after the girls.

'Well, at least you got to cool off in the creek before your temper for him got the better of you, hey?'

'Yep,' he replied distractedly. Tom still had not taken his eyes from the girl. People were congratulating him on his loss and offering to buy him a beer to drown his sorrows. But Tom heard none of it. His focus was on the sway of her body as she followed the other girls through the crushing crowd.

'... I can see you're not listening to me, so maybe you will hear this ...' Drake said as he stopped and stepped in front of Tom, who was still too focused on the captain to listen to him.

'Beth is very special to us, especially Kathryn. So, if you do the wrong thing by her, me boy, it won't just be her father that you will be dealing with. Got it?' Tom smiled a smile of a child who just got caught with its hand in the biscuit jar. 'Good luck. You will need it,' Drake added with a wink before strolling into the crowd.

Tom watched him go, and smiled when he saw the large man had found his wife. Drake pulled Kathryn to him, leaning her backwards over his arm. He gave her a passionate kiss in front of everyone, not once caring where they were or who was looking, before he righted her, his large hand remaining protectively on the small of her back. Drake steered Kathryn through the crowd, people congratulating him as he went, before moving out of their way.

Tom had always been in awe of the way Drake and Kathryn loved each other and their girls. His own parents had not been so affectionate with one another. His mother had always tried to cuddle and sometimes kiss his father, but he was always too busy to notice her most of the time. Her affections pushed away, Tom knew his mother had loved his father, and he had hoped his father had loved her too.

At the start he had. He had believed it was true because it was what his mother had told him, but by the end of her life, it was abundantly clear, his father cared nothing for his mother. Jane O'Loughlin had done her duty and provided the heir to the O'Loughlin fortune. She had added another generation to the family legacy, along with supplying more land to farm. She had also added more money to the company when everything, which was once her family's, was inherited into the O'Loughlin Property Group.

Understanding what happened after that, Tom now knew his mother was then nothing to his father. She was something only to take out and show off when a family needed to be presented socially. The rest of the time, Jane was left at Silverleigh—their family home—while his father was off working or in the city. Tom never wanted what his parents had. He wanted what Drake and Kathryn had, and he wanted to choose that and have it for the rest of his life.

Chapter 4

By the time Beth reached her car, which was parked under some big old gum trees near the end of a long line of other cars and utes in the makeshift car park, her clothes had started to dry with the last of the day's heat. She had managed to avoid most of the celebrational hugs and high fives, leaving the others to receive them from the many well wishes in the crowd. Jess was in full 'Jess' mode, ribbing and teasing the boys about losing.

Leaving them all behind, Beth had made a direct line for the rowing shed to dry herself with one of the spare towels that were always waiting in there. After drying herself off as much as possible, she had headed to her car with the intention of getting her spare clothes, which she had packed to change into once the battle was over—never thinking she was going to be soaking wet—and get changed in the toilets. The later idea had been squashed the moment she had seen the line into the girls' toilet.

The line was about thirty deep and not moving very fast by the looks of it. The festival committee had been taken by surprise with the amount of people attending this year. The proof of it was evident by the lack of female toilets and the quick need to extend the parking area on her arrival as fast as possible to accommodate the constant long line of vehicles entering the dirt river flat grounds. The nearest company with access to portable toilets, was six hours away and unable to bring them in the time needed. Everyone was just going to have to be patient. Later tonight, all the girls would be peeing behind utes and cars or going into the men's toilets anyway, so it didn't matter. Right now, however, she needed to get changed out of her semi-dried clothes.

Looking around to see if anyone was watching her in the setting sun's rays streaming through the trees above her head, her car door open, Beth quickly stripped down her denim shorts and pulled her shirt over her head before madly diving into the back seat of her car. Moving fast in the confined space so anyone happening past would not see her, now totally naked and thrashing around as she removed her wet underwear and hastily dried her skin with the towel, she discreetly tried to keep the towel over her body.

Fumbling around on the floor, she cursed at 'Tommy boy' for pulling her into the water. She had only packed a change of clothes for the night, not a spare set of underwear. Still fumbling, she gave a little squeal when her hands found a dry bra under the passenger side seat. What luck that she happened to have one in the car. What she wasn't lucky enough to find though, was dry undies. She would have to go commando.

Lifting the towel and sitting up straight, Beth quickly clipped up her bra, then tried to get her skintight jeans on. Struggling as she did, her skin still damp, she huffed and puffed, and moaned and groaned, before eventually getting them up. But she was unable to zip and button them closed. Pulling her shirt over her head, she took a quick glance outside and decided it was safe to get out with her pants undone. Jamming her feet into her boots, Beth got out of her little car and quickly zipped and buttoned her jeans, cursing under her breath as she caught one of her long and curlies. She needed to shave it again.

'That was the fastest change of clothes I've ever seen.' Hands frozen at her jean button, Beth whipped her head around. 'Tommy boy' was standing next to a decked-out Landcruiser ute. His now fresh pair of dry jeans hung low on his hips as his bare chest glistened in the setting sunlight. Beth couldn't help herself. She stared at him, all the moisture in her mouth evaporating. His chest was rippled with muscles and sculpted down low into his jeans as his hips narrowed. She had never seen anyone look so defined before. Her hands itched to touch the curves and indents to see if they were actually real.

He shifted in his dry boots and the movement broke the spell she had been under. Mentally shaking her head, Beth smiled at him shyly, an embarrassed blush staining her face a deep red. She had been caught openly staring at him with God knows what look on her face, and by the way he was smiling back at her, he had clearly known what she was doing in her car.

A thought suddenly crossed her mind. Had he walked past her car while she had been drying her naked body? If he had, and seen her, she would just die of embarrassment. Her cheeks now glowing an even brighter red and heating with the thought, Beth turned and flipped her hair upside down to dry it with the towel. She didn't know what to say to him. Somehow, he had robbed her of all her words and now, with that stupid look on his face, which she didn't quite know how to respond to, he began to irritate her. As rare as it was for her anger to do so, it started to rise.

Standing back straight, with her hair flipped back and hanging in damp, messy curly waves down her back, she turned to face him again. 'You know, you shouldn't be watching people get dressed in the privacy of their own car,' she called out to him over the two vehicles that separated them.

He had a smile on his face as his shirt slipped over his head. 'Well, it was a bit hard to not look when you're hardly wearing a thing.' A fresh blush climbed Beth's cheeks and a quick panic made her heart skip an odd beat in her chest, sending a flutter of humiliation down into her stomach. How dare he stand there looking like that and outright declare he had been spying on her as she dressed herself. The audacity of the ... so mad at him, she couldn't even think what to call him.

Slamming her door shut and ignoring him, Beth turned on the heel of her boot, shoving her wallet into the back pocket of her jeans and smoothing her shirt, a hand ruffling her hair, so it dried into its natural curl. She stormed away from him and towards her friends. She was done talking to him. He was just like all the other boys she had ever met—only after one thing and thought themselves God's gift to women. She was glad she was leaving at the end of the summer and had much more important things to think about than silly boys who thought they were men.

Tom ran to catch up with her as she walked with such pace. 'Hey! Wait,' he called after her as she ducked between a couple of cars, trying to elude him on her way back through the entrance gates. Following her idea, he did the same, quickening his footsteps and managing to come out right beside her. 'Hey,' he said again. Glancing over her shoulder at him, she stepped faster to keep distance between them.

'Just go back to your friends and leave me alone.' She couldn't look him in the eye. He had seen her naked and now obviously thought it was an easy way to get her into his swag for the night. *He would have to find someone else for that*, Beth thought as she stepped faster, into a near run.

'Hey, I'm sorry,' Tom said as his fingers gently wrapped around her wrist, slowing her to a stop, and turning her body to face him. The tingle thing happened again, just as it had in the water when he had first pulled her to his body. She could see he could feel the sensation also. His eyes flickered and a little frown creased between his brows.

Studying him way too closely, she cursed at her mistake and pulled her wrist away from him, taking a much needed step away to put distance between them. Her body was acting weird, and she didn't like it. He made her nervous but he also made her feel something she didn't want to label.

Tom was slightly taller than she had realised he was in the water. Being pressed against him, she had been able to look him in the eye while standing on his boot, half floating, half being lifted against his strong body in the water. But now, all she had to do was tilt her head up a little if she wanted to kiss him. The thought made her step back again. Well away from him.

Kiss him? Really? The heat and excitement of the day must be getting to her. She had only just met him and now she was dreaming of kissing him.

'Don't worry about it, okay? You've seen me half-naked and I've seen you half-naked. Let's just call it even and forget the whole thing ever happened.' She tried to sound non-complacent about it but felt the little waver in her voice as she remembered his bare chest. She went to move off.

'Wait. I'm Tom,' he said and then waited for her to introduce herself. And for a heartbeat, she didn't know what to do. She didn't want to give him her name, but then again, she did. Her nerves tingled and leaped, but Beth couldn't figure out whether it was a good nervous or one she should take note of and run. Her hesitation seemed to irritate him, and she looked at the gates of the festival, drawing out his wait.

He looked like the kind of guy girls always wanted to introduce themselves to, so making him wait, was a small victory. The frown between his brows deepened like he was really unsure of why she was not giving him her name. Then she saw the change. His irritation turned to curiosity. The fine line of irritation, now curiosity she never wanted to cross, was done. He was now interested in her more. Dammit.

'I'm Beth,' she said and walked away, leaving him standing there as she finally passed through the gates. She could feel his eyes on her and couldn't help but give a little smile when he called after her.

'For what it's worth, Beth, I liked what I saw.' She turned to face him, but kept stepping backwards. She blushed as she brazenly replied, 'So did I.'

The band was pumping, and the music was loud. Everyone was either dancing and singing at the top of their lungs, or at the bar talking and getting another drink. Jess had talked Beth into staying and celebrating their win for a little while longer. Now, she had to admit, she was glad Jess did. After the afternoon's excitement of their win and then her embarrassment with Tom, she had needed to let her hair down and forget about all of it.

Ever since Beth had seen him across the river that afternoon, the second their eyes met, her skin had been tingling. The feeling had only intensified and put her mind into a frustrating fog when he had held her in the water, turning the feeling into a full body shiver. It had awakened her soul with an odd pulse. And now she couldn't shake him from her mind.

Seeing his bare torso and feeling her body's reaction to his sculptured muscles—the faint dark hair line that disappeared into his low-hanging jeans as he dressed himself in the dying sunlight—was too much. She needed to just forget all about him and celebrate with her friends. But she couldn't stop herself from scanning the crowd, looking for him every few minutes.

Jess squeezed through the crush of the crowd towards the bar, dragging Beth along behind her. The noise was deafening and the heat of the night along with the large number of bodies all pushed together, dancing and moving as one, had started to cause Beth to quickly feel the effects of the last four rum shots. Mixing the shots with the beers she had been consuming since Montana had pushed one into her hands after she had returned from changing her clothes, she swayed a little as she tried to keep up with Jess.

Beth had nearly sculled the entire contents of that first beer, much to Montana's surprise, the second her friend had placed the can in her hands. However, the effects had not been as effective as she had hoped and were made worse, not only because of the rum shots, but because every time she looked around, trying to tell herself she was not looking for him, she would see Tom watching her, and that silly little nervous thrill would race through her body.

Thoughts of Tom's naked chest and that sensation he had given her when they had touched, drifted through her mind again now as she blindly followed Jess. Mixed with the haze of alcohol, it sent a full body involuntary shiver through her. Each time she allowed her thoughts to wander to him, she had needed to take a deep breath and calm herself. As the rum shots started to numb everything, that reason alone, was now why she allowed herself to be dragged back to the bar with Jess. She needed another one to help numb the feeling more.

Jess was becoming very drunk, very fast. Montana and Adelaide had stopped at shot number three and had both been on the beer and water, ever since. But Jess still had not learned when to stop and was in the mood to celebrate their win and her new promotion, with as much alcohol as possible. And tonight, Beth was her drinking buddy.

Usually the driver, even knowing she was opening the café in the morning with Kathryn, Beth didn't care. And as the night wore on, her care facture grew weaker and weaker. This was her last summer here in River Flats, and she had decided to go out with a bang, like Kathryn had suggested that afternoon. When this idea and confirmation of her choice had occurred, she didn't know, but it was now happening, and she was enjoying herself to the fullest.

Kate filled up the shot glasses with rum again and laughed as Jess threw it back and coughed as the sweet, sickly spirit burned down her throat. Beth had the same reaction, and it made Kate laugh even harder at them both. This stunning midnight-haired girl with the most beautiful cobalt blue eyes Beth had ever seen, was a member of their rowing team. But sadly, Kate had had to work in the bar for Willy that afternoon, so missed all the fun of them pulling Tom into the water. Wanting to celebrate with them, Kate had brought the girls the first round of beers of the night, and from then on, everyone else had kept filling their drinks, ensuring their hands were never empty.

Jess handed over another fifty dollar note to pay for the drinks as Kate refilled their shot glasses. Shaking her head, Kate smiled a brilliant beaming grin over Beth's shoulder as the warm tenor voice touched Beth's ear.

'This one's on me.' Tom's hand reached around her waist with a hundred-dollar note clearly visible in it. Her heart was flip-flopping as his other hand gently rested on her lower back, the heat evident through her shirt. Beth forced herself to breathe as Kate took the note with a flirtatious smile.

'The rest is for me, for later?' Kate winked over her shoulder back to Tom.

'Don't degrade yourself, Kate. You're worth more than that,' came his reply for her friend. There was a hint of laughter and respect in his voice. They knew each other—and well by the way they just flirted and bantered with each other in front of her. Beth frowned a little as Kate, happy with his reply, walked off to serve another customer, never giving Tom his change.

'I think I owe you girls a drink for managing to pull only me into the water this afternoon. Such skill you all have.' Beth turned in what room she had against his body, the crush of the crowd and the bar, and smiled up at him. He was watching her closely, his hands now on either side of her hips as he casually leaned his palms onto the bar at her back.

'Well, you didn't think *we* were going in, did ya, Thomas?' Jess pulled his eyes from Beth's with the comment. 'Well, at least we didn't, till you evened things out with Beth.' She nudged Beth in the ribs just as one of the boys they had been dancing with appeared and pulled Jess back onto the dancefloor, leaving Beth standing there with Tom.

'You know she is the only one in the world apart from my grandfather who has ever called me Thomas?' Beth giggled at the indignant look he shot at Jess as she disappeared back into the crowd, before coming back to face her. 'She has done it since we were in kindergarten.'

The crowd let out a large cry and surged backwards towards them, everyone moving and stumbling. Tom's quick thinking by locking his arms, taking the force of the shifting crowd himself, stopped Beth from being crushed between the bar and his body, only just letting himself press up against her. She relaxed her soft body against the full length of his more hardened, warm one, letting him feel her body react and shiver with the feel of him so close. The rum shots and his smell caused her mind to grow a little hazy, and she giggled, turning her head away to look blindly into the crowd around them.

'Beth, come on.' Jess appeared out of nowhere and yanked Beth back into the crowd and away from Tom. As she was dragged away, she could hear him yell at her.

'Where are you going?' Giggling over her shoulder, she just smiled a cheeky, seductive smile at him and winked as he disappeared into the mass of bodies. She was never this brazen or flirtatious. It must have been the rum and atmosphere.

Not one to give up so easily, and taking her beautiful smile as encouragement, Tom ordered another two shots of rum and went in search of her on the dancefloor. Finding her, took him longer than he wanted though. Ashleigh and her friends had halted his path through the crowd, asking him to dance and wrapping their arms around his neck. Removing and gently pushing the girls away from him, he didn't want to risk losing Beth in the crowd any more than he already had. Using Braydon as an excuse to get free, Tom moved away from them.

Seeing his closest mate dancing his usual wild country boy dance with Adelaide Harrison, he moved in a direct line for them. Tom and Braydon had known the Harrison girls since kindergarten and as the girls had been on the same team as Beth, surely Adelaide would know where she and Jess were on the floor. Pushing through the crush, he pressed on.

The music changed and as the next song's intro four bars started, the people around him all moved like an organised flash mob into lines. Tom froze where he was, the two rum shots still in his hands. He was unsure of what was going on. As the next beat of the song dropped, everyone moved in sync.

Line dancing.

Groaning and cursing under his breath, he didn't know what to do as he stood there looking like an idiot in the middle of the dancefloor. He had never lined danced in his life and now found himself in everyone's way.

'You're in the way, Tom!!!' Braydon yelled at him.

Tom turned to see Braydon dancing behind Adelaide. He was about four steps behind her as his friend watched her body and tried to copy what she was doing. Adelaide was laughing out loud as Braydon deliberately bumped into her, nearly causing the people around them to trip over.

The girls all around Tom, bumped into him, the rum spilling over his fingers as they criss-crossed their legs to the left and then back again before turning and stepping forward, walking in time with the beat. The dust their boots were making with the quick beat of the music, was lifting and creating a haze. He couldn't see where Beth had gone and now, he was stuck in the middle of this twisting, turning, two-stepping crowd movement, holding two shots of rum, having no clue what to do. His mind was still only on one thing—finding Beth.

The announcer was calling out and telling those who were in the way of the dancers, to move off the dancefloor. Tom looked over at Braydon and held up one of the shots in his hand. Braydon nodded and met him in the middle of the floor. After shooting the amber liquid down, and sharing a knowing look at each other, they turned in line with the others, but didn't follow the line dance. Instead, Braydon started their dance with the lawnmower move. Tom followed and as the large group around them spun on the beat, the boys found themselves the centre of everyone's attention.

As everyone else repeated the line dance moves, Tom and Braydon kept with the beat and performed their own Aussie-man shuffle. After the lawnmower, came the sprinkler and then the roping cowboy, a high energy leg slapping, and then sexy low-down riding a horse. This move proved to be very popular as wolf whistles and laughter came rippling through the crowd.

Getting inspired and more motivated at the attention they were getting, the boys laughed at each other as they repeated their moves again, this time with more hip action than before. Encouraged by each other's showing off, and the girls in the crowd cheering wildly for them, wolf whistling as the song neared its ending, Braydon reached out his hand and took Tom's, pulling him into a quick waltz turn. Braydon gritted his teeth when Tom touched the side of his waist where the tug-of-war rope had rubbed him raw earlier that afternoon. Tom moved his hand as Braydon quickly recovered, never wanting to show any weakness.

They were both laughing hard as Braydon unexpectedly decided to do a quick backbend dip with Tom. Losing his footing and stumbling, Tom landed hard on his butt in the dust, Braydon on top of him. The crowd erupted with laughter and applause as the song ended and another one roared through the speakers. The latest country rock song. Everyone started to jump and dance around them. The beat of the song was so loud it vibrated the ground and into Tom's chest as he remained still on the ground under the crushing weight of Braydon.

'Braydon! Get off, ya big bugger.' Tom grunted and sucked in some much-needed air as Braydon scrambled off him, holding out a hand for his friend and helping him up. They laughed and slapped each other's backs as they stood and regained their sense of balance. Tom had missed hanging with his mates. It was good to be home, he suddenly realised.

'So, you've got some moves too.' Her voice was barely heard over the noise of the speakers. Spinning around, he smiled when he saw Beth standing behind him, a beer in her hand and a slight sway to her body as she tried to stand up straight.

'Oh, I've got moves you haven't seen yet, baby,' he drawled back to her. Stepping into her space, his hand on her hip, their bodies only inches apart, he could smell the rum on her breath, mixing with a hint of something uniquely feminine. His body's response was instant. Skin tingling all over as his heart thumped wildly against his rib cage. She stood looking up, directly into his eyes and touching his soul, before slightly raising her eyebrows. A challenge.

Tom pulled her flush to him, taking her hand and spinning her around in an over exaggerated turn, with no coordination. Beth clung to him and laughed as she tried to keep up. Her arms raced around his neck, where she buried her face. Tom was laughing along with her. She felt so good pressed to him again. He gripped her tighter a second before letting go of her back and pushing her out and away from his body, her body spinning away from his. Tom never let her hand go, before he pulled her back, her body crashing into his. Turning her under his arm and then back into the tragic waltz he was trying to dance with her, to the fast-paced rock beat, Beth was giggling and laughing out loud, making him do so as well—a thing he had rarely done lately.

She was desperately trying to keep up, but her laugher and drunkenness was making it near impossible. It was down to whatever dance coordination Tom had just pulled from deep inside his body, that she was able to avoid slamming into anyone else. The dance ended with him spinning her out and letting her go as he bowed to her. Satisfied with himself, he laughed again as Beth curtsied to him with a nod and nearly found herself on the ground as she over balanced. Jess caught her at the last minute.

'Look at you, Fred Astaire,' Jess said, flirting with him over Beth's head as she stood. 'You swept Beth off her feet. Just like all the other girls.' Jess walked towards Tom and bumped her hip into his as she looked him up and down with mock desire in her eyes.

'If you ever find a need for sweeping me off my feet, Thomas O'Loughlin, then you know where to find me.' Tom looked at Jess and shook his head, laughing still at what he had just pulled off with Beth, and feeling very proud of himself for accomplishing it. He and Jess had grown up together, just like Kate and the Harrison girls, and she had always been outspoken. She had even sat on his head one day in Grade 1 when he told her that girls couldn't be cowboys; they had to just wear pretty dresses and cook. Jess hadn't liked his words, and she was much faster than he had realised. Catching him, she had pushed him over, sitting on his head until he took the words back.

Three years later, when he had left for boarding school, she had punched him for leaving her with all the 'horrible' boys. The punch had been so hard, it had left a bruise on his arm for two whole weeks. She was always so rough with him, and to prove his memory correct, as she went to walk away, Jess moved to grab him between his legs. Tom sensed the move more than seen it and jumped to the side as her hand swept past, missing him. But she had gotten her reaction and was already gone with a large smile on her face by the time he realised his mistake. She was still a bully and, in a way, she scared him more than he was comfortable to admit.

After watching her go to make sure she wasn't going to come back and leap on top of him, Tom looked up, and found Beth had vanished into the crowd once again. People were dancing around him, and now Megan's friends suddenly surrounded him, all talking and trying to dance with him at once.

'Dammit!' he swore under his breath as he pushed away from his sister's silly, childish friends.

She was gone again.

Thomas O'Loughlin. He was Thomas O'Loughlin. How could she have not known who he was? The O'Loughlin family was the wealthiest in the area and they had properties not just here but interstate as well. Very ... large ... properties. Tom's father was one of the most powerful men in town and his influence spread far and wide. They were listed as one of the top twenty richest farming families in Australia, two years running.

Beth had only met Megan, Tom's sister, by passing her in the street. She had looked down her nose at Beth with her usual snobby manners. That boy, who had seen her nearly naked that afternoon and had now danced her off her feet, was the heir to the O'Loughlin fortune. How could she have been so stupid to have not realised who the hell he was? No wonder everyone was hanging off his every word and all the girls were falling all over themselves to get to him.

Why was he wanting to have anything to do with her? She was nothing special. Was nothing like them. Her family had no money, and she was not part of his group of friends. The people he would hang out with, were not her people. A deep sinking feeling started to burn low inside of her stomach. She had met boys like him. In fact, his own sister's fiancé was like those very boys. Jeff had tried to come onto her one night at the pub, and he was one person who always made Beth's skin crawl.

Jeff had cornered her two years earlier in the bar at Willy's and asked her if she wanted to experience a real man's dick, other than the little one her boyfriend, at the time, had. She had told him very sternly, 'No', and when she pushed past him, he had grabbed her arm and hissed in her ear that she was nothing and his family could ruin hers in an instant. She had never felt so dirty, cheap or unsafe in her entire life. When she had told her boyfriend, Jay, about the incident, he had just told her to leave the bar, and said that by not defending him, she had embarrassed him in front of Jeff. They broke up that night and Beth had decided to concentrate on her studies, vowing no man would ever make her feel that way again. She had value and worth. Never again would she ever let a man treat or disrespect her like Jeff and Jay had that night.. Never again. No matter what or who he was.

Looking over at Tom now, from her hiding place near the end of the bar, Beth could see all the SB girls trying to flirt with, and touch, him. He looked to be trying to get out of there as he searched around the crowd, no doubt looking for her. She kept her head down.

'Who are you hiding from, Beth?' Kate said from behind the bar as she leaned over looking at Beth half ducking behind the large group of older men leaning on the bar, shielding her from being seen from the dancefloor. Kate knew exactly who Beth was hiding from, though still she asked her.

'No one!' Beth hissed back at her, causing one of the tall men in front to look over his shoulder and frown at her. Lifting his beer to his lips, he looked between her and Kate and then back to his mates as Beth scanned the area for Tom again. He was gone.

'Really?' Kate asked, not convinced. Beth looked at her, knowing Kate could see straight through her lie. Her friend stood back up straight, folded her arms across her chest and raised one eyebrow.

'Ok.' Beth stood straighter, now relieved she had dodged Thomas O'Loughlin's attention, and turned her body to face Kate directly over the bar. This was serious and she needed to know what Kate knew.

'Did you know that was Thomas O'Loughlin I pulled into the water this afternoon?'

With a frown and a look that said, *Yeah, everyone knows that. Didn't you?*, Kate looked firstly at Beth and then at the crowd, searching for him, before she came back to Beth, the realisation of Beth's dilemma now clearly shown on her face. Finally, Kate would help her get out of the dastardly mistake she had made that afternoon.

'Everyone knew that, Beth. Didn't you?' Beth shook her head. Her stomach started to roll.

'I didn't. I've never met him. Remember?' Her family had arrived in town when she was in high school. By then, all the SBs were in boarding school. She was never one of them and she mostly stayed to herself. How was she to know who he was?

'Well, I think you've gotten his attention now.' Kate looked over at the crowd again and then back to Beth, with a smile playing on the sides of her lips. 'I think you may need to get to know him, because he's coming this way.'

'What? NO. What does he want with me? Punishment for pulling him into the water?' Beth was beginning to feel sicker and sicker. She had probably breached some unwritten rule that says, 'Thou shalt not pull the O'Loughlin heir into the water or embarrass him in any way or thou shalt be publicly punished.'

'Don't be so over dramatic, Beth,' Kate scolded her, 'It's not you. He's a good one. Trust me.' Her smile turned a little whickered. 'What harm could be done by just talking to him? And you never know, a little summer night fun could be just what you both need. You should enjoy yourself. Especially when he looks as good as that.'

'You're no help, Kate,' Beth bit back at her with a frustrated hiss, staring Kate down with the best angry face she could drunkenly muster. But Kate just smiled wider, her blue eyes twinkling with amusement. She wasn't the least bit intimidated or scared at Beth's attempt to be fearsome. Beth did, however, feel the moment Tom materialised behind her, even before he spoke. Her skin warmed at her back and tingled all over.

'So ...' He used the same tone she had done before with him, as he breathed into her ear. 'Tell me. Are you still going commando?' Beth's eyes widened as she turned a brilliant shade of red, and embarrassment flooded her body.

'You saw?!!!' she screeched with shock. Everyone who was standing near the bar and in hearing distance, turned to look at them. Some had frowns, others just shook their heads and turned back to their friends. Tom just kept his eyes on her, pure humour and daring dancing in their depths. Beth ignored the stares of the others around them, but she lowered her voice so only he could hear. 'And here I was thinking you were a gentleman.' She turned her back on him, now desperate for another shot to numb her total embarrassment. She was never going to speak with him or even think about a summer night's fun like Kate had suggested. The humiliation was too much.

'I am a gentleman, but at this moment, I would love to be your jeans.' His warm breath tickled the little hairs by her ear again, his body brushed up against hers as one of the bar staff nodded at him when he raised his hand at her, his drink order silently placed. The entire time, Beth's body goose bumped and shivered at the images he had just planted in her mind, but her face turned into a blazing hot rush of embarrassment.

He was teasing her, and she was rising to the bait. Her face said it all. Standing as tall as she could, she slowly turned back to face him, trying not to drunkenly sway, and took a long, deep breath.

Wrong thing to do. Her stomach lurched and rolled. Tom's hands quickly rested low on her hips to steady her and stop her from falling back against the bar. With the heat of his body against hers, the wave of sensations he was inflicting with just a single touch, all started to make the world spin faster. She suddenly didn't feel well.

'Are you okay?' he asked as she leaned her head to his shoulder and closed her eyes, breathing in his scent.

'No. The ground is spinning, and you smell sooo good.' She swayed against his shoulder to the side, Tom pulling her more firmly to him. The effects of the rum shots and beers she had been sculling all night, suddenly hit her hard in the cool fresh air where she was standing.

Feeling Tom motion to Kate that he needed a bottle of water, she leaned heavier against his body and breathed in again as he replied, 'You smell good too, but let's get you out of here and away from everyone's prying eyes. If you're gonna get sick, I don't think you want everyone watching. Besides, I don't have another spare pair of boots with me for you to ruin.'

'I did not ruin your boots. You were just too silly to take them off before you went swimming.' Giving a little chuckle and wrapping his arm around her waist, her head lulled on his shoulder, Tom pushed through the crowd to the seats around the corner from the bar and dance area. Beth was now fully leaning on him as her legs couldn't carry her weight anymore. Kate materialised with a bottle of water.

'Beth, you have never been one to get so drunk. What were you thinking?' Kate gently scolded as Tom lowered her to the metal bench seat.

'I wasn't. I just didn't want to be thinking of touching his body.' Beth slurred her words a little as she looked up at the three Kates swaying before her. Blinking to try and see only the one person, she looked back at Tom, now kneeling in front of her, with a frown on her face. 'You really are sooo sexy.'

'You're not bad yourself, but not like this,' he replied with a boyish smile, his thumb pressed to his lips as he leaned on his one knee and watched her.

Kate rolled her eyes and looked down at Beth sitting on the chair. Handing Tom the bottle of water, she asked, 'Are you okay with her? I need to get back.'

'Yep, I will take her home.'

Beth shook her head and tried to stand again. 'No. I will just sleep it off in my car. I have to work tomorrow morning.' She stumbled back into the chair, hard. She had drunk too much and now couldn't look after herself. This was not her. She never did this. Her stomach rolled and she put her head on her hands between her legs to stop the sensation.

'Here, sip this.' Tom helped lift her head and gave her a sip of the water.

'What do you want from me?' Beth asked, looking at him, her face so close to his, as she ignored the water. 'I think you're the most cutest boy I have ever seen and if I wasn't so drunk, I would rip off all your clothes right now and run my hands all over you ... just to see if ...' she waved at his body, '...all of that is real.'

'Is that right?' he smirked at her, his ego getting a boost.

'Yep, but what do you want from me?' Shaking her head at him, now confused at what she was trying to say but hoping it made sense, she looked back at the ground. 'I'm nothing special and you can have any girl here you please. What is it you want?'

Turning her head back up to look at him through squinty eyes, she found him just staring at her, his eyes darting between hers, then to her mouth, before returning to her eyes again. This time she was sure he was as confused as she was about his own intentions. Ever so slowly, Tom moved in to touch his lips to hers.

'This,' he replied softly.

Beth pulled backed, horror in her eyes. He stood, but it was too late. Beth projectile vomited all over him—from his shirt to his jeans, and all over his boots.

Chapter 5

She was dying. Why did she do it to herself? It was all his fault. If he had just left her alone and not seen her naked, she wouldn't have let Jess talk her into getting so drunk. She wouldn't feel like she had moth balls in her mouth and the smell of food wouldn't make her stomach roll every time she had to take a meal of greasy food to yet another table.

All that was nothing compared to the embarrassment of what she had done to him. She would never be able to look him in the eyes again—if she ever saw him. Thank God she was leaving after the summer ended. Now that day couldn't come fast enough. She had vomited all over him.

After throwing his shirt in the bin, he had basically carried her to his ute. While he tried to clean off his boots and jeans, she had been sick again behind his ute. This time he held her hair out of her face and stood behind her, rubbing her back while, on her knees, she tried to turn her stomach inside out. If that wasn't bad enough, she had been sick again all over his passenger side door on the way home. She was crying with embarrassment and utter humiliation as he pulled over and helped her out of his vehicle, not seeming to care that the outside of his ute door was now covered in pieces of food and rum. She had used the last of her water to try and clean the sticky, disgusting mess off, but it wasn't enough. Finally at her parent's home, Tom had carried her to the front door and after much begging and promising she was okay, he left her to sleep it off on the day bed on the front verandah. Her total mortification was now branded into her mind for eternity. If she ever saw him again in this lifetime, it would be too soon. If only the earth could just open up and swallow her whole, she would be forever grateful.

Finally, the day was over. Beth had managed to avoid Montana and Adelaide's questions all day. Kathryn had assigned her to the coffee machine for her shift with one of the younger girls, so talking about last night was not a good idea. Small towns talk when they think they have something good to gossip about. She had learned that within the first few days of being the new girl in the town. The O'Loughlins were gossiped about a lot. Beth didn't need to be part of any of that.

Now, as she waited for Drake to come and take her to the river festival grounds to collect her car, Beth sat on the bench seat just up from the café and sipped her smoothie. It was the only thing she had been able to stomach all day, and sipping it made her feel a little better. The day was hot so the cool breeze from the river near the main street was a welcome reprieve as she sat and relaxed for a minute. Her father had promised to take her out to her car, but an emergency call out had changed their plans, so Drake had stepped in and said he could take Beth out on his way back to collect some of the equipment from the festival.

Drake and her father had become fast friends the night she and her family had arrived in town. Both families usually had a Friday morning coffee and breakfast together at the café, and both families would catch up at least once a month for dinner. Drake and Kathryn were like a second family and she classed Montana and Adelaide as the sisters she never had.

Beth looked both ways up and down the street, hoping he would arrive soon, otherwise Montana would be out here wanting all the gossip and details about last night. She wasn't ready to divulge her complete embarrassment just yet. The sound of Drake's old ute coming up the main street of River Flats, heralded her saviour and with a quick glance back to the café to ensure she was going to be saved before Montana could arrive, she breathed a sigh of relief.

The old ute went past and turned at the end of the street. Coming back, it glided to a stop just in front of her, the afternoon sun blinding her as it reflected off the windscreen. Getting to her feet, slowly, Beth walked towards the passenger side door. It swung open and Tom got out, holding the door open for her to get in. Beth stopped walking, her stomach dropping with dread.

'Your chariot awaits, my lady.' Tom bowed at the waist and winked at her without Drake seeing, daring her to make a scene in front of the older man. Closing her eyes and taking a deep breath, Beth could not believe her luck.

'What are you doing here?' she asked indignantly through clenched teeth as she neared him.

'You will have to slide into the middle, Beth, me girl. Tommy's little ass is too delicate to sit in the middle for me to change gears. That, okay?' Drake called to her from inside the ute as he leaned towards the passenger side door.

Dropping her smoothie into the bin right beside the ute's door, Beth held her head high and glided past Tom. Sliding to the middle, she tried to get as close to Drake as possible, but with her skirt on, she needed to position her legs close to Tom so Drake could easily change gears without her legs being spread. Tom, trying to hide his smirk, took in the street's surroundings seconds before he climbed in beside her. The ute had never felt so small to Beth. Ever.

With Tom on one side and Drake's large-framed body on the other, Beth had no choice but to let her knees and thighs rest against Tom's. Beth could feel the heat of his body through his jeans, midway up her thigh as Drake pulled out onto the main street and headed back down the bitumen towards the river festival grounds. Not wanting to give him any indication that she was aware of him or the sensation the touch of their bodies was having on her, she kept her eyes to the front or out of Drake's window. Occasionally, she could feel his eyes watching her, but she ignored him. What was he doing here? And in Drake's ute of all things.

'So, you pair had an eventful night, I hear, Beth?' Drake rubbed his dark beard, which was splintered with the occasional white stubble on his jaw. A twinkle in his eyes told her he knew what had happened between them already. She turned an ice-cold gaze onto Tom. *How dare he?*

Leaning back into the door of the ute with his hands held up in surrender, he shook his head in innocence. 'Trust me, it was not me.'

'Oh really? Then who was it?' He had a way of making her temper rise so fast. She had never known she was capable of it until yesterday.

'He hit me with it this morning when I arrived.'

'Of course, he did,' she said sarcastically as she turned her attention to Drake, who put one hand up to show his surrender to her as well.

'Who told you?'

'You ought to know by now, that news travels faster around here than the speed of light, Bethy.' She rolled her eyes and focused on the road. The gossip mill was in overdrive already today.

Drake nudged her side and quietly said in a reassuring voice, 'It was Kate and the girls.' He then looked around Beth to Tom and stated louder, 'But mister here told me about your fine skills in your regurgitation aiming. Well done, me girl. At least the town will now be able to gossip about Tom and his bare muscles for a while instead of everything else they make up.'

Beth turned on Tom. 'Really?' she said, disbelief in her voice and all over her face.

'He tricked me, okay? I was late because I had to wash my ute because of your *skills* and when I arrived to help him, he asked me straight away and threatened to hurt me if I had done anything to you. So, I had to tell him the truth. Look at him.' Tom pointed at Drake in mock fear. The tiny smile on his lips giving away, he was in no way scared of the man now driving onto the dirt track to what remained of the festival.

'Oh yeah. Real scary,' Beth said sarcastically as she looked from Tom to Drake and back again. 'Look at him. He is a big cuddly teddy bear.'

'Owi. Don't tell people that or my reputation will be ruined,' Drake said with mock rage at her, a finger to his lips.

'Oh yes. *Your* reputation.' Beth rolled her eyes at him and shook her head as he pulled up behind her car, now the only vehicle left in the middle of the paddock where only last night, it had been filled with vehicles. She needed to get out and get away from both of them. Her head hurt and her stomach had butterflies fluttering, making her already sensitive stomach feel queasy. They were having a big joke at her expense and all she wanted to do was go home and never see Tom again.

That wasn't going to happen. Instead, he got out and allowed her to slide out behind him before slamming the ute door closed.

'Thanks, Drake,' he called.

'Right. Will see you pair later. I had better go and get my girls.' With that said, Drake drove off in a cloud of dust.

Not waiting for Tom, Beth made her way to her car and opened the driver's door. Completely ignoring Tom's presence, she got in and sat. She was going home to bed. Her hand shook a little with her temper as she tried to get her keys into the ignition. Her belly was fluttering, and her skin still tingled where his thigh had been touching hers in the ute.

Oh, what was going on? she thought to herself in frustration as she rested her head back against the head rest, trying to calm herself with soothing breaths that seemed to be anything but soothing. A tap on the window made her turn her head and look at him.

'What is it?' she asked as she rolled down the window and looked at him.

'I don't think you're going anywhere fast.' He pointed at the back of the car. 'You have a flat tyre.' Beth stuck her head out of the window and saw the offending black rubber, flat as a pancake in the dirt. Leaning her head back against the head rest, she closed her eyes to fight the sting of frustrated tears, and took another deep breath. It was just not her day. Opening the door with restrained aggression, she forced Tom to step back, away from her little car. She then retraced her steps to the boot of her car.

'I can help if you like?'

'No. You've done enough,' she snapped, 'I can change my own tyre.'

'Yes, I gathered you could change your own tyre.' Tom followed her to the boot of the car and as she opened it, he beat her to reach in and lift the jack out. His eyes held hers. Faces inches apart. Her stomach fluttered. 'You look like you know what you're doing but I'm here and if I help, you can get on the road faster. How's that?'

Beth fought to pull her eyes from his before looking at the dirt and how flat her tyre was. She was not in the mood to start rolling around in the dirt in this heat. If he wanted to do it, then who was she to stop him playing the knight in shining armour? Nodding her head, she gave him a small smile of appreciation.

He set to work.

'You know, I think we got off on the wrong foot,' Tom said as he climbed back out from positioning the jack in place under her car.

'Really? Why would you say that?' she asked, shifting her outwardly relaxed body from one foot to the other. 'Was it when you pulled me into the water, saw me naked, spun me off my feet, or stood too close that I got sick all over you?'

Standing and dusting his hands on his jeans, Tom smiled at her wickedly and took a step towards her, forcing her back against the car, the burn of the hot metal stinging through her thin, café work shirt.

'Well, I liked three and a half parts of that story.' He was so close to her, she could smell his minted breath.

'Three and a half?' she questioned. It was all she could think to ask him while he was standing so close to her. Belly wildly fluttering, her mind was too concerned with his soft lips to think of anything else to say.

Smiling, he moved away. Squatting back down at the tyre again, he began to loosen the nuts. Looking out and around the grounds, Beth breathed a little easier and tried to stay strong against the assault on her senses he was so determined to rattle.

He knew his closeness had affected her. It was in his eyes every time he got close. Bloody hell, it was most likely written all over her face so clearly anyone could see. Maybe if she looked at him long enough, she might see it pulsating through his body and if she watched his hands, maybe she could see if they itched to run through her long hair, dislodging the band that kept it pulled back into the high ponytail she was wearing again today. Maybe if she studied him hard enough, she might see every time she was near, his heart would thump in his chest and his skin would tingle. Maybe he would feel something different towards her—see she was different—but those thoughts were not healthy thoughts. Tom O'Loughlin would never think anything more of her than what he was thinking last night. She had to remember that and try not to get caught in his eyes any more than what was necessary.

'Yep. Three and a half,' he grunted as he struggled to loosen the nuts, his shirt sleeves pulling tight across his arm muscles. Beth looked away, but not fast enough to see him stifle a smile as he continued. 'Seeing you all wet and pressed against me, your *nearly* naked body, having your hands on me, and then having you hang off me in front of everyone.'

'Oh my God.' Beth rolled her eyes at him and then looked out over the paddock towards the river. The sun had begun to go down behind the trees. 'You boys are all the same.' Tom removed the tyre and was now putting on the spare.

'What do you mean?'

'You all think that because of who you are, you can have anything or anyone you want. You're so used to girls just falling all over themselves to be with you, that you think that is what we all do—what we all want.' Her irritation flared in her voice; she couldn't help it.

'We're not all the same. We all like beautiful girls, especially ones who can't keep their hands off us,' he smirked at her, 'but we're not all the same.'

'Really? All the ones I know are the same. Do you really think you're any different to any of the other boys out here?' She challenged him with a slant of her eyes as she looked down at him then back to her view of the river.

Standing, Tom wiped his hands more firmly on his jeans than before and moved to stand in front of her. His body was so close to hers; they could feel each other radiating heat. His eyes intently scanned her face—her soft, creamy skin; her soft lips with their slightly larger bottom lip; to her little creased lines in her forehead. Beth studied him back with the same intensity. She was beautiful.

She frowned harder at him, waiting for him to come back to her eyes. It seemed important to her for him to see her—to see the real her—just like he wanted for himself. His eyes finally drifted back as his heart beat faster and his hands itched to grab her and pull her to his body. Tom couldn't help himself. His fingers feather light across her skin, he moved a little piece of hair that flittered across her face.

'Give me a chance and I will prove I'm different,' he whispered to her, his breath tingling her lips. She licked them and looked from his lips up into his eyes. She seemed to be trying to see beyond the veil of them into his soul. To see the truth of his words. To see the truth of what he was saying to her. She shifted slightly, her hands locked to her sides. 'Just one afternoon. That's all I'm asking, and if you're still not convinced, then I will leave you alone.'

Holding his breath, he dared her to believe he was different to the other blokes she had met. That he was not just after one thing but truly wanted to get to know the real her. She had to trust him; he had run out of ideas to try and spend time with her. She chewed the corner of her bottom lip as she gave his words some thought.

'Ok then. One afternoon. When?'

Smiling and letting go of his breath, Tom stepped back and finished changing her tyre. 'How about tomorrow afternoon? Come out to the farm.'

'I don't think that would be a good idea.'

'Why? You wanted me to prove that I'm not like the others. How can I do that if you won't give me a chance?'

'Won't you be busy harvesting? I thought the season started tomorrow.' She suddenly looked like a deer ready to run. He knew the implications of her being seen out on his family's property, in this small-minded community. But she was right, harvest started tomorrow, and he would be working nearly twenty-hour days. If she didn't come to him while he was working, he wouldn't be able to see her. They both knew it was crazy, but he had to try.

'Not for you,' he said casually, hoping she would not change her mind.

Beth rolled her eyes at his attempt to smooth talk her. He could nearly see her mind working overtime to get out of her promise. Sensing her hesitation, he added with a teasing smile,

60

'You could say it was to pay me back for the two sets of boots you ruined yesterday. I will put you to work,' he joked.

'I did not ruin your boots,' she half laughed. 'You were just not prepared to lose and are not quick enough on your feet. That's all.'

'And my ute door.'

'Well ... that's what being gallant gets you. I think I do remember saying to you that I would sleep it off in my car.'

He looked up at her from his position on the ground, all joking aside.

'I would never have allowed that to happen. Not in your state. I wouldn't have left you there alone.' Seriousness all gone, he smiled at her with mischief and added, 'Unless I was in there with you and your commando jeans.'

'Oh, you had to bring that up,' she laughed, a warmness washing over him. He had managed to make her laugh at herself without feeling any more of the embarrassment he had seen her show every time he was around.

'Just give me one afternoon to prove you wrong and that I am right. That's all I'm asking, Beth. Just one afternoon.'

Closing her eyes, he nearly let out a cry of relief as she held up her hands in defeat and smiled at his little victory over her. 'I finish at 3.00 pm tomorrow. I will come out after that. That okay?'

'Perfect.' Tom had finished changing the tyre and was putting the flat and jack into the boot. 'Beth.' She looked over at him from her place, still leaning on her car.

'I *will* be waiting.' He smiled and shut the boot.

Chapter 6

Beth had never been to 'Silverleigh' before. The massive wheat-cropping property was located about forty kilometres out of River Flats, with half the trip being on dirt. Beth's little car rattled along as she looked out of the window at the land that seemed to stretch forever. Golden wheat moved like waves across the ocean, ready to head. It was a stark contrast to the other side of town where Drake and Kathryn lived. There, land was more sculptured. The river flats of the properties rose into hills where cattle and horses gazed, and native trees flourished. Out this side of town, the land was flat for as far as the eye could see.

The O'Loughlin homestead came into view and if it were not for the lowering sun reflecting off the glass windows of the home, she would have missed seeing it rise into her view with such spectacular glory. It stole her breath away. The house would have blended into its surroundings throughout the day, if not for the trees and green grass of the perfectly manicured gardens. Its sandstone-coloured stone walls were the same colour as the wheat in the middle of which it stood. The large verandah wrapping around the entire house made the home appear even larger than its mansion-looking appeal already was. Gazing at the magnificent beauty of the home, Beth was now starting to feel way out of her comfort level being here. Her parents' cottage was a three-bedroom, one bathroom home with a nice garden. Tom's family home looked to be five times larger than her home and yard combined.

This was not her world. She repeated this in her head again for the millionth time that day. Thomas O'Loughlin was someone you looked at from afar and never got close to. They kept to their people, and she stuck to hers—there was never any mixing. However, she could not stop herself from climbing into her little car and driving out this afternoon after work. Kates's words of just having some summer fun, and Tom's declaration of him being different, had taken hold and had now started to make her think that if he was up for some summer fun with her—with some boundaries of course— then why not? She would be gone in a couple of months and never see him again anyway. One last summer of fun— maybe one she would never forget—was quite possibly just what she needed.

The gravel crunched as Beth stopped her car at the front gate of the yard. Not knowing where else to park, she thought it was the safest option. Tom would see her straight away and come out. Megan and their father hopefully would not.

Beth opened the gate to the yard after a few minutes of waiting in her car, pretending to fix her hair and search for nothing. She had hoped Tom would have come out and greeted her by now so she didn't have to walk to the door like some salesperson selling vacuum cleaners. But he never appeared. So here she was, walking up the path to the O'Loughlin's front door, with her nerves racing.

The path was lined with rose bushes of all colours—in full bloom. The smell was intoxicating and heady. Looking back over her left shoulder, she spied the workers' cottages in the distance on the other side of the dirt track, that led around the back of the house. The two cottages plus another one that looked more like a social hall, were half tucked up under a few trees and bushes, and if she strained her eyes, she could see lights of what looked like a manager's cottage through the shrubs.

So many people worked for the O'Loughlins. Many more than she had thought. Surely if any of them were to see her here, the gossip mill would run rapid, but it looked like no one was home. She was sure he had meant today.

Her sneakered foot had not touched the first wooden step up onto the verandah, when the screen door swung open, hitting the wall on the house. 'Sorry I was ...' Beth trailed off.

'Here?' Megan stood on the top of the stairs looking down at Beth, arms folded, and her usual resting bitch face perfectly in place.

'Oh ... I ... uhm ...' Beth couldn't find the right words. She had expected Tom.

Shaking her head with impatience, Megan bitterly answered for her. 'Tom had to drive today because one of the drivers is sick. I have been instructed, for God knows why, to take you to him,' she stated with disgust as she walked down the steps, pushing past Beth as she went. 'Come on. Let's get this over with.'

Beth didn't say anything but raised her eyebrows at Megan's open disgust at her being there. Turning on the ball of her foot and following, she knew it was a bad idea coming out here. Getting mixed up with Tom was an even worse idea. Megan's greeting had affirmed it. She should leave now, but her feet kept her moving behind Megan. Knowing her luck and what she knew of his determination, Tom would come and find her tomorrow at work if she didn't arrive like she had promised. She had to keep her word to let him try and prove he was different to all the others—it was, after all, only for this short time today.

They walked around the side of the house and across the gravel to one of the large sheds behind the house. Beth could now see the manager's cottage more clearly. It was in desperate need of some new paint, but it was a quaint little home with one inside light on ready for its occupant to arrive home later that night after their first day of harvesting.

64

Megan opened the door to an old red Landcruiser ute, and climbed in. Beth followed. The ute came to life with a puff of black smoke. The smell of the burnt oil and diesel filled the ute cab as Megan backed the old girl out of the shed, and after putting it into gear, she put her foot down hard, shooting gravel everywhere behind them. Beth gripped the bar on the dashboard in front of her and with all of her might, she held on. Taking a quick right turn after they had passed the sheds, Megan followed a long, straight dirt road further into the property and away from the house.

There was nothing to see but rows and rows of wheat all disappearing into the horizon. Megan had wound down her window when they had both climbed in to let air into the stifled ute. Beth had done the same. Now, as they sped along the track, the wind whipped into the cab, blowing Beth's hair all around her face as she tried to twist it into a bun and pin the mass of curls to her head.

Both girls did not speak for the first ten minutes of their wild drive. Beth didn't know anything about Megan, and Megan didn't seem to *want* to know anything about her. They were from two different worlds. In age, there was only two years separating them. Beth at twenty, was about to start her dream life, and Megan at the very young age of eighteen was about to get married to Jeff, who was twenty-one. And though Megan was young in age, she always looked and acted older. Married at that age was not something Beth would have even considered. Even now it was not in her future, but Jeff and Megan had been on and off since Megan was fifteen years old, so she guessed it was love between them; however, what Megan saw in that pig, she would never know.

Married. That was it.

'Congratulations on your engagement.' Beth turned and smiled at Megan. 'You must be very excited. How are the plans coming along?' It was all she could think of to ask. Anything to break the awkward silence hanging in the ute and settle her nerves, which were raging and making her feel sick.

'Thanks', Megan replied with a false smile, her eyes never leaving the road ahead. 'I was in the middle of planning the formal engagement party when you arrived.' Half rolling her eyes and looking back out of her window, Beth apologised for disturbing her.

'But Tom was adamant that he wanted to see you today. Something about boots?' She glanced at Beth in the passenger seat and shrugged. Her noninterest in whatever it was between her brother and this girl evident as she looked Beth up and down. 'I can never say no to him. He knows too much.' She smiled to herself, and her face softened a little. Her love for her bother was clear in her voice.

'You know, once he sets his mind to something, he can be very persuasive.' She looked over at Beth again. Something in her eyes told Beth that the words had a double meaning. Not knowing what else to say, Beth let the conversation die.

It was the dust rising into view that told Beth they were finally coming close to where Tom was located. They had been driving for nearly an hour and a half before Megan turned the ute without slowing. The rear tyres slid out from under them, making Beth grip the bar in front of her again before they bumped along at the same speed towards the headers coming up the rows. Beth bounced and nearly hit her head twice at the speed Megan was going, but she didn't say anything. Megan just hung onto the steering wheel and kept straight.

Getting closer, she slowed to a near stop and picked up the two-way receiver. 'Tom, you copy?'

'Yep Meg. I'm lead. Stop there', came his voice back over the two-way.

Megan stood on the brakes and stopped. Beth was glad to get out and touch the dirt under her feet. She had made it safely, but she had decided she was never getting back into a vehicle with Megan again.

Leaning on the side of the ute, Beth watched as the headers continued their steady pace up the rows towards her. The front one stopped, then, like a dance, every other machine behind him slowed to a stop as well. Seeing Tom climb out of the header, her nervous energy changed into a different nervousness, and she stood tall as she watched him jog across the paddock to her.

With his smile widening as he grew closer, he glanced at Megan with a smile of appreciation and then, after taking Beth's hand, he jogged her back towards the header. The large, green machine was radiating heat and so much noise, it made it impossible to stand next to it for too long. Tom climbed up the ladder and opened the cab door, reaching down for her, his hand flexing to tell her to take it. He helped Beth up the ladder behind him and into the cool, air-conditioned cab.

'Hi. You came,' he yelled to her as he stepped back to allow her to go first into the cab. With her hand still in his, Beth's heart was racing more at his touch than with the fast and scary ride with Megan. Beth felt a little off balance as she stepped inside the cab.

Taking the tiny seat next to Tom's larger one, she wiggled and tried to stay out of his way as he took his seat and moved the header into gear with a flick of some buttons and a slight movement of the control stick. They moved off down the long row, the grain feeding through the comb of the header, being pushed through the thrasher part, which separated the grain from the stalk of the wheat. The grain entered the harvester's bin, and the now crushed and broken stalks were thrusted out the back and lay in rows on the ground behind them.

The chaser bin driver who was with Tom, followed along beside them. The tractor cab, pulling the chaser bin, was just up a little in front of their cab, and Beth could see the man inside watching the header and the grain unloading into his bin as they drove along so close together. One mistake would cause an accident. Turning to watch the grain like Tom and the driver were doing, Beth could see another five headers, but when she arrived, she was sure there were nine. The chaser bin drivers all started off in the same manner behind her through the rear-view mirror, though they were on their own rows as the dance of the headers now moved back into motion.

On her little seat next to Tom, she could see the full length of the comb and feeder house as the wheat was cut and separated through the header. There were monitor screens to Tom's right, giving him all types of information about the crop. One even gave him a view of his bin as it augured into the chaser bin. Country music played quietly in the cab, and just behind her seat was a fridge with his tucker box sitting on the top of it. Dust filled the air around the cab and hung in the dying rays of the golden sun. They created a haze and you could see the grain dust landing and settling on the header and other machines. More dust in the air would have made it near impossible to breathe if you were exposed to it without the comfort of the air-conditioned cab.

A proud shiver crept up her body and her skin goosebumped as she watched what was happening before her. There was a mesmerising magic to this mammoth job and a romance that touched her heart like she could never have had expected. And all Beth could do was sit there and take it all in, her face awash with interest and awe.

'It's pretty cool to see the first time, hey?' Tom said to her once he had turned the large machine around and started back down another row of wheat. They were now making their way back down the seemingly never-ending paddock.

Smiling widely at him, she didn't care how she looked or the amazement she found in what she was witnessing. She was just relaxed and enjoying herself as she sat on the tiny seat beside him. 'I once watched Kate's dad when we were at a sleep over. I thought he was going a lot slower than this. I guess he only had his one header though and that made it seem slower,' she mused as she watched out her side of the cab. Little birds were flitting around the ground where they had just been, collecting insects and bugs that had been stirred up by the loud commotion.

'Yeah, Trevor has older machinery than us, so it would have been slower. He does well though, usually matching us in the tonnage rate.'

'What's that?'

'Tonnage?' Tom replied, looking over at her. Her interest in this part of his life piqued his interest in her more. He had planned to show her around the farm and then end up at the river so they could talk and get to know one another a little more, but when Dan got sick that morning, he had to step in and drive. Now that Beth was here with him, maybe it was a good thing Dan got sick and he had to drive.

'It's the amount of grain per acre we head. We usually get roughly two tonnes to the acre. Here at Silverleigh, that's equal to about 460,000 tonnes per year. Across the rest of our properties, including here, we harvest about three quarters of a million tonnes of wheat each season.' Tom said it so plainly—just like ordering a burger and coffee—that Beth just looked at him. She wasn't up with how much money that amounted to, but given who he was, it must have been a hell of a lot.

'Just hold, Tom, Mick's coming in,' a voice over the two-way announced. Tom pressed a button and Beth turned to watch as the chaser bin and tractor pulled away and another one took its place, graceful and elegantly in sync.

'Good to go, Tom,' came a different voice. Tom pressed the button again and the grain began to be augured into the bin. The two-way was constantly beeping as Beth listened to the other blokes talk and negotiate their way up the rows.

'Where do they go with all that grain?' Beth had tried to watch but lost sight as the tractor and bin moved away.

'To either the mother bin or direct into the road trains waiting. Dad doesn't like it when the truckies are just sitting around, so he makes sure he has enough to keep them busy. And if they're not back when the chaser boys are ready, then the boys unload into one of the five mother bins we have.' Tom pressed another button on the monitor that was sounding before he continued with, 'They hold about 100 tonnes each.'

'How many of them are here? Road trains that is.'

'We have eight which, when not carting grain, cart our cattle from our stations or other things we need. We also contract out about three more road trains for harvest, just to make sure they never stop. Once all three of their trailers are full, they will drive to where our silos are or to the depot and unload, returning to refill out of the mother bins. With fourteen chaser bins and five mother bins, the truckies are never waiting.'

'This is such a big production.' Beth was amazed at the amount of organisation it would take to have this running year in and year out. 'How long do you go for?'

'Here, usually about a month, then we all move to our other farms. Harvest goes for about eight to twelve weeks depending on the rain and how heavy the crop is, but that's for all our properties. The entire season starts round here now and goes south throughout summer.' Tom spoke as he kept his mind on the monitors and his eyes on the rows.

His body, however, was very aware of Beth sitting so close to him, watching intently how everything around them was all happening. She genuinely seemed interested in what was going on and how it all worked, and she seemed to actually enjoy it all. He had known, when he first saw her across the river, she was different to all the other girls he had met, but something in the way she was truly interested in his life touched him in a way nothing else had.

She was only here because he had half bribed, half forced her to come, and deep inside he had thought she wouldn't arrive that afternoon. But here she was, taking a real interest in what he was actually doing. He couldn't imagine any of Megan's friends sitting there, taking an interest in all of this. They wouldn't be caught dead here. Just knowing that, made something deep inside him stir, and his body reacted.

Moving in his seat to adjust himself more comfortably in his jeans, he asked, 'How was work?'

Their conversation flowed easily into the evening. It was mostly about the farm and local gossip from the festival, friends, and people they both knew. Most of the ones he spoke about, Beth had met or heard about, so when Tom would tell her funny stories about them, she would laugh and claim that it never happened. Tom laughed too and enjoyed the sound of her laugh as it filled his ears.

'... Adelaide and Braydon? Really?' she asked him sceptically after he had told her a story about them on festival night. 'Now I know you're lying to me. Adelaide is my best friend—like a sister. If she had done what you are saying, she would have told me.'

Tom put his hand to his heart and stated, 'May the lord in heaven strike me down if it be untrue that Adelaide and Braydon were seen getting very hot and heavy the night of the festival.' Beth rolled her eyes and giggled, saying she was going to have to talk to Adelaide about it. Their conversation and laughter together, made her eyes dance and her face glow with happiness. She was truly beautiful.

'Did you want to drive?' Tom asked when she looked away from him. His eyes had barely moved from hers as they had spoken. He turned the large machine back around to go back up a new fresh row of wheat. Mick was about to pull away and let the other driver pull up beside them. It was the perfect time.

'Oh no. I couldn't. I would get it all wrong.' Beth hesitated as she watched the grain empty into the chaser bin. Each time it happened, she seemed to be enthralled with the process.

'No. Here.' Tom shifted in his seat and tapped his leg. 'I won't move. I will be here to help. Promise.'

Beth smiled at him as she stood and sat on his knee, her weight not fully on him. He realised she was trying to hold herself off him, so her meagre weight wasn't fully resting on his one leg. She gingerly took the steering wheel.

'You don't have to do much, just keep the girl in line with the rows.' Tom leaned forward as he reached around her, his arms either side of her body to readjust the steering wheel, he pulled her fully onto his lap. The heat of his body pressed to her back, his breath on her shoulder, made her body shiver a little. He couldn't help but smile to himself. Watching her closely, he could see she was trying to focus on the rows in front of them and not on him.

'Is this right?'

'Perfect,' he breathed against her shoulder. 'Just keep doing what you're doing.' Tom continued to stare at her as she concentrated. She had a little smile of excitement as she chewed her bottom lip slightly. With her bottom pressed to him like it now was, it was bringing forth a pure male response within him. Shifting slightly, so she couldn't feel the pressure of what her body was doing to his, Beth turned to look over her shoulder at him.

'Are you okay? Am I too heavy for you?' She started to move off, but he stopped her by putting his arm fully around her waist and stomach and pulling her more firmly into him, locking her in place against his body.

'No. Stay. You're not heavy at all. Just right.' He smiled at her, his lips a mere inch from her shoulder. It drew her attention and for a moment they just stared at each other. If he leaned in just a fraction more, he would be able to place a kiss on her skin and taste her. Moving just a little, Beth turned back to the rows. Smiling a little lopsided, he was sure she had just read his thoughts and pulled back before he did what was clearly in his eyes to do.

'Just hold, Tom,' came the voice over the two-way. Pressing the button, the grain stopped emptying out of the header and the chaser bin pulled away. As Beth continued to steer, her smile grew even bigger as she watched the next chaser bin pull up beside her.

'Good to go, Tom. I'm back.'

'Good on ya, Mick,' Tom replied into the two-way, before asking Beth, 'Do you want to press it?' He motioned to the button and just like a little child, Beth's smile grew as she reached her hand across and pressed the button he was pointing at. Her smile lit up her beautiful face even more when she saw on the screen just above her head, the grain now transferring into Mick's bin.

'You're a pro. Next you will be taking over my job,' Tom teased, his hand gently moving up her ribs to give her a little tickle. The movement caused her to wriggle and move across his body, finally leaning back against him and crushing his hand to stop his tickling. He did.

Beth looked over her shoulder at him and smiled, regaining her breath from his tickles. 'I don't think so. You can keep this job. This is too much to think about all at once for me.'

Tom was so close she could feel his breath on her chin. His brown eyes felt like they were staring into her soul, reading all of her thoughts. The world began to enclose around them as he leaned towards her.

'Where are you two going?' Mick said over the two-way. The spell broke, and Beth sat up and looked around her. Reaching for the steering wheel, Tom corrected the header that had started to drift off course towards the other rows as Beth leaped off his lap and sat on her little chair.

Clearing his voice, Tom replied into the two-way, 'Sorry boys ...' as he looked at Beth with a smile on his face. '... got a bit distracted.'

'You had better not get distracted!' roared a male voice over the two-way. 'You need to keep an eye on that moisture level. What's it sitting at?'

All the colour drained out of Beth's face and her heart started beating faster. It had nothing to do with the kiss she had nearly just shared with Tom—that booming voice at the other end of the two-way, was Matthew O'Loughlin. He was the most powerful and richest man in the community and known to be feared by many. His arrogance and self-importance was well known. She didn't want him to know she was in the header cab with his son or that it was her fault they had drifted off course.

Tom found Beth's hand and squeezed it gently to reassure her she was safe and not to worry. But before he could reply to his father, Mick replied instead, 'I would say that from where I'm sitting, that moisture level is getting pretty high and the air pretty well crackling.'

Tom looked out his window at Mick sitting level with them in his tractor cab. He gave the chaser bin driver the bird salute. It looked as though Tom had also forgotten about Mick being right alongside them, seeing directly into the header cab, watching Beth sitting on Tom's lap.

'What the hell does that mean? What level is that moisture, Tom?'

'The moisture level is sitting at 11.5,' Tom replied flatly.

'Once you get back up here, we will call it a night. Got it?'

'Got it.' Tom slammed the two-way back onto its hook and pressed a few buttons on the monitor before he looked over at Beth, his hand still holding hers. 'Don't worry about him.'

But as they drew to the end of the row, Beth could see Matthew standing next to his ute. The same one Megan had brought her to Tom in. Even in the darkness, she could tell that the owner of the O'Loughlin Properties Group was not happy. He stood with his arms crossed, legs slightly apart, glaring at the header she and Tom were in.

Pulling to a stop, Tom ordered gently, 'Wait here.' He climbed out of the cab and down the ladder, walking to where his father was waiting for him. Matthew did not move from his spot, forcing

74

his son to walk all the way across to him. Beth could see in his eyes, as he glanced up into the cab more than a few times, looking directly at her, that Mathew knew she was in there. And he was not happy about it at all. The two-way beeped louder as the men all talked and communicated together at once. The sound of each header as it neared the end of the rows and parked, mixed with the air-conditioning and vibrating of the machine she was sitting in, made it impossible to hear what Tom and his father were talking about. Their body language, however, told her that the words being exchanged were nowhere near pleasant.

After what seemed like forever, and an endless amount of pointing and looks of yelling on their faces, Tom walked back over to the header, muttering under his breath and throwing a skulking look over his shoulder at his father. Matthew walked towards the back end of the machine. Beth watched Tom visibly calm himself and put on a tight smile for her as he opened the door of the cab and motioned for her to climb out.

He was clearly very upset, but he was trying his best to hide it. Her sneakered feet touched the ground, and Tom took her hand tightly in his, leading her to the ute without saying a word. Opening the door for her, he let her climb in before walking to the driver's side, and slamming the door behind him. Beth knew her choice of coming out here had been a bad idea, and now tonight had just proved it.

Once out of the paddock, Tom reached over to try and take her hand again, but Beth kept them both tightly in her lap, choosing to focus out of her window at the darkness instead. She didn't want him to see the tears that were threatening to fall. She didn't want to be the one causing any fights. She hated confrontation—especially being the cause of it. Having witnessed what fights within a family can do, the last thing she wanted was to cause problems within *Tom's* family. His father was not happy about her being there and getting him distracted. She had been wrong to come out.

'Are you okay?' he asked over the wind blowing through the ute. Beth just nodded and tried to hold back the tears as they drove the hour back to his family's home. She wanted to get out of there before he could stop her. This was all her fault. She was tired and wanted to go home.

The ute stopped right next to her car and before Tom had turned the motor off, Beth opened her door and slammed it shut, near running for the driver's door of her little car. If she didn't go now, he would see her cry.

Tom's hand stopped her opening her own car's door, holding it closed so she couldn't pull it open. She hadn't heard him right there behind her, in her near blind panic to get away.

'Beth. Stop. What's wrong?' he whispered to her, his voice a low tenor, causing her to take a shaky breath in and turn to face him. His eyes slightly widening were the only indication of him seeing her silent tears in the moonlight. His small shock turned to confusion.

'Why are you crying?' he stepped to her. She took a step back and came right up against her car door, as she replied, 'I can't do this, Tom. I can't be the reason for you and your dad fighting. I've seen families ruined because of others. I won't be the cause of you two fighting again like tonight.' She turned back to face her car, pushing his hand away from her door. He obliged, only to wrap his arms around her, pulling her gently back against him.

Stiffening with the contact and the need to do as he wanted, she fought against his will as he whispered, 'Trust me. This has nothing to do with you. He is always pissed at me for something. Tonight, it was because he was listening to the two-way and heard Mick's question. I failed to stay on course and Mick's words made him get pissed at me like normal. That's all.' His hot breath on her temple gave her goosebumps. 'Nothing to do with you. I promise.'

'If I hadn't been here, then you would have stayed on course.' She relaxed a little against the strength of his body

'If you were not here, he would have found something else to get pissed at and besides, I would have been lonely without you.' Tom pulled back just enough to look around her with a sly smile. 'At least we gave Mick something to talk about for a while.' His grin, one of teasing, created a blush to heat Beth's skin and she smiled back at him slightly embarrassed.

'That's all I need. More gossip about my embarrassing endeavours.'

'I like your embarrassing endeavours. Especially when they're with me.' He touched her cheek as she turned fully around to face him. He wiped away the wetness with the back of his knuckles. Beth's eyes rose to meet his.

'Really? Even if that means ruining two sets of boots in one day?' He was so close to her, her heart raced. She wanted to feel his lips on hers.

'Ruin as many as you like. I don't care.' His eyes closed as he whispered the words. His lips touched hers so softly, she wasn't even sure they had touched. Then he kissed her again, tentatively with more pressure. He was waiting for her to respond.

Tilting her head to the side a little, Beth gently responded, her heart beating wildly. She felt dizzy and off balance. This was madness; she should not be doing this. But she couldn't help herself. She wanted to taste more of him.

His hand touched the side of her face, and his lips moved over hers more firmly as she felt herself lean into him. Tom stood more firmly on the ground to support her before he angled his head to deepen the kiss. His hand dropped to her waist, pulling her body to his—hips to hips, chest to chest. Her arms rose of their own accord around his neck, and she pulled him down. Her head spun as he followed her lead. She wanted more. To taste more. Her body started to heat up. She could feel his body responding to hers, right there in front of his father's home.

Beth's heart thundered. This *was* crazy. She should not be doing this. Her inner voice called again trying to get her to pull away. Her heart was yelling, *'NO, stay'* but in the end, she listened to her head and pulled away slowly. Retreating, drawing back, she looked at him and smiled shyly.

'Tom!!' Beth jumped and looked behind him. Megan stood on the verandah, hands on her hips. 'Dad wants you back at the headers now.'

Tom cursed under his breath before he answered over his shoulder to his sister with irritation clear in his voice. But his eyes, still heated from their kiss, never left Beth's. 'Yeah, I will get there when I get there.'

'No. Now Tom!' she demanded back to him. Beth could feel Megan's eyes burning into her. She would have seen them kiss. Megan already hated her and now, after seeing their intimate moment, would hate her even more. Beth was not from their social class; she shouldn't be here and never should have been seen kissing Tom.

Reaching around her, with a resigned and frustrated breath, Tom opened her car door and stood to the side while she climbed in, ignoring Megan as she did.

'I will see you in the morning,' he whispered.

'Maybe,' was all she could say.

Chapter 7

The next morning was a normal one; however, Beth felt a little different. She was at the café before opening, surprising Kathryn and helping set the tables for the morning rush. She had not slept well. Her mind was racing with thoughts of Tom's kiss and his body pressed to hers, but they were mixed with his father's voice and Megan's treatment of her.

She knew her place in this world, where she was seen socially in this tiny little town. What right did she have to think she could ever be friends with, or have anything more with, Thomas O'Loughlin? All these thoughts and images tumbled in her head, and with the lack of sleep, they caused a deep sinking feeling in the pit of her stomach. Some things were just not meant to be, no matter how much you might have wanted them to be different, even just for a short amount of time.

Her afternoon with Tom yesterday had been fun. They had laughed and talked about lots of things—people they knew and random and strange things they both liked, but had never known anyone else to like, and she had had a great time learning about his life on the farm. The way wheat was headed and the organisation it took to get such a large amount all in on time. Harvesting really was a magically synchronised dance with tractors and headers. But why should she be judged because of her circumstances and the way she was raised? Why did it matter what path her parents had chosen in their life? Why did it matter they were not listed as a wealthy family? Why did it, here in this small town in the middle of nowhere, matter what she or anyone else had in the bank? And why were they judged on it? Her annoyance of it all, and the way this small town operated, had never been an issue until today.

Now Beth found herself irritated at the fact that the SBs only went to the other café when Kathryn's café was the best in town. Why was it that one man's opinion was viewed above everyone else's? Why was it that her parents had to lose everything to appease someone, who in the end didn't matter at all, the damage already being done, and never to be undone again? Why couldn't she be friends with whoever the hell she wanted to, no matter what materialistic things they had? If they were friends, then so be it.

Her irritation was clear to see. Beth was slamming things around the coffee machine all morning as her thoughts ruled her actions. She was even snapping at Tierany for taking an order down wrong—causing Beth to have to make another coffee—and then spilling the fresh brew all over the saucer as she carried it to the customer. She was never like this. She was always kind and patient. She never had a temper—never—until she had met Tom. And now everything seemed wrong in the world.

'Beth, are you okay this morning?' Adelaide asked quietly as she slowly lowered herself to the floor next to Beth, who had just dropped a full bottle of caramel topping. It had smashed, leaving a sticky mess everywhere behind the counter.

'No,' Beth said, deflated. She rocked back off her feet to sit on her bottom, up against one of the counter's metal legs. What was wrong with her? 'Why didn't you tell me you got hot and heavy with Braydon?'

Adelaide's face drained of colour, and she stared at her best friend. Those words were not what she had wanted to say, and the way they came out sounded nasty and jealous at her friend. But they were out now, and she couldn't tell Adelaide the real reason she was upset this morning, so deflection was her next option.

'You've been talking with Tom,' Adelaide replied matter-of-factly, ripping off another piece of paper towel and handing it to her. Beth just nodded and non-committedly wiped at some of the caramel.

'It's nothing really. Just a little bit of fun, that's all.' Adelaide avoided Beth's eyes.

'Are you sure of that? Braydon was following you around all night on Saturday. I think he wants more.'

'If he does, he does, but it can't happen. Braydon knows I'm leaving at the end of the summer and so are you.' Adelaide's voice changed a little more bitterly. 'I don't see that being an issue with you and Tom, given he carried you to his ute shirtless and your arms were wrapped around his neck, for everyone to see. I say you have the same trouble I have.' By the sound of it, Adelaide's snarky remark and the irritation in her voice mirrored Beth's frustration. Without another word, Adelaide stood and left Beth sitting on the floor to clean up her own mess, physically and metaphorically.

Growling as she cleaned up her mopped up the sticky sauce, Beth mentally scolded herself at what she had just said to Adelaide. She should have been more careful how she had brought up Adelaide's night with Braydon. It wasn't her friend's fault Beth was so frustrated with the world and they both didn't need reminding of their looming leaving. She suspected Adelaide and Braydon were much more than two people who used to go to school together and just randomly hooked up at the festival.

Both Montana and Adelaide had been tight lipped about him, in fact, no more than a couple of words had ever been spoken about Braydon. And now, frowning at her friends similar situation as hers, Beth walked back into the kitchen with an arm full of dirty dishes and paper towel covered in caramel topping, stacked high on her tray, promising to be more understanding with Adelaide.

She was a good girl. Even more so than Beth. She never usually drank, swore or had ever gotten into serious trouble that

Beth could ever remember. Beth also knew that she had never been with a boy. She had only kissed one – Braydon. It was during a dare when they were in Grade 2, and if Adelaide had ventured there with Braydon, then Adelaide needed Beth to be more diplomatic and understanding. Not this green-eyed monster who had taken hold today, unable to control her own frustration and temper about her world. When Adelaide returned with a bucket of warm water, Beth apologised and hugged her friend before together, they set to work cleaning up Beth's mess.

Tom was driving hard. His temper was raging this morning because of his father's demands. He had ordered him to fix a leaking hydraulic hose on one of the chaser bins last night before he went to sleep, and the small job had turned into an all-nighter. It was just before dawn when he had finally gotten into bed, only to be woken again a few hours later by Meg, demanding he get up and go and unload the bin he had just fixed before they started again for the day. His father's orders were clear and were expected to be followed without question. Tom had completed all that and was planning to drive to Kathryn's to see Beth, and get a much needed coffee, when his father had cornered him.

'I get you're young and it's important to sow your wild oats, Tom, but maybe be a little more discreet with who you choose to bed. Remember whose son you are.' Mathew O'Loughlin had smiled with a wicked smile twisted on his lips. 'We don't need a bad reputation attached to you or any bastard child running around with a slut of a mother chasing you. You know it would reflect badly on me.'

Tom was so pissed and shocked at his father's words, he had just walked away from the man, his own words lost in a sea of churning, unleashed anger enclosing him. How dare his father speak like that about Beth? About any girl? What was wrong with Beth? So what if she was not from his father's social circle. Can't he have friends other than the ones his father chose for him to have?

Climbing into his ute, he had slammed the door and took off, gravel flying everywhere. He had made town in record time, even though he couldn't remember a thing about the trip. He was on auto pilot as his mind filled with rage at his father and all his demands, that even finding Beth a friend seemed to have pissed off the great Mathew O'Loughlin. Tom's faced twisted as he bashed his fists into the steering wheel, releasing some of his pent-up anger, hurt and frustration. Finally, his hands hurting, he calmed a little, letting the ute coast into town passed all the machinery places and rural shops before he turned up the main street and headed for Kathryn's Café.

Finding a park, Tom took a few seconds to calm himself a little more. He could see Drake's ute parked outside the café door and knew the older man would be able to see straight through Tom's thinly vailed façade. Drake had always been able to see right through him and read his moods. Tom needed to get himself right before he entered the café and he needed to not let his father's words get to him. Taking a few more deep breaths, he knew he would need to be fast. If he wasn't back in time to start with the other headers, his father would have more words to say to him—and in this mood, that could be very dangerous.

The bell tinkled above his head when he walked in. 'Tommy, me boy.' Drake took one look at him and raised an eyebrow. 'I would ask how you are, but I can read it all over your face. What's happened?'

Drake looked over to Beth who, after a shy smile at Tom, walked out to the kitchen. 'Your old man again?' Drake pulled out the seat beside him to allow Tom to sit, but he just shook his head.

'Yep,' he replied dryly. 'You know the old bastard. I just need a coffee and something quick to eat today. I'm needed on the header again.' Tom was looking in the direction of the kitchen, waiting for Beth to come back out. He had used coffee and food as a way to get his thoughts back together and to see if she was okay—to let himself be near her and allow her to calm his soul like she had last night when she arrived.

He had been on edge all day due to his father's demands and the humiliation Mathew inflicted on him in front of the other boys he was working with. Being an especially bigger ass—more than normal yesterday—it had taken everything Tom had to grin and bear it in front of all the Silverleigh employees. But once Beth had arrived, he had calmed the second he had seen her, and he was back to his usual happy self. She was like a tonic for his undercurrent of anger and hatred, which had not occurred to him until his drive into town. And now, as he waited for her to reemerge from the kitchen, Tom knew he needed her to calm him again. Her effect had been instant. From the moment he had looked over that river and seen her, she had somehow reached across the water and soothed him. And now, her calmness was like a drug he needed to be able to function throughout the day.

Drake was watching him closely. 'How about you duck back there and see if Kathryn can get you something fast? Adelaide can make you your coffee.' Drake motioned to Adelaide as Tom moved towards the kitchen door behind the counter.

'Tom!' Kathryn was surprised by him being in her kitchen. 'Good morning, sweetheart, what can I do for you?'

'I need some food fast. Can you get me something asap?' Tom smiled at her, but his eyes were searching for Beth. She was not in the kitchen. Kathryn must have read his thoughts and knew his real reason for being in her kitchen.

'Of course, honey. You go wait outside.' She nodded to the kitchen door that led into the alleyway beside the café. 'And I will finish this bacon and egg burger for you and cook the other customer another one. Adelaide will make your coffee and bring it out to you.' She didn't need to tell him twice. Tom was already walking through the back door.

Beth was standing down the laneway a little. She had a smoothie in her hand and seemed to be blindly wandering away from the café entrance, while watching the other entrance of the small alleyway. Her thoughts were vague as she tried not to think of Tom waiting for her in the café. It was better if she just kept her distance from him.

The screen door of the café opened and closed, breaking into her nonlogical thoughts. She was expecting Adelaide; however, the man standing before her, his work shirt and jeans fitting him perfectly, and his sunnies resting on the brim of his cap, had her heart racing instantly. He looked so good.

'What are you doing out here?' she asked, a little taken aback by him finding her out there. Deliberately taking her break early today to avoid him, she didn't want him seeing her in the mood she was in, and knew she needed time to settle before the lunch rush began or else who knew what was going to come out of her mouth.

'I wanted to see you.' Walking towards her, his movements confident and sure, he didn't stop until he was directly in front of her, making her raise her head and look up into his eyes. 'I told you last night, I would come and see you today,' he whispered as he reached out and touched her face, moving the stray hair from her cheek and tucking it behind her ear. His eyes studied hers, seemingly looking for something, but she had no idea what it was.

Neither spoke as they stood there just holding each other with their eyes. The mood he had entered the café in, now seemed to have dissipated, replaced by the need to touch Beth. Unable, it seemed, to stop himself, he leaned in and softly kissed her slightly parted lips. Pulling away and watching her again, he smiled as she closed her eyes and leaned into him, wanting more. Lowering his head, he obliged her. His lips touched hers, soft but firm in his intention, soon turning a little deeper, and Beth allowed herself to lean in and kiss him back.

He wanted this. Dammit, she wanted this too.

The world disappeared around them and Beth felt an instant calm wash over her body and take all the anger and frustration she had been feeling all morning, away with just one simple kiss. Stepping into his body more, she needed Tom to calm whatever it was he had let loose inside of her last night. To take it back.

Angling his head, Tom deepened the kiss, his arms wrapping around her waist. He drew her closer, pressing her fully to his body.

The café's side door closed behind them with a bang of aluminium metal against a solid door frame. It was deliberate. The noise pulled them apart, but neither looked at who it was, both lost in each other's eyes as the world around them slowly expanded again.

'Can I see you tonight?' Tom squeezed Beth's hips and watched as she tried to find the words in her now more confused but calmed state of mind. 'Come out and be with me again in the header.'

Stepping back, Beth shook her head. 'I don't think that would be a good idea, Tom. I need to study and catch up with Adelaide, and sleep.' Looking at the ground as she spoke, she avoided his eyes, pressing the tip of her sneaker into a hole in the cement.

'That's okay', he replied, his disappointment clearly heard in his voice. 'Can I call you then? Are you working tomorrow?' Beth nodded and looked behind him to see Adelaide waiting at the door with his food and coffee, her friend trying to look interested in the guttering of the building above her head. She knew he had to get back to the farm but was not going to leave until he had some kind of promise of being in contact with her.

'Okay. I will talk to you tonight.'

With a quick kiss on the lips, he left her standing there in the alleyway as he retreated his steps, taking his food and coffee from Adelaide as he went.

Beth didn't hear from Tom that night. She kept her phone with her the entire time—even taking it into the shower just in case he called. But by midnight, when she finally gave into her exhaustion and turned off her light, he still had not called or texted her. By the next morning, she woke early and reached for her phone, a little worried she had slept through a very late night call. But still there was nothing. Her mind had started to play over everything that had transpired between them and then her self-doubt kicked in and she didn't like where her thoughts had taken her.

As much as she hated to admit it, she had been carefully scanning and watching the door at the café all that day, and then the next, but still Tom never showed or tried to contact her. Drake had not heard from him either—when she finally plucked up the courage to ask him.

'It's harvest, Beth me girl. Knowing his father, Mathew would have that boy so busy, even sleep would be something he couldn't have, let alone time to come and get a coffee.'

Drake had tried to soothe her with his words. Even Kathryn had alluded to the same thing one afternoon when Beth was still wiping down a table after five minutes of going around in circles with the cloth, polishing the same spot. The table had never been so clean.

Beth was hurt and felt rejected. She understood it was harvest, but it only took a few seconds to send a text. It hurt more because he had promised her he was different. But by ghosting her like this, he had now just proved over these last few days, that he was in fact just what she thought he was all along—just another one of the boys she knew him to be. Just after one thing.

Her anger and bitterness at the hurt and humiliation of him making such a show with her in front of Drake and Kathryn—and Adelaide—made her more volatile. She constantly scolded herself for thinking he was different and that maybe they could've been friends or have some summer fun while getting to know each other. She had even fallen for his smooth moves and kisses.

Seeing one of the SB girls wandering up the street as she wiped over a table late that afternoon, Beth's mind conjured up the image of how she was now probably the laughing stock of the SB group. *Little Beth Kennedy: thought she was going to be one of us. A wannabe social climber.* Throwing the chairs into the table, Beth stormed back into the café and into the kitchen, taking out her hurt and frustration on the dishes and mopping the floor.

She couldn't understand what she had done wrong for Tom not to have at least sent a 'this is not working out for me' text. The silence was maddening. Maybe she should have gone out to see him that night instead of studying. Maybe he had decided to find someone more of his social class to spend his time with. That last thought felt like a rock hitting the bottom of her stomach. Maybe he had played her so well that she was just a game to him. Maybe it was all just a cruel joke at her expense. Maybe he was just as heartless as all the rest. With that thought, Beth turned off her phone late that night and watched out her bedroom window at the lightning in the distance. Tom was just like all the others, and she never wanted to see him again.

Beth slept in the next morning. It was something she rarely did. In the depths of her troubled sleep, an incessant banging on her parent's front door intruded on her dreams. Sitting up, she listened hard as she tried to make out the muffled voices—a male's and her mother's. Concentrating harder, she tried to make out who would be at her home at this early hour.

Turning, she looked at her clock. 9:30 am! It was not early morning; it was *mid-morning*. She really had slept in. Throwing back the covers, Beth leaped out of bed. The meeting with Kathryn at the café to go through some of the recipes she had had trouble with, was in half an hour. She had to get moving or she would be late.

Tom was beyond pissed at his father and sister for what they had done over the last few days. He had wanted to call Beth as soon as he got his phone back that morning, but he then thought better of it. She deserved to see him face to face when he explained what had happened, so he had gone directly to the café, expecting to see her there. But Montana had told him it was Beth's day off.

His temper was at boiling point. He was frustrated at all these little stops to see her, so he drove directly to her parents' home and found himself banging on the door so loudly, even the elderly man sitting on his front steps next door, heard him and looked over with a curious frown at why he was making such a racket.

The door opened and Tom refocused his attention back to the home as an older woman, aged in her early fifties, greeted him. She had the same blonde hair and blue eyes as Beth did. She was a near identical, albeit with just a few more lines and wrinkles, version of her daughter. This was Beth's mother, and Tom had all but knocked down her door, in his desperate need to see Beth.

'Can I help you?' she asked with a small frown between her brows as she looked him up and down.

Taking a deep breath to calm himself, Tom replied, 'I am sorry, Mrs Kennedy. Sometimes I don't know my own strength.' He tried to give his best smile back to her, but he felt it falter as he tried to get a hold of himself, standing on the threshold of Beth's parents' home, not wanting to look like a raving lunatic.

'Is Beth home?' Movement behind her mother drew his attention. Beth stood at her bedroom door looking like she had just woken up, her hair a little messed up, but looking like she had run her fingers through the thick mass laying down her back. Her pyjama top revealed that she wasn't wearing a bra, and her short bottoms revealed her strong, toned, sun-kissed legs. He had never seen anyone look more beautiful than she did at that moment. His eyes didn't move from her. His mouth went dry as a calmness deep inside of him took hold and cleared all he had felt for the last three days.

Susan Kennedy cleared her throat. 'I will leave you two to talk. Nice to meet you ...?'

Tom struggled to pull his gaze from Beth to register what was being said. He held out his hand and shook her mother's in a blind, non-thinking action. 'Tom,' was all that would come out, and it sounded rasped to his ears.

His eyes flickered back to Beth, and he waited as her mother left the tiny living room and went into the kitchen. The house was small, and they had no privacy for him to talk and say all he needed to without her mother hearing. The hum of the kettle beginning to boil gave them some privacy; however, Beth walked straight passed Tom, forcing him to take a step back out of the doorway, back onto the front verandah. Reaching around his body, careful not to touch him, Beth closed both the screen door and then the timber door behind him.

'What are you doing here?' she asked, crossing her arms. She was well aware that she was not dressed to see him, and now tried to discreetly cover her nipples, which had become instantly erect as his heated gaze travelled down the length of her body.

'I needed to see you.' He took a step towards her, but she took one back, her movement stopping any further advancement. She raised her eyebrows at him in a way that made him pause. She was angry and hurt, preventing him from touching her.

'The last I saw you, Tom, was three days ago. Why now? You said you would call but you didn't.' Tom could hear the hurt in Beth's voice. They had only known each other for such a short amount of time—really too short for her to care if he didn't call. But she *had* cared. And it showed—as much as she didn't want it to. But the fact that it *did* show, made him happy. He had wanted to see her every day, to spend as much time with her as he could, driving himself mad thinking it was only he who felt this madness for her so quickly. It had made him question his sanity more than a million times over these past few days, but seeing her now, hearing her hurt, he knew she was under the same crazy spell he was.

'My phone died that night after I saw you and I couldn't find a lead to charge it while I was heading. When I finally got in, it was too late to call you, and I didn't want to wake you, knowing you would have been sleeping.' He watched her closely as he continued. 'Megan had taken my phone the next morning, while I was sleeping. I thought I had lost it somehow.' The anger in his voice increased as he spoke.

'My father had taken all the keys for all the vehicles, so I couldn't leave the farm. He told everyone I was to stay on the property until he gave permission for me to leave.' Tom saw the change start to come over Beth. 'Apparently, I was not focused enough on my job this season and needed to set a good example for the others.' He was frustrated and upset. Running his hand over his face, he took another step towards her, pleading with her to understand.

'I have been wanting to see you ever since I left you standing in that laneway. It's crazy but you're all I can think about.' Beth was still unsure of his words. He could easily read her uncertainty and her feelings about what his sister and father had done to keep him prisoner, at the age of twenty, at his own home—a place that should have been safe and secure. He was a grown man and could make his own decisions, but his father saw him as something to be controlled. And he hated it.

Everyone at Silverleigh was scared of Mathew O'Loughlin. His demands and orders carried a heavy weight, and no one crossed him for fear of losing their job and never getting a chance to find another one. If you turned against Mathew, you could kiss your future goodbye. Delivering a message to Beth from him was too much of a risk and Tom wouldn't let the boys do that. Their jobs and families were too important to go against such as powerful force as Mathew O'Loughlin. That man, Tom had to call a father, ruled with a heavy iron fist, and it was well known his word was an unspoken law. Mathew could ruin a person, or their family's lives, if he thought they had done him wrong. And he had followed through with his threats, not just once, but many times before.

Tom could see Beth's mind working as she chewed her bottom lip. She was too smart and was already piecing things together— things he didn't want her to understand.

'So, because of me, they stopped you having your freedom. They held you prisoner.' Her voice trailed off into a whisper.

Tom stepped forward, shaking his head. He bent at his knees, so he was eye level with her, his hands on her hips. 'It wasn't you. I told him no and he didn't like it. That's all.' Beth studied his eyes intently. She knew he wasn't telling her the whole truth. She could read it in his expression as tears started to sting her eyes— for him and what he had gone through these past few days. But he wouldn't let her blame herself for his horrible family.

'I'm sorry, Tom,' was all she could say as he pulled her to him. His arms slipped around her body, and they held each other tight as he buried his face into her neck.

'I'm sorry,' she whispered softly again. He could hear in her tone, she was blaming herself. Holding her tighter as she stood on her tiptoes and wrapped her arms around his neck, Beth held him just as tight as he was holding her. She comforted him.

Shifting his position, Beth laid her head against his chest—against his heart. Lifting his hand and threading it through her thick, wavy, blonde hair, Tom held her close and closed his eyes to let her calmness still his raging mind, body and soul.

Beth had that effect on him. His temper could be out of control and his thoughts not making any sense, but just seeing her, he calmed down to his usual self and everything seemed right in the world again. He had tried to protect her from the truth of his family's manipulative behaviour, but she had seen straight through his words. She had immediately known the truth of why his phone had been taken, and why he'd been unable to see her. And now, here she was comforting *him*, instead of him comforting and protecting *her* from the truth. He held her tighter to him again.

Sensing the confused stare from Beth's neighbour, Tom released her just a little so he could see her face, the mood too tense now that she was right in front of him. He needed to see her smile and hear her laugh.

'Are you commando all the way?' he teased. The purr in his voice sent goosebumps all over her body, which inflated his ego. Slapping his shoulder, Beth pulled away, letting her arms slip from around his neck. She pulled at her shorts and shirt to cover herself more but made it more obvious that he was in fact correct. His lips twisted with the thought of running his hand up and under her top, to feel the silky smoothness he was so sure her skin felt like. The longing to have her pressed up against him, caused him to desire her more. A redness tinged Beth's skin. She stopped fussing and brazenly stood taller, shoulders back. Smiling seductively, she teased him, letting him have more of his fill.

'I might be, but you will never find out.' She flirted with him, causing a rakish

smile to lift his lips. His eyes travelled the length of her body—slowly—seemingly drawing out something wild and fun and powerfully sexual within her.

'Get dressed and come with me.' He wanted her with him right now. He wanted to put his hands all over her body and explore what it was about her that had him thinking of her every minute of every day.

'Come with me, Beth. We could go someplace where we won't be disturbed, and talk. Just the two of us.' He playfully twisted her hips back and forth as he whispered to her, begging her to understand just how much he wanted to have her all to himself for the day.

'I can't.' She pushed his hands away, and something cooled between them, causing his nerves to leap. 'Kathryn is helping me with my studies today and I need time to think about all of this.' She looked him directly in the eyes and he could feel the barrier he had just brought down between them, going back up. 'I can't be the one to cause you and your family to fight, and I'm not like other girls either.' Her gaze flicked away before she added, 'Others like you're used to, okay?' She took a step sideways towards the door. 'If that's all you want, then go and find it elsewhere. I'm sure you can with any number of girls that swarm around you.'

Frustration welled and Tom tried to remain as calm as possible. 'What are you talking about? I'm not like that.' She was back to not trusting him again. He needed to regain her trust— because of his bloody family. 'I just want to spend the day with you so we can get to know each other better, without anyone else being around and interrupting, that's all. If that's all you ever want it to be—friends—then that's okay with me too.' He was pleading with her. 'Trust me when I tell you this, my family fights are between us and have nothing to do with you. Besides, we had fun the other night, didn't we?'

Beth nodded.

'So, come with me tonight.' He leaned in close to her again, his mind racing and searching for any excuse to spend time with her.

'It rained last night. Enough that we can't harvest today.' Beth chewed her bottom lip as she listened. 'Some of us are going to go skiing and have a bonfire later. I can pick you up and we can just hang out. Two friends.'

Beth was hesitating but Tom could see her thinking about it. He could see her thoughts reflected in her eyes as she debated her answer.

'Kate will be there, and I think Braydon was going to invite Adelaide and Montana. So, you won't be alone without friends.'

'Braydon is inviting Adelaide?' She raised her eyebrows as they smiled knowingly at each other before she answered yes. Relief flooded his body. He had been holding his breath waiting for her to agree.

'I will pick you up later this afternoon. Bring your swimmers.' He leaned in and gave her a quick kiss on the cheek, his lips branding her skin, before he left.

'I didn't know you were friends with Tom O'Loughlin,' Beth's mother's voice called out from the kitchen as Beth closed the screen door, watching Tom's ute drive off down the road.

'We met at the festival. He was the one we pulled into the water, remember?'

'The one that pulled *you* into the water, you mean.'

Beth smiled at her mum and floated back to her room. She needed to get dressed and get to the café.

Chapter 8

Tom arrived back at Beth's house mid-afternoon that day. Anxious and already waiting for him on the verandah, she was wearing a pair of short, cut-off jeans, a white crocheted shirt over her bright pink bikini top, and her thongs. Not quite knowing what to wear, she had called Montana and Adelaide to discuss it. Together they had all decided what each other should wear, talked about their nerves, and formulated an escape plan if things went bad with the SB girls.

She had also packed a small bag with a towel and change of clothes, plus her boots for later that night. She was so nervous; she had changed her clothes and packed her bag with different outfits at least five times before she settled on what she was happy with. Even while waiting for Tom, she nearly went back and changed again. He arrived just in time to stop her. Pulling up into the driveway, he watched her walk down the steps towards him, with a smile on his face.

Leaning over the seat of his ute, he pushed open the door for her to hop in. Sliding in and placing her bag into the back seat of his ute, she looked at him with a little frown on her face. 'What?'

'You look beautiful,' Tom said and leaned in for a quick kiss. The sensation warmed her skin and twisted her nerves about the afternoon and the others who would be there, into a warm, calm sensation he always seemed to bring. Even when nerves and excitement were strong, the calmness he brought her was there. It was about being with him.

'You're a smooth talker who is used to getting his own way,' Beth teased back.

'You ready?' He ignored her teasing with a wink and an even wider smile. He knew he could get away with anything and he knew how to bend everyone to his will with that look.

'No.' She let out a long, loud breath and rubbed her hands on her thighs, removing some of the sweat on her palms.

'You will be fine. I promise.' Taking her hand, he raised it to his lips and kissed it. 'I won't leave you, and Kate, Adelaide and Montana will be there, so you won't be alone.'

Not letting her hand go, Tom held it as they drove the hour out to Braydon's family farm. Braydon's parents' property was past Silverleigh and opposite Kate's father's land, but the driveway was further along than Kate's.

The black bitumen highway was smooth until Tom turned off into a flattened grassed area between two fence posts. He then followed a nearly non-existent grass track, now only visible by the fact that other vehicles had been there before them and had flattened the grass into what looked like a road.

As the scene materialised before her, Beth's eyes grew wide. At other bonfires she had been to—with her own social class—there was a fire pit and camping chairs around it. Everyone brought their own eskies filled with drinks and ice, and maybe the odd packet of chips. If they had decided to have some fun in the creek, then they had makeshift rafts and old tyre tubes from her father's shop. What was in front of her now, was nothing like that.

The first thing she noticed, apart from all the people standing around hundreds of thousands of dollars' worth of brand new utes and cars—all parked, tailgates in, towards the unlit fire—was the height of the bonfire. It looked like a tepee of the native Americans. Wood logs were stacked leaning against one another, reaching high into the sky. Once lit, you would see it for kilometres.

The two utes that were not parked near the others were backing down into a cemented boat ramp at the river. One had what looked like a brand-new jet ski on it. The shiny water craft was ready to unload as the trailer submerged into the water with one of the boys already sitting on it. The large, black machine then floated out onto the water and away from the trailer. The other ute had a large trailer behind it, with an impressive and very expensive-looking jet boat waiting to be unloaded. In the boat, Beth could see a few ski tubes. Everything was bigger and grander here, and she suddenly felt well out of her depth. Watching a few of the boys, all in brand name clothing and sunnies, helping to guide the watercraft into the water, she suddenly felt silly for being here with Tom. These people were not her friends or even part of her friend group. She had no right to be anywhere near this spectacle.

Looking around the area as they idled their way to the spot where Tom wanted to park his ute, Beth realised there were a lot more people than she had anticipated, and more would probably arrive as the day continued into the night. She saw some of the SB girls, all wearing the latest summer dresses and outfits. They looked more ready for a casual but semi-formal picnic than an afternoon of fun on the water—like Beth was dressed for. They all knew Tom's ute, so were all staring and waving at him as he found his spot and stopped. Her nerves started to make her feel sick. This was not such a good idea after all.

Letting each other's hands go, Beth left her belongings on the back seat and shyly climbed out of the ute, ensuring to avoid all the stares she knew she was getting from everyone watching to see who Tom had brought with him for the afternoon. Coming around the front of the ute, she saw him take in the others. With the barest of smiles, he boldly took her hand and led her towards the water.

He was deliberately ignoring everyone and leading her away and, in that moment, Beth tightened her grip on his fingers, causing him to turn back and look at her. Slowing his pace a fraction, so as not to make it seem like they were running from everyone, he walked quickly beside her to the river. Out of the corner of her eye, Beth could see the SB girls staring at her, some with their mouths slightly ajar, others whispering between themselves.

'Geeze, I hope Kate or the others are here,' she whispered to herself. But Tom had heard and before he could reply, his name was called out across the grassed paddock.

'Tom!!!!' Braydon called out to them. He stood in the boat as it was being backed into the river. 'Jump in and we will test her out.'

'Hold up, Noah! Let us in,' Tom called to the driver of the ute. Noah stuck out his thumb and stopped to wait for Tom and Beth to climb into the boat with Braydon.

'Wait for me!' Adelaide called as she appeared from the other side of the ute. Beth let out a sigh of relief. Braydon reached down and pulled Adelaide up into the boat as Tom helped Beth step up first onto the trailer, then over the side of the boat. Following her, his hand barely left her body. Noah slowly backed the rest of the way into the water. Another boy, Beth recognised as Tom's other teammate from the festival—Jack—released the floating luxury machine, allowing it to softly float away from the trailer.

Noah pulled back up the ramp and parked Braydon's ute away from the river, but close enough to easily pull back in and load up later, he waved at them, after climbing out and closing the door. Finding their seats at the rear of the boat alongside Tom, Beth and Adelaide stayed close together, their faces relaxing a little. Their nerves at being there without each other were now gone and the security of being in the boat away from the SBs and with the boys, helped them to finally breathe a little in the security they had just been graced with. Braydon threw out a tractor tyre tube but left the others in the boat, before he started the boat, and it loudly roared to life.

'Hang on!' he yelled back to them. Before they knew it, they were flying along down the river, water splashing up over them as they hit the little ripples in the river and flew around bends, missing fallen trees and logs and even the occasional bird crazy enough to cross their path at the last minute. One caused Beth and Adelaide to instinctually duck, which made both boys laugh.

Her hair whipping around her face, Beth cursed at herself for forgetting her hat in all her changing of her clothes. She had remembered to tie the bulk of it up but with no cap to stop the little bits, it was stinging her face. Tucking it back behind her ear constantly, she tried to keep it back, but it wouldn't stay. Taking his cap off, Tom readjusted the clip and helped her secure it to her head.

At first, she had tried to remove it and give it back to him, but he just shook his head. 'I don't want you getting burnt.' His strong words effectively stopped any protest she could wage. Satisfied with himself, he then openly kissed her cheek, causing a faint blush to colour her cheeks.

The boat slowed and turned so sharply that the side of the speed machine where Adelaide was sitting, nearly washed over with water from the river. Gripping the side of the seat with both hands, Beth held on tight at Braydon's eradicate manoeuvre. The boat, now stopped, rocked with the waves, the motor now idling, as Braydon threw out the long banana tube. 'You pair are first.' He looked at Tom and Beth with a wicked playful smile.

'What? No.' Beth didn't want to be first; she wanted to watch and gauge what the others did. She didn't want to be the first and on full display as they were pulled as fast as Braydon could go back down the river, only to be most likely tipped off in front of everyone. She looked over at Tom for help, begging him with her eyes to say no. But he was no support. Standing and walking towards Braydon, it appeared it was just accepted that they were now to be first.

'Yep. Come on. Off with ya gear.' Braydon winked at her. 'You got the goods. Don't be shy.'

'You just keep your eyes on the river and off Beth's goods, hey?' Tom slapped his friend's back and then pulled off his shirt. Beth and Adelaide both watched. Tom's muscles rippled with his movements as his strong shoulders and muscled chest led all the way down to where his shorts hung low on his hips. His tanned body caused Beth's mouth to dry, and she unconsciously licked her lips.

Flicking his thongs off, Tom turned away without another look at her and her beautiful pleading eyes. Diving into the water, he let the cold briskness of the muddy river take the heat of his body away and cool his desperate need to claim Beth's lips and devour them until she melted against him with need. The image of her coming towards his ute that afternoon had burned into his mind, and he had been half aroused since. She was truly the most beautiful woman he had ever seen.

Breaking back up to the surface a little away from the boat, he waited, treading water, for her to follow him. She had taken her shirt off and was now unbuttoning her little pair of short shorts. Her movements slowed when she bent and slid the denim over her bottom and down her legs. Kicking the discarded item away from her feet, she stood back up and tightened her ponytail, her movements graceful. Tom couldn't pull his eyes from her. He had seen girls in bikinis before and a very select few, totally naked, but Beth's body was like a Photoshopped model in a men's magazine. He groaned silently. Even in the cold water, he could feel himself growing harder.

Giving her sunglasses and Tom's cap to Adelaide, the sun behind her made Beth look like a silhouette as she nervously retightened her ponytail again. Giving an unreadable look at Adelaide, she shot a smug look at Braydon—just to tell him he had not bested her—and then dived boldly into the water.

Sitting on the tube directly behind her, it was even worse. Beth was pressed fully up against him. Her bottom fitted into his groin perfectly and when she leaned back against him and asked, 'You won't let go, will you?' he nearly lost himself like a green teen seeing his first naked girl and knowing he could touch her.

'Not a chance,' he whispered into her ear. Painfully swallowing his reaction to her, Tom moved his body closer again. His arms locked tight around her, pulling her flush against his heated body, he could feel her body's warmth against his cold, bare skin. His arms rested tightly along the side of her breasts, anchoring her to him as he took hold of the banana's handle right next to her hands. Slightly covering hers, he locked her to the bright yellow plastic thing even more. Tom could feel Beth's heart racing. All he had to do was stay focused on holding onto her and the bloody horrible yellow tube now locked tightly between his legs. If he didn't, they would end up in the water more times than he cared for.

Beth adjusted her bottom more securely against Tom's groin, causing his hardness to press solidly into her bottom. Biting the inside of his cheek, and fighting the urge to push back, Tom mentally cursed and locked his jaw tightly. The strength of the flex caused his eye to flicker a little with restraint against his body's natural reaction. His eyes twitched again, and he thought he was going to break his jaw when he felt her give a little shiver as the coldness of the water mixed with the heat of the day, causing her body to react. The pressure of her nipples growing hard in her bikini top against the inside of his arm, caused Tom's body even more pain, and he fought the desperate urge to kiss Beth's shoulder and sample what her skin and river water tasted like together.

'You pair ready?' Braydon called out to them, his arm around Adelaide who was now standing next to him.

Leaning into Beth's ear with a smile, Tom whispered, 'I think they are more than just friends.'

Beth's head lulled back against him a little, and she nodded as her gaze took in their friends. Another wave of goosebumps rolled over her. Tom was not going to make it through the afternoon if her body kept doing this every time he was near her. Grinding his jaw again, he concluded he was going to have to spend the entire afternoon in the water to keep everything cold and as non-reactive as possible.

'Are you ready?' he asked her, and when she nodded nervously, he gave Braydon the thumbs up.

The boat started off slowly, allowing the rope to gently tighten. They started to move. The second the rope was taut, Braydon sped up and soon they were hanging on for dear life to a long, yellow, plastic thing locked between their legs. The excitement and adrenaline pumping through them both made them hold on and laugh. Beth tried not to scream, her concentration focused on holding on, written all over her beautiful face. She laughed along with him, though he wasn't quite sure if it was laughter of joy or to quell her fear at the speed Braydon loved to go back down the river at.

Keeping to his promise, Tom was pressed hard to her, holding her tight and secure within the safety of his arms. Legs like vices over hers, he was never going to let her go as the bend in the river arrived, then the bank of the river appeared, where everyone was gathered for the afternoon party at the river. Adelaide moved to the back of the boat—away from Braydon and prying, gossiping eyes, and let the rope go from the back of the boat.

The banana tube, along with Tom and Beth, freely skidded and bumped roughly along the water wake, over the boat's wash and towards the opposite bank, still going at a rapid speed. Before they collided with the muddy riverbank, Tom leaned to the side and fell into the water, taking Beth with him, laughing.

The force of speed and the rate at which they entered the cold water, hurt. Stealing the laughter of moments ago, it sucked the air from their lungs. Coming up for air, Beth wiped the water from her eyes and treaded water as she calmed her racing heart. Tom broke through the surface, laughing and trying to reach for her as Braydon brought the boat up alongside them.

'Think you pair might need these,' he called and tossed out an old, blown-up car tube. 'Think you both need to cool off before getting out. Especially you, my man.' Braydon deliberately threw another one at Tom with a smile before pulling the boat away to the opposite side of the river and gathering more people onboard for yet another ride.

Climbing into one of the tubes, her legs and arms dangling over the tyre and her arms moving backwards, Beth paddled away from Tom as he loosely held onto the old tube Braydon had given him. Smiling a 'you can't catch me look' at him, Beth laughed when he took the challenge with a smirk and leaped for her. Frantically paddling with a shrill squeal, Tom swam after her in hot pursuit. He was on her before she got more than two strokes away.

Grabbing the tube from underneath her, Tom flipped her over. Even though she was underwater with her ass in the air, a car tyre attached to it, Beth was not going to let the old black tube go. Kicking wildly, she tried to right herself but couldn't, eventually letting go when the need for air become too much. She returned to the surface, only to have the tyre smack her in the face. Tom had tried to steal it off her arm but had accidently hit her instead.

'Ough,' she spluttered. Laughing at what had just happened, Tom moved his arms to get closer to her, the tyre still in his grip. He splashed water into her eyes again. 'Tom!'

'Are you okay?' he laughed as Beth coughed and wiped her eyes.

'No.' She splashed him back, leaping away, playfully. Letting the tube go, Tom leaped after her, pulling her down further.

Taking her deep under the water, the small gasp of air she took before he pulled her down, began to leave her lungs. With arms grabbing anything she could, she found Tom's head and pulled him to her. Their lips smashed together in the water. His surprise made him let her go and they came to the surface coughing and laughing.

Treading, watching each other as they calmed their breathing, the electric current that always seemed to pulsate through her body when Tom was around, rippled and crackled the air around them. The heated look in Tom's eyes gave away that he too was feeling the exact same current. Sensing his arm, more than feeling it as it neared her body, Beth edged away and glanced over Tom's shoulder. Seeing the tyre tube first, and taking advantage of Tom's distractedness with her, she leaped onto it.

'Ha! got it,' Beth cried out as she tried to climb back into it, determined to be the victor over the tube.

'No, you don't!!' Tom grabbed her leg and pulled her back down under the water, tussling over the black rubber. Both determined to not let the other one win, their grips were locked tight on the tube. Coming up for air, their faces and bodies were inches apart. They breathed hard and giggled quietly as they both held onto the tube, neither letting go. Their eyes locked together.

The air around them started to heat and crackle again, this time more intensely. Tom blindly found Beth's waist in the water and pulled her slowly to him, his eyes never leaving hers. Nothing was between them. Her arms entwined around his neck, and her legs wrapped around his hips. He easily treaded water for them both as they still gripped onto the tube. That battle not yet over.

With their breathing a little uneven, Beth could feel his need and excitement for her pulsating at her bottom—and she couldn't deign her own. She could see it all reflected in his eyes as they grew more heated before her. Beth wanted him to kiss her just as much as it looked within the depths of his eyes like he wanted to. She wanted to have his hands run over her entire body, and have his pressed to hers. But after that morning, she needed to trust him again. She needed to know for sure that he wasn't like the others. And that thought cooled her need just a little.

But what was pulsating, right below the surface, of not only the water, but her body, was fighting to crush any of her thoughts about trusting him. Her hands moved into Tom's hair and her nails scratched his skull as she looked down and carefully studied his face. Her body was hot and cold, intertwined with his, the sensation sending heat low and pulsating deep within her body.

Leaning in, Beth kissed Tom softly. Tenderly. Teasing and tasting. He responded gently. Tilting his head upwards to make it easier for her, she deepened the kiss with a slip of her tongue into his mouth. A groan sounded from deep within his throat, and she reacted by pressing her body to his more.

Forgetting where they were, Tom let go of the tube and pressed her hips into his. Without him treading, they sank into the water, their lips still joined. Beth started to laugh as the water slipped over their heads. Letting him go to tread her own water again, they both rose. Tom reached for her, his one arm wrapping her tightly to him. The quiet sternness of his head shaking back and forth told her he was not letting her get away until he was ready.

'You pair had better get a room!' Trent called out from across the river. Beth's eyes widened. She had forgotten they were in full view of everyone. They had been oblivious to those watching on the other side of the river as they played and wrestled in the water over an old car tube.

Tom looked back over his shoulder to Trent as he held Beth to him, turning in the water so she couldn't get away. She now only faced him and not the spectators, but she still witnessed what he didn't. The girls' gazes were green with envy while the boys were laughing and making rude comments about them.

They had heard nothing of it. Until now.

'Go to hell, Trent,' Tom called back before giving Trent the bird.

Beth was horrified. She tried to push away from him without making it look obvious, but he wouldn't let her go.

'Don't Beth.' Tom's grip tightened beneath the water. 'Don't let them get to you. You're here with me, remember? Their opinion doesn't matter. Nobody's opinion matters, but yours and mine. I want you here with me.'

'I can't,' she replied breathlessly, near panicking. 'I thought I could, but I can't Tom. Let me go.' She tried again to get away, but he held her close. Her embarrassment of her actions in front of all these SBs began to overwhelm her.

Firstly, she had been pulled into the water at the festival in front of everyone, then there was the photo with the team, her soaking wet body on the front cover, outlining every curve and indent she had as her clothes had clung to her. Then Tom had seen her nearly naked, she had vomited all over him and his ute, then she had been caught kissing him at his family's property by Megan—not to mention the incident in the header—and now they had been watched by everyone on the opposite bank.

Her humiliation was eating her alive. She had never embarrassed herself like this before and now she had to swim over there and climb out in front of all those SBs and slimy boys, in her bikini, after what they had just witnessed. There seemed to be so many more of them than what she had first thought on their arrival.

She wanted to be there with Tom, but not at the cost of all the SBs' jokes and sneered remarks about her being something she wasn't. It was too much and now, held as she was in his arms, her face now buried into his neck, to hide her humiliation from him, tears filled Beth's eyes. She couldn't help it. She had been feeling completely out of her depth with Tom since she had vomited all over him and he had carried her to his ute. She was drowning around him and there seemed to be nothing she could do about it.

Splashing water over her face to try and hide the tears from him, failed. 'It's okay.' He kissed her forehead and looked back at her. She shook her head, but they kept falling. This was all the more embarrassing.

'I'm not a crier. I promise.'

'It's okay,' he hushed her, trying to soothe her emotional outbreak.

'No, it's not. Ever since I met you, I've done nothing but embarrass myself or you.' Her irritation and temper started to rise.

'You have never embarrassed me.'

'Yes, I have,' she snapped. 'At the festival. You had to carry me shirtless to your ute.' Beth once again tried to pull away, but he wouldn't let go.

'I am now a god, thanks to that.' Tom puffed his chest out. 'I got to carry a very sexy damsel in distress back to my ute with her draped all over my half-naked body in front of my mates and all those nasty bitches who throw themselves at me.' Raising one arm, Tom showed her his muscled 'hero' bicep.

Beth giggled a little. 'A god, you say?'

'Yes. I say. Those little bitches now don't know what to do. They don't know what to do about the gossip we're creating, and the boys are all just jealous that I have you hanging over me.' Beth rolled her eyes at him. 'Now come here and let's give them something to really talk about.'

Tom kissed and nibbled at her neck as she laughed louder and tried to push him away. He let her go and she ducked under the water. Her body slippery, she escaped him, the thoughts from before now pushed to the back of her mind, though still lingering in the darkness there.

'When you pair are finished getting all hot and sexy over here ...' Kate floated over to them on one of the large tractor tubes with Montana. '... you need to come with us and get a drink. We need to get this party started.'

With Tom's help, Beth climbed up and onto the large, black, skin-burning tube, but when he tried to follow her up, all the girls pushed him back off and paddled away laughing.

Relaxing a little being in her friend's company and her protective circle, Beth saw Tom's lips give a pull at one side. He needed to cool down, and they both knew she was safe with Kate, so letting her go with her two friends was the best idea.

The afternoon passed quickly. Kate made sure Beth was introduced and respected by the other girls. Kate was thought of as one of the SBs, even though she had grown up being close friends with Montana and Adelaide. Trevor, Kate's father, had a very large property bordering Silverleigh and Jeff's parents on either side, as well as Braydon's family, who owned the land on the other side of the highway to Kate's. She had been a regular at Megan and Tom's house when they were growing up, since their mothers were close friends. Kate's time spent there was mostly on summer holidays when Tom and Megan were home from boarding school. But that had all changed after Tom's mother's death, and Kate had not been to Silverleigh since Megan returned to live there permanently.

Her friend was also one of those girls who called it as she saw it. She knew all of these SB girls and if they passed her on the street and didn't say hi, Kate would make sure that people in hearing distance would know about it. Even though those girls loved attention, Kate's lecture and ability to cut you down with only a few words, was something that group of girls hated. Even if it was bred into them to be rude.

Kate demanded respect for all those she loved, and today that beautiful girl was the link between them all. The link that made sure everyone got along and none of the bitchiness that came naturally out of the SB mouths, was allowed. At least in front of her that was. After a few drinks and more swimming, everyone was getting used to everyone else. It wasn't all roses, but it was pleasant enough.

While Beth was with Kate, Montana and Adelaide, who had decided to come and be with them, Tom ventured to hang out with the boys. She had seen him water skiing and tubing with Braydon and Noah, each time ending with a spectacular entrance into the water. He would come over to her regularly, making sure she was okay or checking to see if she needed another drink or something to eat, before taking another beer for himself and Braydon and going back to have more fun. Each time, her smile lingered on her lips for longer, and her care for the others' opinions began to diminish.

By the time dusk began to creep in, Beth was feeling relaxed and secure being there. When some of the others decided to race across the river on the tractor tubes, Tom joined the girls' team along with Braydon. Both boys were determined to not be on the losing team this time. Climbing up onto the tube with a little help to balance, and making sure they were not going to fall off, the boys helped the girls, along with a couple of the SB girls—much to Beth's surprise—get on with them. The girls were at the front and the boys were at the back to help give it more power.

Once the word was given to go, everyone madly kicked and paddled, laughing and joking, trying to beat each other with not only their tubes but with their words. It was competitive, but no one was going anywhere fast. The size of the tubes made it way more difficult than Beth had first thought.

Halfway across the river, the other team deliberately crashed into them, grabbing, scrapping, pushing, and shoving until the large, black tube tipped over, causing them all to fall into the water with screams of laughter and curses about unfair conduct. Not ones to lose, Tom and Braydon pushed the girls back up and onto the tyre again and instead of getting fully on themselves, they pushed the girls from behind, hanging half off, half on, making up so much ground, they only lost the race by a few feet.

The others cheered and teased Tom and Braydon about being on another losing team again. Girls laughed and giggled as everyone exited the water full of teasing fun and typical slaps on the back for losing. There seemed to be no social lines anymore. They all walked out and talked together, even walking alongside Beth and the twins.

'Rules are rules, boys,' Trent stated as he walked behind Tom, who was just catching up to her after Noah tackled him back into the water. Trent had pushed the tubes back out on the water to be spiteful. He made Beth's skin crawl a little.

With a quick kiss on the cheek, which made her blush a little as everyone around them ignored Tom's quick show of affection, Tom promised he wouldn't be long as he left her with Kate to go and help Braydon. Because they lost, Tom and Braydon had to load up the boat, jet ski and all the other equipment, while everyone else got changed and grabbed another drink, ready for the night of fun to fully kick off.

All the girls collected their clothes and made for a path that led up beside the river, before it opened up to large boulders in and around the water's edge. Some of the girls who had been faster to gather their things, went first behind the boulders to change as the others just seemed to form a line and wait.

Beth and Montana stood to the back of the forming line and waited for Kate and Adelaide, who were not far behind them. Ashleigh, one of the SB girls, was standing in front whispering to her friends, Katrina and Mackenzie. They had been the rudest of the girls all day towards Beth, and now, as Beth looked back a little nervously, hoping like hell Kate was coming, Ashleigh, pretending to now only see them standing there, turned with a sickly sweet smile.

'Oh, it's you girls. Are you having fun? We love doing this all the time. We get to spend time with our boys and let our hair down,' Ashleigh said in a sweet voice.

Smiling back with a tight-lipped smile, Beth answered so Montana didn't say something they would both regret later. 'Great fun.' Beth's teeth were clenched as she tried her hardest to not show her distain for Ashleigh and the other two.

'I heard the other day that you're all leaving at the end of summer. That you got a scholarship into an elite cooking school in the city, Beth. How exciting,' Katrina commented sarcastically.

The knowledge wasn't any big secret; however, the way the snobby girl said it, left Beth feeling like she had done something wrong. Something that was looked down upon. Swallowing the bile that was rising, and taking a deep breath, Beth stood taller. They were not going to steal her victory of her scholarship away from her and make it something less than it was.

'Yeah. It will be great.' Beth couldn't help her smugness, adding, 'I'm hoping to go to Paris next Christmas to study with my teacher.'

'Really?' they both exclaimed, a little more excited than expected. The sound of it made the fine hairs on the back of Beth's neck stand up. There was something odd in the way they said it but before she could analyse the implications of her own words, Kate and Adelaide arrived, forcing the three to turn around and harshly whisper excitedly between themselves.

After changing into her dress, Beth put her wet things, now wrapped up in her towel, safely back into her bag in the back of Tom's ute. She was about to pull her boots on when two arms wrapped around her waist from behind and lifted her off the ground with a growl. She cried out in surprise as Tom kissed her cheek and neck.

'I missed you,' he purred into her ear, putting her on the ground and turning her within his arms. She could smell the beer he had been consuming all afternoon, on his breath. 'And you were gone for too long, too,' he said as he kissed her full on the lips, running his hand up her ribs, causing her to wiggle and giggle at his words as he tickled her. She could taste a slight hint of rum on his breath.

'Have you been drinking rum?' she asked as he leaned his head heavily against hers and closed his eyes. Planting his feet onto the ground wide, she realised he was balancing himself more.

'Just a couple of shots with the boys, but I feel its hit me hard without any food in my guts. I didn't eat lunch today as I wanted to get to you.' He planted another quick kiss on her lips, his hands roaming over her back, sending heat through her veins.

'Well, we will need to fix that now, won't we?' Her hands on his chest, Beth pushed back a little. Stumbling but correcting himself with one foot, Tom pulled her closer again and nibbled at her neck, this time more forcefully.

'Can't I just eat you?' he purred to her as she gave half a little giggle. His words against her skin sent goosebumps all over her body and made her heart beat faster. She could feel the heat of his body through her thin dress as his hands slowly roamed all over her back and ribs as he continued to nibble and suckle her neck. The sensations and sensual stirring of her body from his touches, was causing her to lose track of her thoughts of getting him food.

'Please?' he whispered.

'No. You're all wet.' She laughed again as he grinded his hips up against hers. 'You get changed and I will get you some food.'

'Can you help me?' He stepped her back against the ute, where she had just put her things, whispering into her ear, 'I need help getting out of my shorts and I fear that if I ask anyone else, they might take advantage of me. You're the only one I can trust.'

'Oh.' Beth pushed him away from her. 'I am sure they would love to have their way with you. Shall I go and find someone to help?' She looked around. 'Oh look, there's Ashleigh talking to Jeff. She won't say no.' They both looked over at the mousey brown-haired girl who was talking privately to Jeff.

'Don't you dare,' Tom said all serious. He really didn't like Ashleigh, it appeared. That was fine by her, she didn't like her either. Looking up into his eyes, Beth smiled and relaxed a little against his strong, warm body.

'Do you still need help?'

'Yes, but I guess I'll cope by myself.' He pouted a little before lowering his head and kissing her slowly. His tongue darted into her mouth to taste her before he pulled back to stare into her eyes, then once again he slowly claimed her lips in a long and soulful kiss that had her clinging to him.

Beth's head spun as Tom took from her what he wanted, his hands cradling her face, her hands resting on his wrists. She couldn't trust herself not to touch anywhere else. Her body wanted him as much as she could feel he wanted her. But she needed more from him—to trust that once she gave him her all, he wouldn't walk away because that was what he had wanted the whole time. Those thoughts and the noise of the others around them drew her back into reality, away from where he had swept her. She stepped around him, leaving him to dress himself.

Beth found Kate near Noah at the BBQ. Kate was in charge of handing out the burgers that Noah and Jack were cooking. This entire bonfire night was a well thought out, well-organised get together. Everyone had brought something that everyone else needed. Kate had the BBQ, and Noah the buns and meat patties. Braydon and Trent had the boat and jet ski, and everyone else had brought nibbles, drinks, beers, music, and wood for the fire. Braydon's older brother, Devon, even had a trailer with a water tank and pump on the back. When Beth had asked Tom why, he had explained that a few years back, the bonfire had gotten away, and they didn't have anything to put it out with. It had burned through a quarter of Braydon's family's wheat crop before they had been able to put out the fire. Now Brian Lewis, Braydon and

114

Devon's father, would not let them have another bonfire without the tank and pump being there.

Kate handed Beth two burgers as she looked at the bonfire, now roaring to the top of the tepee, the flames and ambers floating into the night sky. Beth could now understand how the fire had gotten away, and the need for the water tank and pump.

'You had better take two for Tom,' Noah told her. 'He doesn't normally do rum shots with us out here. Mind you, never seen him this happy before either.' He smiled at her in an all-knowing way.

'We're just friends,' she said, but he didn't hear her as music suddenly blasted across the paddock. Everyone covered their ears until the volume turned down a little, to a better level.

Balancing two more drinks in her hands, along with the burgers, Beth walked back to Tom, now sitting on his tailgate talking with Jack. Lights flashed into her eyes for a second, temporality blinding her, as more people turned up. There now must have been about sixty to seventy people, all there to have fun for the night and relax while harvest had been put on hold for a day or two.

Utes parked where they could, people dancing and even some sneaking off together, it looked like the party was in full swing. Most of them Beth had seen around town, but others she had never seen before. Everyone seemed to know each other. Each new arrival was welcomed with a cheer, or a yell of welcome or wolf whistle as they entered the circle around the fire. Most carried an esky, drink in hand already, as they found their way to their closest mates. Taking a seat beside Tom, his arm going around her, Beth continued to watch the crowd in front of her.

As the night wore on, Kate and Montana got her up to dance. The alcohol she had been slowly consuming, and the fact that everyone there all now knew she was there as Tom's guest, relaxed her enough. She had given in to her friends' whining and was now trying to do some line dancing that all the others were doing, but she was failing very badly at following along. She had already bumped into a few of the others. Laughing at her, they all just kept dancing. It seemed now in the darkness of the night, not all the girls were as stuck up or hated the idea of her being there as much as Ashleigh, Katrina and Mackenzie did.

Feeling tipsy and content, Beth could feel Tom's eyes on her as she continued to dance. Everywhere he looked, her skin tingled. And now, as she took a long sip of her beer, she just stared back at him, watching his brown eyes flicker in the firelight. He had been sitting on his tailgate all night, drinking. People were always coming and talking with him, and he seemed to know them all. Lifting her boot to follow Montana and Kate in front of her, she spun around in a circle to begin yet another wild type of line dancing Montana had conned her in to doing. Watching him again, Beth smiled a little shyly, as Tom's eyes seemed to be only glued to her. Placing his beer on the tailgate and blindly excusing himself from the group of boys standing around him, eyes never wavering from hers, Beth lost her concentration on her steps and stood still. A slow smile lifted one side of Tom's mouth as he neared her slowly, where she now stood in the middle of the makeshift dirt dance floor.

'Can you, do it?' he asked, taking her hand. He twirled her.

'Not now. Can you?' she laughed

'Hell no. I'm not that coordinated.' He laughed and pulled her to him before spinning her back out again. Laughing and trying not to fall over, Beth twirled back and into his body. This time he caught her and held her there. The song stopped and a slower song started.

'Dance with me?' He asked her. His eyes steady on hers.

'Are you sure? Everyone will see.' She looked around them quickly.

'Who cares, Beth? They've already seen more this afternoon. Remember, you're here with me. That's all that matters.' Taking her right hand, he rested it his to his heart. His other hand rested low on her back, strong and firm. She found herself locked against him unwilling and unable to move, even if she wanted to.

'See? It's just you and me. That's all that matters', he whispered and kissed her cheek before pulling back and looking down, willing her to tell him he was wrong.

Smiling shyly at him, Beth just concentrated on her breathing and not falling over as they slowly rocked and turned in the one spot on the dirt dancefloor in front of the blazing fire. A few others joined them, including Adelaide and Braydon.

'See? No one really cares', he said to her quietly. He had not taken his eyes from hers, the others around them, forgotten in the intensity of his gaze. The world receded to just this moment. Nothing but his body to hers, hers to his. The stars and moon, the fire and the heat, their steady rocking, and the music in the background.

Slowly, as they moved, Tom leaned in and claimed Beth's lips. Tender, but sure. Slow and gentle. Nothing more than an unsaid promise of that moment together. Resting his head to hers, he continued to lead her around, in their own little world.

It was getting late and some of the others had started to disappear with each other. Pulling Montana with her, Beth left Tom on his tailgate, and together both girls slipped away for a much-needed pee. Wandering back out of the darkness, Adelaide found them and pulled Montana back into the night with her. Adelaide hated the pitch darkness of the shadows, so peeing by herself was not something she did without her sister being there with her. Leaving Beth to find her own way back to Tom, the two girls vanished into the darkness, back the way she had just come.

The light of the bonfire now visible through the trees, along with the sound of the music still pumping hard and never giving way for the night, Beth casually followed the path back along the riverbank.

With a relaxed, tipsy, alcohol-induced sensation, Beth smiled to herself as a bubble of something good and exciting popped within and flowed through her blood. Strolling casually along the path, she was half waiting for the girls to catch back up, but she didn't want to be away from Tom for too long.

Hearing the sound of someone moving through the grass behind her, Beth glanced over her shoulder, expecting one of the SB girls to be emerging from the dark spot on the path just ahead. Her breath caught, and she stopped, not knowing what to do when Jeff materialised and stepped directly around and in front of her, preventing her from going any further.

Her heart beat wildly as she stood frozen in the dark, covered by the shadows of the trees, Jeff's hand wrapped around her wrist, in a vice grip, sending a shiver of fear and a touch of pain up her arm. He always made her feel uncomfortable and fearful. After his actions at the pub, she had managed to avoid him altogether. Until now. Looking through the shadows, she could see Tom, but he wasn't looking for her. Instead, his attention was taken by a large group of girls all laughing and trying to vie for his attention as they surrounded him. She tried to pull her hand away from Jeff, but he held it tight, taking a step right up to her face. A tightness filled her chest as her eyes flittered back to Tom.

'You know he has bedded nearly half of those girls over there, that are standing around him.' Jeff's breath reeked of rum.

Studying the scene before her more closely, Beth could see Ashleigh resting her hand on Tom's knee as she leaned into him, whispering something into his ear. He didn't pull away, and Beth's heart gave a sharp and painful squeeze as she witnessed more and more, watching him with all those girls, like she was in a daydream. She had been played by him. Well and truly played. And humiliated. He really was just like all the others. Jeff gave a little chuckle as he continued to stare at her pain, now delighting in it.

Clearing his throat, he suddenly moved back a step. 'Enough about that regular shit.' Taking in her whole body with a stare that made her skin crawl, Jeff's fingers still held her painfully as his eyes told her what he was thinking about her body. Panic started to take over. Beth needed to get away from him, and from this place.

'You're looking very beautiful tonight, Beth. Mmm mmm mmm. Tom is a lucky boy to have been able to bed you so fast. A lot of boys lost money on that.'

Beth's skin crawled and she shivered at the meaning of his words. 'Let go of my arm,' she stated through her clenched teeth. She had heard enough.

'Oh, I will, but I thought I would do you a favour and tell you that Tom is such a good boy and always does as his father tells him to.'

'Is that right?' Beth was looking back down the way she had come, hoping Montana and Adelaide were on their way back. They weren't. 'What does that matter to me?'

'Yes. It's right. And when his daddy told him to sow his wild oats, he suddenly found you.' Beth looked at Jeff, his words hitting and hurting her more painfully than his grip on her wrist.

Looking back to Tom and all the girls that were surrounding him, they were all in a deep and serious conversation now. Ashleigh's hand was still resting on Tom's thigh as she stood close to his body. Her eyes stinging with embarrassment and humiliation, Beth watched a little bit longer as she saw all the girls now holding all of Tom's attention. He wasn't the least bit worried, or looking for her. His words had been lies.

'See? He can't with them. Even though he has, his father doesn't know that, but Tom can sow as many wild oats with you as he likes. He would never look at you more than something to root ...' Beth pulled her hand out of Jeff's grip, tears in her eyes. Tears he now saw as he sneered at her and added, 'Told you.' He pushed past her and walked away down the path.

Beth's stomach lurched and her body started to shake. She had been played. Was that the reason everyone had been watching and staring at her all that afternoon? They all knew she was just another girl for him to sow his wild oats with. That he and the boys had a bet at how fast he could get her into bed, made her blood boil, and a stabbing pain sliced through her chest. She needed time to cool down and not make a scene. That was the last thing she needed to do—embarrass herself all over again in front of everyone.

Tears falling, Beth held her hand over her mouth to stop any sound from coming out and give away her distress or where she was. Sticking to the darkness, and circling back around to the front of Tom's ute, Beth crouched down to catch her breath and stop her stomach from lurching. She tried to breathe. The last thing she wanted to do was be sick again and have everyone thinking she couldn't handle her alcohol. She had had enough embarrassment over the last week to last her a lifetime. More than she had realised, it seemed.

Though, as she sat on the cold ground, knees to her chest, her mind racing, everything all started to make sense. Ashleigh's, Megan's and some of the other SB girls' treatment of her. The boys' comments about them when they were in the water earlier. His dancing with her, saying how he didn't care what others thought. That was because he already knew what they were saying. Everyone knew what Tom was really like. Except Beth. Her temper spiked as tears fell. She was the laughing joke of the night, and she wanted nothing more than to be able to leave this place and never come back.

Hearing the girls leave Tom's tailgate to dance, Beth sat very still in the dark, leaning against the bull bar. Feeling the ute move when all the others left too, Beth just breathed and tried to stay calm. She had no idea what to do—how to leave and get home, because walking was not an option.

'Beth, are you okay?' Startled, she lifted her head and found Tom standing over her. Crouching down as she shook her head, no words came out as the fresh tears stinging her eyes caused her to curse at herself for her lack of control. She curled up into a tighter ball, pulling her legs to her chest. She looked around him, not wanting to look into those eyes. Tom reached for her, concern on his face turning to surprise as she pulled away from his touch.

Voices drifted to them as others moved between the vehicles. Tom looked up and around, then back to her, as the voices drifted away again.

'Are you hurt? Did someone hurt you?' His face turned hard as he searched for the reason for her distress.

Shaking her head, Beth hissed at him, trying to stop her tears and gain control over her rolling emotions. 'You are just like all the rest. Take me home, now!'

This was not the place to talk this out with him. She didn't want others seeing her cry and she didn't want to cause another scene. That would cause more humiliation to herself and her family. The distress and confusion on Tom's face was easy to read. He knew something had happened, but he wasn't sure what. He understood they needed to talk away from all the others and that she was not going anywhere with him, except home. Rocking back away from him, hugging her knees, he read her stubbornness clearly.

'Come with me,' he ordered, grabbing her hand and pulling her to her feet, fighting. Locking his hand tightly to hers, ignoring her hissing at him to let her go and leave her alone, he led the way into the blackness of the night. Weaving between and around the other utes and cars in the dark, away from all the others, they walked until they could only see the bonfire and the others in the distance.

Tom stopped and looked over Beth's head, then at her, checking to make sure they were far enough away from any prying eyes and ears. He tried to contain the fear over what had happened to her, from raging through his body. Feeling it vibrating through his hand still locked with hers, Beth tried to settle herself, ready to tell him exactly what she thought of him.

'What's happened? Has someone said something?' He tried to pull her to him, but she pushed him away and stood back another few steps. Her eyes wet with tears, she didn't wipe them away as the moon shone brightly above them. Following her retreat, Tom tried to gently pull her close and make it all okay, but she wouldn't back down now, not when she had just decided to stand her ground for once in her life and make him take her home. She was done with Tom O'Loughlin and his mates. Done with everyone here and this stupid town and its stupid rules. Beth took another step back and saw the frustration and anger begin to bubble under Tom's cool façade.

'I want to go home now. I don't want to be part of this little game of yours anymore,' she said through gritted teeth. She saw he was instantly taken back, but only for a second.

'What the hell are you talking about, Beth?' What game?'

Beth began to shake and tremble, her emotional rollercoaster this past week finally taking its toll on her.

'I don't do one-night stands. I am not something for you to *sow your wild oats* with and I am not something for you and your mates over there ...' She threw her hands in the direction of the fire. '... to bet on how fast you can get me into bed. I am better than that. If it happened, then so be it, but if that's all you're after, Tom, then go and find someone else. You have been with most of those girls; I am sure another tumble in the hay, or header, for all to see, won't worry them.' She moved away from him ready to run.

Tom's jaw ticked in the moonlight above, the warm glow from the now-distant fire, her only guiding light into his emotions as she read the shock and horror that was clear on his face. All he did was stare at her.

122

No words.

She had shocked him with the truth he was never going to tell her. She looked away from him, stepping backwards as she did. She didn't want to be here anymore. His non reply was answer enough. Searching the now distant crowd, Beth looked for a way to escape.

Following her retracting steps, Tom once again neared her, his temper about to explode from what she had just said. Bracing, swallowing the fear that began to race through her, Beth stood still, unsure of what was about to happen.

'Who told you that, Beth?' He reached for her, but she dodged his hand. 'None of that bullshit is true.'

'How do I know it's bullshit? I don't even know you.' Her voice was strained and high pitched, as pain gripped at her heart. She had wanted to believe he was different, but those words Jeff had told her, and his family's actions over the past two days, had broken everything she had wanted to believe of him.

'You *do* know me, Beth. I've been nothing but myself around you. I'm more me around you than with anyone else. You're all I think about when I'm not with you. I've never met anyone like you before and I have no idea what this hold is you have on me, but I don't want to give it up. I want us to be friends. More than friends. But I'm not what you think I am. I don't know how else to prove that to you.'

'You can't. Not anymore.' Her words cut him. She couldn't stand to look at him any longer. Turning away, she spun back around to face him. 'How many of the girls here, have you been with, Tom? How many?'

He advanced on her, standing so close to her that she could feel his breath on her chin. But he didn't touch her. 'One.' His eyes locked with hers. He waited for the inevitable question with his jaw pulsating.

'Who? Ashleigh? Katrina?' Fresh tears welled as she choked the words out.

'I'm very particular where I put my things, Beth. That's an insult.'

'Then who?'

'It doesn't matter.'

'To me it does. Those girls have been nasty little bitches all day because I am here with you—the great Thomas O'Loughlin. I don't want to be compared to any of them when you take me to bed.'

The corners of Tom's mouth fluttered with a little smile as he touched the tops of her arms tenderly. Beyond reason, Beth's emotions soothed and calmed just a fraction as tears stung and slipped down her cheeks. 'Trust me, the girl it was with, doesn't want it known as much as I don't want it known.'

Frowning, Beth said, 'Why? All of these girls see you as the ultimate prize. *The* one to have on their belt of conquests.'

'Let's just say that our experience together was fast and awkward. Like being with my sister.' Looking away to hide his embarrassment, Tom took a moment to let a bout of shyness take over, and for an instant, Beth saw a side of Tom she had not expected to be there. 'It was a horrible experience in her father's hay shed.' Tom shook his head. 'I blew my load the minute I entered her, and we had both been eaten alive with lice, and scratched like crazy from the hay dust all afternoon after.'

Beth giggled a little. 'How old were you?'

'Fifteen. And you're not to breathe a word of that to anyone.' He tickled her ribs. The anger and hurt from before had subsided from her a little. Her fists though, were still pressed against Tom's chest, holding him at bay.

'Oh, I won't say anything. Maybe just to Adelaide,' she teased.

'No! She will tell Braydon, and I will never live it down.'

The smile died from his lips as they stood looking at each other, neither speaking. The untruthful words from before slowly creeped back to memory, the energy around them changing with it as Beth began to close up once again. She knew he could see it and didn't know what to do to stop it. She couldn't trust him. Not anymore.

'Who told you those lies?'

'It doesn't matter. Everyone thinks you are just sowing your wild oats with me. That I am nothing more than a slut and a social climber. I shouldn't be here. I want to go home.' Beth's voice was full of hurt and sadness as she looked at the ground at their feet.

'Who told you, Beth?' Tom's temper was bubbling over. He let her go and ran a hand through his hair and over his face. Frustrated, he did not mention her other words. Had not refuted them. Anger took over all other emotions and Beth hugged herself, looking up into Tom's eyes, willing to see something that told her he wasn't what she thought.

'*Am* I just that to you, Tom? Someone to just *sow your wild oats* with?'

'I'm not that kind of person, Beth. Jesus Christ. When are you going to listen to me? Believe me? Trust me? I just told you what you do to me, and a secret that only two people in the world knew until tonight, and still, you don't believe me. What the hell am I to do?' He turned and kicked at the grass, trying to rein in his temper but failing at it.

'Jeff,' she whispered, her hand on his back to try and calm him down. Tom growled like a tormented beast as he turned to face her with a look that made her shake. 'I'm an honest person; why target me?' she said quietly.

'Honest?' he quipped, his voice trembling as rage rolled through him. 'Honest? When were you going to tell me that you were leaving at the end of the summer?'

'What?' she asked confused. 'I thought you knew. You knew I was studying.'

'I knew you were studying, but I thought you were staying here, not hot-footing it off to some fancy cooking school in the city, and then possibly to France next Christmas.'

'I'm sorry. I thought you knew. Everyone seemed to know.' Tom stepped the half step towards her. They stood toe to toe, his temper barely holding.

'So, what is this between us, Beth? You've made it clear that you're not wanting to be a notch in my belt. Not just another girl. But what is it between us then?'

'It's just two people getting to know one another like you said this morning.' Beth held her ground, though she was a little shocked at his words.

'So, what was that display out in the river this afternoon?' His tone made her flinch, but he didn't stop. 'Just two friends trying not to fuck each other's brains out?'

Beth took a step back, but Tom followed her. 'Don't be disgusting. You know that's not what it is.'

'Well, what is it, Beth? Am I just a way for you to climb the social ladder?'

'Stop it. You *know* that's not true. That's not fair.'

He leaned in close, his eyes squinting with anger and hurt. 'Or what am I? Just some notch on *your* belt? Just another fuck?' Too low. TOO LOW. He knew it the moment the words left his mouth. But it was too late. The words had already cut Beth deeply, gutting her to the very core of who she really was.

With eyes wide, Beth struck Tom hard across the face before she recoiled and stood deathly still as tears filled her eyes. She glared at him coldly, her breath caught in her throat with pain. Holding her head higher, trying to hide the devastation Tom had just inflicted on her, Beth took one last look at him, his jaw ticking in shock, before spinning on the sole of her boot and storming back towards the bonfire.

Tom kicked a rock and sent it flying. If he could have kicked himself, he would have. Never in his life had he ever spoken to a woman like that. How the hell did the conversation get to that level? Yes, he had been hurt that of all the people to believe in this messed up small town, Beth had believed Jeff's bullshit. Then to have Ashleigh come over to him, very smugly, and tell him about Beth leaving at the end of summer. That girl had known she had hit a nerve with him when he had stared back at her – blindly – lost for words, while he fought the frustration of Beth not telling him herself. And to make it all worse, Tom was beyond fearful of himself and how he was losing some part of his soul to Beth in such a short amount of time. He was so scared in fact, he thought he would never feel complete again if she ever left him. That in itself was the raging idiot that now stood watching her walk away, wishing he could take back everything he had just said and hold her until she promised to never leave.

Beth had invaded all his thoughts and dreams since they had first met and when he couldn't be with her and touch her, he ached for her, driving himself insane with a deep burn he had no idea how to quell. He was going crazy over her, and tonight had just proved how mentally disturbed he had become. It was all utter madness.

Not wanting to ever have her leave like this, Tom soundlessly raced after her. He had to stop her and beg her to forgive him, beg her not to leave this way and believe in who he really was. He needed her to see the real him and know those words he had just spoken, were not his real thoughts. His boots sliding across the dew-covered grass, Tom cut in front of Beth, and landed on his knees at her feet. Looking up at her, a little shocked at his actions, Beth recovered quickly, slightly raised her eyebrows, and went to step around him.

He reached for her. 'Beth, please? Stop … please?'

Beth stopped and looked down at him kneeling on the ground in front of her, a hauntingly lost look on her face. 'I want to go home, Tom. Take me home now.' She was crying. Silently. He could hear it in her voice.

'I can't, Beth. I would still be over the limit. It would be too dangerous for me to drive.' He stood slowly, not wanting to push her away any more than he already had. She stepped around him.

He turned as she went. 'Please just hear me out. I'm sorry. I never should have said what I said.'

She spun on her heel and stared him down like some warrior woman facing her enemy. 'You called me a slut and a social climber.' Her words were short and clipped.

'I know. I'm so sorry. I was just mad at Jeff, and then finding out that you're leaving at the end of summer, I was upset and my temper got the best of me. Please just sit and hear me out.' He was pleading with her. Desperately pleading with her.

'I want to go home. Now!' she repeated.

'If I could, I would, I promise, but I can't. Not for a few hours yet.'

'Then I will find Montana and she can drive.' 'Everyone is too drunk to drive, Beth. At least for the next few hours. We all sleep it off till morning, in the back of our utes.'

Beth was still shaking. She had never lashed out physically against anyone in her life. The shock at her actions still rolled through her body, and now, as she scratched her hand, the sting from the slap still itched her palm. Hell, the imprint of her hand on his cheek probably still burned. Her eyes glazing over, all she wanted to do was go home to her own bed and never see any of these people again—Tom especially. As she looked over the bonfire and saw the truth of his words, Beth hoped Tom would see the pain she was in because of him, and hate himself for it.

She refused to look at him. 'Was your plan to sleep with me tonight?' Tom looked at her as she whispered her defeated words, letting them hang in the still night air around them, his breathing steady as he chose his words very carefully.

'I wanted you in my swag with me, yes. I wanted to kiss and touch you all over. Yes.' His words were breathy and seemed to be a tide washing over her defences. Glancing at him, Beth looked away, but his next words drew her back to face him. He stepped forward, so close she had to look up to see into his eyes.

'I would not have forced you to do anything you didn't want to do. I'm not like them. I never have been.' Tom ducked his head to kiss her lips, but she turned her head away and he missed. Taking a breath to still her rejection against him, he added more quietly, 'I want you more than anything else, Beth. You have to know that.' His words were very slowly spoken. He wanted her to really hear him and understand. 'I promise I won't have any more to drink and I will drive you home in a few hours. Please just sit with me. We will stay here till everyone goes to bed and then I will take you home.'

.

Chapter 9

The next morning, Beth lay in bed listening to the birds outside her bedroom window. The sun was only just breaking over the horizon as she stared up at the blank, dull-coloured ceiling above her head.

She had been lying there, under her blankets, staring, since Tom had brought her home two hours ago. They had sat in the grass, where he had slipped over after their fight, until everyone had settled and crawled into their swags or another person's swag. Then, taking her hand – under protest - he had led her to his ute and driven her home.

Continually apologising the entire way back into River Flats, he tried to talk to her—talk his way out of what had happened between them—but she couldn't look at him. The pain was too great, and when he walked her to her door and kissed her cheek, asking if she was working later that morning, she could only shake her head as she entered her home, still not a word muttered. Tom must have sat in his ute for a little while because she didn't hear him drive off until she switched off her bedroom light.

Hearing her father moving around their small, family kitchen now, Beth looked over at her clock. He must have gotten a call out. It was too early for anything else. Throwing back the blankets, she climbed out and sat on the edge of her bed. She wasn't going to get any sleep now that the sun had risen. Her mind was still replaying the events of the night before, trying to work out the truth. But she was merely tormenting her emotions and memory, and getting nowhere.

Running a hand through her hair, trying to detangle the mass of knots and grittiness of the river water from yesterday's fun, Beth felt drained and emotionally beaten. In her heart, she wanted to believe Tom was different, but his words still stung.

'Morning Dad', Beth said quietly as she wandered out into the poky, lime green, faded kitchen.

'You're up early this morning, Pumpkin. You only got in a few hours ago. We were not expecting to see you until later this morning.'

'Yeah, well things change.'

After making herself a coffee, Beth sat down with her father.

'I didn't think you were working today,' he said while taking a sip of his coffee and eating a large scoop of his Weetbix.

'No, I'm not. I just couldn't sleep. Kathryn has given me a few days off to have a rest. I wish she didn't; I need the money.'

Beth breathed in the smell of her coffee and curled her legs up on the seat, tucking herself into a ball to ease her rolling, emotional stomach.

'You will have enough by the time you get there, don't you worry.' Getting up and putting his dishes in the sink, Beth's father smiled warmly over to her. 'If you're not up to much, I have to go to a job and could use the company.'

Smiling back at him, she took a big sip of coffee and nodded. It had been so long since she had been on a call out with her dad. It was time they rarely had together—just the two of them—these days and a little father-daughter time was exactly what she needed.

Dressed in a pair of ripped jeans, an old work shirt and work boots, her hair in a messy ponytail with one of her father's tyre shop caps on to help keep the fly-away hairs restrained, Beth was ready to leave by the time her dad was. Smiling and ready for something to take her mind off the last twenty-four hours, Beth was sitting on the verandah when her father walked out.

The old white ute, loaded up with a tractor tyre and gear needed to change it weighing it down, Beth and her father headed out of town, the same way she had driven back in with Tom a few hours ago. Chatting and laughing at the stories her father was telling her, Beth let the worries of the past few days leave her as she watched her father with such love for him in her heart. He was her hero and the first man she had ever loved. Her father was everything and, looking at him now, as he made her laugh and giggle like a little girl, Beth didn't know how she was going to cope living so far away from him and her mother. They had been her one and only world—her entire life—and in a few weeks, she would be leaving them for a very long time. She doubted that with their business, and her study schedule, either of them would be making the long trip to the city or home very often. And it was moments like this, Beth knew she would miss the most. Just her and her dad as they always had been. A team—and man—she could rely on. The large, heavy emotional lump, that always developed when she thought about leaving, formed in her throat, and she looked away from him, knowing he hated seeing her cry.

Continuing down the highway, her father slowed and turned down the dirt road. The same dirt road Beth had travelled on her way to see Tom the first afternoon she went to Silverleigh to spend time with him in the header.

'Who was the call out for, Dad?' Beth's heart began to beat heavy in her chest.

'The O'Loughlins. One of their headers,' he replied plainly as he focused on the track ahead. Beth's throat tightened as her heart continued to beat harder, drowning out all the noise. The blood rushed through her veins, giving her an outer body sensation that began to take over her entire being. Panic rose within.

'One of the workers called it in this morning,' he added when he saw her shift in her seat a little uncomfortably.

132

Relief. It wasn't Tom.

Her father and the men who worked for him, had been here many times over the years Beth's family had lived in River Flats, and as they passed the house, Beth scanned the parked vehicles, trying to find Tom's ute. The main shed was all locked up. He must have parked in there. She couldn't see it anywhere else. Shifting again in her seat, she concentrated on breathing normally as her father continued to drive down the dirt track, past where she had been with Tom that first night. They kept going further into the property, passed where all the wheat was now gone. Harvested and carted away.

Beth's heart stopped when she saw Tom's ute next to one of the headers. He had changed into his work clothes, and was crawling out from under the large, green machine as her father pulled to a stop near the offending wheel. His surprise and confusion at seeing her there, matched her dread.

'Mr Kennedy.' Tom shook her father's hand when he climbed out of the ute. 'Thanks for coming out so early to fix it.'

'Not an issue. Any time. Now, let me have a look.' Beth's father left his door open, like he always did, and walked over to the header, kicking the flat tyre as he rubbed his jaw. Tom looked into the ute where Beth still sat quietly cursing her choice to come out with her father that morning.

'Morning, Beth.'

Not answering or looking at him, she frustratedly got out of the ute, slamming the door closed. She began to untie the spare tyre they had brought with them. The faster this was done, the faster she would be out of there and away from him.

Tom walked around the same side of the ute and stood so close to her, she could smell the fresh deodorant he had applied that morning. The smell, now only associated with him, stirred her body against her wishes.

'I'm sorry, Beth. I didn't mean to hurt you.'

'You've said that already.'

'I know.' Taking over from her to untie the ropes, he said quietly, 'Let me make it up to you. Please?' She didn't have time to reply. Her father walked around and climbed into the back of the ute.

'Here, Tom. Help me lift this big, heavy bugger down.'

Leaping up onto the back of the ute using one hand, Tom lifted the tyre almost by himself. His muscles stretched his shirt across his chest and arms. Beth looked away, over to the now wheat-free paddocks. Anywhere but him.

Her father and Tom changed the tyre and then reloaded the flat one back onto the ute. Beth kept her distance and focus away from them as best she could, though her eyes betrayed her more than once, and she found herself watching Tom, when he was not watching her.

'I will just make sure I have everything.' Her father walked back to the header as Beth retied the rope to hold the flat tyre on.

'Can I pick you up this afternoon and take you somewhere private so we can talk? I promise, it will just be the two of us. No one will know where we are and when you're ready, I can bring you home. It won't be a late night, I promise.' Tom quickly looked over to her father, who was bending to pick up a stick near the other tyre on the opposite side of the header. 'Let me make it up to you for my mistake. I swear to God, I'm not like the others. Please, Beth, just give me a chance?'

Her father walked the long way around the front of the ute to get back to them, clearing his throat, letting them know he was there as he did.

'No.' she whispered harshly and moved away from him, getting back into the ute. She left him to finish tying the ropes and talk with her father about small pleasantries. Though she tried to remain staring through the windshield, her eyes locked onto the rear-view mirror as the two men at the back of the vehicle continued to speak quietly.

After a few minutes, Tom shook her father's hand and gave his thanks. Walking back to the header, she could see him fighting to hide his hurt.

'You know, Beth, when someone acknowledges they have done wrong and are willing to make it right somehow, especially when it's to show you a different side of them, that's a pretty important thing and shouldn't be just shut down in anger without trying to understand more about that person.' Looking over at her father, she watched him shift in his seat and take his time to pull his seat belt on, the deliberate delay giving her time to think about his words.

Opening the door with a huff, Beth got out and slammed it closed again, annoyed at the truth of her father's words. Huffing and muttering under her breath about being played and how she has to stop letting men get the best of her, she stormed up to the large machine. Finding him under the header, greasing up a part of the engine, she snapped, 'You can pick me up at 4pm' before she turned on her heel and walked away, but not before she caught a glimpse of him trying to hide his smile.

It was true. Thomas O'Loughlin made Beth want things she had never wanted before. He made her skin tingle and her stomach fill with butterflies. No one had ever made her feel like that before, and now, when she should be totally focused on her studies and preparing for her dreams in the city to come true, she was thinking about him and what the afternoon would bring.

Last night he had hurt her badly. Very badly. She had let herself be taken in by his words, and her curiosity to explore what it was about him that made her constantly think of him. She craved him and wanted to do things with him—explicit things she had only thought about in her fantasies. He made her feel strong and confident within herself, enough so, she had now begun to not care about what everyone else thought about her and what her relationship with Tom was.

Her whole life was becoming all about him. Maybe that was the threat she needed to understand. Being with him, she was losing her focus on her studies and dreams. She was being sucked into his world, and was now only thinking about how she wanted more with him than she ever could. These thoughts were dangerous and confusing.

She was scared of the power he seemed to have over her. Tom made her forget about everything else but him. She wanted him. She wanted to be with him and spend as much time as possible with him before she left, but she couldn't do that if she was upset and pushing him away all the time out of fear for what was yet to come. Her father had been right. Tom was trying to show her he was different from all the others. Maybe she did mean something deep to him, just like he was fast becoming to her, just like he had told her last night.

But she wanted him to prove it. To prove it to her without doubt, that he was in fact different from anyone else. So far, he had tried to—until last night. When, mixed with Jeff and Ashleigh's cunning manipulations; hurt, anger and maybe fear, had erupted between them.

Maybe he was scared of losing her so soon, just like she was with him. Tom had shown her, through the kisses he had stolen from her, the touches, his laughter, and the talks they had shared, that he was after more than what she had allowed to cloud her judgement. But through her own insecurities, Beth had twisted his intentions into something she was searching for, to make true within her mind; not what was actually right there in front of her. That realisation and her rolling thoughts, played constantly in her mind all throughout the day, and as she fell asleep on the day bed on the verandah, the intrusive thoughts travelled into her dreams.

Tom arrived early to Beth's house that afternoon. His father had actually let him sleep for a few hours before storming into his room, demanding Tom drive the header again. Standing his ground, he refused. That strong stance had created yet another fight between father and son, one that had them toe to toe screaming at each other, before Megan forcibly pushed herself to stand between them, ordering Tom out of the house and trying to placate her father, telling him she would drive. Mathew O'Loughlin flatly refused his daughter and went to find one of the chaser bin boys to do it, glaring at Tom when he drove past, heading to Beth's.

It had always been the same between them. Ever since Tom learned the word 'no' as a toddler, and stopped following his father around, they had argued almost daily. It had become so bad after his mother had died, that one night his father had grabbed him by the shirt collar, picking him up and slamming him into the wall of the shed. It was the night Tom had told him about his choice in university courses.

So shaken by his father's violence, Tom had taken off at a high speed, vowing never to return again. He didn't even have his licence yet, only his learner's, and he had stolen his father's ute. In the blinding rage of tears, he had run off the road and into a ditch on the other side of town. Fortunately, it was Drake and Kathryn who had found him and taken him back to their place to cool off.

Tom ended up staying for two weeks, in secret with them, telling his father he was in the city, before going back to school. In that small, isolated break from the world, Drake had taught him some strategies on how to deal with his temper, but sometimes it rose up so fast, Tom couldn't contain it. He had only seen his father twice since that day, before he had returned home ten days ago.

They had never spoken about what had happened that night, and Tom had been doing his best to avoid being in his father's presence for longer than being given his orders for the day.

Tom was not one to be walked over; however, he knew his place in his family. He had known it from birth. He was to inherit, and continue to grow, the O'Loughlin property portfolio and manage the extremely large family fortune that came with the title of being the heir, all while doing what he was expected to do as he learned at his father's side.

The thing was, it was his grandfather that had taken the time to teach him about running the properties, dealing with the men and successfully managing the money and investments; and it was Megan, who now did it all behind closed doors. Never Mathew.

His father had been too busy and thought he knew it all while his grandfather had been alive. Mathew had no clue as to the real inner workings of the properties or the handling of the money, only enough to keep the fortune and the outside social views, healthy.

When Megan had returned home from boarding school three years earlier, at the tender age of fifteen, his father had promptly turned the entire running of the company over to her, preferring to be seen in public rather than in the office. How Megan did it at such a young age, Tom was in awe of. But his sister was very smart and observant, and even though she was a girl, their grandfather had taken the time to show her just as much as Tom about running the properties and about how to grow money successfully. Now, with his political dreams starting to form, and Tom finishing the right university course, their father had lost all interest in running the O'Loughlin family business—except for the money and power it gave him. He now expected Tom to take over and run the company, but still under his orders and control.

Knowing his place and how he had no way out of the life already planned for him, Tom had wanted to show his father over the next few years just how capable and ready to take over he was. He had big plans to make the properties more environmentally friendly and sustainable, even experimenting with some other crops of the future to ensure the family's fortune kept growing. He had also wanted to rebuild whatever he could out of the relationships he had with his father and Megan. It was what his mother would have wanted, and they were the only family he had left. Those plans, however, had fast evaporated on his return home.

Walking up the front steps, Tom saw Beth asleep on the day bed, her hair spread out across the pillow, and her body turned away from him. Quietly, he crossed to her, delicately brushing off a lock of stray hair from her face. She shifted a little but didn't wake. Standing there, watching her, emotions he had never felt or could even label, flowed through him. He had felt them growing within him every time he was with her. Thinking of her day and night, and now, as he watched her sleep, the same emotions seemed to take root deep within his body, seemingly locking whatever hold she had over him, *to* him. He had nearly lost her with his stupid temper and the lies of others, and he was never going to make that mistake again. Beth had given him one last chance, and he would never let her down again. If that meant telling her every part of his life, turning himself inside out so she could see the real him, then that's what he would do.

'She has been sleeping most of the day there.' Beth's father stood on the other side of the screen door watching him. 'Would you like a coffee?'

Tom smiled, and with a last look at Beth sleeping so peacefully, he entered her family's home.

Beth woke to the sound of a passing truck. Rolling over, she sleepily looked out across the garden as it passed. Blinking a couple of times, then rubbing her eyes to make sure she was not dreaming, she sat up. Tom's ute was parked at the front gate. Low voices from inside drifted to her through the screen door, making her heart beat a little faster.

Tom sat at the kitchen table talking with her parents. Books, papers, and treasures of her father's, were spread everywhere. The biggest of the books was sitting open in front of Tom, a coffee cup to the side of him. They were talking in depth together. Beth's mother sat on the opposite side of the table, listening with a smile on her face as she watched the two men conversing. Beth could see how excited and animated her father was at having someone who seemed interested in his hobby, actually listening to him. He was pointing and talking all at once, even laughing a little at what Tom had said, before turning a page and pointing out something on the new one, to show Tom. Her father had not been so alive for years.

The friends her father had had were all the same. They would travel and go to shows back home together, but when everything fell apart and her parents had a large debt to pay, her father had been forced to sell everything, including all of his prize artefacts. In the midst of all the turmoil and emotional breakdowns that became a part of their lives, especially towards the end, her mother had ensured her father still had his books and papers. They were the one thing she couldn't let him sell, no matter how much money they would have sold for. It was the only thing her father had brought with them, along with his two sets of clothes and a pair of work boots.

The hardest part in those devastating months, that ripped their family apart, was how his mates from the club, cut him off once they learned about his debt. It had hurt her father deeply, but he tried to never let Beth or her mother see it. Seeing him now with Tom, he was like a little kid again, talking and laughing as he spoke. The scene made Beth's heart fill with joy, and she shifted a little in her spot trying to stop the tears from welling up in her eyes.

The movement caught Tom's attention, and he looked up at her and smiled. Her heart leaped and she found herself trapped in his brown-eyed gaze. She wanted to stay there for as long as possible, held in that warm moment, her whole body filling with a floating sensation as he continued to stare at her.

Seeming to be under the same intense feeling, but more alert to his surroundings, Tom stood, not breaking eye contact with her, his movements alerting her mother and father of her entrance.

'Oh, you're up, Honey,' her mother said as she too stood, touching her father's shoulder. 'You need to pack that up now and let these two get going.' She smiled over at Beth.

'What are you doing in here?' Beth asked Tom before looking to her parents. 'Why didn't anyone wake me?'

'We had plans, remember?' Tom moved away from the table and started to walk towards her. 'Your father offered me a coffee while I waited for you to wake.'

'You like ancient war memorabilia?' she asked with a quizzical look before looking at the table.

'I studied ancient history in my senior years at school, so I guess,' he admitted a little shyly. 'But, I'm not up with it like your dad, though.' He turned and smiled at her father, who looked up from stacking his books on top of each other.

'He knows more than he is saying, Bethy. His knowledge is more of Roman history, but we can expand on that.' He winked at them both before continuing with his task.

Tom turned and smiled at her, whispering as he leaned into her, 'He is wrong. My brain is hurting from trying to recall all that I had learned.'

Smiling, she leaned back away from him, not wanting him to kiss her in front of her parents. 'You know he will now talk your ear off about it every time you come around.'

'Does that mean I'm invited back again after today?' His wolf smile made her roll her eyes. She had walked into that trap. 'Are you ready to go?'

'I won't be a minute. Let me change and freshen up.' Leaving him there, she darted into her room with a fluttering in her heart.

'You look beautiful,' Tom said as Beth emerged from her room in a flowy blue dress that fell to just above her knees, her hair freshly brushed and left to fall over her nearly bare shoulders. A little pair of flats on her feet, completed her look. Tom's eyes travelled down the length of her body, and she saw him shift a little and swallow, like he was all of a sudden nervous.

Tom was dressed to impress, and now that she was more awake, Beth took in his freshly showered appearance. Wearing a clean, nicely pressed shirt and dark jeans that gently outlined his toned body, everything about him seemed different this afternoon, and she fought the urge to forget last night and give him a chance. Letting her walls down and trusting him was her first challenge. And he was making it so easy for her. Firstly, with her father, and now as he led her out the door, her hand in his, he promised her parents he would not have her out too late, before leading her down the path to his ute.

Holding the door open for her, then helping her in, Tom closed the door with a nervous smile. Watching him walk around the front of the ute, he took a deep breath and looked back up the street. He really did seem very nervous. Her own butterflies took that moment to let loose in her stomach, making her even more anxious about this date. She was excited but fearful. The pressure seemed to hang in the air—and they both felt it.

This could be their last chance to get whatever this was, right between them for the summer, and Beth didn't want to ruin it. Still following Tom with her eyes as he reached the door, she noticed he had not only cleaned the outside of the ute, but also the inside for her. Continuing to see all his hard effort, Beth spotted one of Kathryn's picnic baskets—the one her boss made for tourists when they wanted to have a picnic beside the river instead of sitting inside the café. It was their first official date, and he obviously wanted it to be one she would never forget.

Tom drove out of town for about half an hour, along the road towards Silverleigh, before slowly turning into an old, barely visible track, about ten minutes before the entrance to his family's property. The old track looked like it hadn't been used in years. If you were going past at normal speed, you wouldn't have even known it was there.

The grass was high and brushed under and along the side of ute as they ambled their way over a small rise on the flat land and then down towards a very small gully of water. Beth could smell the heated grass burning from where it had touched the hot motor. Eventually, Tom stopped near a freshly mowed—she swore it had been done that day—area of grass just up from the water's edge.

'Wait there,' Tom ordered, jumping out and quickly halting any chance of her moving. Coming around to her side of the ute, a sheepish smile on his face and, holding the door open, he gave her his hand as she climbed out and looked around.

'Why thank you, kind sir.' She smiled at him and fluttered her eyelashes, causing him to puff out his chest a little and raise her hand to his lips for a little peck to her skin.

Retrieving the basket and a blanket from the back seat, Tom offered her his arm, 'Shall we?'

The sting of the lowering sun burned into Beth's shoulders as they walked down a neatly mowed, little path to the edge of the water. Then, taking a left, they continued walking along the little bank, following an animal's well-worn path.

'Where are you taking me?' Beth asked as she followed along behind Tom, the path now too narrow to walk beside him.

Wreaths and bullrushes lined the shore, and a little group of ducklings darted out from between them, making Beth jump as they skittered across the top of the water. 'It's a surprise,' Tom replied after making sure the danger of the ducklings was gone.

Rounding a little corner, Tom stood aside to allow Beth to step up first, onto the old wooden deck built over the water's edge.

The little gully had turned into a large pond area, surrounded by large gum trees and tall, thick grass that shaded the deck, hiding anyone sitting there from sight. You would never have guessed that this little piece of beauty was here.

'Oh, it's so beautiful,' Beth said as she walked to the edge and looked into the water. Little bubbles floated to the top from deep below where a fish or turtle swam. In the trees above, she could hear an old crow calling out. No other sounds could be heard, except the beauty of nature in this little piece of heaven.

Tom laid out the blanket and came to stand at the edge. Avoiding touching her this time, they both looked across the water, watching the mother duck herding her ducklings away from them.

'You know this gives you extra points on top of the ones you earned this afternoon with my dad.' Beth smiled but never took her gaze from the little ducklings floating along the water near the other bank behind their mother.

'I did nothing this afternoon to gain points with you, Beth.' He sounded a little annoyed as he turned and began to unpack the picnic.

Frowning, Beth kneeled and placed her hand over his. 'I didn't mean it like that, Tom. It's just that no one has ever taken the time to talk to my dad about that stuff. He was so happy. The happiest he has been since we moved here.'

'I'm a nice guy, and I was truly interested in it. Not because of you or what points it could get me with you or your parents. I actually really do like ancient history. We can learn a lot from the past. Not many people know that about me.' With a heart beating with nervous energy and a fear of getting hurt, Tom began to lean in for a kiss. But it was too soon. Beth moved her hand off of his and leaned away. Taking the hint, he remained kneeling on the blanket and watched her closely. It was easy to read; he was unsure of what to do or say to heal the hurt between them.

'What else does no one know?'

'Umm ... I like Kathryn's peppermint hot chocolates.' He smiled and sat as Beth agreed with him, wriggling to a comfortable position on the rug, her legs straight out in front of her. 'I also like ancient history, country music, swimming and ...' Beth lifted her gaze to Tom's when she heard him hesitate, '... I love working with horses.'

'Horses?'

'Yeah. Not that I am meant to admit that out loud.' Shuffling to get comfortable and closer to her, Tom mimicked her pose, his back against a post, hand close to hers. 'Cropping is good, and the company is my future; I know that, but working with horses is something that I absolutely love.'

'Is that why you've been away longer than the other boys in the area?'

'Yeah. I was at uni.' His fingers touched hers as they spoke.

'What did you study?'

'Agribusiness management and equine, specialising in stunt and trick training.' Beth was impressed and let it show on her face. Tom shifted under the weight of her impressed gaze. No one, except Drake and Kathryn, had ever asked about his studies, let alone been impressed by them.

'How did you get into that? Agribusiness I can understand, but equine training?'

'Drake.' Tom picked at a piece of splintered wood on the deck and then looked out across the water. His father had not approved of his choice, which was what had caused the argument the day he had crashed his father's ute, and Drake and Kathryn had taken him in. His choice, in his father's eyes, wasn't a real choice he should have been given. Tom had his commitments here and his life was already planned out for him. He didn't need to know anything about horses. Cropping and Ag business should have been his only interest.

'How did Drake get you into it?'

Tom shifted uncomfortably again and tried to gather his racing thoughts. Was he ready to share this part of his life with anyone? Beth wanted to know the real him but was he really ready to show her that side? His true vulnerability? Could he trust her to know the truth and keep his secret—that only Drake knew about?

Looking at her now, the sunlight streaming through the trees, highlighting her hair and making the sandy coloured blonde look like a golden halo around her, Tom already knew the truth. It was simple; Beth made him feel things he had never felt before, and he loved it. She actually made him *feel*. Deeply. Feel the life that he now wanted.

Taking a deep breath, Tom plunged in.

'It was after my mum had died. I wasn't doing so well. My father and I had had yet another fight and I ended up staying at Drake and Kathryn's for a while. The girls were away at a senior camp for nearly three weeks.' Tom looked at Beth, now realising she would have been with Montana and Adelaida at the time.

'He took me out for a ride on one of his horses, and we spoke for hours. He understood my situation in a way that I could never have imagined, and he told me to find something I liked to do while at school—something that was just for me. I didn't follow his advice at first and I found myself in a lot of trouble once I got to uni.' Tom smiled at Beth shyly and picked at yet another piece of splintered wood as she frowned a little, not sure what he meant by 'trouble'.

Catching her look from the corner of his eye, he elaborated. 'I spray painted one of my lecturer's horses in a drunken rage when she failed me.' Beth couldn't help but giggle at his expression. 'So, my punishment was, I had to look after her prize-winning horse, as well as two new ones that had come in to be trained. It changed my life.' Tom put the piece of wood in the corner of his mouth and

146

smiled at a distant memory. Beth watched the change come over him as he remembered. He looked peaceful and content.

'One of the horses was a little paint-coloured pony, who was highly spirited with cheek and naughtiness. My challenge horse, my lecturer called him. She could see I had a special bond with the creature. Maybe we were both reacting to our situations the same way—not listening, and pushing the boundaries, causing trouble everywhere we went.'

Tom didn't look at Beth; he only saw her trying not to question him as he continued. 'So, she set me the challenge that if I could teach this horse some tricks for a movie her friend was working on, then she would pass me for my course.' Tom smiled shyly at Beth. 'I wasn't really good at the study part of the course. The Ag business was second nature, and I was top of my class. Any type of failure was not an option for me or for the expectations of my father.' He looked back over the water. 'So, Splatter and I started working together.'

Beth laughed out loud, her hand covering her mouth at the loudness. 'You named the horse "Splatter". Why? What a horrible name.'

Smiling at her laugh, and enjoying the sound of it, Tom leaned in like it was a secret. Beth copied his move as her eyes twinkled. 'It was because he was a paint-coloured horse,' Tom whispered in her ear. It took Beth a minute longer than she wanted, to get the joke, but she giggled and rolled her eyes when she finally got it, shaking her head in amusement.

'Splatter was a good name for him, trust me.'

'I bet. So, I guess you got it done and passed your course?'

'No. I failed.'

Beth stopped laughing and looked at him. 'What do you mean? You couldn't train him?'

A sadness of joy and heart-filled ache washed over Tom's body with the haunting memory. 'No, I trained him, but he didn't go to the movie set. He had to get there, for me to pass.'

'Why not?' Beth was intrigued as she watched Tom more closely.

'It doesn't matter.' He threw the piece of splintered wood into the water and watched it float away. The memory was bittersweet, but the reality of the truth was something that still haunted him. Knowing what he did, Tom knew that those days with Splatter had changed his life forever. He had not breathed a word of the full truth to anyone. But maybe talking about it now, with Beth, could help.

Feeling her studying him hard, she was waiting for him to trust her—like he wanted her to do. To fully open up. To be the real Tom—the man he promised her he was.

'It does to me,' Beth said as she moved to sit next to him, her thigh touching his. She reached for his hand and held it. Lifting her hand, and intertwining his fingers with hers, they both watched his movements in slow motion. Slowly, Tom raised his eyes, and when they met Beth's, he could see his own pain and sadness, that rolled through his body, reflected deep within them. Beth was staring directly into his soul and he second guessed himself about sharing with her.

'Are you sure you want to know? It's disturbing and very upsetting. I don't want to ruin our afternoon together.'

'I think I can handle it. And if it gets too much, I'll tell you.'

Feeling uneasy about her wish, she had no idea what she had just asked him to tell her. Taking his time to sort through all the memories and how best to tell her, Tom let the glimpses of those days play like a movie through his mind. For him, it had been a chance of a lifetime and a turning point in his life where he had learned that bad things happen and only *you* can choose to be brave enough to deal with the outcome.

Taking a deep breath, he sat up straighter, never letting Beth's hand go as he started his story.

'One afternoon, I was with Splatter, and we had just finished a session. He was rolling around in the sand after his bath, and as I got his feed ready, I noticed a little girl sitting on the steps of the house across the small paddock from the yards. She was watching us. Nothing to it really.' He shrugged his shoulders.

'After about a week, I noticed she had moved to the fence of her house yard. She was always there, every afternoon when I arrived, and she would sit and eat her apple and watch us. I would wave to her to say "hello" but she wouldn't move. She would just watch, nibbling her apple the whole two hours I was there with Splatter. Over the next month, she slowly moved closer and closer to us. I would wave and smile, but she wouldn't wave back.'

Tom smiled to himself. 'One afternoon, I noticed she had moved an old drum out into the middle of the paddock, to sit on, and watch us. She was about fifty metres away from our yard fence, and this time I noticed she had brought herself an extra apple. Splatter was in full show-off mode that day and kept losing focus. I gave up and decided to play with him instead. Drake had shown me how to play tag with the horses, and it was a game I had taught Splatter.' He laughed at the memory.

'The little girl was enthralled and sat there with her mouth open as we played. When I left that afternoon, she was still sitting there watching Splatter. He had nickered to her a few times as I was leaving. Curious as to his attention to her, I hid to watch what would happen after they both thought I had left for the day.'

Beth smiled at Tom as his smile got bigger with his words, 'She snuck up and threw her spare apple into Splatter's ring and raced off across the paddock before he could get to it. Boy, could she run fast. Her ragged, knitted old coat she always wore, even on the hottest of days, was flying out behind her as she took off back to her house.' Beth giggled at the scene he had just painted for her.

'The next afternoon, she had moved closer again. About halfway closer. It was the first time I heard her really giggle and laugh out loud. I had been teaching Splatter to pull a red cloth from my back pocket when I turned my back on him. This day, he did it perfectly but decided to show off by tossing the cloth around and making me jump to try and get it from his mouth. It must have looked really funny.' He gave a small laugh.

'The little girl giggled so hard and loud that when we heard it, both Splatter and I stopped and look at her. She froze like a deer in headlights, and fear came over her. She looked to the house then back to me as she slowly moved off the drum, never once taking her eyes off me. I had never seen anyone look so scared.' Tom's voice softened and became very quiet.

'I called out to her that it was okay. That she didn't need to leave. That Splatter would like her spare apple. But she ran and I didn't see her again for a week.'

'Oh, the poor little girl,' Beth said quietly. Smiling tightly at her, Tom looked back over the water, getting lost in his memory again.

'After about a week, she came back with a lady. They were waiting at the drum but did nothing except watch me work with Splatter that afternoon. I waved at them and called out to her that it was nice to have her company back and it was okay if she wanted to give Splatter her spare apple. The lady sitting with her on the drum had smiled encouragingly at her and, taking her white-knuckled hand for support and reassurance, they walked over to the fence. Splatter pranced around and nicked to her as she held her apple for him to take.'

Tom sat up a little, shaking his head in disbelief at the memory playing through his mind. 'You know, that bloody horse, he stopped showing off, and as slow as slow, he moved and gently took that apple from her hand before backing back. And then, with a loud crunch, he ate his apple.' Tom turned to Beth, his eyes wide and enthralled. 'It was amazing. Splatter had never been that gentle or controlled with anyone.' Beth shook her head at him, disbelief in her understanding at what he was saying.

'It took another week of general conversation with the lady who, it turned out, to be the little girl's aunt, that I learned the truth. I don't think she meant to tell me as much as she did but once it started to come out, it was like a flood gate had been opened for her and I think seeing the smiles and laughter on Kaylee's little face made it flow out easier.'

Tom turned to Beth, his face all serious. 'You know, you're never prepared for the truth of something till you hear it, and then you think to yourself afterwards, "How the hell did something like that ever happen to such a sweet little girl?"' Tom shook his head. His feelings and emotions, and complete disgust and disbelief, blurred his vision with the memory and visions he had conjured in his mind about the truth of what he had been told. His hand grew cold in Beth's as his body began to shake.

'One afternoon, about a month before; Kaylee had spotted me working with Splatter from one of the windows in the house. She had watched him take my rope and swing it around. Seeing Splatter's antics, Kaylee had gone in search of her aunt and told her everything she had witnessed, and had laughed at it. Her aunt told me that that moment was the first time in over nine months that Kaylee had smiled or even spoken more than a few words.' Shaking his head in amazement, Tom's lip lifted into a small smile. 'She had been with her aunt for that long and had never said a word or made eye contact with her, but that afternoon, when she had seen me and Splatter playing, she told her aunt all about it and even drew a picture of Splatter with the rope in his mouth. Over that last month, Kaylee had been talking more and had even requested something.'

Tom stopped and really looked at Beth for the first time since he had started to tell her all about Kaylee and her aunt.

Even though Beth was a little confused, she was listening so intently to Tom rambling away, that apart from those few words earlier, she had said nothing. She had just listened to him, letting him talk about something he now knew was so important—more than farming and social status. Beth was seeing *him,* and it felt so ... freeing.

Her hand was still in his as she watched him with her blue eyes. The sun was dropping down behind the trees, and Beth's skin glowed in the sunshine. She was truly the most beautiful thing Tom had ever seen in his life. And she was here with him, in the middle of nowhere, listening to him talk about how one little girl changed his life forever.

'What did she request?' Beth whispered, enthralled by Tom's story.

'That her aunt come and feed Splatter with her because she was scared of me. She was scared of all men.'

'All men?' The confusion was written all over Beth's face.

'Yeah,' he said sadly, the lightness of before fading and dulling Tom's energy. 'Apparently, Kaylee grew up in an abusive home where she was sexually assaulted by her father and stepbrothers. She had even been starved and burnt with cigarettes. Her mother had tried to stop it, but she was beaten and drugged by her husband. It wasn't until Kaylee was eight years old and ran away, that the abuse was fully discovered. She only looked to be four years old, Beth. She was so small.' Tom squeezed Beth's hand as he fought to hide the tears in his eyes. The anguish in his voice forced Beth to swallow the pain he was causing her by telling his story. But Tom knew he couldn't stop there without telling her everything.

'Child services found her aunt and moved Kaylee to live there, but late one night, her father found her and kidnapped her. When the police eventually found Kaylee by the side of the road a week later, she had been so badly abused that she couldn't speak or walk, and she needed reconstructive surgery to be able to go to the toilet properly.'

Beth couldn't help it. Tears filled her eyes and fell down her cheeks. The horror of Kaylee's story and all the little girl had endured, made the flow continuous. Tom looked away and wiped his own tears away before he looked back at Beth and wiped hers away with the pad of his thumb. A nervous and embarrassed laugh bubbled to the surface as he did. 'I'm so sorry. I told you it was sad.'

Beth smiled through her tears as she whispered, 'It's okay. But I want you to tell me the rest.' Tom wiped away yet another tear as it fell down her cheek.

With a tight smile he hoped would portray confidence in Beth, Tom continued. 'Over the next couple of weeks, with her aunt as support and my new understanding of her shyness and fear, Kaylee became more confident and would sit at the fence on her drum with her aunt as I worked Splatter. She would giggle and laugh at his showing off and tricks that we were practising. Then, at the end, she would give him her spare apple and the core from hers.' A proudness washed through him. 'She even started to talk to me and let me stand near her, on the opposite side of the fence, of course.'

Tom sat up and turned his body to face Beth more, an aliveness and energy in him coming awake and rising to light up his face with a smile. 'For me, it was amazing to see this little girl, who had suffered so much, come alive and be able to talk to me. A man. It changed my life, Beth. Kaylee changed my life.'

Beth smiled at Tom, understanding the whole situation as best she could. 'It sounds as though you helped to change hers a little too. What happened after that?'

Tom looked at her a little shyly. 'At the end of my course, my lecturer came to surprise me and Splatter with the news that the director had changed his mind and didn't want a paint-coloured pony in the movie after all. Splatter was mine if I wanted to buy him. I remember looking over at Kaylee and Splatter playing through the fence and I knew that that horse, who had caused me so much grief but at the same time had taught me so much about myself, life and the magic of what animals could do, could be something much more important in the world than in movies.'

Tom's smile grew wide across his face. It was mixed with a humbleness and shyness he had shown her. 'I called Drake, and he put me in contact with an organisation that could help. Splatter is now with Kaylee, and he is hers forever. Her aunt could not afford to keep him so with the organisation's help, I pay for all his feed and vet bills without them knowing. I failed my course, but hopefully I changed a little girl's life, because she definitely changed mine.'

Beth sat there looking at Tom. Really looking at him. Her breathing was shallow as she finally saw him in a completely different way. Right before her eyes, was the real Thomas O'Loughlin. Tears rolled down her face at the thought of who he was and how stupid she had been for not seeing it the first time they met. He was nothing like any other men she had ever met before. He was full of honour, love, patience, and understanding. He was real and true to his word. Everything he had tried to tell her, he *was*—and all she had ever wanted in a man, was within him.

Not able to contain herself, Beth leaned in and touched her lips ever so gently to his. A butterfly touch at first, sending goosebumps and tingles all over her. But Tom never moved. Pulling back just enough to move herself up onto her knees, she leaned back into him for more. His hands came up slowly and gently brushed her still wet cheeks with his thumbs, sliding his fingers into her hair.

He looked deep into her eyes and breathed. Beth had finally seen him. Finally understood what he had been telling her and trying to show her. He swallowed, and she saw the pulse at the base of his throat quicken and pump more solidly. Eyes closing, their lips touched ... once, twice. Then Tom opened his mouth and tasted her.

His sun-kissed lips heated her soul and lit a fire deep within. Beth wanted to taste more, and like he had just read her thoughts, Tom angled his head and slipped his tongue between her lips, expertly exploring her mouth with a groan. Beth pulled away a little and snuggled down on his chest, her emotions still a little raw. She needed time to process all that had just been shown to her.

'You know I'm very competitive, Beth, and failure is not an option for me—in some things.' Tom's words held raw emotion as he whispered them to her. She had seen the confusion on his face at her withdrawal from their kiss and if she was honest with herself, she didn't understand her actions either. She was driving—not only herself, but *him*—crazy with her uncertainty around what was fast developing between them and all he truly was. It scared the hell out of her, and she wasn't sure what to do. All she could reply with, fully understanding his words were about her and how he would not give up on her, was, 'I know.'

Watching the sun slowly sink down, its rays reflecting off the water, Beth could hear Tom's heart beating in his chest. His arms were wrapped securely around her, holding her to him as her own heart beat just as hard. Her mind was racing at what he had spoken about, and her emotions were all over the place. A tear slipped from the corner of her eye. Her thoughts were about what Kaylee had experienced and how that sweet little girl was still able to find laughter and joy in the world, and Tom's anonymous and continued support of the little girl and her aunt.

He was so much more than the person she had ever thought he was. Looking back over the last week, she could see that now. He had cared for her from the moment they had met. He held her in the water, so she didn't have to tread while he gave her time to regroup after pulling her into the water. He had taken her home when she had drunk too much, and he had even made sure she was taken care of at the river last night by ensuring she had her own friends there as well. And then today, he had let her sleep and waited, while letting her father talk nonstop about his love of ancient war memorabilia. Tom was patient and funny and protective. He was everything she had ever wanted in a relationship. How could she have ever been so blind?

And now she was going to leave in a couple of months. She was going to leave him here to start her dream life. The thought always made her excited, but this afternoon it made her chest tighten. Beth placed a hand over Tom's heart. Whatever this was between them, would never be anything more than friendship. It couldn't be. It was already going to be too painful.

Covering her hand with his at his heart, she felt him take a long, slow breath. 'So, what about you? Why cooking?'

Beth didn't move. Her emotions were too raw over finally seeing the real Tom. She didn't want to look at him when she answered—didn't want to dig up that painful part of her life. Her parents had been ashamed of what had happened and never told anyone how they came to be here in this small country town. Most people knew they had arrived from the city after they bought a failing business to create a new life.

People had tried to find out more, but her parents stuck to their 'less is more' story. And in the end, other gossip took over and they just became the newbie townies. They had struggled to make ends meet for nearly four years, just so they could build the successful business they had today. They had gone without, so Beth could have what she needed to fit in at school—and so they could hide the fact they had hardly any money for food. She was ashamed of it, and she was determined she would never let anyone do to her what her uncle had done to her parents. The hurt was still too raw. Fresh tears built in her eyes. Squeezing tight to stop them falling, she knew she could trust Tom with the truth, but would her parents understand her telling the son of the most powerful man in the area?

Mathew scared everyone, but it was *Tom* she was telling, and in her heart, she knew she could trust him to never repeat her words. He had, after all, trusted her, and she wanted him to see she trusted him.

Without raising her head, she made her decision and began. 'My parents and I arrived in town late one Wednesday night. It had been raining and storming for the last part of our drive and the real estate agent was meant to meet us at the shop. But after we waited for an hour and he didn't show, we drove down the street and found Kathryn's café.' Beth clarified with, 'It was when she had been trialling opening nights before changing back to just days.'

'The café was quiet, with only a few customers. We were so tired and upset with the real estate agent that we sat at the very back of the café in one of the booth seats and ordered a large bowl of chips and some water.' Beth smiled in memory. 'But Kathryn brought us out a full meal each and a round of her famous peppermint hot chocolates. My father tried to tell her that it was too much. He knew we really couldn't afford to buy it.'

Beth sat up and looked at Tom to explain. He just looked at her and waited, his fingers tucking back a stray piece of hair. He didn't seem to notice the tear stains on her cheek. 'See, my parents had a big falling out with my uncle and grandfather and we lost our house and the business they all shared. As a result, my parents inherited an unsurmountable debt. So, with every cent they had left, they bought the tyre business all the way out here and we drove out with what we could fit in the car. It was really only our clothes and photos. We had no furniture because we had to sell it all, and we had only a handful of cooking equipment and a picnic basket. The little bit of cash we had, had to be used to purchase my school uniforms and books and feed us until the business started to bring in money. I still don't know how they did it.' Beth looked out over the water and unconsciously moved back a little from Tom.

'I remember my mum having tears in her eyes when Kathryn told them it was "on the house". After we had finished eating, Drake came over and talked to us. He tracked down the real estate agent at the pub. The idiot had forgotten about us. I guess we were not that important to him.' Beth raised her eyebrows at Tom and shrugged like it was a common thing—she and her parents not being of great importance. 'He had his money,' she said bitterly. Tom reached out and touched her knee in understanding of her dislike for what had happened.

'We slept huddled together on blankets on the floor that night, having no furniture or ways to heat the little two-bedroom apartment above the shop that was now our new home. The next morning, my parents opened the tyre shop business and hoped for the best.

Kathryn sent Drake with a laundry basket full of food and a hot breakfast for us all, and later that day, he returned with some old furniture he had "lying" around. They saved us, I think. People started coming into the shop, saying Drake had told them we had taken over, and money came in that very day. My parents worked 80-plus hours a week to make sure that tyre shop was a success and when they purchased our little cottage home and we moved in, I remember seeing them dance together for the first time in years. We even got takeaway pizzas for dinner that night with Drake, Kathryn and the twins.' Beth looked at Tom and gave a little embarrassed giggle. 'This probably makes no sense to you.' Given that his family was one of the richest farming families in the country, the thought of having nothing or going hungry would never have been part of his life.

'It's okay. I'm trying to understand.' He moved his thumb over her knee. He would never understand what they had gone through. For him, money was something that never ran out. If he wanted something, he could simply go out and buy it. Not having it, was not a concept he would ever have had to worry about, but she was grateful he was trying to understand for her sake. 'So, is that how you found your love for food?'

'Kathryn made food that tasted amazing and made people happy. It brought people together. When I would stay at their home, she was always cooking with the girls, and I would join in. There was laughter and giggles and big messes to clean up, but they were some of my happiest times. When I could, I started to work for her, and I just fell in love with it all. The ability to make people feel something with my food drives me to be better. To create and learn.' Beth could feel her excitement and passion-filled essence rushing up her body and out of her mouth as she spoke. Tom couldn't help but smile at her.

'If I'm good enough at this culinary school, I will be able to travel to Paris at Christmas next year with my teacher and study in France for a few months. It's my biggest dream. If my plans work out, then I will be living mostly in Europe cooking in the world's best restaurants.'

Tom's smile dropped a little as he looked out over the water, which was slowly growing dark with the fading light of the afternoon. Beth had found her passion, and she was going to chase her dreams no matter what. A deep ache began to burn inside Tom's stomach as he realised, he may never be able to feel that same passion as Beth did, again. He had had his moment with Splatter, and now it was over. He had his life planned out for him already. The heir to the O'Loughlin fortune had to follow in the footsteps of all others before him. There was no excuse and there was nothing he could do about it. It was his destiny even before he was born.

Turning back, Tom looked at Beth, her eyes still dancing as she thought about her dreams and all the adventures that lay before her. Their time really was limited to just this summer. When the days began to grow cooler, Beth would go off and chase her new life and he would stay and become the owner of the O'Loughlin fortune and properties. The weight of that responsibility had never felt so heavy and foreboding.

'Beth?'

She looked at him, the strange tone of his voice surprising her. 'If you ever need anything, you call me. I will always be here for you no matter what. I never want you to go without or to go through what your parents had to. I will always be here for you. Do you understand?'

Beth frowned at him. 'I don't need you like that, Tom. I can take care of myself, and I will make sure I don't end up like my parents. Ever.' She looked away before coming back at him, 'I am not your responsibility, and I don't want your pity over what happened to me and my parents. They had the courage, that I don't think I could ever have, to rise above what life threw at them. And they taught me—you have to get up and work for your dreams.' Beth swallowed, her voice a little strained. 'And maybe if you do, life will work out, sometimes in beautiful ways you never thought possible.'

Tom could easily read the hurt in Beth's eyes. She believed he thought she couldn't do it herself.

'I never meant it like that.' He took her hand and pulled her to him for a cuddle. 'The thought of you going through that again makes my guts roll and I want you to know that I am here for you.' He lowered his voice so that his message could get across to her. 'I know that you will achieve everything you set your mind to and one day, maybe, if I ever travel to Europe, I could dine at one of your restaurants. I want you to be happy, Beth. You deserve nothing but the best life has to offer.' He kissed her forehead.

Beth smiled a little tightly at him and answered, 'Thank you. That does mean a lot.' Her guard, he hoped, was dropping again as she snuggled into his chest.

The sun had just kissed the land and began to disappear over the horizon, casting their spot on earth into darkness. Both sat, deep in their own thoughts, in a comforting silence. Tom could feel the change within Beth. He could sense somehow that he had broken down an internal wall she had put around herself as protection. Her warm body pressed to his, he was aroused and could feel it pressed to his jeans. He wanted her in more ways than he could have imagined wanting anyone.

Tom wanted her sexually, that had been evident from the moment he had looked across the river at the festival and saw her standing there ready to go into battle. But as he had gotten to know her, it was her mind, her past, her strength, her desires, her passion, her kindness, and her understanding that drew him to her more each day. She knew who he was, and it made no difference. She wanted nothing more from him than what he himself had to offer. He could give her the world if she wanted it, but that was not her style. She wanted to go and get it herself, and he admired her for it.

With his cheek to the top of her head, he breathed in her scent and his body reacted more. He didn't want this moment to end. Just a boy and a girl together. Nothing or no one mattered. It was just them.

Placing his finger under her chin, he raised her face to look at him. And then he kissed her. It was a kiss of everything he was feeling and wanted her to know, because he couldn't voice it. His voice was gone, his throat was tight with unspoken words and emotions she had evoked in him so much, so he could only show her. His lips were warm and moist against hers as an unspoken passion between them sparked and began to burn long and slow. Tom's hand entangled into Beth's hair and he pulled her mouth deeper to his. A small, pleasurable whimper drifted from within her to his ears, further fuelling him on.

Without breaking the kiss, Beth climbed onto his lap, her hair falling around them, enclosing them within the sanctuary of it. Placing her hands through Tom's hair, she pulled him to her and deepened the kiss again, just like he had done. His hands held her hips to his groin, which only fired his passion and made him groan, grinding her to him more as he sat up.

Tasting her as his, he claimed her lips over and over. His tongue darted into her mouth, and she followed him so she could do the same. It was a playful pleasuring until Tom wanted more. Grabbing her tongue, he suckled it, before tenderly nipping at the side of her mouth and lower lip, making her laugh and moan at the same time.

Angling her head more to the side, Beth dug her nails into his hair and kissed him hungrily. He could feel her heart racing, and her breathing was becoming more laboured. Beth couldn't get enough of him, and he too was ravenousness for her. If he allowed himself, he would devour her right here on this old deck everyone had seemed to forget about, except him.

His hands roamed up her back and down over her bottom, pulling and grinding himself against her. The embers that had been smouldering since they met and touched in that cold river water, leaped to life and burned hot within and between them. Tom's mind had become filled with nothing else but Beth and his need to feel her touch on his skin.

Needing air, Beth pulled back just a little. Too lost in his need for her, Tom's eyes fluttered opened as he tried to focus on her. He was as lost as she appeared to be. Both breathed hard as they looked at each other, desperately searching for a reason to stop, knowing in themselves that it would take the other to do it.

Eventually, it was Tom who had the strength to voice what she couldn't. 'Are you sure you want this, Beth?' His voice, harsh and raspy, could barely be heard above his beating heart. A fractured heartbeat seemed to give him a second to understand, before Beth nodded and reclaimed his lips in a kiss that not only stole his breath, but a deep part of him as well.

Tom's lips burned a hot trail of kisses from Beth's mouth, along her jaw and down to nuzzle the tender spot at the base of her slender neck, his hand finding its way to one of her breasts. The lush mound fitted perfectly against his roughened skin as he squeezed the tender flesh, gently smiling when it grew weighted in his hands. He felt Beth instinctively push against him, wanting more. Pulling his lips away from her silky skin, Tom watched her heavy-lidded eyes, dark and stormy, lost in their focus as he squeezed her breast again. He gloated internally when Beth sat taller with a moan and let her head fall back against her shoulders. Her eyes closed slowly as the sensation of his kneading hand rolled through her body. She was mesmerising. He squeezed again, her head falling forward to claim his lips once more, branding herself to them.

Moving her hips against his, Beth wanted more and more. Seeking the pleasure of the building release her body was craving, she drew him into her kiss, into the essence of who she was. Without knowing what she was doing, Tom had the odd sensation that he was beginning to drown. The more she took from him, the deeper he went. And he didn't care. He could drown right here as the night enclosed around them, on this old wooden deck his grandfather had built his grandmother for the soul reason of asking her to be his wife. Tom didn't care. He just didn't care what happened beyond this moment. If he was to never take another breath, then so be it. He would be happy with that choice so longs as Beth was in his arms.

Untying the little bow on the front of her dress, Tom slipped the strings holding her dress up, off her shoulders. The fabric fell to her waist, revealing her white, lacey bra. Her erect nipples grew harder as the night's cool air reached out and touched her heated skin. Descending down her neck to her collar bone and along her shoulder, following the path where her stings had been, Tom's scolding mouth laid a line of kisses to her skin. And then, with his teeth, he nipped at her bra strap, smiling to himself when he eventually grabbed it without harming her perfectly creamy skin.

He pulled it off her shoulder before returning to kiss where it had been. His hands moved around her rib cage to splay over her back and then down over her hips, squeezing and massaging. He rolled her hips and body to his need. Pressure between her legs was building as she moved her hips against his arousal, pulsating hard and aching to be released from his now tight jeans.

Skin like silk, Beth tasted sweet and salty as his lips moved back to her neck, her face, and eventually her lips. Tom pulled back and waited for her to look at him. They were both breathing hard, but Beth wasn't done. She grabbed his hands and placed them to her breasts and squeezed. Her lips claimed his over and over again as he laughed at her impulsive desire and need for him. But soon the laughter turned into long, low, vibrating groans when the feel of her erect nipples, pressed achingly hard against his palms. The lace of her bra added to the sensation. Tom was dazed, and the drowning feeling was coming in thick, suffocating waves as she kissed him like he had never been kissed before.

Beth moved his hands as she rose to kneel over him, placing them on her bottom as she reached around, her eyes locked on his. He swallowed the lump in his throat as she unclipped her bra and left it. It was now up to him.

Taking his time, drawing out the tension between them as they intently stared at each other, Tom gently kneaded Beth's bottom, his muscles flexing beneath her palms as she now rested them on him for balance. Her body shook with nerves and anticipation. He never once removed his eyes from hers. He could feel hers burning into his.

The moon rising behind her was now their only light, and it made her skin glow. Tom's breath was short and sharp as he stared at her. He had never seen anything more beautiful in his whole life, and it hit him deep and hard inside his chest. She was offering herself to him and was now waiting for him to respond.

His mouth was dry as he tried to speak but it came out as a raspy growl. 'You're stunning.'

Trailing his finger—a very slow, butterfly touch—up her hip, to her ribs, and around to slip under her loose bra at her nipple. Beth's skin goose bumped, causing her to shiver, but she never pulled her eyes away from his—nor his from hers. His thumb circled over the little pebbled nipple, and he watched as she sucked in a breath. Rolling her nipple between his thumb and finger, Beth's eyes closed. She swayed her hips and grabbed her other breast, massaging it as Tom continued to pleasure her.

Holding her hips steady as she moved above him, his own erection pushing against his jeans so painfully, he hissed a little as it too, now moved and pulsated on its own. But Tom wanted nothing for himself at this moment, only to bring Beth as much pleasure as he could.

Nudging her towards him, enough for her to over balance just a fraction, she caught and arched herself on the post over his head, her breasts now perfectly teasing his face. The top of her thighs firmly cradled him through his jeans. Nosing the bra up; Tom's mouth found Beth's nipple and suckled it. She tried to remove the lace from where it tickled his nose and top lip, but he raised her hands and placed them back to the post above his head, shaking his head, firmly, telling her, 'No.'

Arching more, Beth pushed her breast further into his mouth, gripping the post and holding her entire body up against his as he took his fill of her. Finally, removing the bra from her body, he threw it behind her, reclaiming the nipple once again and sucking it right to the back of his throat.

Beth moved her hips to try and find release herself from his pleasures, but he knew it only made it worse for her. He was fully enjoying himself as he released her nipple from the depths of his throat and moved to the other one, suckling and rolling it in his mouth. She whimpered and pulled away, kissing him deeply as his hands drifted lower over her hips and thighs. She was grinding against him so hard; he was growing worried he was about to blow his load like he had at fifteen.

Slipping his hand under her bunched dress, he found a lacey little triangle and thumbed the area as she kissed him hungrily, moaning and growling with her much-needed release. Her impatience was driving him mentally and physically insane. He needed to take her and free her from the wanting desire she was consumed with, but he knew he had to go slow. The risk of her pulling away after this was too much for him to bare in a moment of lust.

Encouraged by her emulating sounds, Tom found the edge of the triangle and slipped his thumb under it. Beth pulled back and watched him with hazed interest as he raised his eyes to hers, his hands gliding over her silky, slick skin. The area was bare. No hair. Looking down at him, she smiled a smile that pierced his heart, and she whispered, 'It feels better when I do it myself with no hair.'

Hers eyes closed slowly as Tom glided over the area again with an uncivilised male growl. He removed his hand and twisted Beth, so she now sat between his legs, her back pressed to his chest.

'Tom. What are you doing?' she asked on a little scream of surprise when he positioned her there.

'I want you to show me how you like it.' He purred into her ear as he kneaded her breast with one hand, the other lifting her dress to expose her through her lacey knickers. She tried to push her dress down and he stopped.

'I can't do that. It's embarrassing,' she said breathlessly.

'Not to me, it's not. I want you to show me how you like it, so I can do it for you too.' He whispered in her ear, his hot breath tickling the little hairs with his top lip. It sent tingles all over her body and through his. Beth shook her head, trying to stay focused as he rubbed her nipple between his fingers again, reheating the passion from before.

'Show me,' he rasped as his hand went over her heated spot. He could feel her wetness and desire for him as her hips lifted to his palm instinctively, and she moaned with pleasure.

Desire, and the begging in his voice, persuaded her enough. Following his hands with her own, Beth tried to remove her underwear. Stopping her, Tom covered her one hand and moved it slowly to slip under the little triangle instead of removing them.

Beth tensed and stopped moving as she felt her own finger, his on top, feel her wetness. Her breath was the only sound around them. She turned her head and looked up at him, their faces only inches from each other. He could feel her breath on his mouth and the rise and fall of her ribs at his chest. She was breathing as hard as he was.

'I want you to show me.' He kissed her slowly, deeply and encouragingly, willing her to trust him with something so private. He slowly drew out the kiss. Their hands locked together at the entrance of her sweet haven. Tom took, and gave her, all he could, wishing she understood everything he himself couldn't in this moment.

'If you don't want to, that's okay too,' he whispered and kissed her again, this time longingly and a little more needy. Moving back a little, Beth repositioned herself. Lifting her leg over Tom's, she shivered as the cool air rushed around their hands and her heated spot. Her hand covered his at her breast, and she showed him how she wanted it massaged—strong and full hand grabs. He felt like he was hurting her, so he hesitated. 'Doesn't this hurt?'

Shaking her head, Beth made him do it again, but rougher. 'I like a little pain with the pleasure,' she rasped as she arched against him when he repeated the move. With her other hand, she caught his finger between her own and together they moved further into her wetness. The heat was deliciously inviting for Tom. And as they both entered her, the sound of Beth sucking air into her lungs sent any rational thought Tom had ever had, out of his head. The only thing left was the feeling of her fingers, with his, deep inside of her scorching hot body. Together they slowly stroked and rubbed and pleasured her until she removed her hand, letting him finish her.

Beth looked up at him from under heavy-lidded eyes. He stared back at her as she pulled him to her for a long, deep kiss that stole his breath away. Beth's cries of pleasure and the release from Tom's soul saw him bringing her to the peak and over it. They continued to kiss long after the last of Beth's body rolled with the ripples of release. Tom slowly removed his hand from her sensual heat. Covering her with the picnic blanket, Tom continued to kiss her until she was ready to let him go.

Beth floated back down to earth while Tom kissed her slowly, ignoring his own need for release. Coming up for air from his lips, Beth took an unsteady breath and rested her forehead to his. Her eyelids were heavy, but she watched him watching her with a little roguish smile. 'I think I need to take you home,' he whispered into her ear, the sensation causing goosebumps all over her body.

Not as graceful or elegantly as he wanted, even causing Beth to giggle and give a little scream when he did so, Tom stood with her in his arms. The picnic rug was awkwardly wrapped around her, and Tom's jeans caught his still very painful and engorged erection, making him whinge and hiss.

Beth saw and tried to wriggle out of his arms, making it worse, but he held her to him. 'No. I want you in my arms for as long as possible.' He kissed her again before stumbling and laughing as he corrected his footing, the extra weight on his body making it a little tricky to walk back along the narrow path towards his ute.

With her arms wrapped around Tom's neck, Beth's head lulled against his shoulder. His legs were steady and strong, his body now accustomed to the extra weight. Tom walked slowly until he reached the ute. Steadying her as her feet touched the ground, he leaned her against the cold metal of the cab while he opened the door.

Lifting her again, Beth wrapped her legs around his waist. With her arms wrapped around his neck, she lowered her head to claim his lips. Slightly overbalancing with the heady kiss, Tom stumbled gently into the side of the ute and devoured her back, fanning the flames from before. Their kisses burning, Beth lifted her head, letting it rest against the top of the ute as Tom kissed down her neck to her bare chest. He planted a kiss on each breast and gave them a little suck. This was all he did—it was all he could allow himself to do, it appeared.

'If I don't get you into this ute now, you will find yourself pressed up against it with me buried deep inside you.' He grunted, and Beth smiled down at him, wiggling her hips.

'Maybe that's where I want to be.'

'Oh God, Beth. Don't tempt me,' he rasped before he quickly kissed her lips and placed her into his ute.

'Don't you want me?' He could hear it as a tease but there was a hint of hurtfulness in her voice as she asked him.

'I want you more then I want my next breath, but I want it to be your choice when you're in your right mind. Not after I made you cum and not here against my ute. You deserve better than that.' He kissed her long and hard, before pulling the blanket around her and shutting the door.

They were driving down Beth's street as she pulled her dress back into place. 'Shit, Tom. My bra is back on the deck.' Her horrified look made him laugh.

'I will go back and get it later if you want. Though I'm not sure how I am meant to explain to your father in the morning, when I drop it off, how your bra came to be off you and in my hands.' He laughed harder at her when her mouth gaped open at the image he had just conjured up in her mind. The thought of him holding her bra and talking with her father made the blood drain from her face. She punched his shoulder, for teasing her.

'Just keep it till I see you next,' she said and kept adjusting her dress, trying to get it to fit right now she had no bra to help hold her breasts in the right position.

Watching her, he rubbed his arm and smirked at her. 'I think I like that idea.'

Beth rolled her eyes and shook her head as Tom slowed and then stopped on the opposite side of the street to her parents' house. He searched the street and then her home, before looking over at her.

'Beth. I need to tell you something.' His voice had lost all the laughter from a second ago as his words grew serious. He knew his next words were going to hurt, especially after their intimate afternoon, but there was no way around it. He needed to tell her.

Beth's eyes grew wide, and he could see her racing with thoughts of what was about to come next. She even looked to have grown whiter in the darkness of the cab, with only the streetlight outside her window shining any light.

'I have to go away with the harvest tomorrow. I leave for our next property at dawn.'

Beth just stared at him, her emotions rolling through her. All she could ask was, 'Why?'

Tom took a deep breath and reached for her hand, bringing it to his lips before he answered. 'One of our drivers had to have an emergency operation and won't be back for a few weeks. We have other drivers, but my father has insisted that I must be the one that goes with the early crew, as the grain at the next two properties is ready now.'

Her temper flared instantly. 'It's because of me, right. I'm not good enough for the great Matthew O'Loughlin.' Beth's anger took over and she struggled to unclip her seatbelt. 'When did this happen Tom?' she demanded as she pulled and writhed on the seatbelt.

Tom's hand came over and covered hers to calm her and help her with her seatbelt. 'This afternoon. And Beth, it's not you.'

Tears filled her eyes, and she climbed out of the ute when the seatbelt finally let go. She slammed the door in his face.

Tom got out and stopped her at the tailgate. Reaching for her, stopping her from running, he cooled his own temper at his father's orders and what they now meant for his and Beth's already limited time together.

'Beth.' He put his hands on her hips and pulled her to him. Her hands were up against his chest to stop his kiss. 'I won't be gone long, and I want to call you every day. I don't want to go a day without hearing your voice. It's going to be hard enough to not see you.' He squeezed her hips and rubbed her against himself. 'Please?' he whispered and caught a kiss.

'Would you tell me if it was really me?' She stood on her tip toes and kissed him back.

'No.' He smiled and kissed her again. It was long and sensual. Beth's body melted against Tom's before he pulled back and rested his forehead on hers. 'But I am telling you the truth. So, can I call you?'

She nodded. 'Every day.'

'Good.' He kissed her again quickly, before taking her hand and leading her across the street to her parents' front door. The night ended with a long, slow goodnight/goodbye kiss, before Tom left her standing on her parents front verandah, watching him drive away.

Chapter 10

'Beth, I think that was the girls who just pulled up. Are you ready?' Grabbing her wallet and doing a last check in the mirror, Beth pulled on her boots. Tom had been gone for the entire O'Loughlin harvest season. She had not seen him in over six weeks—since their night near the river.

Her skin warmed at the memory of his touch and his kisses so hot all over her skin and breasts. She had missed him so much. They only spoke when he had phone service, and she wasn't at work, but it wasn't as much as they had both hoped for. Despite trying to tell herself the lack of communication was a good thing, and it would help when she left for the city in just over a month's time, she had still longed for him. Beth had even cried herself to sleep a few nights when he had not called or texted her.

She had spent too much time checking her phone every five minutes to see if he had called, over analysing and thinking of him and their relationship—whatever the relationship was between them. Then, she would think of her own studies and future and put the thoughts out of her head, but it had become all too consuming. And now, as she jammed her foot into her boot and stood, she tried hard not to think about her heart and how she had felt like a piece of it had been lost the moment Tom left her standing on her parent's front verandah all those weeks ago.

'I won't be late back. I have to work in the morning.'

'Have a good night. Say hi to the girls for me.'

Beth blew her mum a kiss as she walked past the lounge chair and out the front door. A night with the girls was just what she needed.

Beth froze.

Her hand still on the screen door, she blinked twice, thinking she was seeing things. Then she let out a little scream and ran down the steps towards Tom's outstretched arms. He braced himself as she jumped into his waiting body. Beth wrapped her legs around his waist, her arms around his neck, and she kissed him solidly on the lips—repeatedly.

Laughing as his body rocked back, he kissed her back, locking his arms around her, so she couldn't get away from him. Not that she wanted to. 'What are you doing here?' Beth smiled breathlessly as she ran her hand through Tom's hair. His cap had been dislodged when she had jumped into his arms. 'You said you weren't going to be back for a few more days.' She kissed him again, unable to get enough of the taste of his lips.

'I drove all the way back just to surprise you.' He still held her in his arms, never wanting to let her go. The grip he had on her waist told her he had missed her just as much as she had him.

'Fifteen hours?' She was shocked and wriggled free from his embrace, sliding down the entire length of him. She felt his body stir awake at her closeness. The instant she felt his arousal, a low ache formed in her body.

'I couldn't stay away.' He stepped back and looked Beth up and down, before pulling her back in and kissing her longingly slow and more sensual and passionate than before. It sent butterflies fluttering throughout her stomach.

Breaking the long kiss, her whole body humming with him as they stood in their own world, Tom cradled Beth's face between his hands and rested his forehead on hers. He breathed hard but sure, as they just stared at each other. 'I was so scared you might have pulled away from me because of how long I've been away. I was actually nervous about seeing you.' Tom took another breath, but this one was a little shaky as she released the depth and truth of his words. Shaking her head, with the sting of tears misting her eyes, Tom quietly added, stealing another earth shattering kiss from her, 'But this ... holding you is everything.'

'For goodness sake; let her breathe!!'

Tom let his lips slowly drift away, his head against Beth's until she regained focus. Her eyes opened slowly to gaze into his, and they both laughed. Beth looked around him to see Montana hanging out the window of Adelaide's little car, giggling. A blush crept up and coloured Beth's face, tainting it deeper, when Tom kissed her cheek. He then put his arm around her as he turned to the girls.

'See? Still breathing.' He kissed Beth's cheek again. 'How are you girls?'

'Better now after seeing your sexy ass,' Montana giggled as Adelaide pulled her back into the car, scolding her twin sister at her boldness.

'We're heading for a few drinks at the pub. Want to come?' Beth said, turning her back on the girls to face Tom.

'I think Montana has already started.' Tom placed his hands on Beth's hips and pulled her to his body. 'I can't stay.' He kissed her again. 'I just wanted to see you. I need to meet the trucks to unload all the machinery, and Dad has some urgent jobs that need to be done after, but are you free tomorrow night? Megan has decided to have a mini engagement party at the pub, and I want you to come.'

Beth shifted uncomfortably in front of him. 'Umm ... don't you think she will be upset about me being there? She doesn't like me. I'm not up to her social level, remember?'

'I want you there. That's all that matters.' He kissed her slowly, persuading her by his kisses, which were winding magic into her defences. 'Say yes.'

'Are you coming or not, Beth?' Montana called from the car.

Beth smiled up at Tom. 'What time do I need to be ready?' With her hand resting over his heart, she felt his heart beat faster.

'Say 8pm?' He took her hand and started for the girls' car.

'Okay. I will be ready.' Tom opened the door for Beth, before kissing her again and closing it for her. 'Behave tonight,' he warned the girls sternly, adding a wink to tell them he knew they wouldn't.

Montana's reply was to salute Tom in return.

Beth's nerves were raging wild, causing her to shake slightly as they walked up the steps to Willy's pub. Tom's hand on the small of her back for reassurance and support was the only thing keeping her moving forward, and her legs from buckling from beneath her body. Opening the door for her, he smiled reassuringly seconds before everyone at the bar turned and looked at them, then cheered and wolf whistled as she entered.

'You got yourself a great catch there, Tom,' yelled one of the older men sitting at the bar.

'Yeah, yeah boys. Give it a break.' Tom smiled at Beth, returning his hand to her back, and steering her through the crowd to the back area where Megan had booked her and Jeff's casual engagement party.

Walking through the large barn doors into the 'shed,' people turned and watched Beth enter the room, Tom just behind her, his hand never leaving her back as he thumbed the dress soothingly across her skin. A few of Megan's friends scowled and whispered behind their hands as they looked Beth up and down. She felt a rush of nausea sweep over her.

Wearing a black little number that clung in all the right places, but was modest at the same time, her hair was half swept up into a messy and elegant twist with the other half hanging down her back. Beth felt that she had dressed correctly for the occasion, but now she found herself unconsciously brushing at the sides of her dress, wishing she had chosen something a little less dressy and clingy.

When Tom had seen her exit her home, he had just looked her up and down with his mouth open before eventually finding his voice and exclaiming how stunning she looked. Kissing her on her cheek so as not to mess up her freshly applied lipstick, Tom took a long look at her, while she twirled under his arm and giggled. Satisfied with his approval, Beth watched as Tom then pulled out a little black box from his dark-coloured jeans, and presented her with a solid white gold bangle covered in a light dusting of diamonds imbedded into the stunning piece. They gave the bangle just enough glitter to catch the light, without being too showy. As Beth slipped it onto her wrist, gushing at the elegant piece's beauty, and thinking how he shouldn't have, Tom made her promise to never take it off.

Fidgeting with the weighted piece now, Beth could see every eye in the room watching her. This was not the place for her. And the more she fidgeted with the bracelet, the more people seemed to be watching her, which in turn made her feel sick, so she fidgeted with her dress and bracelet more. Pressing a firm hand on her back, Tom's smile was one of reassurance and of a silent word to stop fidgeting, as an older couple, Beth didn't recognise, came up to Tom and began a conversation.

Introducing Beth to them without a thought of who she really was and her presence in his life, Tom continued to talk openly with the couple. He had obviously known them for years, but still Beth felt awkward and out of place. This was a family event, and to the outside world, she was just a friend to Tom, regardless of what was happening between them when no one else was around.

Others she did not know continued to come over slowly to talk to Tom. Each time, he introduced her proudly, ensuring they all knew Beth was with him and she was important. His hand returned to her back after each handshake with a gentleman, or a hug and kiss on an older woman's cheek as he greeted each one.

176

Beth was so thankful Tom was keeping her close and protected, knowing and understanding her nerves at being where she felt she didn't belong. He didn't seem to care what others thought or how their relationship was running out of time. He was proud to have her there, on his arm, and show her off. Watching him closely, her heart warmed and swelled for him as he confidently spoke to all those who abided for his attention. This world was not for her. This was his world, and she did not belong. But as each person came and went, Beth's body relaxed a little more and she grew to understand that just for tonight she would just enjoy having Tom next to her.

'Well, you finally decided to turn up. And look, you bought new jeans and a shirt for the occasion.' The couple who had been talking to Tom, discreetly moved away. 'But look at this sexy little thing on your arm. I'm now thinking it wasn't for our Meg, but so you can drain your balls later, that you got all dressed up, Tommy.'

Matthew O'Loughlin half stumbled up to them, stopping so close to Beth she could feel his foul, hot rum breath on her face and down her dress as he blatantly looked down at her breasts. She did not step back, as Tom's hand was there, and neither did she cover herself with her hand to stop his outward intake of her body. She would not give him the satisfaction of seeing how much that one movement had unsettled her. Tom stepped half in front of her, pushing his father back a step, without making a scene.

'That's enough, *Dad*. You need to give Beth more respect,' Tom said quietly under his breath so only his father could hear.

'Now, now, Tommy.' He firmly tapped Tom's cheek with jest, but it was more of a warning. Beth could feel the tension between them, feeling that at any moment they could come to blows and cause a massive scene in front of the crowd, ruining Megan and Jeff's causal celebrational night. Leaning into Tom's ear, Mathew spoke gruffly. 'We're in public now. Settle down, boy. You'll get too riled up and won't be able to perform later.'

Mathew winked at Beth over Tom's shoulder as his son glared at him. 'We can't have your poor performance getting out to potential brides now, can we?'

Tom stood his ground in front of Beth, his father having to lean against his shoulder to get close to her. 'If he can't perform as an O'Loughlin should, come and find me and I will show you what a real man can do.'

The smell of rum wafted over her and made her ill. Beth's stomach lurched and her hands shook. Reaching for the back of Tom's shirt for reassurance, Beth could feel the steel in his muscles as he physically protected her from his father's crass words. Mathew's gaze went to her breasts again and back to her eyes as he stepped back, a predator's smile on his lips.

Sneering, he added, 'You know you want a real man and not a boy.'

Mathew's gaze turned to Tom, and they shared a look that only they knew. Tom's whole body radiated with fury and anger as he held his father's gaze. Neither was going to be the first to look away and give the impression of submission. Eventually, it was Mathew who looked away first, a smile on his lips as he winked at Beth.

'Nice trinket on your arm too.' He raised his eyebrows as he smiled a nasty little grin and moved away.

Not wanting to think about the meaning behind his last words, Beth took a shaky, deep breath as Tom turned to her. Taking her hand, he looked around to make sure no one was looking at them. People averted their eyes away and went back to their conversations.

Looking back at her, Tom's voice was harsh and full of anger and disappointment. He touched her face gently, his hand shaking a little in hers. 'I am so sorry for that. When he gets on the rum, he has no manners and what he thinks is funny, is usually degrading and horrible. He won't remember it in the morning.'

'He might not remember in the morning, but I will,' Beth said in disgust. How could Tom and his father be so closely related?

'He won't come near us again tonight. I promise.' Tom leaned in and gave Beth a slow kiss on the cheek. Her skin heated, but her heart ached for Tom, as the sting of tears threatened. 'You're here with me, remember? No one will come near you.'

'You make that sound bad,' she giggled, trying to ease the tension pulsating through them.

Kate came up with Braydon.

'That looked intense you two,' Kate said, looking between them both as Braydon handed them a drink. 'Think I might drag Beth out on the dance floor to loosen things up a little.'

Before Beth could say no, Kate had her by the hand and out on the floor. It was darker there with only the disco ball and soft lights above them. Beth was unsure of what to do. She didn't want to make more of a spectacle of herself than she already had walking in with Tom. People were still watching her and talking, even more so now after what had just happened between father and son.

Feeling exposed and vulnerable, a ripple of fear so hot it made her stare at the exit door, Beth thought of leaving, but she couldn't do that to Tom. She couldn't embarrass him by deserting him in the middle of his sister's engagement party, in front of all these people who respected him. No, she would stay and stand her ground by his side.

'Loosen up, Beth.' Kate grabbed her arm, turning her in a wild woman waltz move, making her laugh out loud at her friend. Kate was one person you could always depend on when she called you a friend. Kate was straight and direct and always told it how it was, but she was protective and loyal to those she loved. Beth was glad Kate loved her.

'Well, well ... I think I have found myself to be the lucky man who gets to dance with two sexy girls tonight.' Braydon swaggered up to them, a beer in both hands—one for him, the other for Kate. He smiled a cheeky grin that made Beth relax more. She was with friends and she was safe, she reminded herself.

After handing Kate her beer, Braydon took Beth's hand and pulled her tightly to his body. He crazily Aussie-country-boy waltzed her in a circle. She had to keep her balance against him as he was unsteady on his feet. He must have been drinking hard since he and Kate had arrived.

Swinging her around again and away from Kate and anyone else who was watching them, he whispered, 'Don't let them get to ya, Beth. I've never seen Tom so happy.' Before she had time to comprehend his words, Braydon spun her out gently, his fingers slipping from hers. He moved on to show Kate his moves. Watching them both, Beth giggled and smiled at their fearlessness of all the others watching.

Kate was looking at Braydon with a 'come and get me' look as she swung her hips low in a sexy, grinding move. Braydon threw his head back and laughed. Stopping his progression towards her, he copied her low dance move. Not as graceful as Kate, he stumbled a little, then continued to walk to her, grabbing her hips and pulling them against his before she laughed and pushed him away. Their attention fixed to Beth, her eyes widened. She shook her head. She knew what they wanted.

'No.' Beth shook her head, hands up to stop their asking eyes.

'Come on, you sexy thing you. Shake it for me,' Kate encouraged. Beth kept shaking her head. Not here and definitely not now.

'You know you want to.' Kate drawled up to her, her ruthless smile making Beth scared of what was to come. 'If you don't, you know what will happen.'

'You wouldn't.'

'Try me.' Kate turned and wiggled her ass in front of Beth. Two years ago, Beth was working as a waitress at the river festival grand ball. Kate was there and extremely drunk, and she had caught Beth on the outskirts of the dance floor, grinding her body, very sexually, up against her. Beth had tried to push Kate away and retreat to the kitchen, but she couldn't. Not wanting to encourage Kate further in front of all the SBs who were watching the two of them on the side of the dance floor, Beth didn't grind back against Kate.

Kate, being Kate, she licked between Beth's breasts and up her neck, shocking her so much Beth had dropped the entire tray of glasses she had been carrying, smashing them, sending glass fragments all over the dance floor. And if that wasn't bad enough, Kate also groped her ass, in full view of the entire town, when she had bent to pick up the tray and what she could of the glasses. Beth had not spoken to Kate for a week after that and, thinking about it now, she had never gotten an apology from her friend either. Looking at Kate now, still grinding along with Braydon as they waited for Beth to do the same, she was certain that if she didn't grind back, Kate would do something similar to what she had done at the ball.

After a quick look around to make sure no one was looking, Beth lowered her hips and grinded back to Kate and Braydon, who loudly wolf whistled. 'Yeah baby. Whoop.'

An arm wrapped around Beth's waist and pulled her back as a drink appeared in front of her. She fell back against the solid wall of muscle.

'Will you do that move for me later?' A little laugh escaped Beth's lips as she felt Tom's hot lips on her neck. Her body tingled all over. 'Have I told you how sexy you look tonight?'

'No.' Beth teased and let Tom hold her to his body as they swayed together.

'You look absolutely beautiful. The prettiest girl here,' he whispered in her ear, his breath sending goosebumps all over her body. Lulling her head back against his shoulder, he kissed her gently, heating her veins, pooling a deep ache for him low in her body.

Later that night, the dance floor was full and nearly everyone was drunk. Beth had only had a few drinks and was now drinking water. She didn't want a repeat of the festival and to ruin yet another set of Tom's boots.

Tom had been pulled aside by the couple, Mr and Mrs Shackleton, who she had met earlier, though he was still watching her on the dance floor as he spoke to them. She could feel his eyes on her. Spinning out of Braydon's arms as he pulled Kate into another dance when the song changed, Beth's eyes caught Tom's across the room. Together, they locked and held. Watching him bring the glass in his hands to his lips and take a long, slow sip as his eyes travelled down the length of her body and back again; the interaction touched and heated her from across the crowded floor. Tom knew the effect he was having on her, and behind his glass she saw his seductive smile lift his lips. It caused her knees to grow weak.

'Come to the toilet with me, *girlfriend*.' Kate grabbed Beth around the neck in a headlock and kissed her cheek before dragging her out of the shed doors, letting her stumble along laughing, and up the steps, just outside the pub's backdoor. Large potted plants gave privacy to the toilet entries and, as usual, there was a line up for the women's. A lady was tapping her foot impatiently as she waited outside for the girls inside to finish. Everyone around the back of the pub could hear the girls inside giggling and slamming doors, all drunk and preventing everyone else who needed to go, from entering.

Two stumbled out, holding each other up, laughing and spilling the drinks in their hands, all over the floor. Leaving Beth to stand on her own, she waited while the lady and Kate, who had started to do a little kid's toilet jig, go in first. Ashleigh and Katrina came up giggling and openly bitching about her, right behind her back. They were just about as drunk as the other girls were, though they seemed to be holding it together better. Beth

182

just rolled her eyes. She wouldn't confront them, wouldn't cause a scene or upset anyone, and soon, it wouldn't matter—she wouldn't be seeing any of them again for a very long time.

This made Beth feel sad as she thought about leaving and saying goodbye to Tom for the last time. The lady came out, *tsking* and mumbling about the state of the toilets, stopping any more sad thoughts. And before Beth could move forward, Ashleigh and Katrina pushed in front of her. Shaking her head at their rudeness, she let them go. If that's how they got some twisted power over her, then so be it.

Kate stumbled out, wiping her hands on her dress. 'No paper towel left,' she complained before looking Beth up and down with a drunken frown, noticing she was still waiting in line—alone. 'Are you ready?'

'No. I won't be long though.' Beth tilted her head towards the toilet's entrance door. 'I let those girls in before me.' Kate followed her gaze and nodded, her eyes saying she knew Beth had not let them go in first.

'Don't be long otherwise that sexy boy of yours will be coming to find you. He hasn't taken his eyes off you all night.' Licking her finger, Kate placed it on her own bottom and made a hissing sound like her finger was branding her skin. Then she unsteadily walked back down the steps to the shed.

When Beth walked out of the toilets, no one was waiting, and she had been the only one in there. A rare phenomenon.

'Beth.' Jeff stepped out from behind one of the large potted plants and blocked her path back to the shed. Startling her, her heart began to race, and fear slithered through her body. 'You're looking very sexy tonight in that dress.' He took a few steps towards her, the beer bottle, hanging loosely in his hand, going to his lips as he took a swig. The way his eyes raked over her body made her very nervous and feel as though she had been undressed.

Instinctively bringing her hands up to cover herself from his gaze, Jeff raised the corner of his lip in a sneer. Beth began to panic. He knew she was uncomfortable, and yet he seemed to like it. A sick turn on. Nausea began to roll through her body. Looking over Jeff's shoulder, Beth hoped someone was coming to the toilet. She prayed Tom was searching for her. With a curl to his top lip, Jeff followed her gaze. Checking that no one else was coming, he turned back with a nasty smile on his face.

'Tommy. Oh, so precious, Tommy boy, is a little busy at the moment, Beth. He is doing the family thing, having photos with Meg. He might be awhile.' Jeff took another step forward and Beth took an involuntary step back. Smiling maliciously at her, Jeff's eyes flickered. She was trapped. Beyond the female toilets, was a little nook where the cleaning room was. She had to get past him to get to safety. To get to Tom.

'Let me past, Jeff. Stop being an idiot.' Beth looked around him again, but he started to stalk her, backwards. Beth retreated as he dropped his beer into another potted plant and kept coming for her. She looked towards the toilets and made a quick step for them. Jeff grabbed her before she could reach the door, his body now blocking her escape both ways. His hands painfully gripped both her wrists and locked her hands behind her. Walking her backwards, as she struggled, Jeff used his body to push Beth into the cleaning room nook and out of sight from anyone coming to use the toilets.

'Get off me, Jeff!' Breaking one hand free, she tried to strike at him, but he grabbed it and pushed her hard against the wall, knocking the wind from her lungs. This made it impossible for her to scream in that moment.

'You fuck him so easily. Why not let me have a turn?' he hissed in her ear as he pinned her to the wall with his body. Getting her breath back, Beth screamed and tried to push him away. Jeff grabbed her wrists in his one large hand and pinned them back against the wall so she couldn't move. Her body was now painfully locked between Jeff and the wall at her back. Fear and panic sliced through her as her fight or flight adrenaline kicked in.

'Get off me!!!' she screamed at him as loudly as she could. Turning her head as he tried to kiss her, Beth lifted her knee, trying to make solid contact with his body anywhere she could.

'What the hell are you doing?' The growl was low and fearsome. Before Beth knew what was happening, Tom grabbed Jeff, spun him around and connected his fist to Jeff's jaw with a sickening cracking sound. Jeff's head twisted around, and his eyes rolled back into his head with the brutal force. He hit the wall and slid down it. Tom grabbed him by the collar, ready to go at him again, when Braydon's hands grabbed his shoulders. The larger man struggled to pull Tom back.

Willy, the publican, stepped in between them. 'That's enough boys!!'

Tom violently shrugged Braydon off, yelling at him to 'get off' so he could go to Beth. Stepping over Jeff's dazed body, giving him a forceful kick to the ribs as he went, Tom materialised in front of her.

'Are you okay? Are you hurt?' Tom was frantically looking all over Beth's face and body as she began to cry, her arms wrapping around his neck. She buried her face into Tom's neck as more people came out to see what was going on. She was trembling as he shielded her from everyone crowding the little nook.

'Get him out of here. Now!' Willy yelled to the other men as he hauled Jeff up by his shirt and pushed him into them. 'The rest of ya, clear out!'

Willy waited for everyone to go back to where they had appeared from as he helped to block everyone's view of Beth. He was a large man with muscles that stretched his shirt when he crossed his arms. He had purchased the pub after retiring from the army a few years ago. The rumour was, he had been SAS, but no one ever asked. By the way he was standing guard, blocking the view of Tom and Beth, it was more than evident that he meant what he said and if anyone disobeyed, he was surely capable of removing them himself.

Ensuring all the spectators had left, Willy turned to them. Tom was still shielding Beth, his arms wrapped tightly around her as his anger churned. He cradled her safely in his arms. She was visibly shaking and felt like shock was taking her under a wave she didn't know how to swim through. With a gentle but firm hand on his shoulder, reassuring him that they were indeed alone, Willy touched Beth's hair. His anger and distress at what had happened in his pub was clear on his big, round face.

'You had better take her home, Tom,' he said quietly. His fondness for Beth showed in his eyes and voice. 'Don't leave her alone tonight and make sure her parents know what's happened. John and Susan won't want to hear it through the grapevine.'

Shaking Willy's hand, Tom put his arm around Beth, and with Willy shielding them as much as possible from the front, Tom led her back past the toilets and towards the back side door of the pub—the nearest exit with the least amount of people around it. He didn't want everyone staring at her by going through the main bar area or past the party.

'What the hell did you do, Thomas?' It was Megan. She was sneaking back into the party through the same door they were trying to get out through. Trent was behind her. 'Where is Jeff?'

Turning Beth's tear-stained face into his neck with his hand so she didn't have to face Megan, Tom growled at his sister. 'I don't know, Megan. Probably licking his wounds.' Her accusation that this was all his fault, peaked his anger so fast he leaned right into her face as he spoke through gritted teeth so tight his jaw had begun to pulse. 'Maybe if you both were not fucking other people ...' His eyes darted to Trent's and then back to hers, telling her he knew where they had been, '... then maybe he wouldn't have attacked Beth. You pair deserve each other, Meg.' He leaned back, holding Beth closer to him. 'Now get out of my way; I have to take Beth home.' Tom shouldered between Megan and Trent, ignoring her huffing and puffing at him.

After a few steps, he demanded over his shoulder, 'If Jeff can see straight and work that jaw enough to talk, tell him I want to see him at Kathryn's café in the morning to publicly apologise to Beth. He knows what will happen if he doesn't arrive.'

Chapter 11

Driving down her street, towards her home, Beth stared out the window. She had not said a word since Tom had reached her trembling body, locked against the wall with fear, and hauled her into his arms. Watching her carefully out of the corner of his eye, Tom was worried. Beth's hands were locked together in her lap, and her shaking appeared to have stopped. But she was still very fearful and appeared almost lost.

Bitterness and anger rolled with his thundering heart, his guilt for not being there to protect her eating and tearing at his insides. He should have been more aware—she had been gone for too long. Mackenzie and another girl had had him cornered and he thought Beth was with Kate. Then Ashleigh and Katrina had joined the group surrounding him, all touching and vying for his attention. He was too busy trying to get away from them to notice how much time had really passed.

He had seen Kate come back to the dance floor and watched for Beth to follow her back into the room, but she hadn't. Remembering how his skin had prickled, he had forcibly pushed through the group of girls to go in search of her. It wasn't until he had stepped out of the noise of the party that he had heard her scream and started to run. Willy and Braydon appeared from nowhere behind him, but he was already on top of Jeff. The scene of Beth fighting as she was pinned to the wall, will remain with him forever. The mere thought of Jeff's body pressed to hers as he tried to kiss her, made him clench his hands into fists again.

He had failed to protect her. He had let her down. And now, as she sat opposite him in his ute, tears staining her cheeks, his heart tightened so much it felt like the muscle would never beat again.

Tom reached across the ute for Beth's hand, but she just looked at it blindly. The shock of the night and her emotions becoming too much, she began to cry and shake again. Through her tears, she looked up at him. 'I don't want to go home, Tom. I just want to be with you.' Her voice broke, and she began to openly cry. 'I can't be without you tonight; I'm too scared.' The whispered words hit Tom hard.

Bringing her hand to his lips, Tom held her cold fingers there, breathing warmth into them as he continued to roll down the street, past her house and out of town.

At their little spot by the gully, the grass now regrown back to its thick state, Tom stopped the ute and turned off the lights. They both just sat there, silently staring out the windshield, into the blackness of the night.

Tom waited for her to speak, but the longer she didn't—the longer she just stared into the black night—the more he became worried about her, about his choice of bringing her out here and not taking her home to her parents. But in that moment, she had begged to be with him. And he—and only he—would never deign her. He could never say no to her.

Calming his rolling anger and pain, Tom got out and gently closed the door of the ute. Taking some deep breaths, he knew he needed to remain calm and be all Beth needed tonight. Dealing with the rest of it, would be done tomorrow. He would make sure of that, but for her, tonight, he needed to keep himself and his emotions all under wraps.

Coming around to Beth's door, he opened it and tried to give her a small smile of encouragement. Beth plainly returned his look. Her tears no longer fell, and she seemed to have recovered a little now they were by themselves with no one able to find them.

'Are you really okay?' Tom wanted to pull her out of the ute and cuddle her, never letting her go; however, doing that might have scared her even more and she might end up being scared of him. He had to find a way to reach her, comfort her and let her know she could trust him again. He wouldn't let her down again. Ever.

Smiling a little, she turned in her seat as he stood back. 'I think so. Can you please just hold me tonight? I just want to be with you and no one else.'

'Are you sure?'

She didn't have to nod twice. Tom pulled her to him in a tight cuddle, so strong and secure for them both. Beth began to giggle, the sound causing him to relax a little and release his grip.

'Why are you laughing?' Tom looked down at her face, relieved to hear her laugh and see a smile on her beautiful face.

'Because you're holding me too tight. I couldn't breathe.' She snuggled back into his chest.

'I won't leave you, Beth. I promise.' He could see her trying to understand the depth of his words. She raised her head and looked at him for a second before leaning back into his embrace. She was leaving at the end of the summer—he knew that—but he would not leave her. Breathing with the feel of her safely in his arms, he just held her while he had her.

Raising her head to look at the stars above, Beth breathed deeply and studied the little glitters of light so high. Tom too looked up at the phenomenon of the southern sky, the spellbinding beauty of twinkling balls of gas so close yet so far away from them. It reminded him of just how small they were in this ever-expanding universe and just how insignificant the people who treated them so badly really were. For the first time in a long time, Tom just stared up at the stars, before gazing back at Beth.

No part of his plans ever included this. Her. Being here with someone like her was something he had never thought he would have. How had he found someone who caused his heart to dance with just a single thought? To cause him to want and need things he had pushed to the furthest regions of his mind? She now stood holding a bright evanescence beacon to show him he could possibly have what he wanted. How he could make that happen was still a mystery, but while he had her, while he could hold her in his arms and call her his, nothing was impossible.

How he had gotten so lucky to meet her, he would never understand, but looking back up at the sky again, somewhere up there, beyond the mind's consciousness, someone had decided that she, Beth Kennedy, should appear across a muddy river and pull him headfirst—literally—into her life. For that one, now precious, second, his life had been forever altered, and he was never going to be the same. Something profound was developing between them, and the rest of life dulled compared to it.

Her skin glowing in the moonlight, lips soft and inviting, Tom watched her. He couldn't take his eyes off her as his heart raced, and warmth spread through his being, calming and relaxing. He was floating just above his body. Beth's eyes flicked to his and held, drawing him to her. He slowly leaned in, giving her time to stop him if she was not ready. Her eyes fluttered closed as he neared, giving him her unspoken permission.

His lips touched hers, and the ground shifted under his feet. He could taste the beer he had been drinking all night, mixing with her sweetness, as he held her firmly and continued to slowly draw her into his soul. Wrapping her arms around his neck, Beth slid out of the ute and stood on her tip toes to taste more of him. Tom slipped his hands to her waist and pulled her to the length of his body. Her hands slid into his hair, and he vibrated with a little groan as she lowered her feet back to the ground, taking him with her, tasting him and needing more.

The heat and warmth, muscle and strength, and pure security and protection of Tom's body was all hers, and would be forever if she would have him. He was hers, and as the thought swam through the tidal wave of emotions, she was causing him, he groaned and held her tighter, stirring the inner flames of their relationship to life.

Lifting her small frame of a body easily, Beth's legs wrapped around Tom's hips. He pressed her to the side of his ute as his kisses trailed a blaze along her jaw to her ear, where he nibbled. Melting against him, with a tiny moan, Beth turned her head to allow him better access to her skin.

Tom didn't know why it happened—what had caused the image—but as he was tasting her, hearing her whimper a little in pleasure, a vison of her pressed up against the wall with Jeff flashed through his mind and cooled his desire in an instant.

Slowly lowering Beth to the ground, he stepped away from her and looked at the ground. Her hands clung to his shirt as confusion showed in her eyes as to why he pulled away and rejected her desire for him.

'I'm sorry, Beth. I can't. Not after what happened tonight.' He stepped back again, her fingers losing their grip in the material at his skin. Shame and anger of not protecting her left a bitter taste in his mouth, and his body tensed with the visions that continued to play through his mind.

Beth cuddled herself at the memory he had just forced her to replay. He could see her body shiver and felt the coldness that seemed to surround them both as he drew away from her. Looking at him backing away, a deep hurt stabbed at her, instantly showing in her eyes before her temper flared at him.

'So, what? I'm not good enough for you now?' She spat the words at him. Her arms dropped to her sides as she clenched her hands into fists. 'Not worthy of you to touch me because of what Jeff did. Is that it?'

'NO!! That's not it at all.' Frustration and thinly vailed, controlled anger infused his words. Tom was shocked she would think that. Blinking at her, he wiped a hand over his face.

'Then what is it? Why would you pull away just now when I am offering everything you have been after since we met?' Lowering her voice, controlling her temper, Beth dared to ask what she had tried never to think about. 'Is it because everyone knows what you're after and now it's not a game? That going against what they want isn't fun anymore?' Hurt and rejection laced her words and stabbed at Tom's guts.

'That's bloody cruel and a load of bullshit, and you bloody well know it, Beth.'

'They don't want me around. They don't want us to be anything—even friends—and they're doing their absolute best to make sure I'm seen as nothing more than the slut or social climber they think I am.' She yelled at him, high pitched and full of pain from finally voicing all she had been subjected to from the moment they had met.

It was the truth, and he had failed her in that way too. A deep sinking feeling hit like a boulder landing on top of Tom's shoulders, and he felt the weight of all Beth had endured for him and how she was still willing to endure the pain, for his love. He was not the man he had always prided himself to have been. For her, *he* had failed.

Tears stung Beth's eyes, and she turned her face away from him. She was now done with this conversation. Stepping to the side, she moved to climb back into the ute. Tom's arm stopped her.

'Don't you dare ever say that again,' he angrily whispered to her. His chest brushed her shoulder and her body recognised the contact. Tom clearly saw it in her eyes as she tried to glare at him as he attempted to prevent her from running.

'Why? It's the truth.' She was not going to shed the tears that were welling up in her eyes. Strength and willpower held her firm.

'I don't care what others say or think. You know that.' Tom's breath sent tingles over Beth's body. Even with her temper, her body reacted to him.

'I was the cause of the fights tonight. I can't be the cause of that between your family. You know the reason I can't. We can't do this anymore, Tom.' She moved away from his body, making no eye contact, her back to him. 'In a month, we have to say goodbye anyway. It's not worth creating problems just for a month.' Her battle to keep her tears down, failed.

Tom gently spun her back around, so she had to face him. Lifting her chin so he could see into her eyes, he kissed a tear away as it slid down her cheek. He then rested his forehead to hers. 'I know we only have a month, Beth.' His words were slightly unsteady. 'It's worth it to me.'

Shaking her head at his words, her eyes closed, she pulled back away from him. 'How can you say that, when seconds ago, you just pulled away from me when all I wanted was you. For *you* to hold me and make it all alright.' Deep hurt sounded in her voice, and Tom finally began to understand. She thought it was her. It could never be her. Pain and anger, hurt and frustration— all he had caused her and then failed her tonight. He didn't know how he was ever going to make it right or why she would still want him. His own tears threatened.

'Why would you want me to? I failed you. I wasn't there to protect you. If I had, Jeff wouldn't have been able to do what he did.' Tom's anger at himself and Jeff burned so hot, he felt sick to his guts. Swallowing the bile rising took all he had as he clamped it down for her. 'I want you, Beth, more then you will ever know, even in ways I don't understand myself, but I let you down tonight. Even more than that, I've let you down every day since we met. I failed to keep you safe when I had promised I would.' He looked away and steadied himself, trying to get the right words to come out.

Frowning, Beth placed her hand on his chest, over his heart, drawing him back to face her. He could feel his heart pumping strong and steady in his chest as her warmth seeped into his body, calming the rage. 'You did, Tom. You stopped it all before he was able to do more than scare the shit out of me. You heard my scream and came gallantly in.' The corners of Beth's beautiful lips twitched with the first sign of a smile. 'And you knocked him so hard, I think you may have broken his jaw and nose.' Rubbing the knuckles of his right hand, Tom felt the swelling and cuts that, up until that moment, he had not even noticed were painful. 'He will be seeing stars for days, if not weeks,' Beth finished tenderly.

'I don't know what the hell to do to make it better. To take it all away for you.' Tom's frustration came out in a growl, but Beth didn't flinch. In fact, she was staring at him like she was proud of who he was. He was frowning at her, now completely confused. She fisted her hands into the side of Tom's shirt and stepped closer to his body.

'Make me forget,' she whispered and, taking his hand, she led him to the back of his ute, jumping up to sit on the back of the tray. Tom stood in front of her and watched as she slipped off her shoes, letting them drop to the ground. His chest tightened along with his jeans as she slowly unpinned her hair, letting the mass fall over her shoulders, framing her face. Her eyes never leaving his, he swallowed the nervous lump in his throat, suddenly unsure of what to do.

She waited. Waited for him to make the choice and take what she was offering him.

Her breathing was shallow as his eyes scanned her face for what seemed like forever before he stepped forward. His body now between her legs, he ran his hands through her hair and held her, trying to see into her soul—trying to read her thoughts so he could understand what she wanted from him and why. They both wanted what she was physically asking, but why? He was so confused. The more he stared at her the more he questioned it.

'Are you sure you want me?'

'Yes, more then you will ever know. Even in ways I don't understand myself.' She copied his words as he looked at her. She wanted him and her whispered words broke the restraints holding his heart. Now freed, it thundered against his ribs. His lips crashed into hers and he kissed her deeply, needy and fast at first. It was like needing a long drink after being in the desert for years without water. Taking his fill in those few desperate moments, he restrained himself and slowed.

Their passion ignited, Beth's hands in Tom's hair. She clung to him, ankles locking around his legs to stop him from moving away. His jeans scratched the inside of her thigh as he stepped into her more, her dress rising to rest at the top of her thighs. Still, he continued to kiss and taste her. Suckling her top lip and nibbling her bottom one, he caught her tongue when she darted it into his mouth, before following hers back, where she did the same to his. Tom's mind was no longer focused on anything but Beth. Her touch. Her taste. His need for her.

The embers that had started here, in this place, weeks ago, started to burn hotter as he continued to plunder and take from her all that he needed—and give her all that he had. She was melting into him. Nothing mattered, nothing *could* matter but losing his soul to her.

Slowly, something drew him back, back from the maddening power she had over his entire being—over his mind, body and soul. He forced himself to come back to where they were, back to the coolness of the night and the ground under his boots, back to the sounds of the crickets in the grass and the frogs in the little gully. Slowly, he came back and remembered what she was giving him.

Raining little kisses on her lips and over her face, Tom pulled away. 'Wait here,' he rasped, his own voice sounding strange to his ears.

Leaving her a little confused and dazed, sitting on the ute, he jumped up onto the tray and rolled out the swag before leaning down to her and pulling her up, so she could stand with him. Stepping to her, pressing his entire body to the length of hers, he looked back over at the swag, then to her.

'A place for me to hold you like you asked.' Tucking a piece of stray hair behind Beth's ear, Tom followed his finger—first with his eyes, then with raining butterfly kisses along her skin, causing her body to shiver and goose bump.

'I want more than that. I want to lie in your arms all night, Tom; Beth whispered, her hands fisted into his shirt to hold herself steady. Tom nodded and followed a fiery, branding line from her ear, down her neck and to her collarbone, kissing her bare skin as his fingers pulled the dress off her shoulder. He blindly returned his lips to hers for another long kiss.

With trembling hands, he found the little buttons at the back of her dress, smiling as each one popped open under his skilled fingers, allowing the dress to stretch just enough to let him remove the sleeve from her other shoulder. Branding another line like before, causing her to shiver again with his kisses, he once again returned to her lips.

Going this slow was driving him crazy, and when Beth pressed her body against his and moved her hips, he knew it was the same for her. Teasing her and never wanting this night to end, he moved with her. They grinded and pressed against each other, hungrily feasting, needing more than the other could give. Tom glided his hand down Beth's back and over her bottom to cup and knead it.

His jeans tight over his straining erection, he grew harder as Beth pulled his shirt from his jeans and skimmed her fingers over his stomach and hips. Sending shivers up and down his body, a deep gravely moan vibrated up his chest from deep within him and out of his mouth where Beth caught it and sucked it into her lungs with an erotic whimper. Unbuttoning his shirt with an unsteady hand, she pushed it from his shoulders and let it fall to the tray of the ute. The fabric now gone, it allowed Beth's hands to wander all over his chest and back down to cup him through his jeans. Tom stepped back a little, with a hiss as his hand encircled Beth's wrist and pulled it away from him. 'Not yet,' he rasped on a laugh.

'But why? Oh ...' Beth was lifted into his arms, twisted around and then laid onto the softness of his swag. His actions had been so swift that she let out a little squeal and clung to his neck. Laying her down ever so gently, Tom loomed over her, his hands entangled in her hair as it fell all over his pillow, her shoulders bare. For a long moment, he took it all in.

Finally, lowering himself to her body, he kissed her again, deepening the kiss until she was lost and melted into the thin mattress. Finding his way down her neck, Tom kissed the tops of her breasts. The soft mounds desperately tried to escape the confines of her dress. Beth reached for him as she arched her breasts higher, wanting more of his teasing. Unsatisfied with the restraint the dress was causing her, she sat up and pushed him back.

Rocking back onto his ankles, with a smile at her as she tried to reach behind to loosen the buttons, he let her struggle for a little bit before leaning back in, claiming her lips again. His fingers removed hers and he took over the task of unbuttoning the rest of her dress, finally allowing it to fall down her arms to her hips. She pulled her arms free and clutched his head before falling back onto the mattress, taking him with her. Catching himself above her, so as not to crush her body with his heavier weight, he lengthened out the kiss, thoroughly tasting her over and over. He couldn't get enough.

Smoothing a hand down over her ribs, waist and around to her bottom, Tom kneaded roughly like she had shown him how she liked it, before following the path back to her ribs and her still lace-covered breasts.

Eyes closed, Beth felt his every touch brand her skin. Her gaze locked with his, it was like their bodies had become one as her need for him and his for hers, grew with each touch. Her nipples, hard and pebbled, were aching to be touched and released from their lace confinement. Beth moved so she could free herself, and Tom gasped as she arched up into his hand, causing him to smile roguishly. Ducking his head, he took her nipple in his mouth and suckled it.

A cry from her lips made him take it deeper into his mouth. The friction of the lace and the feel of the hard little pebbled nipple at the back of his throat, had Beth holding him to her. With her hands in his hair, Tom looked up at her with her nipple still in his mouth. She looked back down at him, her eyes half closed in pleasure. He pulled back, stretching the breast and the lace of the bra. He saw the flash of pleasure and pain in her eyes before letting it go. It snapped back and she cried out.

Reclaiming her mouth, Tom reached around and tried to find the clip to undo her bra. It was all lace except for a little strap of material. Stopping the kiss to concentrate, he tried again to feel his way to open it. Beth giggled at the concentrated and confused look he gave her when he still couldn't accomplish it. He frantically searched with both hands, but still, he couldn't find it.

Pulling her up into a sitting position and looking at her, Beth couldn't help but giggle harder. It wasn't there. Tom looked back at her, and she laughed out loud at his aspirated expression.

'What the hell?' He looked again.

After a moment, she whispered with a giggle, 'It's here' and pointed to two little butterfly wings on the front of her bra. Slowly, she unclipped the wings as he watched, a little bit shocked at having missed it, and surprised at finding out bras could open at the front. Whispering his amazement, the laughter of before vanished into sexual tension between them. It was so intense that Tom tried to swallow the dryness from his mouth as Beth slowly undid the little butterfly wings, her eyes burning into his. Bit by bit, she pulled the bra apart until her two perfectly formed breasts were revealed.

Clearing his throat, Tom looked at her as a sly, wolfish smile formed on his face. 'Well, that's a new one on me.' He leaned into her hungrily and needy, and she leaned back, slightly moving away, with a soft giggle.

'You planned that.' He grabbed her hips and pulled her back to him playfully as she twisted and turned to get away. Beth laughed and twisted back the other way, only to find her hands intertwined with his and pinned above her head. Her lauger turned into panting before they both stopped and stared at each other. Lying like he now was, between her legs, his weight pinning her body to his swag, the air around them sizzled and crackled.

Tom could see the heat and passion swelling in her eyes as the bottom of his rib cage pressed into the top of her thighs, he could feel the heat from her sensitive spot, touch his bare chest through her underwear as she lay there pulsating with need and desire for him. Kissing her belly, his eyes never leaving hers, he kissed her hip and then the other one, returning to her belly button. He ran his tongue around the little hole before tasting the inside.

Raising her hips slowly against him, her need increasing, Tom slowly raised his own body, now on all fours. He lowered his head and rained kisses all over her stomach and along her ribs, around her breasts and in between the soft peaks, savouring every taste and fleck of skin Finally, he took one of her nipples into his mouth and bit it tenderly. Beth cried out and tried to sit up, but he held her down and smiled, softly grinding the hard little nub between his teeth.

Her moans and body arching, turned him on even more. Letting her hands go, his fingers found the other nipple and he rolled it between his thumb and forefinger with different pressures. Her hands were in his hair, pulling and massaging as he brought her pleasure.

Breathing hard, he could sense Beth was nearing the peak fast. Finding the top of his jeans, she unbuttoned them. He smiled wickedly at her as he lifted his head, nipple still between his teeth, before letting it go, the sensation making her lose her thoughts of his jeans, and buck. Her hands went to her own breasts. She kneaded and rubbed them, soothing but prolonging the sensations, bringing herself pleasure right in front of him.

Watching her self-pleasuring nearly made Tom's night end right there. Lowering himself to her body, he kissed her deeply again. He could feel her still rubbing her breasts, and his nipples while he did. His own self-control was becoming too thin and weak against her.

Running a hand up the inside of her thigh, he felt her quiver. Rising higher still, he found a very thin, shear lace strip between his fingers—and her wetness. She was burning hot and ready for him through the wet lace. Pulling her underwear to the side, he slipped a finger deep inside of her and she arched so high, she nearly overbalanced him. They both gave a flustered little laugh and continued to kiss. Beth's hips grinded against Tom's hand as he took her further and further up to the peak.

'Please, baby ... I need you now. Please ... now,' she panted against his mouth. Her tightness clutched around his finger as he stroked. With a long, deep kiss, Tom pulled away and trailed kisses back down to one of her of nipples. He suckled until she cried out and crushed his head to them. The cool night air and the wetness from his mouth made her nipples look like stiff little peaks. Continuing his downward path as Beth rubbed her breasts again trying to find release, Tom made lazy circles with his tongue over her stomach before continuing south to the top of her smooth mound. Laying a trail of hot kisses down the inside of one thigh and then back up the other, her musk surrounded him, making his own need so painful, he winched.

Looking back up at her, he found her heavy-lidded gaze, the deepest of deepest blues looking back at him, her chest rising and falling in anticipation. Lowering his head, eyes still locked with hers, he kissed her once above her opening, then licked. Beth cried out with pleasure and moved up onto her elbows, watching him, her hair falling all around her. Lifting and bending her legs out more, Tom opened her wider to taste, lick and suck at her heated, soft wetness some more.

There was wringing moans and soft throaty cries from Beth as her body pulsated and twisted against Tom's mouth, the pressure and pleasure building within her. Tom continued with his ravenous onslaught to lick, nuzzle, bite, and suckle her as much as he could as her cries grew louder, echoing around the silence of the night. It was music to his ears. She was now so close to the peak, the edge was coming, he could taste it.

'No ... no ... I want you with me ... now!' she panted and tried to claw him away.

'No,' he growled and continued with his feasting of her. Beth's cries and moans of pleasure filled Tom's ears as her body wreathed and twisted. But he held her down. 'I want you to cum. I want to taste you,' he said frantically before biting her tenderly, then licking it better and sucking her harder.

Beth couldn't contain herself as he forced her to hit the peak of the mountain and fall off the edge, in loud cries and breathlessness. Her legs squeezed his head between her thighs as she surged over the peak and floated higher into oblivion.

Her body was liquid and sated. Her muscles weak, she fell back against his pillow, releasing Tom's head, her breathing fractured and heavy. She floated slowly back to Earth, like a feather floating on the soft whisps of wind in the still night air.

Smiling at his conquest and covering her sweet spot with her dress, Tom kissed her belly, breast and lips. He couldn't help but be very pleased with himself as Beth lazily reached for him, gently pulling him to her for a long, liquid kiss. She could taste herself on his lips and it stirred her arousal again, sending him into a painful spiral as he hovered above her.

'How about you get out of those jeans and let me have my way with *you* now?' She smiled up at him, heavy lidded. Tom loomed over her sated body and watched her float back to the present.

'I don't think you're ready for that yet, Baby.' He hung over her in pain, but he was content to continue to watch her, kiss her, and be whatever it was she needed.

'You just do as your told, Thomas O'Loughlin, and let me be the judge of that.' Beth pushed him up playfully, and he rocked back onto his ankles, knees resting on the mattress. He watched her groggily sit up. Kissing him again, she pulled away and pointed to his jeans. 'Off!'

Obliging her, he slipped off the back of the ute and, pulling off his boots and slipping out of the rest of his clothing, he tried to calm himself. He had wanted her, to claim her for himself for so long, and now that the time had come, he didn't know if he was going to be able to perform like they both wanted him to.

Taking another deep breath, he turned to jump back up, but stopped—shocked. Beth was standing on top of the tray, completely naked in the moonlight. She truly was the most beautiful girl he had ever seen. He had thought that ever since they had met, but he didn't think she could have gotten any more beautiful—until now. She was not shy about her body around him and as she stood there on the back of his ute, the moonlight illuminating her skin, it allowed him to look at her in all her perfect glory. Tom's body reacted to her instantly and it painfully stretched out before him.

Beth just stared down at him, her clothes now laying somewhere on the tray behind her, as the cool night air surrounded and touched her skin, her body still warm from Tom's attention before. Taking him all in as he stood before her, completely naked, his lean muscled body reflecting off the moon's light, it created a hard lump in Beth's throat. She had seen him shirtless and in shorts before, but this was something totally different. His muscled torso rippled down and over his hips to his strong thighs. His manhood now fully released, was larger than she had thought possible. Chewing her bottom lip, she contemplated if he would be able to fit within her tiny body. Swallowing the lump in her throat, her eyes travelled back up and over his body, eventually meeting his passioned-filled eyes.

Not able to bare her intense gaze any longer, Tom moved to jump back up to be with her. 'No,' she commanded and gracefully bent down and picked up the blanket off the swag. She lay it on the end of the tray and pointed to it, wordlessly telling him she wanted him to sit on it.

Doing as ordered, with a confused but curious look on his face, Tom now sat with his legs dangling over the side of his ute tray, unsure of what was going on, as Beth leaned on his shoulders, manoeuvring herself so she was kneeling just above his lap, facing him. She could feel how large and long he truly was against her apex as she sat positioned just above it. His hands were around her bottom, supporting her so she couldn't fall.

'This is new,' he stated, still not sure how it was going to all work with them both sitting like this.

Leaning down, a playful and seductive smile on her face, Beth kissed him until he groaned. Lowering herself just a little more so he could feel the heat of her, she moved her hips, making him moan with the sensation. He squeezed her tightly, his self-control on its last legs as he pulsated at her entrance.

'Do you want me?' she teased and rose, giving him the impression she was about to climb off of him. The air cooled her heated area, sending a shiver over her body and vibrating over Tom. Holding her strongly in place, pinned to his body so she couldn't move away, he nodded as she kissed him again. It was long and hot, teasing and arousing.

Beth's tongue darted into his mouth as she nipped playfully at his lip, seducing him into a melting mess. Pulling back, she waited for him to look at her. His dark eyes fluttered open, pleading in silence, begging her to stop her game and take him deep within her blessed body. To ease the torcher and take him as hers. Making him wait a heartbeat longer then she should have, she melted down a little, but stayed strong. 'How much, Tom? Tell me.'

'I want you. You know that. I want you more then you could ever know.' He grinded out between her passionate kisses. 'You're driving me insane, Baby. I can't think, can't breathe, can't think of my own name, I only want you. To brand me for life and take my soul. Jesus, Beth, I would gladly die for you if only you would end my suffering,' he whispered through clenched teeth. His words were garbled as Beth moved and teased him with her warm, wet apex.

Seeing the whole truth in his eyes, the earth shifted under her, and she wiggled down against him, her hands threading into his hair as she gripped him. She pulled his head back so she could watch his eyes as she lowered herself just enough to take him inside her a little.

'Oh, my ...' he hissed through clenched teeth, '... fucking God, Beth. I want you till the day I die. Please ... I need you,' he begged through his teeth as his restraint was at its limits. Pulling her against him, he dropped his head so he could taste her nipple again. She arched back on his arms, her hair tickling his legs. Biting her nipple, then suckling it, he smoothed it with his tongue before repeating his actions on the other nipple. Beth cried out.

Something was changing within her, and she didn't understand. What he was doing, not only to her body but to her heart and mind, was creating a shift she couldn't stop. She didn't want it to stop, but fear sliced through her along with the pleasure he was bringing her. It blinded her mind and stole her heart.

Bending his head back again, the world had stopped shifting. With their breaths mingling, hearts beating, they just stared at each other. They were the only ones in their world. The only beating hearts as the world shifted beneath them again, clicking into place, and everything stopped. Not a sound was whispered except for the sound of their hearts beating together. As one. Together as one forever. Beth lowered herself slowly, onto Tom. Not once did he look away as her world shattered into nothing but him.

Adjusting herself a little, Beth let him fill her like nothing else had. Her eyes closed as she impaled herself on him—deep. Very, very deeply. Tom didn't move. His jaw was locked so tight it pulsated at the sides as he held her to him and allowed her to get comfortable with his size. Taking her lips in a kiss that stole her breath, Beth began to move.

Rotating at first, testing, discovering, getting a feel for him, she began to lift just enough to slide back down onto him again, continuing to slowly bring them both to the top of the mountain at a pace she could handle.

Holding onto her as he stayed controlled, panting and moaning together, Tom held her bottom and sucked her nipples each time she rose. Her nails dug into his shoulders, and she could tell he was extremely close and losing his mind. When next she rose, he lifted her nearly off, then let her fall, taking him even deeper again. She cried out in pleasure, her sounds echoing around them, their mating turning into a frenzy, until they both hit the peak and flew crashing into one another over the other side. Cries and growls of pure pleasure, their worlds never to be the same again.

Tom held Beth's melted body as she lay slumped against him. Their breathing slowed, coming back to normal, but they were still joined. She could still feel him slightly pulsating deep within her, though not as before. Her body was calming down, the float back down to earth was slow and magical, and she tried to remain there as long as possible. Their minds were still somewhere off in the oblivion of the golden glow.

Brushing her hair from her shoulder, Tom kissed Beth's skin, sending goosebumps over her body. But she didn't move. She couldn't. Reaching back for the other blanket to wrap around her and keep her warm, Tom failed in his movements. Gathering what strength he could manage, Tom lifted them both and slid back across the cold metal tray to the swag. Beth lifted her head and smiled a lazy satisfied smile at him.

'If you still have strength, I haven't done my job right.' She kissed him and he moved inside her, but she was still coming back from her heavenly experience, too sated to respond.

'I am just superhuman,' he joked and kissed her lips, stirring her body some more.

'I will just make sure you can't walk tomorrow,' Beth said with a laugh as he rolled her onto her back, laying her out on the swag.

'We will see who can't walk tomorrow.' Tom teased and kissed her tenderly as he pulled the blanket over them both. Snuggling against him, her eyes grew heavy, and she felt herself drifting off to sleep in the safety of his arms.

Chapter 12

The next morning, it was Beth who felt she couldn't walk. They had spent the night in each other's arms, alternating between sleeping and making love, then this morning Tom had driven her home. While she had showered and gotten ready for work, he had told her father what had happened with Jeff, promising he would be there this morning to make sure Jeff showed up to make his apology and would never touch Beth again.

Jeff did show up. Right in the middle of the morning rush. Drake and Tom had sat at the coffee bar talking, and Beth guessed Tom had told him about Jeff's attack, because by now, Drake would have normally gone back to the farm to work his horses. However, this morning, he was still sitting there in his spot, talking, keeping an eye on both her and the door.

Beth could feel the tension vibrating from both men as the morning had gone on. Her own nerves, despite the floating feeling Tom had poured into her veins last night, were on edge. It wouldn't take long for the gossip to get around town about what had happened and for people to make their own opinions known about the situation; judging and blaming her for what Jeff had attempted. Part of her wished Jeff would not show up, but another part wished he did because then if Tom got upset, at least Drake was there to stop things before it came to fists again. It was like waiting for a bomb to drop, never knowing when. The tension was building with each passing second.

Taking a large order of coffees to a group of local businessmen, Beth watched Jeff amble in, holding a hand to his ribs. He was leaning to one side, trying to protect what she suspected was maybe a few broken ribs, looking a little sorry for himself. His jaw was swollen and discoloured, the large grotesque split on the corner of his lip looking painful and infected as his complexion was near greenish. He was not well at all.

Trying to smile at one of the groups of older ladies sitting near the door, Jeff's smile was lopsided, and he was now missing a tooth. Taking in the many customers in the café, now all looking at him with frowns and questions clearly on their faces, he first saw Tom at the coffee bar with Drake.

The look on both men's faces, protective and ready to kill if he did anything wrong to Beth, made Jeff swallow as he searched around the café for her. Finding her serving a table full of men, she inwardly smiled when she saw his recognition of the gentlemen at the table, now making this situation even worse for him. These were the men of the local and state environmental boards, along with local businessmen. Most of them knew Jeff and his family, as well as the O'Loughlin family, very well. Looking the way he did now, the public apology he was about to make, was now made a lot worse as these powerful gentlemen were about to witness it.

By the time Jeff had made it to Beth's side, Tom was close behind him. She had not been able to move away from the table after giving them their coffees and breakfast.

'Beth,' Jeff said quietly and as clearly as he could. 'Could we maybe go outside and talk?'

Gaining strength in the presence and safety of the café, and the men present, including Tom and Drake, Beth shook her head. 'No. Here is fine if you wish to speak.' She was going to make him pay.

Tom came up behind her, his hand on her back for support.

Jeff shuffled in his spot as he cleared his throat. 'I'm sorry for the misunderstanding last night.' He glanced at the men and then to Tom, who was not happy about his choice of words.

Knowing he needed to add more, he continued, 'I was drunk, and I am sorry. It won't happen again.' He smiled at her again, but the smile never reached his eyes as his lip split, oozing a little fresh blood. Instead, the malice and hatred for being there—forced to say words he did not mean—was clear in his eyes for all to see, no matter how hard he was trying to hide it.

'Your face doesn't look that good, Jeff.' Tom couldn't help but tease him as he stepped around Beth, creating a protective barrier and making a clear statement in front of everyone witnessing the two, soon-to-be, brothers-in-law's conversation. 'At least my hand is looking better then what it smashed into.' To prove his point, Tom quickly raised his fist to Jeff's face. Jeff's instincts kicked in and he dodged the movement. Tom gave a smirk, knowing now that Jeff was in his place and scared of him. He turned to the men at the table.

'You all heard—clearly—Jeff's apology to my girlfriend about what happened at Willy's pub last night.' They all nodded and looked between Tom and Jeff, not quite sure what was going on, but they would soon piece the story together once they heard the gossip. No doubt, a few beers at Willy's this afternoon after their golf game, would have them finding out the truth. Jeff reluctantly smiled at them through gritted teeth, before snarling with his eyes. He nodded at Beth.

With his embarrassment and humiliation written all over his face, knowing that Tom's deliberate choice of words would ensure Willy's would be busy today and abuzz with what he had done, Jeff turned and walked out.

'Are you okay?' Tom asked over his shoulder to Beth. When she nodded, he walked to the door, quickly following Jeff. With a panicked look to Drake, Beth held back tears out of fear of what was about to happen outside. The feelings rose within her, but Tom was already out the door.

Kathryn appeared by Beth's side and, with a comforting, firm grip, she held Beth's shoulders as she smiled at the men, trying to distract them as they all watched Jeff, Tom, and then Drake, all walk out the door. 'How about you men try some of Beth's key lime pie and cream? My shout for a Sunday morning.'

Nodding blindly as they returned their focus to the two women standing before them, Kathryn and Beth's eyes darted between each man sitting at the table. They forced their best smiles, trying to cool the situation down before Kathryn steered Beth to the kitchen. Reassuring her with hushed whispers, that, with Drake there, nothing would happen to either of the boys, and Tom needed to do this. This confrontation was more about them than her.

Beth had just finished plating up the pies and cream in the kitchen when Tom entered. Throwing herself into his arms, she held him tight to her. Her mind had been filled with thoughts of him and Jeff coming to blows in the middle of the street and Tom getting hurt. Shaking with those thoughts, and now as he held her, she burst into tears.

Holding her tighter again against his body, Tom kissed the top of her head as Kathryn rubbed her back soothingly and whispered, 'Take her home, Tom.'

Beth heard and shook her head, wiping at her face. 'No, I want to stay.'

'Your shift is over, Beth. You can't work like this. Tommy will take you home.' Drake had spoken in his concerned but authoritative father voice—the one everyone obeyed.

Tom took her home.

Over the next two weeks, Tom made sure he was there to pick Beth up after work every day—except for the few days he had flown to the city; her father had picked her up on those days. Tom would then stay and help Beth study or cook, mostly getting in the way and eating all her food whether it was good or not, and when her father would get home, Tom would sit and talk with him about ancient history, wars and the local gossip around the town. News of her and Tom now being declared a couple had spread through River Flats like wildfire, and she had been called a gold digger and slut more than once by some of the SBs—not that she would tell Tom that.

He had become very protective of her since that night at the pub. And when she had asked about his declaration of calling her his girlfriend, he simply explained that once news got around of what Jeff had done, and her being his girlfriend and not just a summer thing became common knowledge, it would make Jeff's life hell. She had tried to reiterate to him that this *really was* only a summer thing, but his response was to smile and kiss her forehead, thus ending the conversation.

Today, Tom had picked Beth up around lunchtime, and as they drove down the dirt road, dust hanging in the air from a vehicle travelling in front of them, Beth's nerves were at their peak.

She had tried to tell him numerous times that her attendance today was not a good idea; however, Tom had told her that if she didn't attend on his arm, people would think they had broken up, and she was *just another girl* to him. He didn't want her viewed like that. So, against her better judgement, Beth now found herself going to the O'Loughlin's end-of-summer party at Silverleigh.

Anyone who was anyone, was going to be there. People had begun flying in that morning in their helicopters and private jets. Talking to Kate about it, Beth discovered that the afternoon's party was where a lot of social networking was done, and for Matthew O'Loughlin, this one was going to be very important. He had invited people who could help him launch his political career.

This was also going to be Tom's official introduction to these people as the heir and next CEO of the O'Loughlin company. In truth, this was really a high-profile business meeting disguised as a relaxed Champagne afternoon summertime party. She had no right being there. They would have to say goodbye in a matter of weeks, and she was not part of his future beyond that. To be seen on his arm was wrong, but he wouldn't listen.

Beth was relieved Kate was going. It would mean she at least had one other person to talk to instead of Tom, who, she had the feeling, would be talking to a lot of people, and his father probably expected her not to be involved in any of the conversations.

Tom drove around to the other side of the house, near the pool and outdoor area, so they could enter from within the home and not appear like they were arriving as guests. Megan had insisted.

Beth climbed out and shut the door of Tom's ute, but didn't let it go. She was still shaking. It wasn't just the people who were there; it was also the first time she would be seeing his father, Jeff and Megan since the night at the pub. What she had heard through the local gossip of what the SBs were saying, Megan had tried to spin the story of Beth leading Jeff on and taking advantage of him before Tom had found them. It was Jeff who was the one who tried to protect her from Tom, getting punched in the face in the confusion and lies of Beth's story to her brother. Jeff was the victim, not her.

Some had believed the story—the ones who needed Megan's social status. Others had chosen not to say anything at all. The town, it seemed, had become slightly divided about it all. But no one voiced opinions due to fear of the consequences that doing so against the O'Loughlin's could bring down on them.

These people here today were going to be judging her as the girlfriend of Thomas O'Loughlin. Was she all that was expected for the heir to one of the wealthiest family fortunes in the country, or was she a gold digger and manipulator, playing the field hoping to snag a privileged life for herself? If Megan had told them her twisted version of Jeff's still-darkened eye and how the scar on the corner of his lip came to be, then they would not be looking at her favourably. It would then affect their view of Tom, and that would in turn affect his future. This had become way bigger than the summertime fun and friendship it had started out as between them. This was now becoming all too serious—lives were being affected, and she was leaving in two weeks. This was insane.

'Let go of the door, Beth.' Tom's hands were at her back, where she had gripped the door handle behind her, his body pressed to hers, calming her a little. 'It will be okay. Kate is here already. Nothing will happen to you today. We have all been lectured to an inch of our lives from Megan to behave. Jeff and I in particular.'

'And your father? Does he know you invited me?' Beth looked around as one of the waiters walked out the side door of the house with a crate full of Champagne bottles and dumped them loudly into one of the large old forty-four gallon drums hidden from sight.

'He does, and he was happy about it.' Beth raised her eyebrows at Tom in surprise. He really didn't think she would believe that lie, did he? Leaning down and kissing her until her toes curled and she let go of the door, he smiled against her lips, still stealing little kisses from her.

'That's a dirty trick, Thomas O'Loughlin.' Beth smiled back against his lips. 'Maybe I should go straight to your room and wait on your bed until all of this is over.' She nipped at his lip and slipped her tongue into his mouth, making him groan and pull her flush against his body.

'Don't tempt me.' He nuzzled her neck and kissed her quickly. 'Now, we had better go in before I change my mind, and we end up at the gully with you naked in my arms.' She gave him one of her seductive smiles. He kissed her again and groaned in frustration before taking her hand and walking into the house, out through the back door and into the famous O'Loughlin end-of-summer garden party marquee.

Tom was stopped and greeted by people even before they had stepped off the bottom step of the verandah. He introduced Beth and praised her as an up and coming chef. The men talked to Tom, and Beth's interest in food seemed to intrigue their wives and partners. She found herself easily conversing with them, her nerves settling a fraction. They even asked after her thoughts of the food being served. Not revealing to them that most of the copious amounts of food being waited around had been prepared by herself and Kathryn over the past two days, and that the chef in the kitchen was only there mostly to look the part and plate it all up, she highly complimented the food.

Spotting Megan being the gracious hostess and making sure it looked like her and Jeff were the couple of the season, Beth watched them closely, admitting they had their acting parts very well-rehearsed. Jeff would kiss her cheek when she walked up to him as he spoke with others, and he would then put his arm around her. Beth had heard them talking about the wedding and honeymoon, and their plans on where they were going to settle down, which was here at Silverleigh. This had made her start to question Tom's future living arrangements, but she put it out of her mind. It was not her concern because in two weeks she would be gone.

Ashleigh and the other girls were there. They kept their whispering behind their hands to themselves. Finding their childish behaviour just that, Beth didn't care anymore what they said or didn't say, or whether it was the truth or not. The people Tom and she had spoken too already that day, all seemed to have liked and accepted her. Those girls didn't matter.

Kate had found her earlier, making sure she was okay. Her friend had been on Braydon's arm. Apparently, it was Megan's way of keeping them under control and out of trouble; however, Beth couldn't find the logic in that. Together they would have spiked the punch or done something to the food, just to liven up the party. On second thoughts, maybe it was right to pair them up. Then the poor old punch wouldn't be spiked twice.

As the afternoon wore on, Beth began to relax more. Jeff and Tom had been circling around the party, keeping a near-perfect distance between themselves, and Tom's father had been busy talking and schmoozing his guests, acting like the perfect gentleman. Beth recognised some but not all. She didn't know much about politics or the who's who of Aussie wealth.

But Mathew had been watching her closely all afternoon, even though he pretended he wasn't. When an older woman joined her at one of the tables, her husband in deep conversation with Tom about cropping and soil health, Mathew had been a little surprised—and even nodded his approval at her—when she and the older woman began to talk. Beth had noticed the lady not really blending in with all the other woman throughout the day as her husband talked. She seemed to prefer to just stand and listen to what the men were discussing.

After Tom had introduced them to her, feet hurting in her heels, Beth had promptly sat on the chair closet to Tom and let the two men talk. The lady, smiling with what looked like relief, did the same. After a polite few words, they had ventured to then talk at length about food and a European foodie trip that the couple had done a few years back. Beth and the woman had talked for nearly an hour when her husband and Tom were joined by another couple. Tom took the opportunity to move on to others he was yet to speak with.

Beth stood, saying her goodbyes to the lady, but her head spun a little. Not wanting to cause a scene, she leaned on Tom in a discreet way, taking his one hand with both of hers. He looked at her a little concerned and when they were out of ear shot of the couple, she admitted she hadn't eaten much all day, and the Champagne she had been sipping all afternoon was now going to her head. Gently moving her away from the heat of the crowd towards the open doors of the marquee, Tom steered Beth towards his father. Beth's hand gripped tighter to his.

'It's okay; he is on display. He won't do or say anything. Plus, he needs to be seen with us today, otherwise people will talk that there is an issue in the family, and we can't have that,' he said through gritted teeth and a fake smile.

Beth just looked at him strangely. This fake world he was expected to live in was horrible. It was all about how it looked from the outside and what each person could get from the other. No one cared to see how uncomfortable Tom was or that his family was fractured and broken, only held together by the glue of money, manipulation and control. Beth's stomach rolled and she began to really shake.

'Tom. Beth, my dear.' Matthew O'Loughlin really should have been up for an acting award. Gold Logie for sure! He embraced Tom in what looked like a loving father-son hug, but Beth could feel the awkwardness of it. He then, to her astonishment, leaned in and kissed her cheek. Beth couldn't hide her surprise at his actions. She could feel it plastered on her face. With a nod to the people he had been speaking with, he dismissed them, showing favour for his son and his son's girlfriend.

'Dad. Can you stay with Beth for a moment? I will be right back.' Tom kissed Beth on the cheek and whispered, 'I will get you some real food. Stay with Dad. He will be on his best behaviour.' Her hand locked in his, he gave it a reassuring squeeze before sending his father a warning look, which he ignored.

'Of course, my boy. We can have a little chat.' His dad's fake smile was certainly in place; however, his choice of words made Beth a little more unnerved than she already was. She looked after Tom, losing him in the crowd. She searched for Braydon and Kate, but they were nowhere to be found either. She was all alone with Mathew, and she didn't like it.

'How about you and I walk to my office, my dear? It's cooler in there with the air-conditioning going, and Tom will no doubt be held up and take a little while to return to your side. We will be back before he notices you gone.' He leaned in closer to her with a smile that made her skin crawl. 'You do look a little whiter then normal.' Taking Beth's hand, he placed it in the crook of his arm, holding it firmly so she couldn't move away from him, he led her from the party.

'Are you enjoying yourself? You have never experienced anything so grand or with so many influential people, I'm guessing.' His tone had changed, and it made Beth become very wary of him. She tried to remove her hand from his arm, but he held it tight.

Strolling casually around the back of the marquee, Mathew led the way a little behind the house, before walking up some steps to a little side door. Holding the door open, he pushed Beth though.

The room was cool and richly appointed with leather seats and a large, dark-stained timber desk. His office. There was only one door in and with an audio '*click*,' that door was now locked.

Beth spun around. Her heart began to race painfully in her chest. She was trapped in his office, out of hearing range of the party, and Tom. Beth's skin crawled as Mathew's eyes slowly drifted down her body. Standing tall, she tried to remain calm as he pushed away from the door and casually walked towards her as he spoke.

'You know, Beth, I must be very honest with you.' This was the real Mathew O'Loughlin talking now. Before her eyes, he morphed into the man everyone feared. 'You must have a golden pussy by the way you have my son following and panting after you like some mongrel bred dog. Maybe you can show me exactly what you're giving him.' His eyes flicked to her breasts, then lower, before returning to her eyes. 'That I am somehow missing out on.'

Beth felt sick and began to violently shake. He saw, and his lips ticked at the corners into a smile of a predator. 'I believe that you were going to let Jeff have a turn, but Tom found you before you could, and poor Jeff was left seeing stars for days.' Mathew backed Beth against the solid desk. The back of her thighs hit the top of it, making her lose her balance and sit on it. Something in his eyes told her he liked the position she was now in. Before she could get off, he stepped to her, the top of his thighs pressed to her knees.

'Tom wouldn't try what he did to Jeff on his father again. That boy learned that lesson a long time ago. He does what he is told now and lets me have whatever I want, no matter what it is.'

'Go to hell!!' Beth all but spat at him.

He laughed at her. 'I always get what I want, Beth. When I told Tom to go and use this summer to sew his wild oats, I meant with many girls, not just one. My mistake, I guess. However, you have had your fun and gotten a very expensive little trinket along with the one on your arm.' She touched the bangle Tom had given her. It had been the only thing he had given her. She didn't know what the other expensive trinket was he was talking about.

'You being here today, has given all those people out there something I never wanted them to know—the impression he has a girlfriend, and a very serious relationship at that. Not just some cheap ass pussy on the side, like your meant to be, being the whore that you are.' Beth flinched at his wording. He reached to touch her face.

She pulled away.

'You have had your fun with my son, and now it's over.' He leaned in closer to her, his breathe on her face, his hands by her thighs, touching her skin, his thumbs rubbing over the smoothness of her legs. 'You will leave and never have any contact with him again. These crazy ideas he has had, and his trip to the city he did a few weeks ago, makes me think that your power over him, has to end.'

Beth tried to speak and tell him she had no idea what he was talking about, but her voice wouldn't work. Her throat was restricted and dry from absolute fear. She was trying to stay strong against him, hoping that Tom would come and find her. But she was fast losing her nerve.

'I know you have your heart set on that little school and a trip to Europe at the end of the year. And to afford it all, you have been working very hard to save as much money as you can.' He leaned in further, causing her to lean back over the desk a little, her arms now locked straight to hold herself up. Mathew smelt her neck as he continued speaking. 'So, I thought I might help you out if you help me out. A mutual benefit of exchange. Our own little agreement, per se.' He reached into his coat pocket and pulled out an envelope. 'Here is enough money to set you up and pay for your trip to Europe, and more.' Beth just looked at the white envelope in his hands, her heart pounding so hard in her chest she could barely hear his words. 'This is your payment for opening yourself up and helping *my* boy stick his dick somewhere over the summer.'

Heat blazed in her eyes and over her body as his crass words filled her with shame and embarrassment, causing her to feel dirty and worthless. Her body shook as shear panic rose within her. Mathew's hand moved up her thigh midway between her knee and where the hem of her dress now sat. Squeezing painfully, Beth sat up involuntarily, her face nearly touching his. She pulled back and tried to dislodge his hand, tears in her eyes.

'If you don't end things badly with him, that little business your parents fought so hard to work and keep going, will end, and the bank will be forced to take their home and everything they own ... again.' His knowledge of her parent's finances shook her. She swallowed hard to stop the bile coming up her throat. He leaned in so close his lips nearly touched hers. She held her mouth tightly closed and turned her head away.

Taking her jaw, he forced her to look back at him. 'And you, my little whore. All your dreams will be gone. You will never get another job anywhere apart from scrubbing some mangy toilets in the middle of nowhere. Do you understand Beth? Do we have an understanding?' She didn't know what to do to get away from him. Her mind was racing. She felt faint.

How was she to ever hurt Tom so badly? If she didn't, it was her parents that would suffer. She had no choice. Taking her non reply as acceptance, he added, 'I always get what I want, Beth.' To make his point, Mathew squeezed his hand painfully into her thigh again before smoothing the tender inside of her leg with his thumb. Beth, frozen with fear, didn't move. 'One word of this to Tom, or anyone, and I will follow through on my threat, and more.' His hand slid up under her dress as he leaned into her ...

Chapter 13

The long drive had taken its toll on her. She could see the lights of River Flats in the distance and her nerves and sickness increased. This was not what she had planned. None of her life had gone as she had planned. She had hoped they would have had more time but that was now not possible. It was over. He had been taken too fast for her to even get her head around what it had all meant. Now, here she was driving back to say her final goodbye.

Tears filled Beth's eyes and she allowed them to fall. She had cried so many times already on this drive back—what was a few more? Her street came into view, and she looked into the back seat. Emily was sleeping in her seat, her little head leaned to the side as she held her teddy loosely in her arm. Chelsea was curled up on the passenger seat, her head on a pillow, softly snoring. So much for her keeping Beth company.

The last three hours had been silent and peaceful as Emily had finally slept; however, for the last two days, it had been a nightmare. Usually, the drive from the city only took a solid day of driving, but with Emily, it had taken them a lot longer, with more breaks and an unplanned stop over. They had pulled up at a motel last night, unable to take anymore, and then overslept this morning, which was why it was nearly midnight and they were only just arriving. She had texted her mum from the last town to let her know where they were and as Beth pulled her little car into the driveway, her mum came out to greet them.

After a hug and lots of tears spilled, all three women unpacked the small car. Chelsea had woken to help, getting the bags with Beth as her mum woke Emily and brought her inside.

Chelsea had been her saviour. When Beth had arrived in the city and had nowhere to go, it was Chelsea who had helped out and taken her in. They had fast become friends and now, she was here for support, before catching the bus back tomorrow night making sure she would return in time to teach her class for the final term of the year. Walking up the steps, memories came flooding back. Most were good, but some were too painful to think about.

'I have made your room up. I didn't get a cot, sorry.' Her mum started to tear up as thoughts of her husband and the reason she hadn't bought a cot at such short notice brought back the very reason Beth was here.

'It's okay, Mum.' Beth hugged her and tried to stay strong. 'Emily can enjoy sleeping with me for a while. She usually ends up in my bed by morning anyway.'

'The bathroom is that way, Chelsea, if you wanted to go for a shower and crawl into bed. You both look like you need some sleep after your long days.'

Susan Kennedy showed Chelsea where the towels were and as if on autopilot, walked to the kitchen and boiled the kettle. Beth changed Emily into her pyjamas, after giving her some toast, and put her to bed.

Beth's room had not changed since she had left. It even smelled the same. Taking a deep breath and shutting out the memories that also came with the room, she pulled the door closed a little so Emily could settle better.

After making up the spare mattress on the floor, Beth let Chelsea go to bed. She needed time to herself to get her mind right before tomorrow; it was going to be a very emotional day and through it all, she needed to be strong.

Sitting in the silence of the night, on the day bed on the verandah, Beth's mother brought her a cup of tea. The night was warm, and they just sat talking quietly about the funeral arrangements, the way the day was going to run and their memories of her father.

John Kennedy had never understood her reasoning, but when he had come to the city and received the news, they had connected and tried to rebuild their relationship again. It was never like it had been, but Beth had gotten to see him before he got the infection and passed.

'Are you going to go to bed now?' Beth asked when her mother stood.

'I think I should, though sleeping is hard these days. But I need to try. I will need my strength for tomorrow.' Beth stood and gave her mum a kiss on the cheek. Their relationship had been just as strained too—if not more—but right now, they needed each other for all the strength, courage and support they could muster. The sun would be up in a couple of hours and then a day they never thought would happen so fast, would be upon them.

Crawling into her bed, Beth cried and hugged Emily to her. She understood the truth of her mother's words. The pain a loss like that can bring, made her own memories slice painfully through her chest again. She pushed them down—way down deep—so they couldn't resurface. Not while she was here anyway. Not until she returned home and was able to just let it all go.

For now, she was back in River Flats until her mum was okay and had recovered enough to stand on her own two feet. She knew she couldn't be here any longer than what was required. As soon as her mum was able to cope without her, she and Emily would go back to the city. She would find a new job, and they would go back to the life Beth had built for them both.

The following morning, Beth sat in the front row of the church. The hard timber seat made it difficult to find a comfortable position beside her mother, who was dabbing at her tears. They both wore black dresses. Her mother had her hair pulled back into an elegant bun, and Beth had hers half up and half down. They were both holding tissues in their hands, trying their best to just breathe. Opting to be seated first in the church, both sat facing forward the entire time as the church filled with friends and those who came to pay their respects to her father. Beth could hear whispers behind her—her name repeatedly being hushed—but she ignored it all.

As the minister talked about death and God, Beth sat staring at the pine timber coffin at the front of the church. Holding her mother's hand, she wiped at her tears as they silently fell. Drake had been asked to give the eulogy, speaking respectfully of her father. He told funny stories that made everyone laugh, and he spoke about how much John Kennedy loved his family. It was beautiful.

As the last hymn was sung, the pallbearers walked quietly up to the coffin, all darkly dressed, their faces stained with tears. They took their positions. Beth recognised the four men from her parent's tyre shop. It was their way of showing their respect for their boss.

Beth numbly watched as Drake appeared. And then her heart stopped. Tom followed and stood on the opposite side of Drake at her father's coffin, his back to her. Beth's hand, dabbing her watery eyes, began to visibly shake. Some strange part of her had thought he would not be there. Had hoped he would have stayed away. But he didn't. In fact, he was one of the men carrying her father's coffin out of the church.

The minister stepped in front of the men and together they easily lifted the coffin, sitting it on their shoulders. Beth watched as Tom took that moment to look directly at her. Their eyes locked and she could tell he was fighting back tears. Her heart ached and raced in panic as they continued to stare at each other. It was no more than five heartbeats—enough to make her feel sick—but they had locked their sorrowful eyes onto each other.

Pulling her eyes from his as they stepped forward behind the minister, all in perfect sync, Beth helped her mother to stand, and they followed the coffin slowly out of the church. She didn't see anyone. Her focus was only on taking one step after the other and not letting herself or her mother fall as the weight and pain of where they were and what they were doing began to weigh on them more and more.

'Step one, two, three.' Beth continued to count as her mother's body grew more weighted on her, stifling her soulful agony. Susan gripped Beth's hand and let her daughter walk her out of the church into the brightness of the hot day. Silently, they followed the coffin to the waiting hearse outside the church, watching as tears slipped down their cheeks as the pallbearers placed the coffin in for her father's last drive.

Kathryn materialised beside them. 'You pair can't drive out to the cemetery. Not like this. Drake will, okay? Now come with me before all the do-gooders come up with their fake well wishes. That's for later.' Kathryn took hold of Beth's mother's shoulders and led her away from the circling crowd to their car. Beth was a little lost, her feet unable to move from her spot, until Drake, right behind his wife, took her arm and followed Kathryn and Susan away.

Due to the heat of the late-morning sun, the burial was quick. Beth stood there under an umbrella the funeral director had given her, shielding her from not only the sun but the stares of everyone else. Throwing her rose—the one she had specially picked that morning from her father's garden—and a handful of dirt onto the coffin, she watched as they lowered her father into the ground, her tears continuously falling down her cheeks to her feet.

Others slowly walked past and did the same. Some whispered their goodbyes to her father, others touched her mother's hand.

She didn't make eye contact with any of them, oblivious to it all as she just stared at the hole in the ground. Her heart was breaking more and more with each centimetre the coffin dropped lower. This was not the way it was meant to end, not the way he was meant to go.

After an hour of greeting, hugging and saying 'thank you for your thoughts', Beth needed some space and time alone. It was emotionally draining, and she had lost all hope of her polite smile, giving the impression of her being okay. Who was she trying to impress anyway? She had just said a final goodbye to her father, the first man she had ever loved. Surly no one would think she was really okay. Leaving her mother and Kathryn to continue with all the well wishes, Beth slipped through the kitchen and out the back door for some much needed air.

The kids who had attended the funeral, were running and playing in the church yard play area. She could hear their laughter and giggles as she found Chelsea with Emily, who had been sleeping when the service was going on, playing on the swing. Beth had thought to keep her at home but like her mother had said, the gossip would be better handled if everyone found out at the same time. Because Emily had slept through the service and had now been playing out here since they had arrived back from the cemetery, no one knew yet that she belonged to Beth.

Chelsea saw Beth standing near the back door and walked over to her, Emily content to play with the 'big' kids by herself. 'How are you holding up?'

'As best as I can. Mum is getting better as the day goes on. I'm just numb.'

'She is starting to heal. That's why we need to have funerals. To start the grieving and healing process. You need to let it all out and heal too.' Chelsea shifted in her spot and looked over Beth's shoulder.

'I believe someone may want to talk to you.'

Beth knew who it was. She had felt his eyes following her the whole day. It came as no surprise he had seen her escape. Confirming it was him, she looked over her shoulder to the corner of the church hall where they were holding the wake. Tom stood there, waiting patiently. Beth turned away and tried to steady her breathing. He had changed since she had seen him last. She had thought him a man then, but he wasn't; he had been a boy. His shoulders were now wider and more defined under his black dress shirt. His face and eyes were darker, and his closely trimmed beard gave him a seductive edge.

The man who stood back behind her with his hands in his pockets, rocking back and forth in his boots, was something completely different to the boy she once knew. Her body reacted, tingling, heart skipping, a warmness flowing through her veins, but he wasn't the same. And neither was she. Tom didn't move. He just waited for her to give him some sign that it was okay to approach her. After another quick glance, one he missed as he was looking at the dirt at his feet, she turned away and steadied her breath.

'Is that him?' Chelsea whispered as Beth nodded, tears welled in her eyes as emotions she had been fighting began to resurface.

'Just say hello.' Chelsea nudged her gently, knowing her friend was feeling very fragile, as she looked back to check on Emily. 'I'm getting a drink for us all.'

Closing her eyes, Beth could feel Tom approach her when Chelsea disappeared through the hall's back door.

'Are you okay, Beth?' It was a simple question she had been asked a thousand times that day, but hearing him ask it, in his slightly deeper voice, made the lump in her throat she had worked so hard to keep down all day, come up and break. She had no control over it at all. Her eyes closed. She shook her head as the sob escaped her lips. She couldn't help it as it rolled through like a solid blow to her chest, taking her down, knocking the wind from her lungs. Her knees gave way, and she started to fall to the ground.

Tom watched her struggle as the sob broke though. Before he could think of his actions, he wrapped his arms around her tightly, one hand on her head as she sobbed into his neck, the other around her waist as she sullenly leaned on him. He let her cry it out. He let her release the pain and anguish he had witnessed her hold down all day. She clung to him, her hands fisted into the side of his shirt at his hips as the tears fell and her body shook against his chest. Still, he held her. Standing strong and protective of her, Tom held Beth to him because her legs couldn't hold her anymore. He gave her the safe place she needed so she could cry in his arms.

He had wanted to ask her a million questions, but the only one he could formulate in his head as he watched her talking with her friend, was if she was okay. His emotions for the last week had been unpredictable and his temper shorter than normal. Holding her now, all his painful emotions faded away. Right now, in this moment, nothing else mattered.

Taking a very deep, shaky breath, Beth pulled herself together as best she could and stepped away from Tom, her eyes avoiding him. He could see she had not meant for that to have happened. Knowing her like he used to, she was most likely mentally lecturing herself at what she perceived was her own weakness and embarrassment for letting him hold her. He had only said four words and she had fallen into an emotional mess. Whatever was between them had to wait. Beth had needed someone to hold her, and Tom was glad it had been him who was there to catch her. But now, as she smoothed her hair and dress, the walls to allow him that close again were bricking back up right before his eyes, and he had no idea how to prevent it.

Apologising for staining his shirt with her tears, she stepped back away from him more, wiping her nose on a tissue and then dabbing at her eyes, Tom had to force himself not to follow her retreat. Instead, he let the corners of his lips form a gentle smile as he quietly spoke. 'I'm kinda used to you ruining my clothing and boots.'

Giving him a small smile, Beth turned away, taking yet another step back, the emotions of their past now too raw with him standing so close to her, it seemed.

'Thank you for helping my parents when my father got sick.' She was now watching the children playing under a tree—two little girls running around a large gum seemed to have caught her particular attention. 'And for helping today. It meant a lot to us.'

Seeing she wanted space, Tom stepped back, leaned against the wall and stared out at the playground, though he only focused on her. 'It was nothing.'

She turned and looked at him so seriously he nearly stood to attention. 'Never say that.'

'Mummy! Mummy!' A little girl with blonde, curly hair came running over to them as fast as her little legs could carry her. 'Looks whats me found.' She held out a leaf as Beth squatted down and gathered the little girl between her arms so they could examine the leaf together.

Tom felt he had been punched in the gut several times, his breathing coming in small gasps as he fought to clear the sudden confusion that filled his mind. Not once had anyone bloody told him Beth had had a child. Not one bloody person. His temper started to rise as he stared at mother and child in front of him. Feeling as if the earth had sped up, he touched the wall at his back and planted his feet more firmly on the ground through his boots. Blinking to try and stop the spinning, he looked back at Beth and then to the little girl, who took that moment to look around Beth and up at him. She smiled.

'Wants to see?' She held up the leaf and broke away from Beth to show Tom. Fighting the rolling wave of emotion, he shakenly

230

kneeled to her level and studied the leaf with her. She was saying something about the cats eating the leaf. Confusion reigned as he fought to clear his mind and listen to her words as she spoke.

Catching the words she was trying to say, he laughed at himself for not understanding, and the world slowed back to its normal speed. She was talking about caterpillars.

Praising how smart she was, Tom glanced over to Beth, who was staring at them, her arms folded tightly across her chest. The leaf touched his nose, and he focused back on the little girl with a little frown. 'What's your name?'

'Emdlee. What's you?' She frowned at him with her head to the side as he smiled at her.

'My name is Tom. Nice to meet you ... Emily?' He looked at Beth with a raised eyebrow, hoping he had understood the little girl's pronunciation. She nodded to him with a small, tight smile.

'How about you go and put the leaf back for mummy?' Beth smoothed her little blonde curls before Emily ran back towards the tree.

Standing, Tom watched her go, his mind spinning with a million more questions then he started with. 'Where's her father? Shouldn't he be here to support you?' Staring at Beth's back, he waited for her to turn and face him, but she didn't. He could hear his own anger and bitterness in his voice and felt like he was back at day one, trying to figure out what the hell had happened between them. And now, as he watched her little girl running back to the tree with her leaf, he felt more like it was a horrible dream than reality. That at any moment he would wake and find himself alone in his bed again.

'She only has me .... oh, and Cee Cee.' Correcting herself, Beth looked over her shoulder at him. 'Chelsea, my roommate. The one who was standing here before,' she clarified before looking back to watch Emily, who was now nearly back with them. Beth's back was ramrod straight, the emotional moment from before, and her need for him, now completely gone.

Tom was totally confused. Who the hell would leave her in that situation? His need for answers rolled violently through him. He stepped near her. 'Beth, we need to talk.' She stepped away, swooping Emily up into her arms.

'Come on, Em. We had better go and check on Nanna.' Beth looked back to Tom, ignoring his statement. 'Thanks again for today.'

'You know, I'm feeling a little sick of my own cooking and these four walls, this morning,' Beth's mum stated a couple of weeks later as Beth sat and watched the sun rise. It was her special time to think and get her mind right before Emily woke up for the day. Beth's mother had been joining her the last few mornings. Silently, they would sit until the sun fully rose, then they would talk quietly. It had not been a rule either had stated, but it was like the sun rising required their silence—their full attention to hear the day awaken to the new possibilities it had to offer.

Over the last week, her mum had had a regular flow of friends to her door, each bringing a plate of food to share and talk over, but Drake and Kathryn had been the most regular. They either both or separately, had been around every second day checking on them, making sure they were both coping with their tragic loss and the grief that came with it.

On the days Kathryn came alone, Beth would bundle Emily into her pram and go for a long walk along the river path and back home around the back streets. She was careful to avoid being seen around town, where people could talk and gossip about her being back.

Kate had called around twice and missed Beth both times. Beth was glad. She didn't want to see her friend or face the questions she knew Kate would fire at her—demanding answers Beth couldn't give. Could never give.

Her mother was coping with her loss much better than Beth had been. It was her mother that was the strength in the first week, often finding Beth sitting quietly in the middle of the night on the day bed on the verandah, crying silently so as to not let anyone hear her sorrow. Tom had unlocked a flood gate of built-up sorrow and despair she had not only been feeling for her father but for her life and dreams, now lost to the raging river, never to return again.

That day had been harder than she had ever thought possible. She had put on a brave face for everyone, but him. He had broken through her walls with a simple sentence, and shattered her strength. Holding her, she had wanted to climb inside of him and never leave. To shelter in his protection and strength for all eternity. And it had taken all her willpower to pull away from him—and stay away.

He had been shocked over meeting Emily, and the discovery that she was a mother. She hoped it would have been enough to have him walk away forever and not want to speak to her again; but that was not the case.

Twice, when she had been on her walk with Emily, and seen his ute parked at Kathryn's café, she had panicked. The first time she had diverted away so as to avoid running into him. Walking further along the river, he had been sitting on a bench, watching the water flow past. Standing when he had seen her, she had immediately turned around and walked away from him. The second incident, she thought she had been aware of his game, walking instead straight past Kathryn's café. He had seen her walk past as he was leaving, calling out to her, but she pretended not to hear him and kept walking, though at a faster pace. Keeping her distant was safest for all.

Looking over at her mum, and smiling tenderly at her, remembering that her mother had spoken and was now waiting for her to answer, Beth replied with, 'Me too.'

This week, the grief felt a little less. It was still painful and brought tears to their eyes daily, but they had started to look better and were even laughing a little. Emily's antics helped. Her father's death had been unexpected, but expected. After his diagnosis, they had prepared for the worst but were hoping for the best. His intensive round of chemo had left his immunity so weakened that a simple infection had taken his life within two days. Beth had had no time to even try to drive and see him before he passed. It was one of her biggest regrets—one she would never forgive herself for. That was why she had to make sure her mum was okay before she left to go back to the city. She could never live with herself if that was to happen again.

'Maybe we could go to Kathryn's early.' She looked out at the garden. 'Before it gets really busy. The river festival starts tomorrow so it will be too busy until next week.' She could see Beth shift in her seat, her hesitation evident. 'We could eat and be gone before the locals turn up if we leave now.'

Emily wandered out of the house rubbing her eyes. The screen door slammed behind her as she climbed up for a cuddle on Beth's mum. Her snuggly teddy was protectively squeezed to her chest. She had become so close to her nanna, and Beth knew that it was Emily's presence that had helped her mum heal since they had arrived.

'I need to see something other than these four walls. Kathryn's would be perfect for us both, I think. Besides, I am craving one of her pancake stacks with loads of berries and her caramel topping.' Standing with Emily in her arms, her voice firm, which meant she wasn't going to take no for an answer, Susan added, 'You need to stop hiding here too.'

She was right. Beth had been hiding and using the grief of her father's death to stay away from everyone. The only people who had seen her were the ones that had come to visit her mother and pay their respects. Those and the ones who had passed her on her walks with Emily. Though she doubted that many would recognise her. She had stayed to the very back streets and had covered her hair and eyes with a cap and dark sunnies.

It was Kathryn's pancake stack that drew Beth out and not her mother's orders, Beth told herself as she found a booth in the very back corner of the café. Drake was sitting at the coffee bar when they arrived, but was now making his way over to speak with them. Settling Emily in one of the highchairs, Beth was going to sit so her back was facing the rest of the café; however, her mother had decided that was her spot, leaving Beth facing the entire café. She would be the first person people saw when they walked in if they looked around. 'Dammit!'

'Beth. Susan,' Drake said, touching Emily's chin when she looked up and smiled at him. 'Hi sweetie.' Emily had fallen in love with Drake the day after the funeral. He had arrived with a bag of lollies for her and some books about horses. He had then sat and read each one about five times with her. Telling her about *his* horses and showing her his ropes in his ute, had only started the admiration. They had then played peekaboo and hide and seek for the rest of the afternoon, while Kathryn had visited with Susan and Beth. Emily even showed him her leaf collection. Only special people got to see her leaves. He had fast become one of her favourite people.

Finding the colouring-in papers and pencils in the shelf at her back, Drake found the horse one and handed it to her. Her little squeal of delight made him smile, and in front of Beth's eyes, he turned into a big teddy bear.

'Here we go, ladies.' Kathryn placed three large coffees down on the table and sat down next to Susan with a smile and a gentle squeeze of her hand.

'You knew we were coming?' Beth asked as she placed a teaspoon of sugar in her coffee and stirred slowly.

'I just had a hunch that by now your mother would be craving my pancakes.' Kathryn smiled at Susan, who leaned her shoulder into her closest friend and smiled back. 'Plus, I have to introduce this little angel to my famous pancakes.' Kathryn looked to Drake, who had squatted down next to Emily and was now helping her colour in her horse bright pink, her love for her husband showing in her eyes.

'That's if I can get between these pair to feed her, that is.' They all laughed as Drake stood and looked at Kathryn all serious.

'This is serious stuff. Don't knock the colouring.'

'Yes, yes, we won't.' Kathryn waved to one of her girls to come over and take their order, just as one of the festival coordinators came in and signalled to Drake that he wanted to talk.

The pancakes smelled so good that Beth leaned in to smell them when they arrived at the table. 'I have missed these,' she said and began to cut up one for Emily, piling it high with the berries.

'That's good. We have missed you too,' Kathryn said and tucked into her own. Talk turned to the festival, Montana and Adelaide and how much Drake and Kathryn missed them, before eventually turning to the local gossip. Beth's mother was enjoying herself as the café got busier, but Beth wanted to leave before others saw her. She didn't want to have anyone come over and have to make polite conversation with them. She was only here until her mother was okay and then she was going back to the city. Seeing Susan talking and laughing now with Kathryn, made her stop all thoughts of herself. This was part of her mother's healing. Getting back out in public and being around friends.

'Icky.' Emily held her hands up to show Beth. Her little fingers were stained red and purple from the berries and were glued together by the caramel topping. Standing, Beth took out a wet wipe from her bag and started to wipe Emily's hands.

A strong, hot coffee and one of Kathryn's bacon and egg rolls was what was needed this morning. Tom was sick and tired of being tired and unable to sleep. His temper had been so short these past two weeks, and this morning when the horses had escaped through the open gate—he had forgotten to latch due to his haze of a head—he had had enough. The horses were now in the wrong paddock, eating grass, and would most likely buck the shit out of him tomorrow. But with his mood the way it was, he would most likely welcome the thrashing they would give him. Maybe it would tire him out enough that he might actually sleep without thoughts of Beth running through his mind.

He had kept his distance from her since the funeral. He had intended to just enter into small talk with her there and then call around to her mother's a few days later and find out all the answers he had to all his questions. He had not anticipated how large the funeral would be or the fact that she would be forever needed at her mother's side.

At his mother's funeral, he and Megan sat in the corner with their grandfather and watched it all happen around their father. His grandfather eventually took them to get ice cream before driving them home. His father arrived back late that night, drunk, never even checking to make sure they were okay. His mother had rarely been spoken of since.

At Beth's father's wake, Tom had stood near the back corner of the hall and spoken to those who had approached him, his eyes never leaving Beth's for more than a few seconds. He was waiting for her to get a private moment so that he could talk to her. Seated on the other side of the church, Tom had watched Beth struggle to be strong for her mother, his heart aching for them both. His legs, under the church pews, had grown restless with a burning need to go and comfort her. She had not seen him enter the church, and her shock at him being one of her father's pallbearers had been evident on her tear-stained face when they had locked eyes. If he had not had the weight of the coffin on his shoulders, or the whole damn church watching him stare at her like the damned fool he was, he would have walked over to her and held her to him, never letting her go.

Seeing her sneak out to the kitchen, he had excused himself and followed, but through the side door to avoid more gossip starting. Walking around the corner, he had stood and taken in her beauty as she talked with her friend. She had not changed a bit—only gotten more beautiful. The part that had his world spinning so fast it had made his head and heart hurt, was finding out she had a child. She had moved on and he had stayed where he was.

His temper flared, and he slammed his ute door as he got out near Kathryn's café. If he slammed it anymore, the metal would one day go through to the other side. His vehicle had taken such a beating over the last few years, his frustration and anger taking over more times than he cared to admit, and the poor old ute bore the brunt of it. He would never sell the girl though—it held too many memories of Beth to let it go.

Calming himself as he pushed through the café's door; he was not really in the right mood to be in public, but the allure of a strong coffee made him check himself twice and pull it all together.

Tom saw Beth before he saw anything else. His body was tuned into hers like a moth to a flame. Standing near the very back corner booth, wiping her daughter's hands and laughing, her smile lit up her face. He took those precious milliseconds to just take her all in. She was wearing a light pink summer dress and thongs. Her skin was tanned and glowed. Her hair was tied high on her head in a ponytail and its curly length hung over her shoulder, tickling the little girls face as she giggled.

Tom's feet started to move towards her before he could think. He wanted to hear her voice. To have her look at him and smile. To just have her attention like old times.

'Tom!' Drake called above the noise of the nearly full café. Shaking himself from his blinded state, he stopped. People had been watching him stare at Beth and he had not even noticed a single person apart from her since he had entered.

He hadn't seen the café full of people. Most had seen him and were now waiting and watching, wondering what he was going to do. Drake had seen him and was now calling him to get his attention, most likely saving them both from further gossip and potential embarrassment.

He never cared about what others thought of him, but he cared about what was said about Beth. Tom didn't want her to feel anything but comfortable talking to him when they did talk. And they *would* talk again. He was only trying to find an excuse to do so. Her being here was his chance, but not with everyone looking on. Diverting to Drake under his heart's protest, Tom moved through the café, away from Beth.

'Take a seat with me, me boy.' Drake pulled out a chair for him as he made his way to the coffee bar. The young girl at the coffee machine was already making him his usual, and his name was called to tell the girls in the kitchen that he was here for breakfast. Anywhere else and it may have seemed odd, but in this small town, at this café, it was a regular occurrence. Many locals had standard orders, and the girls would just call out that they were here, and like magic, the food would appear not long after, just the way they liked it.

Sitting, Tom never took his eyes from Beth. She was now aware of him being there and was trying her best to avoid looking his way, angling her body to face Emily only. Her focus was on colouring with the little girl, while her mother sat with Kathryn, talking. Empty plates and cups sat neatly in front of them. They would be leaving soon, especially now he had arrived. He could see it in Beth's eyes; she wanted to be out of there as soon as possible.

'Have you spoken to her yet?' Drake asked, his voice low so only Tom could hear. Shaking his head, Tom looked at him and then back to Beth. He should just walk over there and say hi. His temper started to rise.

'How could no one tell me that she had a child?' Tom couldn't hide the anger in his voice. He was so mad at everyone for keeping it a secret, he hadn't really ventured into town much for about a week, nor spoken to anyone apart from Megan—who was anything but helpful—to find out why not one person in this godforsaken town had thought to mention it to him.

'No one knew, me boy,' Drake said behind his coffee before taking a sip. 'She hadn't even told her parents till the end. By what Kathryn understands, Beth is ashamed of it all. That the father abandoned her and that she has struggled with raising that beautiful little girl all by herself. In my eyes, its anything but shameful.' Drake's fondness for Beth still showed on his face as he continued, 'She swore her parents to secrecy, thinking that her father would have longer. She is under a lot of pressure, Tom. You need to give her time to work through everything that has happened. Time to let her trust us all again. To build trust that whatever happened is not going to be held against her.'

'I just want to talk to her. She won't even acknowledge my presence let alone let me try and build trust with her again.' His frustration made his voice louder than he wanted. The girl at the coffee machine, and the couple sitting at the table near him, looked in his direction, their eyebrows raised in question at his tone.

'She is very aware of your presence, me boy. Trust me. She just needs time before you guys speak; when she is ready and feels safe to do so.' Drake added sternly, 'You can't rush her or force it, otherwise she will run again.'

Over at their table, Beth could feel Tom watching her. He had been since he had walked in, sensing it the second he had entered the café. Watching him out of the corner of her eye, she'd pretended not to, but her body had not agreed. Her heart had skipped a beat and started to race as her hands shook slightly. Tom had always been able to make her body do that, even before he had touched her or even spoken to her. Her body would just come alive with him simply being in the same room. The years apart had not changed that. Kathryn looked over at her and then over to where her husband and Tom sat, before looking back at Beth, then to Susan, a knowing look between mothers.

'I had better let you pair get on with your day. You're coming to the festival, right? Drake has a team in the cross river tug of war this year and is determined to hold onto the trophy. He will need all the support he can get, but ...' she winked at Beth, '... don't tell him I told you that.' She moved out of the seat and stood waiting for Beth and her mum to stand. Giving them both a cuddle, she helped them through the café to the door. Nobody would stop them that way, and it helped put a barrier between Beth and Tom. Not that he tried to move, but Beth saw him standing as she walked through the door.

'Let her go, mate. Not here. It's not the right place or time.' Drake had placed a firm hand on Tom's shoulder, forcing him to sit back down again as he watched Beth and her mum leave the café with Emily. Picking up his coffee, he took a long, large gulp. His temper flared at Drake for stopping him from following her, Beth ignoring him, the people staring and talking behind their hands, and the complete frustration still at not knowing what the hell happened to her to make her run. It all roiled him up. The coffee burned his mouth, throat and guts and he welcomed the pain. At least this pain was better than the pain of being so close to Beth and not being able to touch her.

'I just wanted to talk. Surely, I can do that without it going around town or her running from me,' he said after slamming his coffee mug on the counter. A gentle hand on his shoulder and a whispered voice made him stop and remember where he was.

'She needs to trust again and feel that it's safe to talk to you. Just give her time, honey.' Kathryn moved from Tom to Drake's waiting, outstretched arm. Her husband wrapped her to him, kissing her cheek. Tom just watched, blank faced at their private, intimate moment, his emotions rolling over what to do to reach Beth, and hurting at his yearning for wanting what Drake and Kathryn had. The fact that he couldn't cuddle and pull Beth to him when he wanted, and the fear that he may never have what the couple beside him had—and that he had thought he had it with Beth and didn't protect it enough—ate at him again.

'Besides ...' Kathryn gave him a little smirk, '... I thought you promised her father that you would help take care of the yard and mow it when needed.' She looked outside and Tom followed her gaze before looking back at her, the dawning of her words taking hold. 'Susan was just saying that the yard was needing a mow and some trees trimmed.'

Kathryn's eyebrows raised at him in her knowing way. Tom gulped the last of his coffee and swallowed the rest of his breakfast before standing.

'How about you get those horses back in at home first, and some jobs done before you go and help a lady with her yard this afternoon? Taking your time and doing the job right, might make you very hungry and in need of food and drink.'

Drake pulled Kathryn against him and nodded as he spoke, his eyes full of mischief and meaning. Tom nodded and smiled. He knew what was not being said. Suddenly, the day looked much brighter, and those horses needed taming and to be put back in their correct paddock.

Chapter 14

The sun was setting as Tom tied the last rope over the large load of grass and hedge clippings. He had spent the last three hours working in the heat of the afternoon just to try and see Beth. Susan had come out and thanked him for his help before she was called back inside as a car pulled up in the driveway.

He recognised the car as the McDonalds. Helen was a close friend of Susan and Kathryn's. Those ladies would be talking all afternoon. He had hoped that Beth would come out to him, but she stayed inside, though he knew she had been peaking around the curtain all afternoon. He had seen her twice, but the other times, his body had reacted just like it used to. She always had that effect on his body.

Emily had come out and sat on the steps to watch Tom mow and trim the front yard as she ate her biscuits. She had waved enthusiastically each time he had walked past, but when he had emptied the catcher and walked back to have a drink with her, she was gone. Beth had obviously been waiting for him to disappear before coming out and bundling her back inside the house.

'Tom. You have done a beautiful job. Thank you.' Susan walked up to him, her hair blowing gently in the slight breeze. She had strolled out the house with Helen, who was now driving off with a toot of her car horn. They both waved at her. Finishing tying the knot, Tom lifted his cap and wiped the sweat from his forehead. He surveyed his work as his annoyance at his plan for being there not working, momentarily gone. He had done a good job, even if he did say so himself. The satisfaction and knowing he had done it for Beth's father made it even more fulfilling.

'Would you like a cold beer and a burger?' Susan touched Tom's arm gently and smiled a knowing smile. Tom couldn't hide his smile back at her as she turned to the house. Susan didn't want to give herself away. She was a very smart woman and knew the real reason he was there in the heat until late. He also had the sneaking suspicion she had deliberately told Kathryn about her yard, knowing Kathryn would tell him.

'Beth is cooking up a storm. Way more than we will eat.' She turned back to him and said, 'I'm sure you could use it. Come in once you're finished. I'll have your beer ready.' He wasn't going to say no. This was exactly what he had hoped would happen.

After checking his load was secure, and giving Susan what he thought was enough time to tell Beth about his invite, Tom walked up the back steps and through the laundry door. It was located next to the kitchen. He could hear Beth as he quietly closed the screen door and removed his boots.

'Mum. I know what you're trying to do, but please don't interfere with this. Tell him that there isn't enough and send him on his way,' she pleaded. She didn't want him there, and for a split second he thought about making up some fake excuse and leaving, but he pushed that aside as fast as it made itself known. He wanted his answers, and he wanted to be near her again. He couldn't explain it. To him, Beth was like a shot of rum directly into his veins. She warmed and calmed him. Made him lose all his senses in such a way he couldn't get enough. She was what he needed most in this life.

'He has been here all afternoon, and you need to accept that I have invited him in as my guest.' Tom had never heard Susan speak so sternly or with such authority. He had come to know her as a mild-mannered woman, never raising her voice. But at this moment, she was making sure Beth understood she was not going to send him away. 'It's too late he will ...'

Tom opened and closed the back screen door, clearing his throat loudly like he had only just entered. He made sure they knew he was there in an attempt to end the conversation before a full argument could start between mother and daughter. Stepping into the kitchen, Susan handed Tom his beer with a warm smile and, after taking a long sip, he sat at the table, watching Beth's back as she finished making the burgers.

Looking between the two, Susan shrugged her shoulder at him. 'I will go and get Emily to wash her hands.'

Emily was sitting in the lounge room playing with some blocks and toy animals. Watching, Susan walked over to the little girl, bent down, scooped her up, then looked back to Tom and nodded her head at Beth, encouraging him to talk to her while she dealt with Emily.

Tom's body filled with nerves and he found any words to say, difficult. They were finally alone where she couldn't run or have others interrupt them, and for the life of him, Tom couldn't think of a single word to say. He wanted to say a million things, but nothing would come out. He had wanted this moment for the last three years. He had played it over and over in his head of how he would react, what he would say, what his emotions would feel like. But never had he dreamed of sitting there watching her, confused and not being able to say a single damn word. Beth was standing as straight as a rod, her shoulders tense. She was busy and he knew she was trying her best to ignore him.

Collecting a jar out of the fridge, she never looked his way— not even a side glance—her eyes focused on what she needed. Once it was collected, she turned her back on him again as he watched her struggle to open the jar. He stood, a smile fluttering at his lips, and silently walked up behind her, his arm coming slowly around her to gently take the jar from her hands. 'Let me,' he whispered near her ear.

Beth's whole body stopped. She froze at his sudden nearness. The little hairs on her neck tickled with his breath. Her heart raced and her body tingled. Letting go of the jar as he took it, he brought it back past her just as slowly as before, his arm brushing her elbow. The touch, only brief and light, warmed her skin. She didn't move until she heard the *pop* of the jar opening. He was too damn close. Before he could hand it back, via her side again, Beth turned, took the jar from him, and with a quick 'thank you', she turned her back to him again.

He was too close. Too close. And she wasn't strong enough against him to not let him see that her body still reacted to him with want and desire. She needed to keep her distance. This was why she didn't want him having dinner with them. Why she had stayed inside. Her willpower against him was so weak that she had been peeking out of the curtains almost all afternoon, watching him mow her parent's lawn. Her body reacted and pulsated to his every move, driving her nearly so mad that after she collected Emily from the front steps, she had needed a very cold shower. Now he was at her back, the heat from his body radiating into hers. The air around her felt thick and heavy. He was too close, and she was starting to panic.

Shifting her body to the side, she grabbed plates from the cupboard and placed them down on the bench, bumping into his solid warmth as she did.

'So, what can I help with?' he asked, looking around at the bench.

'Umm ...' She looked around as she tried to get her thoughts back into what she was doing, and away from Tom.

'If you could grab the chips from the oven as I put these back into the fridge, we should then be ready to sit.'

Tom grabbed the oven mitt and put the tray of hot chips onto the bench. Beth moved behind him as he stepped back, but they collided in the tiny kitchen. Moving fast and catching her so she didn't fall, Tom turned her and leaned her against the bench.

Trying to catch her balance, Beth placed her hands down onto the bench with instinct, Tom's hand falling on top of hers to also catch himself. Beth cried out as her fingers touched the red-hot tray of chips. Her two fingers burned as she stuck them in her mouth and sucked them.

Damn his closeness and distraction. Beth squeezed her eyes shut with the pain of her fingertips being sizzled at 220 degrees Celsius.

'Here. Give me a look.' Tom stepped into Beth, their bodies touching, as she looked up into his eyes, their dark concern holding hers. She couldn't look away. Heart pounding in her chest, she forgot how to breathe.

Pulling her hand slowly from her mouth, Tom looked at her two little red fingertips. It wasn't bad. They were just a little sizzled. Though, as she watched him study her fingers, she knew the moment he saw she still wore the bangle he had given her. His eyes darted to hers, and she saw the flash of realisation in his eyes. She heard the roughness in his voice when he spoke.

'It's not too bad.'

The air began to crackle around them, and the world shrunk until it was just them. Their eyes locked together, neither looking away as their hearts raced and their breathing became slow and heavy. Without a word, Tom raised her sizzled fingers to his lips, his eyes never wavering from hers. He pressed a kiss to them. Beth sucked in a breath and allowed her eyes to drift close at Tom's warm lips on her skin.

'Mummy!' Beth flew back from him, her hand ripped from his lips. She avoided the still-hot tray at her back as Emily ran into the kitchen and directly into her arms. Beth lifted her and turned to collect her plate from the bench.

'Here you are, honey. Your chips are just cooling.'

Beth avoided her mother's gaze as she placed Emily into her highchair. She had forgotten where she was. Forgotten that Emily and her mother were only in the bathroom — on the other side of the kitchen wall. Her mother would have seen Tom kissing her fingers. She couldn't look at her. She would not give her mother that satisfaction, especially not with her heart and head still reeling from his soft touch. Her fingers were still burning and tingling, but not from the heat of the tray.

'I thought I heard you yell, Beth,' her mum asked her as she took a seat at the table. Tom grabbed himself another beer from the fridge and lifted it to his lips. Beth knew he was just as affected by their intimate moment as she had been and *that* was a dangerous place to be.

'Yep, I burnt my fingers on the oven tray. Nothing to worry about.'

'I see Tom was helping with the first aid.' Susan's eyes danced as she kept her face serious. She was teasing Beth and Tom, but Beth didn't like it and scowled at her.

Ignoring the mother-daughter moment the girls were having, Tom took a seat opposite Beth at the table, brushing the top of Emily's head as he did. This caused her to smile up at him as she tucked into her mini burger, sauce dripping down her hands.

Throughout the meal, Susan spoke the most. Beth avoided Tom's gaze and stayed as quiet as possible. She had not wanted him there. She was too tempted by him, and it wasn't good. She was leaving soon and didn't want him to get the wrong idea. Didn't want to hurt him again.

Nothing had gone to plan before, but she was determined that this time, it all would, and she would leave for the city, only returning when necessary. Her mother always loved going to the city, so Beth wouldn't be back here unless absolutely needed. Tom was here, and they couldn't let whatever it had been between them in the past, get in the way now and complicate her plans.

But watching him with Emily, Beth's heart squeezed and raced, and she felt the sting of tears in her eyes at that long-ago memory flashing in her mind's eye, causing her to shake. Swallowing the bile that rose, she sipped her water and focused on her daughter. Emily had taken most of Tom's chips and even some of the salad from his burger. Tom had pretended to try and bite at her little hands, or fight for his food, but Emily would always laugh and giggle at him. When she got it in her mouth, he would mock shock or sadness, only making her giggle more, or she would argue that he was only pretend 'saddy'. He was a natural with her, and by the end of the meal, Beth wasn't sure who had had more fun or made more mess at the dinner table—Tom or Emily.

Her little girl had taken such a liking to him that Beth felt her heart squeeze for her daughter. She was such an outgoing, confident little girl, who loved to have fun and explore. She had become close to Drake over the last two weeks and now, it seemed, with Tom too. When they went back to the city, her little girl would never see these men again, and that saddened her more.

In the city, Emily only had Beth and Chelsea. She had her teachers at her childcare centre, swimming and gymnastics classes, but they were all females. Men had never been a part of her daughter's life, and now, seeing her with Drake and Tom, Beth realised Emily had missed that part of growing up. That having a man around to play the rough and messy games with her, to wrap them around her little finger as she had with Drake—and it seemed Tom too—was hard to acknowledge. But it had to be this way. As hard as it was, nothing could change.

After dinner and dessert, Emily started to rub her eyes. She was ready for bed. This was Beth's way to escape Tom. After saying goodnight to him, making it clear she was not coming back out, Beth took Emily to her bedroom to put her to sleep.

Beth saw Tom look to Susan for help, but thankfully her mother just shrugged. Beth was all she had left in this world—and their relationship was rocky. As much as Beth knew her mother loved Tom like a son, she was not going to risk her relationship with Beth any more than she had already tonight, for him. And rightly so. Mother and daughter needed each other.

Waiting until Emily was nearly having a temper tantrum, Beth gave in and went to find her mother. Hoping she had given Tom enough time to leave, Beth opened her door and moved through the small house.

'Mum...' Beth came through the lounge room as she called, 'Emily wants you to read ...' she trailed off as she saw Tom still in the kitchen. She had prayed he had left already but dammit, he was still there in the kitchen making whispered small talk with her mother as he washed the dishes and she dried them.

'No worries, my dear girl. I love reading lots of books to my granddaughter.' Susan turned to Tom as she dried her hands. 'If you wash, Tom; Beth can take my spot to wipe and put things away.' He smiled at her and nodded.

Walking past Beth, Susan gave Beth a cuddle and a kiss on the cheek. 'I will put Emily to sleep and go to bed too, I think. I'm feeling very tired.' Beth shook her head just enough that only her mother would notice it. Ignoring it, Susan added, 'Beth will see you out later, Tom, and I will see you at the festival tomorrow.' He turned and waved a wet soapy hand at her, very happy to be there, helping.

'It would do us all good to go, I believe,' she said to herself as she walked off to Beth's bedroom and closed the door.

Beth was not happy about her mother's scheming and plotting. She thought she was doing the right thing, but she wasn't. She had no idea what she was risking, and Beth had no way of telling her. Picking up the tea towel, Beth began to dry the wet dishes. Together, they worked in silence.

From the corner of her eye, Beth could see Tom trying his hardest to engage her in conversation. Each time he would look at her, she turned her back on him, placing a plate or cup into the cupboard. Her reaction to him before was still too raw, and her emotions were still scattered and unpredictable. But truth be told, this silence, now stretching out before them as they worked in the quietness of the room, made Beth feel every glimpse of his eyes as well as his heartbeat. His closeness was stirring her body awake and she didn't want to test her inner strength against him. If he touched her again, looked into her eyes, she might crumble like she did at her father's funeral. And that could *never* happen again.

'Are you going to the festival tomorrow?' He eventually asked, though his voice was raspy, like he just couldn't formulate any words. Clearing his voice, he shifted his stance at the kitchen sink.

'Mum wants to,' she said as she placed a plate in the cupboard.

'But *you* don't?'

'I think it's for the best that I don't.'

'Why?'

It was a simple word, but it was heavy with everything that lay between them. She felt the weight of it, and the crushing in her heart at the thought of things not being the way they had been between them. She needed him to leave. She needed to go and have another shower so she could cry. To cry out everything that had happened. To let the tears, she had refused to cry, let loose and fall. She had been so worried that if she did start again, she would never stop. But this. It was becoming all too much. Being here at home again, Tom so near, yet untouchable, her mother without her father, her fear about what others were saying or will say if they got the chance. Everything. Everything made her feel like crying. She began to feel the burn of the tears. She wouldn't shed them now. Not in front of Tom. She had to be strong.

She couldn't answer his simple question, so she just shrugged.

Not happy with her avoiding his question, and trying to brush it off with a shrug, he tried again.

'Thought you might like to come and watch me get dragged into the water again.' He placed the last plate into the drying rack and started on the frying pan. 'Drake has conned me and a few of the boys into doing a charity tug-of-war against him and his mates. Kinda like an old versus young boys match. I could use the support and cheer squad.'

Memories flooded her of that long ago day and how in those moments across the river when she first set eyes on him, her whole life had been put onto a different trajectory. If only she had just stayed back at the café and studied, her life would not be what it was today. She could have been living in Europe and doing everything she had dreamed of—all the choices she had made from the very first moment of seeing Tom, never having happened.

'I think you will be fine. You will have all the girls cheering you on and more than willing to help you dry off and get warm again.'

Placing the now-clean frying pan on the drying rack, Tom looked at her. He stared intently until she stopped wiping the last plate and looked up at him.

'But not the girl I want.'

He allowed his words to sink in. For her to take the full measure of what they meant and what he truly wanted. Beth's heart squeezed and flip-flopped in her chest. She had understood the meaning of his words and what he was telling her, and then painfully swallowed the restricting lump in her throat.

He took a step towards her.

'Beth.' His voice was a low whisper as he saw the first sign of tears start to fill her eyes.

She took a step back and shook her head. 'NO'.

He stopped and just looked at her. A cutting emotion of her rejection flashed across his eyes as he watched her struggle but still wouldn't let him near her. They just stared at each other.

The sound of her mother opening her bedroom door broke the spell. And Beth quickly turned away from him. 'Emily wants Tom to read her a book now.'

Beth's head flicked around. All traces of her tears were now gone, perfectly replaced with wide eyes. 'She's only stalling going to sleep. I will deal with her.'

Tom reached out and caught Beth's arm. 'No. I would love to read to her. I love doing it for Megan's girls. It's always fun.'

'No. You were just leaving, remember?' Beth said sternly.

'Yes, I'm going. But it won't take long, then I can go and leave you for the night.' The promise that he would leave after reading Emily yet another book, made Beth give in and nod.

Beth sat and stared into the darkness. The street was so quiet. The whole town seemed very quiet tonight. She had been sitting out on the day bed for the last few hours. Her mother had showered and gone to her room after Tom began to read to Emily. Beth had cleaned up the kitchen and when all had fallen silent in her room, she had peaked in and found that Tom had not only succeeded in getting Emily to sleep but also himself. He was sprawled out on his back on her bed. One of his arms was tucked under his head, and the other lay protectively around Emily, who was asleep on his chest—drooling.

Beth had stood at the door and watched them sleeping. Watched the steady rise and fall of Tom's chest as he slept in her room on her bed. She couldn't move further into the room; her feet wouldn't allow it. So, she had stood there and watched as her heart squeezed so tight she finally let a few tears sneak out of her eyes and slide down her face. Her emotions were still too raw. She now sat, huddled in her favourite spot, not letting herself feel anything.

The house was dark except for a tiny night light in the lounge room. She heard her bedroom door open slowly and then Tom curse as he kicked the corner of the lounge chair. That bloody corner had caused her little toe more trauma over the years than it deserved. Beth followed the sound of him moving slowly towards the front door. He must have guessed where she was after looking at the empty lounge chairs. She didn't move from her dark corner when he opened the screen door and stepped out. Beth secretly hoped he would not see her and leave. It had to be this way.

'You should have woken me.' Tom's voice was low and raspy with sleep as he sat down near her. Moving the light blanket she had over her curled up legs, so he didn't sit on it, she hung on tight to the beer in her hand as the streetlight reflected off the other two empty bottles beside her. She knew he couldn't see her face in the shadows.

'You pair looked so peaceful sleeping; I didn't have the heart to disturb you.'

'You may regret that when you crawl in later with the grass clippings.'

'I've had worse,' she said with a distance tone to her voice. Taking another long sip on her beer, she kept her eyes to the street. In the distance, she heard a car making its way down the black bitumen. Lost in her thoughts, and without thought of her past habit, Beth wordlessly handed over her beer to him.

Tom took a sip and handed it back. 'Beth ...'

'Not now, Tom. Please?' she whispered as she looked over at him. The car drove past, its lights illuminating Beth's face. It was then that he saw the tears rolling down her face. Her eyes were soaked with wetness.

Reaching for her, he said, 'Beth ... come here.' His whispered plea reached her, but she leaned away, shaking her head.

'I can't.'

'Why?'

'Because I'm afraid that if I do, I won't be able to stop.' She skulled the last of her beer and stood. Tom followed her, standing to stop her from leaving.

'It's okay. I can take it.' He reached for her again, but she stepped back. He followed her retreat.

'No. Tom, please?' she whispered, her voice breaking on a sob as he reached for her again. Pulling her to him, Tom wrapped his arms around her shoulders. Fighting weakly, Beth's hands rose to his chest to put a barrier between them.

With an arm tight around her waist, the other pressed her head softly to his chest, Tom held Beth to him and let her cry. At first, she tried to stop. She fought hard to stop the flow, but eventually his strength and security won, and her soft crying turned into large, body-shaking sobs.

Tom stood there with Beth sobbing heartbreakingly in his arms. His heart was thundering with pain for all she had been through. For all the sadness that, until now, she had tried to keep locked away deep within herself. He could feel the anger and frustration rise within her when she softly beat his chest and tried to push him away, but still he held her to his body and let her fists clench and softly pummel him.

The wetness of her tears began to soak through his shirt and touch his skin. It was as if her pain was branding his skin and soul. He tightened his grip around her, fighting his own raw emotions that he too had locked away. When the anger and frustration subsided, and pure pain and heartbreak rocketed through Beth's soul, her body sagged, falling into Tom's, and her cries became louder and more sorrowful.

Kissing the top of her head, and cooing to her, Tom vowed to himself that he was never going to let her go. He was never going to let her suffer this much pain again. No matter what it took, he would never let her go through this ever again.

Beth's legs grew weak as she clung to him in a desperate need to feel safe and have someone be her strength for her. For him to take the weight from all she carried, and for once be the one that was held, soothed and supported, and allowed to just let it all go.

Tom could be that for her. He was that for her in this moment, and as his arms tightened, scooping down, he lifted her into his arms and sat on the day bed with her on his lap, more tears and cries emulated from deep within her heart.

Tom's arms were like a steely vice around her so she couldn't move away. It seemed that, in those moments, she never wanted to let him go either. With her arms around his neck, her head against his chest, hearing his steady, strong heartbeat, Beth let her tears flow. Her sobs slowly subsided after a few minutes and she just let the tears fall as they wished. Reaching for the blanket she was just under; Tom placed it over her and pressed a kiss to her head as he settled back against the day bed.

Eventually, Beth's tears slowed and calmed down as she lay curled up in Tom's lap. Her nose was runny, and she tried to wipe it discreetly, but she had nothing. She needed a tissue but didn't want to leave the comfort of Tom's arms. She felt safe within the confines of them.

Shifting her a little, Tom untucked his shirt from his jeans and reached beneath the blanket, accidently touching her below her breast as he unbuttoned two of his shirt buttons. The sensation sent a burst of tingles through her body, causing her heart to skip a beat.

'Here, use my shirt.' Tom lifted the corner of it up for her.

'No, I can't. That's gross.' She smiled a little at his thoughtful kindness and wiped her nose again on her dress.

'I've had worse.' He poked her ribs a little as he teased. Wriggling, Beth sat up. The loss of connection between her body and his, flicked her nerves.

'I can't believe you would bring that up right now.' She pushed at his shoulder as she giggled. 'I am still so embarrassed about that, and you *know* it.' She tried to wriggle out of his arms, but he held her to him.

'I wasn't referring to that ...' he laughed, '... but now that you have reminded me of it ... yes, that too. Geez. That was an expensive day.' He mocked frowned at her. 'I lost two pairs of boots and a good shirt. All because of you.' He poked her playfully in the ribs again, right where he knew she was most sensitive. She fell into him as she wiggled, then she sat up a little again.

With their faces only inches apart, Beth's breathing was heavy as she looked into Tom's eyes. She could feel his body's response to her movement and knew that he was not trying to hide it nor was he making it known to her. The knowledge that she could still do that to him, and the feel of him pressing against her, stirred her blood and sent heat pooling low through her body.

Sensing Tom not moving, she guessed he didn't want to scare her or break the small amount of trust he had so successfully won back tonight—against her will. Beth now found herself on Tom's lap, looking into his eyes, breathing the same air, with a desire that was growing with each heartbeat.

Without any thought to her actions, Beth's hand rose slowly, and she gently touched Tom's face, her thumb smoothing over his closely trimmed beard. Tom's eyes slowly drew closed at Beth's touch, before reopening, revealing such depths of darkness and wanting. Beth's thumb slowed even more, barely moving across the oddly soft hair against her palm. The streetlight behind her allowed her to see him better than he could see her in the shadow of her body. But she saw him, as her other hand pressed over his rapidly beating heart. Lowering her head, her eyes closed. She hovered just a fraction from his lips, their breaths mingling. Beth hesitated.

Tom never moved.

It was taking every bit of control and strength he had and more, to not to. He had to let her come to him. To trust him again. To know that she was safe with him. Her lips barely grazed his. Once. Twice.

A heartbeat.

They pressed again, this time more firmly. Tom still didn't move. Beth moved back just enough to look at him, and he knew she could see his eyes were locked on hers. He didn't hide the fact that they were filled with passion and need for her. He felt Beth quiver a little, his hand on her hips giving the tiniest of pulls towards him. It was enough to encourage her and let her know that he wanted more, but she would have to do it.

Leaning in, Beth's eyes closed as she kissed him. The softness of her lips to his, made them both sigh, and as she opened her mouth more to taste him, Tom darted his tongue in to fully taste her. The spark that they had started years earlier came alive and started to burn. Tom's hand found Beth's hair tie and pulled it out, releasing the soft waves and causing the blonde layers to fall over and around them, cocooning them into their world. Running his hand through her long mass, he entangled his fingers and pulled her deeper into the kiss. She was all his. She always had been since that first moment across the river, and now he wasn't going to let her go. Ever.

Frantically, with shaking hands, Beth unbuttoned the last of his shirt and exposed his chest. Letting her hands roam freely over his defined muscle expanse, Tom's body warmed to each delicate touch and exploration of her soft touches. Groaning with the sensation, was like adding fuel to a fire. It exploded to life between them and began to devour their souls. Kisses became desperate and needy. The very air they breathed came from each other — and it still wasn't enough.

Not breaking the hungry and desperate kisses, Beth repositioned herself so she now straddled Tom's hips, her hands pulling and tugging at his shirt to pull it from his body. Leaning forward, Tom struggled with it, his hands catching in the cuffs, before eventually freeing himself from the material and throwing it across the verandah. They both laughed as passion and desire overtook any rational thoughts they had. Their need to touch and rediscover each other, was their only thought.

Finding the edge of her dress. Tom slid it off Beth's shoulder. Breaking the kiss, he trailed and nibbled his way down her throat to the exposed skin above her breast. Nipping and kissing, making her skin goosebump and her body shiver, he continued his track across to the other side. Her nipples were tight and pushing through her bra and the thin material of her dress. A simple touch and Beth seemed to be in pain with her need for them to be freed.

Tom could feel Beth's body moving over his, seductively with need. His own desire was becoming a force of its own that he was struggling to control. Slipping his hand beneath her dress, he lazily skimmed across her silky flesh to her lace bra. He found her rock hard little pebbled nipple and, with a smile of pure evil, Tom pinched it gently. Beth leaped up with a tiny cry of pleasure and then fell forward, nearly smashing Tom's head into the back of the day bed's frame. She then fell back again as her body rolled with the pleasure he was giving her.

Sliding her hands up his chest, Beth slipped her fingers into Tom's hair. Holding his head, she forced him to look up at her. His view turned him on even more. Her eyes closed and she pushed her breast further into his hand, encouraging him to squeeze again, creating another body wave as she whimpered and devoured him with a kiss that made him breathless and hum with need for her.

Rising to her knees, Beth's hands found the top of Tom's jeans between her thighs. She tried to unbutton them. Tom's hands wrapped around her wrists and pulled them away.

'No,' he growled before kissing her hard on the mouth, taking her breath away. His He moved to her breast again, his eyes watching her every movement.

Tom wanted to have his memories of her eyes and body rolling over his; to hear her whispered cries of his name on her beautiful, lush lips as he brought her to explosion with his finger deep inside of her pulsating body. He wanted all they had before and all he wanted of her now. Locking his jaw, the raw emotions building up from deep inside, he continued to pleasure her, indulging in her every move, lip bite and little gasps. Blindly gliding his fingers to the side of her knickers, Tom ripped at them. The delicate fabric tore, and they both stopped and looked down at what he had done.

Tom's horrified look turned to one of pure satisfaction of his work. 'I guess that will make things easier,' he drawled in her ear before he nibbled it.

Her giggle and squirming pleased his male senses beyond belief. Tom stroked her wetness slowly and gently as she intently searched his eyes, her forehead pressed to his. The world receded more, closing in around them until it was only their touch and passion, heat and desire.

Stroking her again, Tom watched as Beth's eyes closed slowly with pleasure. She was wet and ready for him. He desperately wanted to unbutton his jeans and plough himself deep within her body. To take her right there. To feel himself buried and lost within her. To lose himself fully to her again and again, never wanting to leave.

The thought made his heart twitch and something changed within him. He needed to know just one thing, and he wanted it now. Slipping one finger into her, he felt her heat as a little noise escaped her. Beth clung to him, rolling and grinding. He continued to stroke her as her need and tension tightened around him. Beth was passion and wanting and needing. She was lost in what he was doing to her body as she twined her hands in his hair, kissing him deeply, before resting her forehead back to his, breathing hard with little whimpers.

'When was your last time, Beth?' His voice was gravelly but demanding. He asked again when she didn't answer. She was too lost in her need and the pleasure he was bringing her.

'When was your last time, Beth?' She still didn't answer. He knew she had heard, but was refusing to give in to his demands for answers. He slowed his movements and pulled back just enough so that she had to look at him. Her eyes opened and he could see she was fighting tears and passion all at once. He stopped his movements and removed his hand from within her. A frown creased his brow. 'When, Beth?'

'Why? Why do you need to know?' she whispered back, her passion cooling fast. He pressed a quick kiss to her lips, trying to rein back his need to know but also keep her passion simmering. Keep her with him and not send her running.

'When, Beth?'

She looked away from him and began to move her body away. He pulled her back, his fingers in her hair at the base of her skull. His temper flared as he kissed her deeply to soothe the beasts inside. He was bullying her, but he didn't care. His need to know, his need for her to tell him—something—anything—overpowered any rational thought.

'When?' he asked again, kissing her, his fingers stroking her intimately again, slipping deep within her warm body. Pulling away from him with a gasp, Beth levelled him with a sultry, dirty look.

'You don't ... fight fair ... mmm ... you're a bully, Thomas ... O'Loughlin!' She was breathless as he restoked her passion and kissed her hard. Pulling back, he watched her climbing towards the peak. His own need strained painfully through his jeans. He welcomed the discomfort as he watched her getting closer and closer to the edge.

'When, Beth? Tell me!' he gritted through his teeth.

She looked down at him, her eyes heavy with passion and close to climax. She kissed him deeply before she pulled back and replied through gritted teeth and tears, 'When I fell pregnant with Emily.'

Beth exploded and tumbled over the peak as Tom plundered her with his fingers. She contracted over and over as her cries were swallowed by his kiss, taking them deep into his soul. They were both shaking with the intensity of the moment.

Beth was liquid. Her body had no strength as she lay on Tom's lap, the effects of her release slowly rolling through her body. Even her anger at what he had just done, was not affecting her. She had told him the truth but now, as the afterglow tainted her mind, she shut down that memory of the past and let Tom hold her as her body shivered with pleasure one last time.

Shifting, so she was more comfortable on his lap, Beth could feel Tom's own need beneath her bottom, but she was too weak to help him. Slowly, she felt her eyes close with the gentle sound of his beating heart.

Chapter 15

Tom entered through the gates of the river festival later than he had wanted. He had planned to be there just after lunch and wait for Beth, Susan and Emily to arrive, but he was now a few hours late and hoped he had not missed them. Knowing Beth was anxious about going, and would most likely go early and leave early, he wanted to stop her and hopefully spend some more time with her and Emily before they left the festival.

Last night had gone better than he could have ever thought. He had learned Beth had not been with anyone except Emily's father, and that the idiot had bailed on her before he knew about Emily. Stupid bastard. Why it had mattered, he didn't quite understand, but the knowledge certainly had changed things for him.

The one piece of information feeding his male ego the most, was Beth still desired him with as much passion and need and maybe even more than before, and she still wore his bangle. She had never removed it, like she promised.

Replaying last night's events for the millionth time, the memory brought a smile to his lips and gave him a lightness he had not felt in many years. Moving forward on his mission, he still needed Beth to tell him everything, to give him all the answers he needed to understand. But first, she needed to trust him—and that was why this afternoon, and his timing were so important.

Beth had fallen asleep on his lap, and he had held her there, to his heart, until nearly dawn. Until the first bird song had stirred him awake. His arms had lost all feeling and blood flow, but he couldn't bring himself to let her go. He had dozed a little off and on, waking just to make sure it wasn't a dream. That she had truly been there, sleeping on him.

Eventually, lifting her as carefully as he could, Tom had carried her to her bed and laid her gently beside Emily. Covering them both, he had just stared at her before she had stirred and rolled over to hug her little girl. Leaning down, Tom had kissed the hair near her ear and whispered, promising he would see her later that afternoon, before quietly sneaking out of the house. Flexing his still-tender arm, from holding her, Tom paid his money at the entrance gate on a high. With his mission set, he went on his search for Beth.

The crowd was massive. People were everywhere. Moving anywhere fast was not happening as Tom weaved his way through the crush. Tourists had been filing into River Flats over the last few days—booking out the campgrounds, caravan park, motels, and even some places along the river—that the authorities had turned a blind eye to for the weekend. It seemed like even more had arrived this morning, ready for a weekend of festival fun. Tom had deliberately missed the ball last night, and the parade this morning, his time with Beth yesterday being way more important than making sure he was 'seen'.

The afternoon activities were in full swing now as he listened to the loudspeaker call the dragon boat racing. His tug-of-war competition was due to start in a couple of hours, right before the night entertainment began. He wanted to make sure he had been with Beth for a while before it started, so she could feel comfortable enough to cheer him on to victory. He wanted her to be front and centre to watch.

It took Tom another half an hour to locate Beth, and in the end, it was Braydon who had told him where to find her. His frustration was written all over his face as he had been stopped and quizzed repeatedly. 'Have you seen Beth? Are you okay with her being here? How is your father? Can we catch up for a drink and maybe more later?' was all it seemed to be about. The last one was from Katrina and Mackenzie at different times.

They had stepped in front of him, holding him up more as he tried to push through the crowd. Over the last year, they had become very touchy-feely with him and as much as he had politely told them no, and it was never going to happen, they never seemed to get the hint. The others were just after gossip. Telling them nothing and moving on, Tom was glad to see Braydon, Noah and Michael heading his way. After a brief catch up, Braydon pointed him in Beth's direction. Ignoring his friends' concerned gazes, he made a direct line towards her.

Eventually finding her, she was sitting by the river's edge at the very end of the festival's fenced-in area, watching Emily play in the water along with a lot of other children. Susan was standing back a little talking with a group of ladies he knew all too well. Stopping, Tom surveyed the others around, before watching Beth for a long moment. She seemed to be more relaxed than he thought he would find her, as she lazed in the afternoon shade of the towering gums along the bank of the river. Talking with another mother, her laughter lit up her face when the other lady said something funny. Something had changed within her, and his heart settled from his panic of missing her, to a comforting, peaceful beat of calmness. The kind she had aways brought out in him.

Letting his feet carry him to her, he reached her side, squatted, and touched her back tenderly so she knew it was him. Turning with a little jump, Beth flashed a smile on him that had his heart skipping a beat and racing. She was genuinely happy to see him.

Taking her welcoming as a good sign, he leaned in to kiss her cheek, but she discreetly pulled away, her conversation with the other woman never stopping as her eyes darted around the nearby crowd in hesitation of his outward show of affection.

Covering his mistake by pretending he had slightly over balanced, Tom sat down beside her as Emily came running out of the water with a little squeal of delight at seeing him. She flung herself into his body for a wet hug.

'Oh, hello beautiful girl. You're all wet.' Tom half laughed but gave Emily a big squeeze as her little arms wrapped around his neck and squeezed him with all her might, the water from her body and togs soaking through his shirt and touching his skin, cooling his body a little.

'Yeps. Wants to come play?'

Tom touched her chin when she pulled back to stare into his eyes, very closely, her nose almost touching his as she squeezed his cheeks together with her little hands. He smiled, but instead his lips formed a puckered duck look that made her giggle and let him go. 'Maybe later. How about I watch you play?'

A laugh from her new little friend made Emily run back to the water, splashing and jumping up and down. Ignoring the few confused stares from some of the locals, Tom watched Emily playing and laughing. Beth's little girl was just like her mother— beautiful and full of life.

With contentment flowing through his veins, Tom stretched out beside Beth, happy to watch Emily while Beth was engrossed in conversation with her new mum friend. The afternoon heat warmed his body and dried his shirt as he continued to watch Emily and ignore the looks of others as they walked past him. The few people he caught watching Beth and him, he just nodded at but withdrew himself from them with his eyes if they slowed enough to think he wanted to talk. He didn't. And he didn't want to have people come up and make Beth feel uncomfortable. While she was happy, he was happy. Though, as he looked back through the crowd when an uproar further down the river rippled through everyone, and he saw Katrina and Mackenzie coming his way, Tom sat up and placed a protective arm near Beth's back, leaning closer to her. The simple move of protecting both himself and Beth saw him witness his sister's two friends' faces turn sour before they turned and left—no doubt to gossip to whomever would listen about what they had just seen.

Beth looked around as Tom moved closer, her body already on edge with him sitting so close to her in public. She once again scanned the area for anyone looking. She knew he was going to find them and be with her, and after last night, it wasn't a matter of *if* he found them, but *when*. So, her plan was to allow him to find them, and act like friends. That way she couldn't create unnecessary gossip about what was happening between them. She not only had to show the locals, but she had to show Tom too.

All they were, were two people who were just friends. That's all it could be. After last night, she knew she had lost her battle of keeping him away. Scolding herself all day for her weakness, she had re-evaluated her position with him. Maybe while she was still here, they could be friends.

Weighing it up in her head, she knew she had no option; she didn't want to embarrass or hurt him now by ignoring him in public. When they were in private again, she would just explain that last night had been a mistake.

'Tom!!' Braydon called as he and another man Beth didn't recognise, made their way directly towards Tom. 'There you are. We have to get ready.'

Tom stood, and when Beth looked up, Tom helped her to her feet. She was a little unsure of Braydon and how he would welcome her after all this time.

'Beth!!' Braydon only just let her get to her feet before he picked her up off the ground and swung her around. 'It's about bloody time you came back to see me.' He kissed her cheek and put her back down, holding her at arm's length to check her out. He winked at her and wolf whistled slowly. 'Geeze girl, you're even sexier than before. No wonder Tom here is sticking by your side.'

Braydon pulled her back to his larger body, his arm draping over her shoulder. They both turned to face Tom. Beth blushed with embarrassment as Braydon stirred Tom up, loving every second of it as he did. Tom just rolled his eyes and grinned at his friend.

'Don't get too comfortable, mate. She is here to see me.' Tom shot her a smile that heated her entire body.

'Well, since no one is going to introduce me. I'm Michael,' the other man standing next to Braydon said, leaning over and shook Beth's hand. Then, with a cheeky grin at Tom, he pulled her from Braydon and gave her a tight cuddle. 'She's actually here to see me, boys,' he said proudly, before Braydon and Tom ribbed him about not even knowing her, and to get his smooth moves off their girl.

She was so shocked at both of Tom's friend's actions, she burst out laughing. They had welcomed her with such love and friendship—even Michael, who she had never met before. Taking his time to let her go, she could see Tom over Michael's arm, laughing and letting his mates stir him up. Wanting to join the fun, Beth snuggled back into Michael's embrace, her arms wrapping around him tighter. She buried her face into his chest. Tom saw her move and with a lunge, he pried her from his mate's grip with humour in his voice.

'Yeah, yeah, yeah. You can let her go now.' Beth let him pull her back to stand next to him, his hand gently relaxing on her back.

'Drake is wanting us to get ready. We are programmed to start in twenty minutes. You coming to watch, Beth?' Braydon asked her directly as Emily wandered up to hug Beth's leg.

'Hey. Who is this?' Braydon bent down to be eye level with Emily, no shock on his face at the little girl appearing at Beth's side. He must have heard the gossip.

'This is Emily,' Beth said as she cuddled her daughter to her leg. Emily had gone shy with Braydon's sudden attention.

'Hi Emily. I'm your Uncle Braydon. Pleased to meet you.' He held out his hand for her to take, completely ignoring the raised eyebrows and questioning looks from Beth, Tom and Michael about his declaration of being family.

'*Uncle* Braydon?' Emily slowly took his hand and gave it a squeeze, her smile small and curious at this large man in front of her.

Not wanting to scare her, Braydon stood as Emily took that moment to sneak behind Beth to Tom, her arms raised in a gesture to be lifted, her eyes never leaving Braydon. Tom complied without a second thought and lifted her into his arms, enveloping her in the protection of his body. Emily buried her head into his neck, hiding away from Braydon.

'Oh, so you have stolen yet another heart again, Thomas O'Loughlin? Typical,' Braydon mocked, a hurtful look on his face.

'Yep. We've become fast friends over a leaf and my chips,' Tom replied, rubbing Emily's back as he gloated. 'Haven't we, Em?'

'We had better get going,' Michael said with authority. He had been watching the interaction between Emily and Tom with a polite smile on his face that never reached his eyes like before. Beth couldn't read him, but she had seen the assessing looks he had given her, and she knew Michael was internally questioning her and Tom's 'friendship'. Emily only added to his thoughts of what she could only think was concern as the man's eyes flicked to Braydon, and they shared a look of worry between them.

'I will follow along,' Tom said as he turned to Beth. 'You're coming to watch us beat Drake, aren't you?'

Looking after Braydon and Michael, she noticed a lot of the locals watching her and Tom, whispering behind their hands. She had forgotten all about the crowd when Braydon and Michael had arrived. Realising Tom was holding Emily, and the scene it was creating, it provoked even more talk.

'Umm ... maybe I will stay here so that the noise will not upset Em.' Reaching for Emily, Beth tried to take her daughter from him. Panic had started to rush through her body and she frantically scanned the crowed, shaking, but Emily snuggled closer into Tom's arms.

'She will be okay.' He rubbed Emily's back, searching Beth's eyes with concern. 'Won't you, Em?' Little blonde curls bounced as she nodded her head.

'I really don't think it's a good idea ...'

'Are you ready to get wet again, Tom?' Kathryn walked up behind them, slightly startling Beth.

'I think it's your husband that is going to get wet. Hope he brought a spare pair of boots.' Tom winked at Beth as he spoke to Kathryn.

'Well, I for one am looking for a laugh. Aren't you, Beth?' Susan looked at Beth. Seeing the apprehension and fear on her daughter's face, she frowned a little, then looked between them both, unsure of what was going on. 'Come on. Let's go.' Taking her daughters hand, Susan let Tom clear a path for them, with Emily still in his arms, towards the river.

'No matter what happened before, just give him a chance. You're here to enjoy yourself with friends who have missed you,' Susan whispered.

'It's more complicated than that, Mum,' Beth whispered back and tried not to let everyone's looks and whispers get to her.

Susan patted Beth's hand. 'That might be true, but right now, all that can be put behind you. Promise me you will just enjoy tonight.'

'I will try,' she smiled nervously, her eyes on Tom, watching his protective grip on Emily never waver as he moved through the crowd. Her heart squeezed in pain. She was so confused and fearful, she stumbled over her own feet as her thoughts replayed the memory.

Crushing it and shaking her head at her mother's confusion of her tripping on air, Beth looked at Tom again, and her thoughts turned to last night. Her body still tingled and heated as they floated through her mind. Her heart and head contradicted each other, and confused her once again. She knew what she *had* to do. But what she wanted to do was a completely different thing.

Beth understood what her mother and Kathryn were trying to do. They loved her and wanted things between her and Tom sorted out. But that could never happen, and pushing them together, making him think it could be more than whatever this strained and awkward thing was between them—that it could be anything like it was years ago—was so wrong. So, so wrong. She would be leaving once her mum was able to cope on her own. She had to return to her life in the city with Emily. It just had to be this way.

They were nearly to the end of the deck where all the boys were waiting. Emily had lifted her head and was ruffling Tom's hair after stealing his hat and giving him her pretty little pink one. Oblivious—or knowing Tom, he didn't care—to the looks he was getting from others as they continued through the crowd, he just tickled Emily and held her tight when she wiggled, giggled and squirmed with delight.

'Love the hat, Tom. Pink is definitely your colour,' Noah teased him, though his eyes were focused on the little girl in his mate's arms. His question was easy to read on his face as he looked behind Tom, and Beth neared. Noah's facial expression changed immediately, and he smiled at her tightly, unsure of how to act or what to say. He turned his attention away from her.

'You got my shoes?' Tom asked Noah as he handed Emily to Beth. Unable to help himself, he ruffled her hair and swapped hats before she could get back to him.

'What shoes?' Drake came up and gave Kathryn a kiss before tickling Emily's chin.

'Oh, I know all of your tricks, old man,' Tom teased as he slipped on a pair of runners Noah had given him.

'Do you now, Tommy?' Drake raised his eyebrows at Tom and the boy's shoes. 'Jeans with runners. Nice look,' he smirked.

'Better then you grandpas blinding us with your lily white legs.' Tom pulled his sunglasses over his eyes as he took in Drake's glowing white legs. 'Oh, and by the way, you have to flip us for which side you get too.' Tom smiled at Beth. Drake turned to her with a fake, stern look on his face.

'You been talking about our secrets, Bethy me girl, have you?'

Beth held up her hand in defence and shook her head, briefly looking over at Tom. He had remembered what she had told him about the deck and shoes. Looking back at Drake, she smiled innocently. 'I have no idea what you're talking about.'

'Yeah right.' He turned back to Tom. 'Alright. On one condition. Beth flips the coin, and you have to be the leader so I can watch you go in again.'

'You're on!' Tom shook his hand and smiled at Beth as he gave her his wallet and keys from his pockets.

Drake pulled a coin from his back pocket and handed it to Beth. With a wink, he said, 'Heads I win, tails you lose.'

Tom was about to agree, his hand outstretched, before he pulled it back. 'Hang on, hang on, hang on. I wasn't born yesterday. Heads *you* win. Tails *I* win.' Tom shook his head at Drake and rubbed Emily's back.

'So long as you're sure, Tommy. So long as you're sure.' Drake laughed and turned to face Beth. 'Bethy, flip that coin for me.' Drake stepped back so Beth could flip the ten-cent piece. All the others gathered around, all intent on seeing. It landed tails side up. Tom jumped up with excitement, fist punching the air.

'Yeah. We choose crowd side. You old boys are on the river side.' He was beaming.

Drake had roped Willy, the publican; Trevor, Kates's father; and big Johnny from the local supermarket to be part of his team. They were roughly around Drake's age and were all as strong as bulls. Tom had Noah, Michael and Braydon on his team. The boys would need everything they had, including the advantage of the runners and the little rises in the wood on the crowd side of the deck to beat the 'old boys'. This year, even Braydon was keeping his shirt on.

It was going to be a battle of will and strength. Knowing Tom and Drake, neither were going to give in without a fight. They were both as competitive as each other.

'You girls are my lucky charms,' Tom stated proudly, his words only for her ears, before giving her a quick kiss on the cheek. Beth looked at him in horror, only to have him give her one of his 'butter-wouldn't-melt-in-my mouth' smiles, which always made her knees go weak. But a slice of panic still rippled through her. After ruffling Emily's hair over her hat, Tom stepped up onto the deck with the other boys.

Kathryn cleared a path to the river's edge, further down the wooden deck, so they had a clear view of all the action. Beth, Susan and Helen, who had joined them, followed. They now all had a front row seat to watch the battle begin.

And it *was* a battle.

From the moment the gun went off, the crowd went wild. It was more evenly matched than Beth had expected. Youth, stamina and muscles against bigger, determined, older men. Beth's heart leaped into her mouth at the start as Tom nearly went in within seconds. But his anxious cry to Braydon to lock it in only made Drake fight harder. Lost in the high enthusiastic energy and adrenaline-pumping excitement of the crowd, Beth began crying out instructions, and clapping her hands to Tom and the boys.

She could tell they were listening as they moved their positions slightly and gained a few precious inches of rope back from Drake.

Straining and grunting against the shear pulling power of the men across the river, those older—and so called wiser—men thought it would have been easy against a younger, smaller team across the water. But Tom and his team were holding their ground, just like the girls had done that day when she had first met Tom.

Looking over at Drake, she could tell he was closely watching across the river. Kathryn was calling out encouragement to them across the dirty, muddy water, along with the entire crowd, as the roaring increased with each passing second of this charity tournament. It was so loud that it vibrated through Beth's chest. Emily had her fingers in her ears as she watched, wide eyed at the crazy antics and noise of her mother and those around her.

Seeing Tom move closer to the edge, Beth searched her mind for ways to help. Braydon was losing his grip. Michael and Noah were red and sweating, their teeth grinding as they knew they would go in soon. Remembering what Drake had made them do to get Tom in last time, Beth knew she had to act fast.

Handing Emily to her mum, she leaned over to yell at Tom, 'Remember his trick, don't fall for it again.' Tom nodded and smiled across the river at Drake.

'You're going in, Drake!' Tom yelled at him, the noise around them drowning out his words. But Drake knew he had called something out. Yelling direct orders to his team, Beth watched as Drake's eyes widened as he realised Tom's plan too late.

The big man went in with an almighty, very ungraceful, splash. His legs over his head, Drake belly flopped painfully into the depths of the cold murky water. Trevor and Willy followed, while big Johnny was the only one who managed to stay high and dry. He was laughing so hard and loud, you could hear him across the water as the crowd erupted with cheers and roared laughter.

Tom and the boys dropped the rope and were chest bumping each other and cheering along with the crowd in celebration. The deck under their feet shook and vibrated as they took in the glorious moments of their win. Coming up to the surface, Drake shook his head and after having a few joking words to Willy and Trevor, the three men in the water splashed in Johnny's direction. They were no doubt upset that he had remained dry, and they didn't. Their loss now witnessed, and being the good sportsman he was, Drake casually swam over and climbed the ladder. Offering his hand in a congratulatory gesture as he approached the boys, Tom looked at it suspiciously for a few seconds before taking it.

Wrong move!!

Drake bent down and threw Tom over his shoulder, racing for the water. It was only a few steps but it didn't give Tom enough time to get over his shock before Drake, along with an unsuspecting Michael, who had been standing near the water's edge celebrating, threw them both into the water. The force over balancing him, Drake landed back in the water with a large splash. The crowd erupted with even more screams of laughter and cheers as all three hit the water, surfacing coughing and spluttering and cursing each other.

'One day, Drake, you're going to pay for that!!' Tom splashed water at Drake as he laughed and looked for Beth in the crowd. She was laughing so hard watching them, her cheeks began to hurt. Their eyes met and she could feel the intensity of his gaze on her as he swam towards the ladder.

Her body gave a little shiver as he climbed back onto the deck, his clothes clinging to every curve of his chest and arms. She could see the definition of his muscles. His eyes, dark and sultry, locked back on hers as he made his way directly towards her. Beth got a sudden feeling, like she was being stalked by a hungry lion, and she didn't know what to do. Her heart leaped as she stepped back and bumped into her mum and Emily. She couldn't move.

Before she could think of another plan, he was right there, dripping wet, mischief written all over his face. Grabbing her, she thought he intended to throw her into the water. She gave a little scream and tried to push him away, but instead of throwing her into the water, Tom pressed himself against the full length of her body. His soaking wet clothes and body drenched the front of her dress through to her nipples. They instantly hardened against his chest with the coldness of the water and his body pressed to hers so intimately. He looked down at her when he felt them. Desire flared in his eyes.

'Oh, you're all wet. Get off me.' Beth laughed and pushed him back. Laughing and teasing her, he grabbed her again, holding her tight, the front of her dress now soaked. He stepped away and whispered in her ear, 'Now I have an excuse to get you fully out of your clothes—and not just your lacy undies this time.' He pulled back as the heat flared on her cheeks.

The crowd behind them roared, and Tom turned as Big Johnny and Willy picked up a struggling and screaming Braydon. It was not an easy lift, but they each had an arm and a leg and threw him in the water, high-pitched screaming all the way. Noah followed him in as Trevor and Drake had him the same way. Turning back, and with a long look down Beth's body and a smug smile on his face, Tom turned away and went to get the trophy he and the boys had won. The giant cheque, already signed by himself and Drake, was presented to the local kindy—this year's nominated local charity for the event. The newspaper then took their pictures and interviewed both men.

An hour later, Beth sat in the dying sunlight, trying to dry the last of her dress. Emily had found a large play area and had conned Tom into playing with her. Beth sat watching them. Her mother had gone with Kathryn and Helen to check out the market stalls and get some food for dinner. Some of Beth's old school friends, and people she knew, had drifted by and said hi to her. Others, from his social group, had found Tom and spoken to him, but no one talked for long.

The apprehension and nerves from earlier in the day had settled and Beth had begun to enjoy herself. Knowing she would be leaving again soon; the ease of catching up with old friends was good for her. Maybe in the future, if she ever came back home, she could do so without some of the fear.

Still, she worried about the gossip getting around about her and Tom, but she hoped that with her leaving again very soon, it wouldn't matter. They were just old friends catching up and having fun at the river festival, just like everyone else.

'Hey stranger. Thought you could use this.' Beth turned to see Kate standing behind her, a couple of beers in her hands. She held one out for Beth, which she took. 'Mind if I sit down?' Not waiting for Beth to reply to her question, Kate sat down next to her.

Both opening their beers and taking a sip in silence, Kate followed Beth's gaze to where Tom was pushing Emily on the swing.

'Beth, we used to be close friends. Never best—that was always Montana and Adelaide's job—but you need to hear me out.' Kate was still Kate, Beth thought as she took another sip and prepared herself for what was coming. 'I take it the rumours are true?'

Beth looked from her to where Tom and Emily were. 'That depends on what the rumours are.'

'That you got knocked up when you got to wherever the hell you took off to, and that the father didn't want anything to do with you or the kid.' Kate turned from watching Tom, to face Beth. Pulling her knee up on the seat so her whole body was facing Beth, she continued with, 'It's a small town, Beth. They need their gossip. And after this weekend, there will be plenty of other gossip for them to twist and talk about. But is it true?'

Beth mimicked Kate's position and faced her down. She was not intimidated by Kate. She had always tried to love her friend just as closely as Montana and Adelaide, but Kate was hard to get close to. 'Like you said, Kate, it's been twisted. But it is complicated.' Beth took a sip of her beer and watched as Kate did the same. They weighed each other up. Eventually, her long-time friend smiled over the rim of her beer at her, but there was a coolness in those cobalt eyes.

'You do need to hear what I have to say, but you're not to repeat it.' Kate looked over at Tom. He was helping Emily climb up the ladder to the taller part of the play equipment. She looked back to Beth, 'I don't know why you up and left. That's your business and yours alone. However, it was low, Beth. Real low.' Beth went to protest, but Kate held her hand up to stop it. 'Just hear me out as your friend and his.' She nodded towards Tom. 'He was really messed up when you took off in the dead of night. He tore up the town looking for you and then took off to the city to find you. Drake ended up going down and getting him to come back. I will spare you the details of it all. That's for him to tell you if he wants to, but when he got back, he was pretty messed up, Beth.'

Kate stared at Beth, making sure she understood the gravity of what was being said. 'He was drinking heavily and causing a lot of trouble with his father and Megan. A lot of nights I had to drive him home from the pub because he wasn't capable of doing it himself. Most of the time, he could barely stand or walk.' Beth looked over at Tom. He had not said a word. No one had told her anything about it. 'The final straw came late one night. He had really written himself off and he couldn't walk. He was legless and beginning to pick fights at the pub. He had even managed to get Willy offside, getting himself thrown out of the pub with instructions for me to take him home. I was struggling to get him to my ute when Michael arrived. He's the new hottie police officer here in town. He was on Tom's team for the battle against Drake before,' Kate clarified for Beth, when she saw the frown crease Beth's forehead.

Michael was a police officer? Beth had thought he had some authority about him. Kate continued, 'Anyway, Michael and I took him home and after I left, Michael stayed with him. I don't know what was said, but after that Tom started to really get his life back in order. He has become the old Tom, to an extent, again. Today, I saw the true old one back before us.' They both looked over at the playground. Tom was pushing Emily on the swing again. He had realised Kate had joined Beth, and his face clearly stated that he was worried about what they were talking about. Kate turned back to Beth.

'It's you that has brought him back. But Beth ...' Kate's voice was stern, and she was determined to be heard. '... if you intend on leaving again, for God's sake talk to him and tell him the bloody truth. He loves you beyond reason. He deserves better than you runnin' out on him again. We all love you. Both of you. We don't want to see either of you get hurt again. A love like what you pair have is rare. Be careful how you break it.'

'Mummy.' Beth turned from Kate, a little misty-eyed but with a smile on her face to greet Emily. Her emotions were running high, but she couldn't show it as she promised Kate she wouldn't let on to Tom what they had spoken about.

'Emily!' She scooped up the little girl. 'This is my very good friend, Kate. Can you say hello?'

'Hello. Mummy, I'm hungry.'

'Oh, good to hear. I have some chippies and nuggies for you,' Susan said as she walked up behind the group. 'Oh, Kate dear. Glad to see you.' Kate stood and cuddled Beth's mum.

'Yep, you too. How have you been?'

'Oh, you know. As best as I can. I'm glad you and Beth have had a chance to finally catch up again after missing each other at the house.'

'Yep, just talking girly talk, though she did just promise me that she would join me for a dance and some drinks tonight so we can have a real catch up.' Kate smiled at Beth, her blue eyes twinkling, knowing she had just forced Beth to stay for the night and celebrate with her.

'Oh, that's great.' Susan looked to Beth and smiled. 'I can then spoil my granddaughter more without her mother knowing.'

'I had better get back to the bar, otherwise Willy will be kicking my butt. I will see you two later.' She motioned to Beth and Tom then, bending to Emily, Kate said, 'Nice to meet you, Miss Emily.'

Chapter 16

Kate's words still rang in Beth's ears as she watched her mum walk off with a very sleepy Emily. They had eaten dinner and watched the trick riders on the water do their thing before the fireworks display.

Tom had taken Emily into his arms and held her as she watched in awe of the display lighting up the night sky above their heads. The whole festival had gone dark except for the magical display of colour set to music. Emily had covered her ears at first, but Tom had soothed her with his words and eventually, she had—her arms and teddy bear wrapped tightly around his neck, her face squeezed to his—loved it. Beth felt Tom's arm go around her waist and she let herself get pulled into his body as they watched together. She didn't want to make a scene of pulling away in front of so many people, so she let him hold her close. It felt safe and secure. It felt like home.

When they had first met here three years ago, he was just a boy, and she was just a girl. Over the years, he had grown into a man. One she was fast learning was strong and full of conviction. One who kept his word and understood all those around him. Tom was a man she desired and wanted more than she ever thought possible and he was more than she deserved. She was going to hurt him again, and this time she knew she had been the one to allow it—by leading him on again.

Beth had known he was seeking her out—waiting at the café or along the river walk, and by coming to her mother's house. And in her own selfish need for him to want her, to chase her, to hold her and make her feel all that he was—safe, secure, protective, and able to hold her while she had let herself collapse—she had let him.

Without understanding the full extent and emotional turmoil her own actions, Beth had let her guard drop and she had let Tom in behind her wall last night. His patience and playfulness with Emily, his touch to Beth's body, was the beginning. And then he had put a full assault against her shields and held her, letting her cry out her pain, grief and anxiety, until there was nothing left but him.

He had held her and broken down all her defences.

Even while he cradled her, he offered her his shirt for her to blow her nose on. He was there, offering everything he had. Tom had managed to break down her carefully crafted walls and get inside to her heart all within an afternoon, and now she couldn't—and *didn't want to*—remove him from where he had stormed her walls and won.

His words and voice soothed her, his touches and heat calmed her, and then last night, after she had let all the hurt, pain, anger and frustration at the world and for her choices, all go, Beth had touched him back. Her mind had screamed 'NO!!!!' but her heart had only wanted him.

Now, as they had stood watching the fireworks, Tom's arm around her as he also held her daughter, Beth felt the harsh cold stab of anger and self-betrayal at what she had let redevelop between them, slice through her. It had been a massive mistake. She was going to be leaving in the next few weeks and he was not going to be part of their lives again. She couldn't let this go on any further. But right here, right now, seemed the wrong time to make that known. To tell him she was sorry for leading him on and that she would be leaving again, and how this little thing— whatever it was that had reopened between them—was going to have to end. Again. Forever this time.

Kate's words hit hard—deep inside Beth's chest like a boulder hitting her from behind without seeing it coming. A painfulness weighed on her shoulders, so crushing it overcame her, and she had to concentrate on not crying or making any outward sign of her rolling emotions. She couldn't do that to Tom again. She couldn't ruin everything he had worked so hard to build for himself. She would leave this time and make sure he knew she wouldn't be back in this town for her mother, her friends or for him. Risking having to hurt him like she was once again going to do, was too much, and Tom had already endured that pain and suffered beyond what she had ever imagined.

As the last of the fireworks lit up the night sky in an explosion of rainbow colours, and the smoke and tainted smell drifted across the crowd and tickled Beth's nose, she made the heartbreaking decision that she would have to ruin Tom's life— and break her own heart—once again, because of the mess she had made by allowing him to get so close. But this time her heart would be broken beyond repair, and hopefully, he would never look at her like he was now.

Explaining her decision and speaking to him about it, was not something she could do here—or tonight. But tomorrow, it had to be done. Taking a shaky breath and letting it out slowly, Beth recalculated her decision to stay and be with her friend.

Tonight, she would dance with Kate and catch up with her old friends, saying goodbye, minute by minute, to them and this town, without anyone knowing. And then, tomorrow she would tell her mum and call Tom. By the time the day ended, she and Emily would be on their way back to the city—to Chelsea's—where no one would find them, and Tom would have had no chance to hinder her decision, leaving Beth to, once again restart her life. But this time she would know she had made the right decision for everyone—even at the cost of her own heart.

So tonight, she would enjoy herself and talk to Tom tomorrow. Her words would have to be chosen correctly so she could prevent, as best as possible, his heart breaking as much as hers already was.

Susan had come over to them from her spot next to Helen, Drake and Kathryn, who were all standing towards the back of the crowd, and taken Emily from Tom when the fireworks finished. Emily was so tired she didn't care that Beth was staying without her. She just waved and snuggled into her nanna with her teddy.

'Are you ready to hit the dance floor? Or shall I take you for a drive to a certain old wooden deck?' Tom stepped behind Beth and pulled her back against his body.

Feeling the heat of his strong body against her back, her body instantly warmed to her bones. However, the thoughts of him driving her to their spot on his family's property to be together in the way he wanted, was a terrible idea. Ignoring the cold dread and shutting down her last memory of being at Silverleigh, Beth turned and quickly kissed him on the lips before backing away. His one hand was still gripping hers as she walked backwards. Tom stepped slowly forward with her, a sly smile forming on his lips, as she easily read his mind of where he thought her thoughts were going.

'Kate would miss us.' Beth playfully pouted at him and his smile faulted before he shook his head to debunk her words. 'I promised her I would have drinks with her.' Beth argued with him as still, she slowly stepped back. Her hand in his, Tom followed. 'Now, are you coming?'

Breaking free from his grip, Beth sprinted off, darting between locals and tourists. She lost him in the thick moving crowd. Laughing, she ducked between two market stalls and weaved through the next two rows of shop owners and vendors. Searching behind her, her smile grew as she realised she had lost him. Quickly making her way around the back of the bar, she kept her eyes out for him. Tom was nowhere to be seen. She had beat him there. Gloating at her little victory, Beth leaned on the bar, puffing a little from her exertion. She looked over the large crowd, all settling in for a night of dancing and fun.

'About time you showed up. Where's Tom?' Kate slid her over a rum and coke from where she was sitting on one of the bar stools.

'Oh, he will be along soon. We had a race.' Beth took a long sip of her drink. A warm hand slid up her thigh under her dress. She jumped and turned, spitting and spilling her entire drink on top of Tom's head.

'Oh, jay … suss, Beth!!!' Tom cried out.

He had bent down to run his hand up her skirt, a way to scare and punish her for running off on him. Standing straight, he shook the sticky mess from his hair and shirt, spraying everyone around him who had witnessed his rum bath and had burst out laughing. Beth stood there with her hand covering her mouth, trying not to laugh at him. Her whole body shook with laughter.

'Just like old times.' Kate laughed as she watched Tom look at Beth, horrified.

'Oh Tom. Not again!' Braydon boomed over the noise of the crowd as he led the way, Michael and Noah following him. By the looks of it, they had been coming around behind Tom to the bar and had saw what had happened. They too were laughing hard. 'At least this time it's not spew.'

'Oh, shut up Braydon!' both Tom and Beth said at the same time. Michael looked between them both as he pushed past the boys to stand next to Kate.

'What about vomit?'

'You don't want to know,' Beth said and shot Braydon a look of death. He ignored her.

'Oh, my new friend. Let me tell you a delightful little story about how these two met. It was long ago, when a fair maiden named Beth looked out across the river to an ugly duckling called

Tom,' Braydon lullabied as everyone shook their heads at his story telling. 'Then she whipped his ass and pulled him headfirst into the river.' His voice back to normal, he punctuated his words, making the story sound heroic. He then changed back to his lullabied tone. 'But not to be out done, our ugly duckling pulled our fair maiden into the water ...'

'Oh, dear God, Braydon. Get on with it.' Tom stood near Beth's side. He smelt sickly of rum and coke as he ordered another round for her and the others.

'Well, okay then. I was trying to make it all romantic and stuff for our resident Romeo here.' He turned to Michael, slapping him on the back as he continued his story. 'Beth got really drunk, and Tom tried to be the hero and got himself projectile vomited on. So, this required him to not only remove his shirt, but to also carry the now legless Beth across the festival, to his chariot, where she was sick all over another pair of his boots, ruining the second lot for the day. The first pair was ruined when she magnifically pulled him into the water. But she then, on the gallant ride home, managed to decimate the inside and outside of his luxury ute.'

Beth hung her head in her hands, embarrassed. Braydon had told of her and Tom's meeting perfectly and with such flare, all those around who had been listening, were now laughing. More at Tom than at her, but Beth still tried to hide behind her hand.

'Yeah, yeah boys. That's enough.' Tom handed around the drinks he had brought. Beth's was last. 'Try to keep this in the glass this time and not on me. I have no more clothes with me tonight ... unless you wanted me naked, that is,' he whispered into her ear.

Tom's breath sent shivers down Beth's spine, his words heating deep within as her skin tainted the slightest red. He kissed her on the cheek quickly before he focused his attention on the group conversation. With his arm around her, he did not intend to leave her side.

Kate, Michael and Beth were deep in conversation about music when the DJ finally got organised and started the first song rocking all over the festival grounds. The bass of the music made Beth's chest rattle, and everyone had to yell to be heard over the noise. One of the organisers raced up and spoke to the DJ. The music dropped down a few decibels so people could still talk but the music was loud enough to dance to.

'Come on, Beth. Let's dance.' Kate sculled her drink and dragged Beth out onto the dance floor. The crowd was thick, but Kate cleared the path with her 'Will you get out of our way?' voice. They were in the middle of the dance floor, jumping and dancing around to beat of the music before the first song had ended.

The rum, and of course the two shots she had done with Michael and Kate at the bar, were now warming her veins and relaxing her worries. Beth danced and jumped around with Kate, and as each song played, the more they laughed and talked, the more Beth felt at home. It was so good being here with her friend.

Jumping around and grinding on each other, then moving and letting the music move their bodies wildly, Kate bumped into a group of males who were all dancing with a very large group of girls. Giggling and apologising to them, Kate laughed out loud to one of the young boys after a quick word with him, her hand on his arm, her eyes wide, before she danced her way back to Beth, saying that the one she had bumped into had instantly hit on her. Kate said he was barely out of nappies, giggling with mock horror of it. She made Beth laugh and sent an ache through her body at how much she had missed her friend.

Her body alive and full of energy, moving and letting the music beat sync with her heart, Beth was still aware of the heat Tom's stare was causing to her senses. He had not removed his eyes from her, even though he was still talking with all of his mates at the bar. Beth knew he was watching her every move. The sensation was warm, and it had started the embers that had always been between them, to burn. Her skin flushed and shivered at the replay of what had happened between them last night, and she felt the familiar rush of heat grow between her legs.

'He hasn't taken his eyes off you for more than a second, Beth,' Kate yelled into her ear so she could hear over the music. 'I hope you know what you're doing.' Kate jumped back, spinning, and smiled wickedly at her before coming back to her ear. 'Maybe you do know what you're doing by having that sexy body touching and pressing up against you. To see that naked body again would give me wet dreams for a year, I reckon.' She pulled back, laughing, as Beth swatted her shoulder, a tinge of red creeping up and colouring her face deeply.

'Let's just say it was never bad,' Beth yelled back with a laugh and bumped into another person. Everyone was doing the same. It all was just great fun as Kate raised her eyebrows and fanned herself with her hand. An arm wrapped around Beth and pulled her back against a solid wall of muscle and heat. The smell of rum filled her senses.

'What's never bad?' Tom asked over her shoulder before kissing her neck, making her squirm and wiggle as he pressed her firmly to his body.

'You in the sack,' Kate, who had moved to dance closer to them, said. Beth laughed and turned her head to look at Tom over her shoulder.

'Kate wants you to take her to bed and have your way with her so that she will believe me that you're as good as I'm talking you up to be.' Tom looked between Beth and Kate. The look he gave Kate was one that Beth couldn't quite work out. Kate looked him over with mock desire and walked up close—so close her friend stood only inches from them both as they swayed together along with the music. Then, without warning, she leaned in against Beth's body and kissed Tom on the lips. It was just a quick peck before she burst out laughing and whispered to Beth, 'That was like kissing my brother.'

Tom's eyes nearly rolled out of his head in shock. 'Well, if that's how you feel, I will just have to take Beth to bed then.'

Kate danced up to them again, her eyes set to Tom's, a smile of devilry and cheek all over her face. 'You just remember that I know exactly what Beth is talking about.' She winked at Tom as he turned red, a sight that Beth had never seen before. He became flustered at Kate's words.

Laughing, Kate threw her hands in the air, screaming as the song changed to one she obviously loved.

'I don't want to know what that was between you pair, but do I get a say in this?' Beth drawled in Tom's ear.

Tom turned a questioning look on her. 'What?'

'About you taking me to bed?'

'Nope, you're all mine. Now and forever.' Tom bent to kiss Beth's lips, but she turned her face, and he got her jaw instead. She didn't want to give others more gossip than they were already witnessing. He laughed.

'Later, Beth. Later. I will get you another drink. Kate? You want one?' With two thumbs up, Kate twirled Beth as Tom made his way back to the bar where all the other boys were gathered, talking and watching the dance floor.

When Tom didn't come back with their drinks, Beth turned and searched the crowd to see where he was. She couldn't see him with the now very large group of people he had been standing with earlier. With a questioning look at Kate, both girls stopped dancing in the middle of the dust dancefloor and started to search, both in need of a drink. And if Beth was being truthful, she needed to feel him.

'There he is. He has been cornered, leaning up against the bar by the SB girls. You should go and save him.' Kate was pointing to the large group surrounding Tom. She was right. The SB girls had cornered Tom, blocking his view of the dance floor and of her. So desperate in their need for his attention, they were not letting him leave.

'No, he will be fine,' Beth replied, a little distant as her words lost their volume and jealously speared through her. 'He should fight his own battles.'

'I think it's a battle he's already lost. He won't turn them away and embarrass them in front of all the others. Megan would have his balls, and his father would have his throat, and those girls know it. His too much of a goodie to just up and move away.' Kate could see Beth was torn about what she should do. It was written all over her friend's face.

'Just go and claim what you know is yours and deal with the consequences tomorrow.' Kate, who had begun to dance again, stopped, and they both watched the large group for a few more seconds. Softly, she nudged Beth's shoulder. 'I can bet a million dollars that he would be forever grateful. Those girls need to be put in their place once and for all.'

Beth didn't want those girls near Tom. As much as she knew it was wrong and how he should be given the chance to meet someone else and let her go—how this was the perfect situation for her to use tomorrow when she left his life forever—Beth couldn't stop herself. Even as her feet carried her through the crowded dance floor and through the bystanders at its edge, she knew this was going to be the very worst thing she could do. To lay claim over him. Now. Right here in front of everybody. It was the absolute worst thing and would give everyone the wrong impression, Tom included. But she couldn't stop. Wouldn't stop.

Tom saw her coming and the relief in his eyes made her smile inwardly. Forcibly pushing her way between Katrina and Mackenzie, Beth positioned herself directly between the girls, now having to take a step back from Tom's body to allow Beth room in front. Reaching for her, Beth turned as Tom pulled her body back against his. She was his shield as his arms wrapped around her hips. He kissed Beth's neck intimately in her sensitive spot. Her body reacted just as he knew it would.

'Hi girls. How have you been? Long time no see.' Beth smiled sweetly as they tried to hide their anger at her laying out so plainly, to all in the group and to anyone else, that she was with Tom tonight, and he was definitely with her.

'Oh, hi Beth,' they sneered. 'It's been so long. Three years?'

'Yes, that's right. And you're still here enjoying life to the fullest, I see.' Tom squeezed her hip a little, hoping she understood he was supporting her and giving her the confidence she needed for this battle. He had read and understood her game plan the minute he had seen her coming. She was making her claim, and he couldn't have been happier. This was a side of Beth he had never known was there. Hell, *she* didn't even know it was there. But discovering it right now, like this, she felt strong and confident, and sexy as hell.

'It's always so good to know where your home is and appreciate what you have. Don't you agree?' Mackenzie stated sarcastically.

'Yes, of course.' Beth gave them a fake smile of friendship and a shrug.

'We hear you have a daughter, but her father didn't stick around. That must be hard, doing it all by yourself now that you're all alone.' Katrina covered her mouth and giggled behind her hand, looking away as Makenzie spoke her cruel words.

'It *is* hard, but you know what ...?' Beth leaned in a little, careful not to break Tom's firm hold around her, '... I think I would rather be doing it alone then having to share my man like you two and Megan do with Trent. He must be exhausted having you three little girls to keep happy.'

If Beth could have taken a picture of Katrina and Mackenzie's faces, she would have. Their mouths fell open, and their eyes widened before they turned on each other and started yelling accusations of who Trent was cheating on and who did who wrong. Everyone who was in earshot of their little conversation and had heard what Beth had said, clapped their hands and cheered.

Without thinking, Beth let the adrenaline and true satisfaction of the power she felt in that moment—finally standing up for herself to these girls who had made her feel like such a nobody—take over her. She turned within the circle of Tom's arms, grabbing his face and kissed him fully on the lips. Her body pressed to his, her hands slipping into his hair, she kissed him passionately. His surprise and hesitation only lasted a heartbeat before he kissed her back, his hands possessively holding her head to him. It washed out the noise of the cheers and wolf whistles from all those around them, who were cheering on the girls getting put in their place and her kissing Tom so publicly.

The realisation of what she had just done—broke the spell— and caused her to pull back ready to retreat. Tom held her firmly in place, forehead to forehead. He was not going to let her go and run. Looking deep into her eyes, he smiled, and when Beth rested her hands to his chest, she could feel his heart was racing at all that had just transpired between them so publicly. She could feel his heart rate soaring and the dread stifling hers.

'Maybe I should get cornered by other women more. That was truly spectacular.' His lips brushed the top of her nose.

'Don't you dare. Next time, I will leave you to fend for yourself.'

'So, there will be a next time?'

Beth didn't answer. She had made a massive mistake. He now believed she was going to stay. Her stupid mistake of letting her jealously overrule her better judgement was now going to hurt him more—and publicly. Mentally cursing herself, she only just smiled as Braydon came up and gently touched her shoulder.

His thumb rubbed her shoulder blade as he smiled widely at her, but she read the mischief in his eyes as he spoke.

'Oh, get a room, you pair.' Before he ordered his drink from the man standing behind the bar.

Tom straightened and reluctantly let Beth go to where Kate was standing with a curious look on her face. 'Do you want your drink now?' he called to her.

Beth nodded to him as he turned to the bar. Braydon looked back at her before turning and saying something that was for Tom's ears only. Beth watched the interaction closely, with a slight frown on her face. Tom had the same frown on his face when he faced Braydon in answer. They both turned to look at her before Tom slapped Braydon on the back and grabbed his drinks, answering his mate with a smirk of reassurance. Tom then walked over to Beth.

'What was that all about?' she couldn't help but ask. It seemed like an intense conversation and something in Braydon's look at her, made her stomach drop just a little.

'Braydon just being Braydon. He's a really good friend— the absolutely best, that's all.' He brushed off her question and soothed her concern just a little as she sipped her drink. The music changed into a slower song. Tom looked up and around the crowd then back at Beth. Taking her drink from her before she had a chance to take another sip, Tom handed it to Kate and led Beth out onto the dance floor.

'Dance with me?' he softly ordered.

Stepping into his arms, her arms wrapping around his neck, Beth let Tom pull her to him. Other couples moved around them, but they didn't notice. Staring into each other's eyes, the heat slowly burned between them. Beth could see the passion and need for her, liquify Tom's eyes. Her own desire and arousal was pooling low as the world around them disappeared, their lips coming together gently, hearts beating as one.

Her breast vibrated against his chest. He laughed and looked directly down her dress. 'What was that?' he smirked as Beth reached into her bra and removed her phone. Reception was only very limited, and it was an unconscious thing that she had brought it with. It had become a habit in the city after Emily was born—to carry her phone everywhere she went. She was surprised that it had buzzed.

Sorry. Emily is very upset and is calling for you.
What do you want me to do? I can't settle her. Mum

Beth looked up at Tom and showed him the message. Together, they left the dance floor and started to quickly walk towards the gates.

Chapter 17

'Did you enjoy your night last night?' Beth looked over her coffee cup to where her mother was standing at the kitchen sink washing up the breakfast dishes. Emily was outside playing in the sandpit under the large gum tree.

'Yes. Why?' She didn't like the tone in her mother's voice. Even though Susan had tried to deliver it as just a general conversational starter, it came across as a little invasive. Surely her mother would not have already heard anything about last night by this early hour.

'Oh nothing. Just asking.' She looked up and waved at Emily through the window.

'No. You're wanting to say something but not cause an argument.' Beth knew her mother's ways. When her father was here, he would always be the one to help create peace and harmony when needed. Not that it was needed often, but when her mother wanted to really speak her mind, her words sometimes came out wrong, and Beth would not like it. They would fight and it had been her father who would help them see each other's points of view. Now that he wasn't there, this was something new they would have to figure out.

'I want you to just hear me out. That's all.' There it was. Susan Kennedy was not as sly as she thought she was. She had been dropping her opinion in little ways, hoping that Beth would get the picture. She had. Her mother was now just going to say it all to make sure Beth had picked up on her not-so-subtle hints.

'Ok then. Hit me with it. But please just be nice.' Beth stood and placed her empty cup into the water and reached for the tea towel. If her hands were busy, she would have something to wring if needed instead of losing her temper at her mum. Susan gave her a side glance.

'You have kept your reasons for leaving to yourself. Even from me and your father. We know something big must have happened between you and Tom to make you feel that your only option was to leave and keep everyone away. Even us.' Susan wiped away a tear with her rolled-up sleeve so as not to get dishwashing soap in her eyes.

Beth felt a nasty little lump start to form in her throat. 'We trusted that whenever you were ready, you would come back to us. Eventually, you did in a way. Even when your father got ill, we never asked you about your choices and we respected you for them. We are both very proud of you and the great mother that you are.' Another tear slid down her mum's face. Beth felt tears stinging her own eyes.

'I know it must have been extremely hard to be by yourself and alone for all this time, and how hard it has been for you, coming back here for your father's funeral and staying on to make sure I was okay. Those choices took great courage. But Beth ...' She turned her whole body to face her daughter. 'If you are planning on leaving soon, and going back to your life in the city, you need to be honest with yourself and with Tom.' Her voice became very stern. 'That young man was devastated when you up and left without a word to him. He's had to make some pretty big changes to his life and yet here he is trying his absolute best to get you to trust him enough to tell him the truth of what happened. What made you up and leave in the dead of night, scaring the hell out of us all?' Beth shifted on her feet. Kate's words from last night, her own guilt, and now with her mother's words, it all started to make her feel sick.

'He has even taken to Emily with such devotion and care because she is yours. He loves you, Beth. That type of love is rare. He doesn't see Emily as anything but an extension of you. I feel he is already in love with her too because of his love for you.' Susan looked back out to Emily in the sandpit before pinning her daughter with a serious look. 'If you care like I think you always have about that young man, don't lead him on. You have been brought up better than that. Tell him the truth. Even if it is only him you tell, tell him. He deserves the truth, doesn't he?' Susan looked out the window. 'See what I mean?'

Beth looked out. Tom had materialised and was now sitting on the edge of the sandpit talking with Emily. Beth had not heard his ute pull up or the side gate squeak open. He had just appeared.

Emily was showing him her tractor and her horses she was playing with. He must have said something that excited her as she leaped up and gave him a cuddle then pulled him to stand. Obliging her, he let her lead him around the side of the house. Beth heard the squeaky gate.

Her mum was right. Tom deserved to be told the truth that she was leaving again soon. It was the only truth she could tell. After last night, she knew her time here was up. Her mum would cope. She had her friends. Tom would be upset but at least he would know this time and she would leave without causing any further harm to anyone. She would tell him when they were alone and in private. If he was to get upset, which she knew he would, at least no one would see but her. She would even make sure her mother had Emily.

Tom came round the corner of the house again. Emily was doing her best effort to skip along beside him as he carried a piece of board tied with rope. A swing.

Beth's heart squeezed. Her mother was right. The time had come. Dabbing at the wetness around her eyes, Beth walked out of the kitchen to her bedroom. She needed time to sort her words.

What do you say to someone when the words that needed to be said will destroy them and change their lives forever? Changing her mind, she went to the bathroom. Showering while she cried was always healing.

Emerging from her shower, Beth still had not thought of any appropriate words that would dull the pain of what she needed to say to Tom. Bracing, ready to find Tom in the house waiting for her, Beth was surprised to see the house empty and no sign of her mother or Emily. Walking out the back door and around the side of the house, Beth stopped.

Tom was transferring Emily's seat from her car to his ute, under her mother's close watch, while Emily was exploring the contents of the inside of his ute with such glee and excitement. By the looks of her face, she had found his secret stash of orange choc drops.

'Aaargh. What are you pair doing?' All three stopped what they were doing and looked at Beth. Though it was Emily who went back to doing what she was doing, her mother and Tom just looked at her. With a smile that stopped her anger and confusion, Tom walked to her and gave her a kiss on the cheek. She had turned her head at the last moment so that he missed her lips. She saw the hurt and confusion flicker in his eyes, but she couldn't do anything about it. The worst was still to come. She needed to stay firm and strong on her boundaries with him.

'Tom has suggested that Emily and you go and see his horses. So, I suggested that you should all spend the day together.' Susan, happy with herself for the suggestion, gave her an encouraging smile. 'I want to go to the shop today when no one else is there and catch up with the paperwork.' Her admission made Beth frown.

'Are you sure you're up to it?'

'Well, I won't know unless I give it a go. Besides the boys won't work for free if I don't pay them, especially with harvest season about to kick off again this week.'

'I will come with you and help.' Beth didn't want to go with Tom—especially, absolutely and definitely not to Silverleigh. She wasn't ready to tell him she was leaving. She wasn't ready to hurt him again so badly. She hadn't even worked out how to tell him yet. Her mother was pushing her by sending her off with him, and it was starting to make her feel sick and panicked.

'No, you go and have a wonderful day. I will see you when I see you.' She touched Tom's arm and gave him a smile. One that Beth couldn't understand the meaning of. 'Bye Em. Have fun with the horses.'

'Come on, Princess. Let's go.' Emily climbed into her seat and let Tom buckle her up and wipe her face over with a wet wipe he had pulled from her little bag. Her little teddy in one arm, her toy horse in the other, Emily was all set. Beth's mother had packed for a day and night by the looks of it. A deep sinking feeling came over Beth and settled in her chest.

'Comes Mummy!' Emily yelled to her, her excitement making her voice a shilled squeal in Tom's ear. Stepping back, he put a finger in his ear and wiggled it, looking at Beth with a little smile.

'She has a good set of lungs.'

'Tell me about it.' They stood about a metre apart from each other. 'I don't think us going out to your family's farm is the right thing to do, Tom.' Beth folded her arms across her chest, a cold shiver lacing her body. She began to shake with fear, fighting her demon memories.

Stepping to her, his hands resting on her hips, he wiggled them against his own. 'Trust me today, okay? That's all I'm asking.' He kissed her quickly on the lips before she could turn her head away. 'Please?' Tom's eyes melted Beth's defences, and with a silence, she let him lead her around to the passenger side door. She hopped in. Raising her cold, shaking hand to his lips, he kissed it.

'Where are you taking us? This is the wrong way out to Silverleigh.' Tom looked over and took Beth's hand, giving it a reassuring squeeze.

'To my place.'

'Your place?' she frowned. 'You have your own place?'

He gave a little laugh. 'Yes. Dad wouldn't be caught dead with horses on the home place. So, I brought Reggie's old place off Drake a couple of years ago.' She let her surprise show. No one had told her about that little piece of information. Her mum must have thought she already knew.

Tom's farm was different from what she had imagined. Given who he was and his family's wealth, it was a little surprising. Tom had redone all the fences and had built a new set of stables and yards. The house had been painted, and the house yard was neatly manicured, but it still held its charm from the last time Beth had been to Reggie's with Drake and the girls. It looked just like a well-maintained farm. You wouldn't know that someone of Tom's financial benefits lived there. What needed to be replaced had been replaced, and what needed to be there for his needs had been done. But nothing was showy. When you drove up to his family's property, you knew the people who owned it were wealthy. Here, not so. But that was Tom. He was who he was. Money wasn't something that made him who he was; it was just something he had. Beth looked over at him and he kissed her knuckles.

'Horsey, Horsey!!' Emily screamed and wiggled in her seat to get a better view of them. Slowing to a stop on his driveway, near the stables, Tom laughed as he removed Emily from her seat. As soon as she was put on the ground, she ran towards two very large, black horses, who raised their heads.

Seeing this little human running for their paddock, squealing, they ran the other way, bucking and throwing their heads around. Emily stopped and began to cry.

'Emily! This way, Princess.' Tom scooped her up and gave her a cuddle. 'Those are just a little too big and playful for you yet. Come and see what I have in your size.' Walking back past Beth, Tom reached for her hand, leading the way towards the stables.

Inside, Beth slowed to give her eyes time to adjust to the dimmed light of the stables. Walking directly ahead, Tom's boots clicked on the cement. Beth was taken back as she looked around the large building. It looked just like Drake's but only bigger and newer. A few horses hung their heads over the stable doors and nickered to Tom as he walked past. Hay, horses and horse poo filled her senses, but it wasn't offensive. In a weird way, it was comforting.

This was Tom 's world. This was the world he had wanted and told her about. Not his father's property or cropping, but this. Her mind began to spin in what had changed his father's mind to let Tom have this world. To buy Reggie's property, especially off of Drake, when Mathew had been so adamant that Tom's future was Silverleigh and the O'Loughlin empire. It had been made very clear that nothing else would be allowed. Something had drastically changed between father and son and Beth had a deep sinking feeling of knowing—maybe it had something to do with her.

Emily's excited thrill drew Beth from her thoughts. In a little area just outside the stables, she found Tom saddling a little pony that looked like something out of an American country and western movie with Indians. It had brown and white patches all over it and it was eating happily while Emily jumped around.

'Meet Squirt.' Tom rubbed the horse's hind quarters. 'He is a new addition I purchased about a month ago.'

Beth was hesitant about Emily getting on a horse, and it showed in her pretty features as she leaned on the fence railing. 'Is he safe for her to ride?' Coming over to her and relaxing his arms over hers, Tom leaned in and stole a kiss. When she didn't pull back, her thoughts still mildly on Emily and Squirt, he lengthened the kiss, sending a tingle all over her body. Drawing back, when he smiled against her lips, he knew he had broken down her walls she had put back up again that morning. Adjusting his cap, his smile widening as he stepped back and picked up Emily. Tom cleared his throat and tickled Emily, who was all but leaping out of her skin.

'I would never do anything to hurt Emily *or* you.' His meaning was clear.

For the next hour, Tom walked Emily and Squirt around the little arena and out along a little shaded path and back again. Emily never stopped talking or wiggling. Both Squirt and Tom had much more patience than Beth. She had never seen Emily so animated.

After finishing her ride with some protesting, and bribing Emily to feed some of the other horse's hay and even giving Squirt a bath, Emily was covered in wet horsehair and soap. She was loving every minute of it. Tom was too. He never pressed Beth for conversation. He would touch or kiss her every time he was near, but that was it.

At first, she tried to push her body's reaction aside, but her body and mind wouldn't let her. With each touch, look and movement of his body, Tom was stirring her desire for him. And he bloody knew it. She could see it in his eyes. The kisses were slowly getting longer, and his hand touches were more frequent. The embers were igniting. As much as she tried to fight it, she couldn't. But she needed to. She had to tell him she was leaving in a few days. Doing what she so desperately wanted with him, was only going to complicate things more than they already were.

As the sun rose to its peak in the sky, Tom surprised them both to a picnic lunch he had made by himself, suggesting they take it down by the river to eat. Her mother had been very sneaky and packed both Beth's and Emily's togs. After a quick change, holding hands tightly, Tom led the way to the river that flowed through his land.

The walk was calming. As much as it could be with Tom so close. Emily walked along in front, stopping every couple of metres to look at something she had found or saw, or to ask a question. Beth's hands were full of 'special' rocks and leaves Emily had found, and Tom even held a gumnut that she was sure the gumnut babies used to live in before it fell from the tree.

The water flowed over rocks and through small narrow passes, making bubbling and gurgling sounds. Birds chirped and sang as they went about their business of collecting food for their newly hatched babies, or spiderwebs and sticks to protect and secure their nests. It was a beautiful, warm day, made only better by being there with Tom.

Finally making it to the spot where Tom suggested they could eat and have a swim; Beth was more settled in her emotions. She was still unsure of what to say, but in her mind, Tom would understand and not take her leaving as badly as last time—like Kate had said he did.

Lunch was simple but nice. He had done his research via her mum or Kathryn, she guessed. Vegemite sandwiches, grapes cut in half, and Arnott's Chicken Crimpy biscuits for Emily, were packed along with cold meat sandwiches and soft drinks for Beth and himself. Emily sat right next to Tom—her absolute new favourite person in the world—who was stretched out on his side on the blanket, his head resting on his hand. She was hand feeding him her cut grapes. Beth laughed when he screwed up his face and complained about her fingers tasting like vegemite. To that, he was told to shoosh and eat his fruit; it was good for him. Emily then proceeded to push another one into his already full mouth.

'I know where she gets her bossiness from,' Tom teased after he had finally swallowed all his grapes.

To Beth's surprise, Emily snuggled down on the blanket beside Tom and went to sleep. Something she rarely did. Beth lazed beside her with her eyes closed, the sun too good not to lay out under its heat. She heard Tom move and then water gently splashing. He had gone to swim laps like he used to in school. She could hear the rhythmic sound of his strokes back and forth across the river, lulling her to sleep.

Swimming laps had not been what Tom had wanted to do that afternoon with Beth; however, it was what was needed. Beth's behaviour today was withdrawn and reserved from him, like she had been at the funeral and at her mother's house when he had first arrived to have dinner with them.

The woman in his arms last night was not with him today, and his frustration at not being able to read her like he used to, was getting to him. He had thought, and desperately hoped, that by bringing her out to his place, away from everyone and all interruptions, she would begin to open up and talk to him. To finally tell him what had happened, what he had done three years ago to make her run and cut all communication with everyone in her life. He had been through that day and all the ones leading up to it all a million times in his head, but still he was no closer to what had happened to her to cause her to run the way she did— and neither was anyone else. Kathryn, Drake and Susan, no matter how or what they said or asked of her, they all knew no more than he did. Whatever had happened, whatever he had done wrong, she still did not trust him enough to tell him.

With each stroke through the water, Tom's thoughts travelled to the night before and how at the start Beth had been worried about people gossiping about her return to town and being with him. She seemed better after talking with Kate and then, when she was welcomed, quite literally back with old friends, she was the Beth he remembered again, but with more confidence than he had ever seen. Remembering how she had put Katrina and Mackenzie in their place and then laid her claim to him in such a public display had made him believe whatever had caused her to run, was now not as powerful as it had been, that she could see that whatever had made her run, was now not there. She was safe and protected with him and her true friends. She could trust him, no matter what.

Doing yet another somersault as he swam, Tom tried to understand. He tried to keep his emotions at bay—and calm so she didn't flee again. If Beth could see that all he wanted was her, no matter what, no matter what had happened in the past, then surely, she would tell him what he had done wrong so he could learn and didn't risk losing her again. That she would stay. Both she and Emily would stay. Her mother would love them both being here and it would help Susan in her sadness and grief over her husband's death. Beth and Emily being here was where they belonged. Here with him.

She was confusing the hell out of him with her contrasting emotions and fear that kept creeping up and blocking her getting close to him. His frustration swelled within him. Fighting it down, Tom turned and swam back across the river. Nearing the bank, a little splash near the water's edge signalled his laps were over.

The walk back to the house was quiet. Emily had played in the water a little but was very teary and clingy with Beth. The last few days were catching up with her, and she didn't want to walk or explore on the way home, instead clutching to Beth's neck as they followed the path back. Tom had offered to take her, but Emily had cried and buried herself into Beth more. Taking the bags in one hand and Beth's hand in the other, Tom led them back along the path, helping her to step over rocks and roots so she didn't trip or fall.

Squirt saw them walking back up the lane and trotted up with a neigh and a snort. Emily lifted her head and gave a little giggle but then rested her head back on Beth's shoulder. Her little arm outstretched for her new friend, but she was just too tired to do anything more. The little pony continued to prance and neigh, following them as they walked around the fence and up the little walkway between the paddocks to the driveway. Horses on the other side of the lane trotted over to see what all the fuss was about from the little pony. Once they saw there was no food or treats, they went back to eating grass. Not impressed.

The noise Squirt was making disguised the noise of the vehicle coming up the driveway. It was nearly on top of them before Tom and Beth noticed, startled a little by the scarlet Landcruiser when it stopped directly in front of them, its tinted black windows blocking out who was inside. With a firm squeeze on Beth's hand, his eyes not meeting hers, Tom stepped slightly in front of her—not that it looked like that to the person in the ute. It would have looked like Tom was stepping closer to the vehicle to talk to the occupant. The window slid down, and Beth's heart stopped. Her stomach rolled and lurched, nearly causing her to lose its contents as her knees and entire body began to shake. Instinctively, she covered Emily's face and held her little girl as close to her body as she could.

Mathew O'Loughlin sat in the driver's seat.

Tom's father looked at the scene directly in front of him, his eyes going down the length of Beth's body. She instantly felt dirty. With only her bikini top on and a towel wrapped around her waist, Beth felt panic rising within her—fast. Her hands started to shake violently and her heart beat so fast and hard, it felt like it was ready to burst out of her chest. Schooling her features, she kept her emotions from showing, as Mathew looked her up and down again, mentally undressing her right in front of his own son. Tom cleared his throat and Mathew looked from Beth to Tom and then at Emily. No surprise showed in his face, but Beth saw the flicker in his eyes as his mind worked overtime.

'Dad,' Tom stated dryly, all emotion void from his voice.

'Tom.'

'What are you doing here? You know the rules. So, what do you want?'

'To check on you. I came out two afternoons ago, after no one could get hold of you, and you were gone. Then yesterday too. Just wanting to make sure MY boy was okay.' Mathew looked at Beth as he emphasised the word 'my'. She stepped back just a fraction and then mentally cursed herself. Mathew saw the movement for what it was, and his eyes flickered. One corner of his mouth lifted just a fraction with satisfaction of her retreat from him.

'I don't need to tell you where I was.'

'I can now see where you were.' Mathew turned his focus to Beth. 'Did you have a good night last night? I heard you pair left earlier than everyone else.'

With her teeth gritted, Beth ignored him and shifted Emily to her other hip, as far away from Mathew as she could without retreating. Emily reburied her face into Beth's neck. Her daughter didn't like Mathew, and Beth couldn't blame her. Emily had such a great sense of people, and her shyness and fear for the man in the ute, just proved that both Beth and Emily were right about Mathew O'Loughlin.

His hand on her hip, Tom turned his back to his father and faced Beth, essentially blocking Mathew's view of Beth and Emily. Tom was not pleased with his father's sudden arrival—it showed in the depths of his eyes. 'How about you go up to the house?' He could feel Beth's tension and the difficulty that carrying Emily was having on her. 'I will be up in a minute.'

Before Beth could move, Tom leaned in and kissed her on the cheek. Her stomach dropped and she thought she was going to be sick or faint as all the colour drained from her face. Mathew had just witnessed his son's tender moment with her. The truth that one small action just spoke, made his eyes flare with rage at her. He was furious at Beth for being there with Tom, and Mathew made damn sure Beth saw his displeasure behind his son's back, as Tom stroked her daughter's head tenderly.

Beth walked up to the house without a word being spoken to either of them. She stayed focused on each trembling step in front of her, fearful of falling with her shaking, weak legs. Leaving Tom with his father, she got away from the man that now made her skin crawl and panic rise so painfully within. Beth's heart began to physically ache with fear. Her focus strongly on the white cottage home, she never looked back.

Mathew drove away from her steady and careful track to the house and pulled up closer to the stable. She heard him as he got out, and felt the daggers in her back when he watched her go. Even Emily turned back to face the front so she couldn't see Mathew glaring at them. As both men walked into the stables and through into the machinery shed, their boots on the cement gave not only their destination away, but also the frustration and tension they were both feeling. Beth tried to settle her racing heart and breathe normally as she opened the door into Tom's home.

Having gotten changed for their swim in the stables, much to Tom's confusion as to why Beth wouldn't go near his house, Beth now entered the home Tom had created for himself. But the second she entered through the main door, her eyes swelled with tears, and she covered her mouth to stop the little sob that tried to escape.

Tom's home was beautiful—and bigger than she had realised. From the front, it had not changed structurally since Reggie had owned it. Tom had painted the front exterior and cleaned up the cottage to give it a beautiful look, but now Beth realised the extent of the renovations Tom had done to extend the back of the home.

Walking in, there was an office to the one side and a media room to the other. Following the short hall, which opened into a large, open plan kitchen, dining and living space, Beth found the kitchen of her dreams. It was a luxury country kitchen with a very large island in the middle.

Emily wriggled out of Beth's arms and wandered into the living space, finding a large toybox and a set of toy stables with horses—all pink. Tom must have had them for when Megan and her girls came to visit. Emily squealed with delight and sat down, not knowing what to play with first.

Setting the bags on the bench, Beth explored the kitchen, running her hand along the granite countertop, which was cool to her touch. The gloss white cabinets and six-burner stove stood gleaming in the lights hanging from a beautiful light fixture above the bench. Exploring further, she found a large butler's pantry hidden behind the kitchen, that was like stepping into a dream. Megan or another girl must have helped him with the design. Beth stopped that thought at the jolt of jealousy it produced immediately. She didn't want to know if Tom had had another woman here. That was none of her business. Though the thought still hurt.

Exploring the rest of his home, she found three bedrooms. Two had beds in them, the other was empty. She had seen at the other end of the house just past the kitchen, Tom's bedroom, but she was not going to venture in there, no matter how tempting.

The sun had set, and it was now dark. Beth had bathed Emily and had found some little sausages and salad for her to eat. Emily had nibbled on them but not eaten much before she had curled up on the couch and gone to sleep almost instantly. The long busy days of the last few weeks had finally caught up with her. She had even whinged and cried as Beth had bathed and tried to feed her. Emily was just so exhausted.

Sitting outside on the steps in the dark, Beth could see the lights in the stables still glowing. Her nerves were raw, and she still felt sick. Mathew O'Loughlin had brutally threatened her to stay away from Tom or else his consequences would be followed through. But now, here she was, not only with Tom, but at his property—in his house.

Mathew would piece together what he thought was going on and come up with her spending the night and possibly even being here permanently. He had obviously heard about her bold declaration of claiming Tom as hers last night, and it was most likely his reason for being out here this afternoon. His anger was clear to her when his suspicions were found to be true. She knew for sure—she was now never going to be able to end things again with Tom—nicely. There was now never a reason for her to return here, even if her mother was to remain in town. Mathew would follow through with his threats. Once Beth brutally broke Tom's heart like she was now going to be forced to do, she would never be welcomed back to River Flats—and she couldn't blame any of them. She wouldn't want to see her face back here either.

Her hands still shaking at what was to come, she felt her own heart breaking at who she had to become to make everything all right because of her own selfish choices. She was not that person. She didn't intentionally hurt anyone. She did all she could to protect them, but they would never understand. Beth had known that her leaving without a word last time was going to hurt her parents and Tom—and possibly others—but what she didn't know or understand was the amount of hurt that her choice had actually caused.

Looking back now, that summer was only meant to have been some fun with Tom, and nothing more. A last bit of joy and freedom before being an adult, working hard to chase her dreams and living the life she had envisioned. However, after leaving, Beth knew in herself that that summer of fun had become more for her. In fact, that summer had made her view of the world completely different, and she had relished in the fact of leaving and getting away from all she had endured because of her love for Tom. Yes, even though she had told herself it was nothing more than a fling for him; it was real love for Beth, and she had paid with her mind, body and soul for that love. Kate's words had finally brought the truth of what that summer had meant for the both of them. The real truth of Tom's feelings and those she had tried to deny or not even think about.

Tom had truly loved her, and if she allowed herself free rein of her thoughts and what his actions told her, he was still very much in love with her now. Her own sadness and longing for him in those weeks and months after she had left, meant she felt just as much as he did. But she couldn't go back to him. She couldn't call or contact him. No matter how hard it had all become, no matter the tears and heartbreak, she knew she couldn't. So, Beth locked herself away from any kind of love, except the love she had for Emily. The hurt was just too much to bear again.

Being here now, letting herself think they could be friends, she now understood her vital mistake. Telling herself friendship was something they could do, that friendship was okay, and her heart could cope with being friends with Tom. It was meant to have been easy. But the lines had become blurred, and they had slipped back into something that resembled a relationship—and a promising one at that.

Last night, she had laid her claim to him. And now, tonight she would have to take all those unspoken promises back and hurt him beyond words, and they would have to become strangers in this world, never to be anything but two passing souls walking this earth.

Feeling sick, Beth watched Tom and his father's shadows move within the stables. Anger built. Why wasn't she good enough for Tom in Mathew O'Loughlin's eyes—for her love and commitment to Tom to mean more than money and status? Why did he see her as a piece of dirt? Love and commitment was what made a life happy and fulfilled. To know that you're doing what you love, for and with the people who truly love you, just for who you are and not what you can give them socially or materialistically. Love was something freely given and not bought or manipulated or chased as a prize. It was pure, innocent and magical.

But what did that matter? She couldn't give Tom anything now—or risk him even thinking she could. Mathew would certainly carry through with his threats if she didn't destroy Tom's heart enough for him to finally let her go for good. But to do that, tonight Beth had to try and make Tom hate her as much as she possibly could. And the first step in this heartbreaking process, was to let him go.

Raised, heated and angry voices drifted to her. Straining to hear what was being said more clearly, Beth tried to understand who and what was being said. She couldn't. Her stomach sank a little more as she heard metal hit the wall of the stables. Her first reaction was to go and make sure Tom was okay, but her feet wouldn't move. She was scared of what she would find or what she knew was being said. Before she could force her feet to move, Mathew O'Loughlin walked out of the stables and looked directly her way before getting into his ute, slamming the door and starting the engine. His spotlights, on high beams, blinded and stung Beth's eyes as he spun the ute around and drove off down the driveway.

Beth knew she shouldn't have been there. Tom's place was not where she was meant to be. She needed to go back to her mother's house and pack. Her mother would be okay; she would have to be. Beth's time here in this middle-of-nowhere town had come to an end and now she needed to take her daughter and herself back to the city, find herself a new job—since she lost hers when she came to her father's funeral—and move on with her life. She had to let Tom go and live his own life without her. She also had to let that summer long ago become a distant memory. She was causing pain for too many, and more for herself.

The lights in the stables turned off and she could see Tom's dark shadow slowly walking towards the house. How was she meant to do what she had to do? To hurt him so much that he would only ever think of her with hatred. He didn't deserve this.

Tom was a good man and now she had to be the evil one. Some part of her screamed to tell him all. Everything about what had happened and beg him to forgive her for what she had done that afternoon at his family's summer party. But another part screamed and begged her not to. Too many others would be hurt if the truth was ever to be known. No, it was better that she was the villain in this story. Everyone else would be safer that way.

Seeing him run his hand through his hair and over his face told her that he was frustrated and possibly very upset at what had just transpired in the stables. The need to hold him grew strong, but Beth remained where she was, her hands gripping the glass of water in her hands tightly so she couldn't reach out and touch him. She leaned back into the shadows on the stairs, not knowing why. He would see her once he stepped onto the path leading up to the front steps. Maybe it was for safety. Maybe she hoped that while she was hidden by the shadows, it would prolong the inevitable.

Too late. The movement lifted his head as he walked directly to her. He didn't stop at the bottom step. Instead, he stepped up the two and leaned in and kissed her lips. Beth pulled away, leaning back, but Tom followed her retreat, his knees coming to rest on the step just below the one she was sitting on. His body was over hers as he took what he desperately needed from her.

She had been sitting there waiting for him. Just her being there gave him peace like no one else ever had. He could kiss her all night long if he wanted to, and now there was not a thing she or anyone else could say about it. He wanted and needed her for his next breath. What he desired from her right now, he needed more than her kiss. He needed her all night long.

Kissing her deeper, Tom followed Beth down as she tried to retreat away from him. His temper, still heightened from his long, heated discussion with his father, flared and turn to irritation, hurt and anger about her refusal to tell him all he wanted to know. All the whys he had had to live with for the past three years. He wanted them; and he wanted them now. He would not take her back to her mother's house until she told him all he wanted to know.

It was not what he had planned but now, as he kissed her breathlessly, his temper simmering with everything he was unable to control, Tom domineered the kiss and wanted the answers to all his questions. And he wanted to have what he believed they still had between them before she had left him in the dead of night.

Beth pressed her hands to his chest as Tom leaned her back until she was painfully pressed against the sharp edge of the timber steps just above where she had decided to sit half an hour ago. His lips hard against hers, he was unrelenting with need and hunger. He was taking more then she could give him and still, he demanded she give him more.

Pushing again, Beth struggled to gain a breath in the kiss, and her lungs began to burn. Desperately, Beth pushed her hands harder against him. Tom moved back just enough for her to breathe more easily. Repositioning his lips on hers, he pulled her against his chest and let his hands roam freely over her back and done to cup her bottom. Her little moan in the back of her throat made the corners of his lips lift, feeding his male ego.

Beth was all heat and passion. Wanting and needing him like she always did, her mind reeled against her actions, but his hands stopped all her thoughts. The roughness of his callused hands drifted up to cup her breast. She could feel her heart pounding in her chest, her hands shaking as she touched his. She gently pushed them away. Tom lifted his head and looked into the depths of her eyes. Beth watched his heart constrict.

Not letting what she just saw be acknowledged, Tom's gravelly voice harshly growled at her, 'I have been wanting to do that all day.'

Recapturing her lips, not letting her speak, Tom lessoned his demanding need, and this time, when he kissed her, her body gave a little shiver. Wrapping her arms around him, her tongue darting into his mouth before returning. He followed hers and together they danced.

The embers that had been smouldering all day, began to burn, lighting a flame that was set to overtake them if left unchecked. Sliding his hand up her thigh and under her dress, Beth sat up straighter, her beasts now pressed tighter to Tom's chest, her hands in his hair, holding him to her.

The power of who was leading whom, and who needed whom the most, changed with each touch, with fear and anger an undercurrent to their moods, but in different ways. Beth tried to soothe it for them both, but the more Tom kissed her, the more it grew. He was becoming more needy with each kiss. Passion, mixed with the desperate undercurrent, made her nerves leap and turn from passion to fear. A haunting fear of the past—and memories. Tom's hand squeezed Beth's thigh a little painfully, and he morphed into someone else for a second. Beth's fear locked her body, and she suddenly felt sick and scared.

Moving just slightly so she could break the kiss and move away, Tom reacted and gripped her thigh harder just near her heated juncture. She let out a little cry of pain and anxiety and he let her go, rocking back away from her, his eyes showing that he hadn't meant to hurt her and was shocked at his own actions.

Beth's heart squeezed at what she saw, and at the same time a part of her mind reminded her that if she was going to end it tonight, like she now had to, kissing Tom was not what she should be doing.

Tom stood and took her hand.

With her eyes filling with tears she wouldn't let fall, Beth pulled her hand away from his and looked away before darting back to meet Tom's eyes.

'We need to talk.' Those four simple words hit hard. Her tone and her eyes said everything he never wanted to hear from her. Tom's jaw tightened and pulsated as he nodded and walked past her up the steps.

'At least let me shower first.' Opening the screen door, Tom walked in, letting it close behind him. Beth closed her eyes as her heart started to harden. She needed it to turn to cold, hard stone for what she was about to do.

An icy chill crept up and over Tom's skin as anger burned low within him. His shower didn't give him any perspective either. He had walked in and seen Emily sleeping on his couch, her little hands tucked under her chubby little cheeks, and her little blonde curls, so much like her mother's, fell all around her.

Walking over and gently smoothing away the locks from her face, he studied her. Thick eyelashes and her porcelain skin gave her an angel look. Somehow, over the last few days, this little girl had stolen his heart—just like her mother had three years earlier. He was not going to let them go without a fight, but something in Beth's tone gave him the chills. He didn't want to hear anything else from her beautiful lips, except how she was staying and the truth of why she ran all those years ago. He couldn't feel pain like that again. He wouldn't survive. He would follow Beth and her daughter anywhere she wanted to go, just to be with them. He needed to approach this with care and a cool, calm head.

Beth heard the shower turn off as she piled salad and the sausages on a plate for them both. Not that she wanted to eat. She would probably be sick if she did, but it had kept her hands and mind semi busy as she waited for Tom to finish his shower. Waited to hurt him beyond repair.

'Mmm ... that looks good.' Beth's heart stopped, and her mouth went dry. Tom was padding past her in only a lose pair of jeans that hung very low on his hips. 'Forgot my towel,' he stated with a little grin. His skin was wet and glistened in the light. His muscles rippled and flexed naturally as he walked. His body had changed and hardened over the years, into something that now made Beth's mouth dry and other areas super wet.

In the dark the other night, she had noticed but didn't really see it until now. He was heated muscle, flesh and bone. Her hands tingled as heat pooled low in her stomach. This was not helping her. She needed to cool herself down and get her mind back onto what she was about to do. Washing her hands, the cool water only cooled them as thoughts of touching Tom heated the rest of her.

Seeing Beth in his kitchen made Tom smile. He had designed it for her, even knowing she may never see it. He had held out hope that one day she would come back, and they would sort things out and be together. He had planned all the house renovations just for her, recalling all she had ever said—every little snippet of information they had spoken about—and he had put it all together to create a home just for her. As morbid as it sounds, when he found out her father had cancer, he had been upset, but he had hoped the news would bring Beth home. Home to her parents. Home to him.

Wrapping his arms around her waist as she washed her hands, she tried to move but he locked her to him, kissing her neck. Through her dress, Tom could feel her warmth against his now dry, bare chest. It comforted him and he began to sway and move. Her hips pressed to his, he took her hand, twirling her around under his arm, and bringing her back to him, face to face. Her cold hands against his hot skin, sent tingles throughout his body and her little laugh calmed his soul.

Pressed to the length of each other, Tom continued to sway. Beth's eyes smiled up at him, and he remained staring into hers as he moved her backwards, her body bumping into the large, island bench. Bending at his knees, his eyes still on her, Tom lifted her to sit on the granite countertop. Beth's shriek made him smile as she dug her nails into his shoulders to hold onto him.

With breaths mingling and hearts racing, Tom placed his hands on Beth's cheeks and kissed her. Lightly at first. Tender and tasting, only opening her mouth enough to nibble and nip at her bottom lip. Her hands clung to his wrists as she let him melt her, slowly and seductively. The embers from before lit up and burned her slowly from deep within, from where Tom's hands were holding her, to low and deep within her body. He was going to set her body on fire if he continued to kiss her like this.

Creating a haze over her mind, Tom continued stealing everything from her until her world consisted of nothing else but his lips on hers. One of his hips pressed against the inside of her knee and he pushed. She opened her legs, allowing him to step in between them. His bare stomach was now pressed inches away from where her thighs met. His body's heat fuelled the already scolding area as his tongue darted into her mouth, and she let out a little moan. Tom smiled against her lips and did it again. Beth sagged against his hands as he stripped her of all her built up reserves against him, and still he kissed her deeply, causing her to lose all thought.

Tom was hanging onto Beth for dear life. He couldn't move his hands. He needed her for his every breath. Nothing else seemed to matter but her. He knew he had questions, but he couldn't remember them. He knew they needed to talk but couldn't find the words. Only that he needed her to breathe. Her hands on his told him she needed him the same way. Without each other, they would never survive.

Moving his hand, he touched her ear, gently stroking the softness of it. Then, with a butterfly touch, he trailed down her neck along her slender shoulder, lower still, finally finding what he was after. Tom gave it a gentle squeeze and she broke away, sucking in her breath. Beth's eyes were heavy lidded and unfocused. He squeezed again and she pulled him back into another kiss—heat, fire and need.

Pushing his other hand to her other breast, Beth dropped her hands back behind her body to steady herself. His lips parted from hers so he could watch. Finding her already erect nipples, Tom rolled them through her dress until they pebbled in his fingers. Her head fell back with a moan as he worked, her hair falling like a waterfall behind her. Letting go, he leaned in and nibbled her neck, his hands tangling in the waterfall of waves. He glimpsed Emily sleeping on his couch. His body cooled.

'Let's take this elsewhere.' Without waiting for her to respond, Tom lifted her.

Beth's legs wrapped around his waist as she kissed him deeply, seemingly not wanting to have the heat they had created before to cool. Walking them blindly into his bedroom, Beth didn't notice any of the furnishings or his clothes laying over the floor and chair in the corner. She didn't notice the large bed or its soft blankets. And she didn't even notice that the one picture they both had of each other, was now framed and sitting on his bedside table.

Tom was all she could focus on. His touch. His strong arms, wrapped under her dress, carrying her confidently to his bedroom. Her lace underwear was the only barrier between his touch and her pleasure. It was erotic. Getting close to the bed, Tom tumbled onto the soft mattress, rolling himself off her body. Beth gave a little giggle and followed him over. Finding his lips, she captured him again. His arms tightened around her. His leg bent as hers fell between them. She positioned her knee at his groin and applied a little pressure, driving him crazy. Twisting again, he rolled her on her back, her hair falling like a halo around her. His arms stretched out, and he hovered above her and drank in the sight.

Tom's eyes told her it all. He was an open book to her. She could see the passion and desire. She could see the hurt and vulnerability. She could see the love and devotion, and she couldn't look at him anymore. She turned her head, feeling the lump in her throat growing at the memories that flooded back to her. She remembered what she had to do. She couldn't let this happen.

His finger touched the side of her face gently and turned her head so she was forced to look at him. 'I know,' was all he whispered before he lowered his lips slowly and kissed her deeply.

The fire from before had cooled but now took hold and leaped to a raging inferno. Reaching behind her back, Tom unzipped her dress and slid it down over her shoulders. She wriggled so her arms were freed, and the dress was now wrapped around her waist. Unclipping her bra, but not moving it, Tom instead branded hot kisses to mark a path from her shoulders to the top mounds of her breasts. With a one-finger tug in the middle of her bra, he licked between her breasts. Her hands tangled in his hair and she gripped onto him as he repeated it again and again, slowly and heated. Her body shivered and goosebumped all over. Kissing his way to her left breast, he suckled her tender flesh. Beth arched and pressed her breast into his mouth where he sucked her so deep, it hurt with pleasure. Her little cries filled his ears and the room around them.

Finally releasing it, he turned his attention to her other one. His onslaught was spinning her out of control. Clawing at him, his name was repeatedly on her lips as she arched and bucked underneath him. Tom's own need was straining against his jeans. With only the hard denim on, his sensitive parts were rubbing against his zipper so painfully that he was sure that when he finally removed the denim from his body, he would not be able to satisfy her as he would be too injured. But as Beth begged him for more, Tom put the pain out of his mind and set his full attention back onto the woman in his bed, breathlessly whispering his name.

Removing her bra, Tom slowed his movements and gently kissed each tender and purple, tortured nipple. They were flushed, aching and swollen from his attention. Slipping his hand up Beth's thigh, he kissed her back into nothing but a wanting mess.

With the movement of her hips rolling up to meet his hands, he broke away from the kiss and watched her facial expression closely, waiting for the moment he touched her. His hand found her heated mound. He squeezed roughly before slipping beneath her delicate material. Her eyes fluttered closed then opened as he witnessed how truly lost in their molten depths, and in her, he truly was.

Heavy lidded, she licked her dry lips. His eyes followed the movement as his fingers slid over her heat. It had a slight prickle to it, only adding to the sensation for them both. Beth was hot and wet and pulsating as his thumb stroked her little mound. She nearly lost control on him instantly. Sitting up, she wrapped her arms around his neck and took his lips hostage against hers.

'Tom. Please *Please!!!*' she repeated over and over between her kisses. Hanging from him, she forced him to lock himself into position so he didn't fall over. He was after all only balanced on his knees and one arm. Entering a finger deep inside her, Beth contracted around him. A groan rasped from deep within Tom's throat and vibrated out against her ear, sending her body into more spasms and goosebumps.

'Do you want me, Beth?' She tried to focus on his words as he fingered her deeply. He added another finger, and her world receded. She was trying to cope with the intensity of the pressure and the sensations rocking through her body.

'Do you want *ME*, Beth?' he asked again against her ear. His harsh whisper tickled her and sent even more shivers over her body. She heard him clearly this time. Looking deep into his eyes, she fought against the insane plundering of her senses and nodded vigilantly. Her breath was heavy, her chest heaving with the emotion of all he was doing, taking and asking. The weight of his question drilled into her mind. He needed her to need him. He needed to hear that she wanted him as bad as he wanted her—and she did. She wanted it all with him. Everything. She wanted to be with him forever. Beth stopped the thought before it could spill out over her lips. His gaze penetrated into her.

'Say the words. Say you want me. I need to hear it from your lips, Beth' he gritted out. The rough, strangulated sound told her how desperate he was.

'I want you, Tom. Only you ... it's only ever been you,' she whispered, breathlessly.

Tears threatened, and Tom saw. He truly saw everything she had in her heart for him. Slowing his movements and need just a little, he kissed her long and hard as he continued to bring her near the peak of release she was begging for. Two tears slid out of her eyes, and he kissed them away, the truth of her words being too much to bear. He had gotten the truth from her—the one, and really *only*, truth that mattered. And he rejoiced that she could see it in his eyes as he brought her higher to the peak. Her body tensed and she was ready to fall over the edge, but Tom stopped and withdrew his hand. Beth looked up into his face, panting, as he kissed her quickly and stood.

Unbuttoning his jeans carefully, he let them drop as he watched her face. He saw her swallow and run her tongue over her lips as she looked him up and down. Pulsating under her stare, he waited. He wanted her to beg him, to reach for him. Yes, it was his male ego, but he wanted to know for sure her words were true. That through all this time apart, it was still him—Tom O'Loughlin—she wanted. Needed.

Tom still stood there in all his glory. Totally naked and beautiful as Beth moved to the edge of the bed. Still, he did not move. They just stared at each other. No words were spoken.

Swinging her legs over the side of the bed slowly, her dress falling to the floor, Beth stood and took two steps to stand directly in front of him. He didn't reach for her, his arms locked tightly by his side, his eyes never leaving hers. She touched one finger to his chin and pulled his face around so that their eyes remained locked on one another as she walked around him. She let go and stepped behind him. He swung his head to the other side to watch her continue back to the front.

After a moment, she did—completely naked—and stopped right in front of him, allowing him to look down at her. Opening his mouth to speak, Beth stopped him by gently grabbing his pulsating rod before he could say a word. He hissed and pulled away at the contact. Satisfaction filled her.

'Do *you* want *me*, Thomas O'Loughlin?' Before she could finish her words, Tom picked her up and sat her on the edge of the bed, kneeling in front of her.

The seriousness in his eyes, and the depth of his soul that she saw, nearly made her cry as he replied gruffly, 'Let me show you.' His smile grew wolfish, and she let him see the shiver that streaked through her, causing his smile to grow even more as he pressed her back to the mattress with one hand. His mouth touched her where his fingers had been moments ago.

Beth cried out with the contact as Tom began to feast on her, suckling and licking, tasting and eating every part of her as her hands tangled in his sheets, her legs tightening around his head as explosive sensations rocked her. He licked and nipped at her little nub, causing her to cry out even more. The peak was coming so fast, she tried to drag him away.

'I want to feel you inside me when I go. Please drive me home,' she pleaded but he shook his head, burying deeper between her legs and feasting harder and faster. She was arching and bucking, but Tom held her still. Beth's body arched and rolled as her body rocked with the pleasure he was giving her. She was climbing faster and faster until she crested and fell over the peak with a cry of pleasure, release and satisfaction. Her legs squeezed Tom's head as he suckled her hard, drinking in all her juices. She fell limp to the bed, her body spasming as she floated like a feather back down to earth.

Her body like liquid gold, Beth felt Tom lift her. Her legs were over his arm, her head cradled against his chest. He placed her up the bed and crawled over her. Parting her legs for him, he entered her slowly. She was tender and still sensitive, but she needed to feel him deep within her. She was so tight from her contraction that Tom had trouble entering her. Waiting for her to relax, he kissed her slowly and gently, setting to work rebuilding the fires within her again as he nudged deeper and deeper within.

She scolded him and he had to use every little bit of restraint he had left not to embarrass himself. She moved her hips wider, and he plunged into her, groaning with a gravely cry. They made love frantically, and when he pushed them up and over the peak, Beth gripped onto Tom as their world shifted beneath them.

Together, they lay clinging to each other. Beth felt as if her bones were hot liquid and jelly, humming and sated. Using the last of his strength to shift off her, but not letting her go, Tom wrapped his arms around Beth so her back was to his chest. Bringing the sheet up to cover them both, he cradled her to him tightly. With his hand on her breast, his body was protectively and possessively wrapped to hers.

Tom drifted off to sleep nearly immediately after covering her. Beth slipped into an after-sex nap but then awoke and was listening to his steady breathing rhythm. She had not wanted this to happen. Her thoughts replayed his every touch, his every word and expression. He had begged her to want him, and she had. She had wanted him with everything she had. She still did. Not just physically but in every way a person could want another. She wanted it more now than she ever had. She wanted him more than she had ever let herself want him.

To lay beside him every night as she drifted off to sleep, and to wake up next to him each and every morning—that is what she truly wanted. Nothing else, just him.

Wiggling onto her back as he tightened his arm around her in his sleep, she could see his face in the dimmed light from the kitchen. She could see how beautiful he truly was. However, no matter how much she wanted him, she knew the truth. She couldn't have him, and she couldn't tell him the truth. She couldn't destroy that many lives. It had to be her life that she destroyed, but unfortunately that meant Tom's as well.

She should have stayed away. Stayed cold and detached. But she couldn't. He knew how to warm her, how to make her melt and lose all thought with just a look or touch. She was in love with Thomas O'Loughlin. She probably had been since she set her eyes on him across that muddy river. He had stolen her heart and given her his, and now she was going to have to rip them both in half permanently. Her eyes filled with tears, and she let them fall onto his pillow, crying silently trying to disguise her body shaking as she let her heart shatter into a million heartbreaking pieces.

Tom could feel Beth crying gently and quietly beside him as he awoke. Her warm, naked body pressed to his had stirred his desire awake. That desire had cooled the instant he felt her body shaking as she cried in his arms. Hauling her over to lay on his chest, she clung to him and cried more. Still silently, he felt her warm tears roll onto his skin.

'I wish you would tell me, Beth' he whispered and kissed the top of her head. She shook her head and tried to crawl into his chest where she knew it would be safe. Where they could be together all the time, protected and safe. More tears fell.

Tom held her and stoked her shoulder, his heart tightening as he felt hopeless. He had always thought he would push her for answers, but he had melted the moment he saw her in the church, trying to be brave and strong for her mother. She was always trying

325

to be brave for others, but with him, she seemed to just crumble and cry. To his male senses it meant she felt safe and protected with him, but if that were true then why did she not tell him the reason she had left? To him, anything that had happened back then couldn't stop what was happening now. Surely it couldn't prevent them from being together now. Sitting up, he needed to tell her how he really felt. Maybe that would help her understand and tell him.

Beth sat up with him, wiping her tears so Tom couldn't see them in the semi-darkness of the room, and lowered her head. She covered her breasts with the sheet as he wriggled so his body was facing her, his hand taking hers, so that if she ran, he could stop her. She needed to listen to him.

'Please just listen,' he whispered to her. 'I know there are things that have happened between us. I'm not sure what they were, but they were big enough to make you run from me.' He ducked his head to meet her eyes when she couldn't meet his. 'I know that you're very scared and unsure, but being here tonight, I think you know that I would never hurt you. I would never let anything or any—' Beth cut him off.

'No. Don't say it. Please don't.' Beth yanked her hand from his and rolled away off the bed, taking the sheet with her. 'Just take me home now, Tom.'

'Beth. Just stop.' Panic rose within him as he got out of bed, pulling on his jeans as he stumbled towards her. She was standing in the corner of his room, her back against the wall, watching him approach. She was like a startled deer. Her hands were shaking as fresh tears welled in her eyes and then streamed down her flushed cheeks.

'Just tell me what the hell it is I've done wrong,' he pleaded as he watched her look around him. 'For God's sake, you owe me that.' Try as he might, he couldn't keep the frustration from his voice. His panic and anger were taking over, and he was working hard to keep it all reined in.

'I know!' she yelled back, taking him back a bit. She cursed as they both remembered Emily sleeping on the couch next door. Taking a steady breath, she tried to stop herself from shaking. Something deep inside of her was breaking and tearing her apart and he began to feel his own heart begin to shatter.

'I know I do,' she whispered to him. He was now standing in front of her, holding her hips through the thin sheet, her whole body was shaking uncontrollably at what she was trying to say. The emotions racked her body. 'You deserve it all.' She raised her head and looked into his eyes, her own now overflowing with tears, blinding and blurring her vision.

A bump and scraping of a table being slightly moved across the hardwood timber floor, stopped Beth's words that were caught in her throat. The deathly scream that followed made them both run for the door.

Tom beat Beth to Emily's limp, scolding hot, tiny body. Something was definitely wrong. He looked up at Beth. 'GET DRESSED NOW!!' he yelled before he moved Emily's body from the cold floor of his home, back to the lounge chair. Her eyes were not focused as she let out a sudden scream and started to cry hard. She was rambling and incoherent. He couldn't work out her words. She seemed delirious. The bump on her head, from falling off the couch, was already a large, raised, purple egg on her forehead. Beth came running out from Tom's room, zipping her dress up, his shirt in her mouth.

'She needs a doctor. And now,' he called to her. Beth's face paled even more. 'Get a wet cloth to try and cool her.' Tom picked up Emily as he directed Beth on what to do.

Emily was limp in his arms. She had stopped crying and now seemed to be unable to keep her eyes from closing as she looked up to him with her big blue eyes. Her breath seemed to be shallow and wheezy. Tom knew he had to keep her awake. He tried talking to her as calmy as he could get his voice to sound soothing, but his heart was racing. He couldn't let panic overtake him. He had to stay calm and keep himself—and Beth—thinking straight.

'Emily? Emily? Princess? Please wake up for me. Open those beautiful eyes and show me your smile,' he repeated as he walked to the door with her in his arms.

Stepping onto the path, Emily gave out an odd little cry and moved. Tom only just managed to catch her before she vomited. He had moved fast enough that she missed his jeans and the boots he had managed to jam on his feet. Her little body shook and contracted with the effort. When she was finished, she fell back against his chest—white, hot and not moving.

Tom looked at her. He spoke and tapped her delicate little cheek a bit, but Emily didn't respond. He couldn't hear her breathing. His heart stopped as Beth let out a blood curdling scream. Tom kneeled to the ground and checked Emily's pulse. It was still there—faintly—but she was gravely ill. They needed a hospital and doctors now.

Chapter 18

Tom had never driven at that speed nor had he ever done a trip from his house to town so fast. He had made Beth sit in the front seat with Emily on her lap so he could keep an eye on both of them.

Beth was near hysterical. The only thing keeping her from breaking was Tom telling her to keep wiping the cold, wet cloth over Emily and talking to the limp body in her arms to keep her awake. Emily had fixed her eyes on him as he drove, and Tom spoke to her, his hand reassuringly holding hers when he could. But taking corners that fast required both his hands, and his full concentration, on the road. Emily hadn't cried, but she had kept her eyes solely on Tom in a deathly gaze he wasn't sure she was actually seeing through.

The River Flats hospital was small. It only had two doctors and about a dozen nurses, but they treated basic emergencies and illnesses. Anything more than that, required people to be driven to the next largest hospital. In extreme emergency cases, they would be flown out, which Tom was already organising in his head. If the medical helicopter couldn't get there in time, he would have the O'Loughlin plane ready in minutes if Emily needed it.

There was a small emergency room with parking directly out the front of the large, one-storey brick building. Tom pulled up at such a high speed, he nearly collected the bright yellow cement barrier pole on the sidewalk. Leaping out, he raced around and took Emily from Beth's arms.

'Go ahead and get help now!' he told her in a voice that had her moving without question. Kicking the door shut with his booted heel, he looked down at the little girl in his arms before kissing her head, avoiding her raised purple lump. 'You hang in there, my girl. I need help with the horses, remember? You can't leave me or your mum.' Tears welled in his eyes, but he pushed them down. He had to stay strong for both Emily and Beth. 'You got that?' He kissed Emily again as he entered the emergency room.

A nurse came running for him, Beth close behind. With a quick look at Emily, delicately turning her head from side to side and talking to her, the nurse slowed in her movements a little. Her panic abating, she spoke to Emily and even managed to get half a little smile out of her when she tickled her feet.

Looking up at Tom, she said, 'In here' then led the way through a large set of swinging, wooden doors. They walked down a little hall then into a small room with a bed and two chairs. The wall at the head of the bed had an array of little yellow and blue boxes screwed to it, filled with medical supplies. There was a little machine on the opposite side to where Tom stood holding Emily. The nurse walked to that side of the bed and said, 'Just lay her on the bed.'

'NOOOOOO!!!!!!!' Emily clung to Tom's shirt as he moved to lower her onto the white, sheet-covered mattress. Her tiny hands fisted into the material of his shirt he had slipped over his head after putting Beth and Emily in this ute. It was half unbuttoned, and Emily was now holding onto it with both hands, fighting to not be let go.

'It's okay, it's okay.' Tom tried to soothe her, but she wouldn't let go.

'It's okay, little one. If you want to stay there, you can.' The nurse pointed to the seat near the bed. 'How about you two cuddle here while I take a look at your head and see what's making you cook in your own juices. You're very hot, Sweetheart.'

Tom looked around the nurse to see Beth hovering, her arms wrapped tightly around her body, not sure what to do. Emily was gripping to him and not her. He could see the despair it was causing her, but didn't know what to do to help her.

Another nurse came in with a clipboard and pen. She stopped next to Beth and began asking details about Emily. Tom tried to focus on the nurse tending to Emily, but he found himself half listening to Beth speaking with the other nurse. He could hear little bits and pieces of Beth's conversation.

'Where was Emily born again? The city?'

'Yes. At 'The Royal.' Beth never took her eyes from Emily as she robotically answered the nurse's questions.

Tom missed the next couple of questions as the nurse, after asking Beth about any known allergens, gave Emily a needle. Emily had whimpered and clung to him. The nurse patted his shoulder when she was done.

'She will settle once that kicks in. The doctor's on his way.' She walked back around and started to fiddle with the machine. Tom's arms tightened around Emily as his attention locked back onto Beth. She was still focused on Emily and robotically answering. Her panic had subsided, but he could see her hands slightly shaking and her skin was still very pale. She was fighting shock.

'Sorry, when did you say?'

'12 August. She was roughly a month early.'

'Oh, okay. That explains why she is a little small for her age. If you could come with me to the office, we can finalise the rest of the paperwork.' The nurse looked over at the one now manoeuvring the machine around the bed to Tom and Emily. It was an unspoken look.

'Your daughter will be fine, Miss Kennedy. You will be back in a few minutes.' She took Beth's arm and helped steer her out of the room. Tom nodded reassuringly to her as he watched her being led away with the other nurse.

Walking back into the room, Beth saw Emily sound asleep, still laying in Tom's arms with her teddy snuggled to her chest. Her little cheeks were flushed with a now low-grade fever. Avoiding Tom's eyes, she stroked Emily's little curls from her face.

'She seems better now,' Beth rasped, ignoring Tom as he tried to catch her eyes, continuing to stare at the little bundle in his arms.

'Exactly how old is she, Beth?' Tom's voice seemed far away and didn't make sense. Beth's body was still locked tight, and her mind was still not focusing on anything else but Emily and how she had missed her being so sick. She had prided herself on being the mother who always knew when her child was sick or not feeling well. She ran through the last two days in her mind and now as she really thought about it, the signs were there—and Beth had missed them.

She had been too focused on herself and Tom that she had missed Emily getting sick. Guilt sank her heart and made her feel ill. Her stomach rolled and she became angry for letting herself lose focus on her beautiful daughter and for her real reason for being here in this town. She had come out to say goodbye to her father and support her mother, that was all. Once that was over, she was leaving. She had never planned to even talk to Tom, let alone allow what had happened between them over the last few days. If she had been focused, she would have picked up sooner that Emily was so sick. Then this—her precious baby girl would not be in a hospital hooked up to a drip and drugged to stop a severe fever. How could she have let this happen?

'Beth?'

'Not now. Okay? I just can't.'

'Can't what?' The tone in Tom's voice made her finally look at him. It was the first time she realised the tightly wound tension radiating from him. His words were spoken through gritted teeth and his eyes were burning into hers. He stood and placed Emily, sleeping, on the bed.

Something was wrong with him. 'What?'

'Right then.' The Doctor walked into the room. Beth and Tom were staring at each other. The tension in the room was thick but the thickly accented voice broke the spell. Tom shook his head and left the room, leaving both the doctor and Beth confused.

After the doctor left, Beth lay with Emily on the bed, her thoughts only on holding her little girl close to her. Emily was her world and nothing and no one else mattered. Her daughter was safe and would heal, and Beth needed to get her priorities right.

Beth woke a few hours later to the sound of Emily chattering. Stretching, she felt muscles she had not used in a while, protest. Her mind searched for the reason in her sleepiness.

Tom.

Their night together. Then the horror of it.

Beth's eyes flew open, and she sat up looking around her. Emily was sitting at the foot of the bed picking at some fruit and toast as she drew a picture with Susan. The drip was still attached but Emily looked a lot better.

It was still very early morning; the sun was only just starting to rise above the treetops outside the window, but the heat of the day was already penetrating through the thick glass of the only window in the room. Susan and Emily both looked at Beth. Emily's big smile told her that her daughter was feeling much better than Beth first thought.

'How did you know where we were?' Beth asked her mum as she shifted on the bed, so she was sitting close to Emily, but not close enough to stop her drawing her picture. Beth checked her forehead, making sure the fever had gone.

'Tom called last night and said that you needed me. He was gone and you two were sleeping when I arrived.'

Beth kissed the top of Emily's head; she did not reply to her mum's unvoiced question. 'So, you have been sitting here since?'

'Of course. You're my daughter and granddaughter. The most precious things in the world to me, though I didn't think to bring another set of clothes for either of you.' Susan smoothed Emily's hair and smiled at her colouring picture when she held it up for her inspection.

'How about I sit here and watch Emily while you go home and shower? That way you can bring everything Emily needs and be back before the doctor does his rounds.'

Beth hesitated. 'You need to freshen up and change your clothes. Vomit doesn't make for a good perfume.' Susan wrinkled her nose a little, then added, 'Have some breakfast while you're there. The food here is not up to your standard.' Susan winked as Beth took a smell of herself and had to agree with her mother.

Looking at Emily, she was unsure about leaving her. But her mum was right. She would need to get some clothes for herself and Emily. If she left now, she would be back before the doctor did his rounds in a couple of hours.

'My car is parked out front.' Her mum tossed her the keys and Beth caught them mid-air.

'Is that okay if mummy goes and has a shower and gets you some clothes, Bub?'

'Yep. Bring my horsey?' Emily never looked up from her picture.

'Yep, I will. You be good for Nanna and the nurses.' Nodding her head, Emily showed Susan her masterpiece then went back to doing the finishing touches.

Tom stepped up the last step onto the verandah. His jaw was aching with tension, his head swirling with questions that made his jaw clench tighter again. His body had turned cold, but he did not shake. He was deathly calm as his emotions and what he now knew was the truth rolled under the surface of his severe control.

His throat hurt from where he had screamed and yelled in hurt and anger, trying to remove all his frustration out of his body before coming here. His knuckles were cut up and two were swollen from repeatedly punching the timber post of the fence. He needed his control and to remain as calm as possible to extract the answers he needed.

On his drive home, he had replayed Beth's words over and over in his mind. He had to be wrong. He had to have heard her wrong, but with the feeling deep inside, he knew he wasn't. There was no other explanation. His calculations had to have been right. He had repeated her every action and every word in the conversations they had had over the last few days, and now her lack of words—or her very clever use of them—angered him to the point that he had needed to take it out on something. To pummel the shit out of something. So, instead of feeding the horses, Tom had taken all his emotions out on the post.

Continuing to punish the post, he had cried and screamed until he crumbled to the ground, still screaming as pain rocketed through his body. He had cursed and swore to kill anyone who ventured near him in that moment. Eventually, he had calmed and leaned against the post. Thinking about her and how everything now nearly made sense—nearly—Tom had driven to where he now was.

There was only one person who knew the truth—and the answers to all of his questions. He had thought he would hate her but try as he might, he couldn't. He only knew that there had to be something to make her do what she had done. To keep a secret like that, all this time.

Hearing the shower turn off as he reached the screen door, Tom reached out and tested the handle. It wasn't closed, he invited himself in and stood just inside the door to wait.

He didn't have to wait long. Beth opened the door, and all thought and emotion left his mind for a heartbeat. Beth emerged from the bathroom in a short satin dressing gown, her skin still dripping wet, making the garment stick to her body. It outlined her every curve and more. Every bloody damn curve he had touched and kissed last night. Every ounce of her, writhing beneath him as she took him deep within her body. Tom took a steadying breath to not only control his instant desire for her— but his temper too. It was a volatile mixture, and one that could lead them anywhere. Anywhere but the truth if he let her.

The movement scared her, and she jumped a little and screamed. 'Shit, Tom. You scared the hell out of me.' Beth touched a hand to her breast to quell her racing heart. 'What are you ...?' Her voice trailed off as Tom took a step towards her.

His eyes had turned black and cold. He walked towards her with an anger he had never felt within him. She took a step back as instinct kicked in. He was like a beast about to capture his prey that had eluded him for far too long. Seeing her retreat, Tom stopped halfway across the room.

As the clock on the wall ticked, so did his jaw as he reined in his temper—and need for her. He took another steadying breath as his eyes fixed onto Beth's and held.

'Is she mine, Beth?'

Beth stopped breathing for a second, and Tom saw the flicker of realisation in her eyes. She knew he knew ... she didn't say a word ... didn't move ... didn't break eye contact ... she had completely frozen.

'IS SHE MINE, BETH?' he roared at her. He had never yelled like that at a woman before, and he bit back the words as they started to come again. It took everything he had to stay rooted in his spot in the middle of her parents' lounge room and not tear the place apart with the raging tidal wave crushing over him. He could see the tears filling Beth's eyes as she flinched at his tone. But she never took her eyes from him as the wetness now rolled down her cheeks.

She slowly nodded her head and whispered, 'Yes.'

'Jaysus Christ, Beth. What the fucking hell?' He threw his hands up in the air, with such anger, it was vibrating from him. Beth began to violently shake in fear of him. He would never hurt her intentionally, but with her one whispered confession, he could now destroy her life forever.

'Why? Why would you do that to me?' His voice broke and she could see he was now fighting his own tears as emotions overtook him like nothing ever had. His heart was breaking and shattering into a million pieces right before her. Her own heart was aching as it too broke apart with the pain she was causing him. She had never wanted to cause him this much pain. She had never wanted him to find out at all. She couldn't risk the truth, but somehow, he had found out. Tom's heart was violently—devastatingly—shattering into nothing directly in front of her—all over her deliberate and forced lies. And now her secrets were doing everything she had fought so hard not to do.

She still did not move.

'Why Beth? WHY? I would have supported you. I would have never left you. For God's sake, why would you do that to me?' Those last words were gritted through his teeth as he fought with his raw and untamed explosion of hurt.

'I didn't know until after I had left, and then it was too late.'

'Too late? Too freaking late?' he roared again at her, 'You left hours after I dropped you home that night. You left a note to your parents, barely saying anything apart from that you couldn't stay and had to leave. That you would be in contact with them when you knew it was safe.' Tom frowned at Beth as he screamed at her. 'You left me nothing. NOTHING!!' He stepped forward, beating his chest. 'Did I really mean that to you? *NOTHING*. That we had nothing?'

'No,' she whispered.

'I went after you. Did you know that?' Beth shook her head. 'I looked for you for three bloody months. I searched every café and food venue for you. I showed your photo to everyone I walked past like a damn deranged psycho!' He turned and paced in the small space of the lounge room. 'Drake ended up finding me and dragging my ass home. Where the hell were you?'

'Packing shelves at midnight at Coles. It was the only job I could find, so ...' she trailed off as she unconsciously played with the bangle he had given her.

'... that you could find a way to hide if anyone should come looking for you?' he finished, scoffing and shaking his head.

'It wasn't like that, Tom. And don't you dare keep yelling at me or you can get the hell out.' Her bite made him stop pacing and look at her, running a hand through his hair and over his face.

'I was crazy out of my mind looking for you, Beth.'

'Do you think it was easy for me?' she suddenly roared back at him before taking an intimidating step towards him. 'I had to leave. Don't you get it? I had to do what I could. I had to find a place to live that wasn't in my car, and a job so that I could eat. Then I found out I was pregnant with Emily, and I knew that everything I had worked towards was gone. She was all I had left of you, and I had to protect her and everyone else. I worked two jobs through the week and mornings at a café on the weekends just to keep a roof over our heads and food on the table. I wanted to call you, but I couldn't. Don't you get that?'

Red hot temper rose within him, and he couldn't think straight. His words came out without thought. 'So, you only wanted to use me, and then when it got serious, you bailed. Maybe you were only after one thing and at the last moment, you couldn't do it.' As soon as the words came out, Tom vilely regretted it.

Beth took the last step to bring her up face to face with him. Her tears had stopped, her eyes chips of ice. 'I am no gold digging slut, Thomas O'Loughlin. And you bloody know it.'

'Beth, I'm—'

She stepped back, her voice low, calm and full of conviction. 'You need to leave NOW!' Turning away, Beth stopped, then turned back around to face Tom. 'If it wasn't for Chelsea and her offer to live with a complete stranger, and then her support through and after

Emily was born, who knows where Emily and I would have ended up. We had nowhere else to go. I couldn't come back. I wanted to call you and tell you about our daughter and how beautiful she was, but I knew I couldn't. I knew my position. I knew yours.'

Beth started to shake as she wrapped her arms around her body. She was naked underneath her thin dressing gown, her body still wet from forgetting to grab a towel before she hopped in the shower. She felt like she was standing in front of him, naked. Exposed and fearful. That her fight was drowning her, and she still had no life raft to save her.

'Why Beth?' Tom's voice shook as he tried to calm his temper and understand all she wasn't saying. 'Why couldn't you call and tell me? I would have come for you. I wanted you, Beth.'

'I *couldn't*. Don't you see? I couldn't,' she screamed back at him, her anger and hurt and frustration of it all over the last three years starting to take hold and roll out of her again. 'No matter what I did, someone was going to have to pay for our mistake ...' She corrected herself, '... *my* mistake.'

Tom frowned and sucked in a much-needed breath. 'What mistake, Beth? Our daughter?'

Beth shook her head, and the tears fell harder as she whispered, her throat throbbing. 'For falling in love with you. For loving you with all my heart.' Her legs grew weak, and she began to sway, her head spinning at all the emotions and stress of the past weeks.

Tom felt like he had been punched in the gut. She loved him. Still did. His heart tried to sing, but he didn't allow it to. Not yet. He took a step towards her, and she took another one back. This time her legs hit the lounge chair, and she fell back only to be caught and hauled into Tom's strong arms.

Tom gripped her upper arms tight. Looking down into her blue eyes, he hovered before gently kissing her. A feather weight before a deep burn within deepened the kiss. It stole her breath

339

and became an insatiable need. It was like there was a beast within him. He needed her, and he took all that he wanted and more. He needed to taste her and feel her in his arms to soothe his rollercoaster of emotions and confusion that were taking over his mind and body. Her warm and wet body were pressed to his, turning his anger from a moment ago to pure sexual desire for her. His hands roamed her body. He lifted her, her legs wrapping around his hips. His hands grabbed her face, holding her to his lips.

Staggering back onto the other lounge chair, he didn't let her go. He held his lips clamped to hers as the chair creaked under their weight when they landed hard. He just kept taking and taking, holding her lips to his own. Beth dug her nails into his shoulder as her need to breathe and catch her breath from him raised a panic within. He wasn't letting go. She dug harder, causing him to finally release his hands from her face, resting his forehead to hers as she tried to breathe. Her heart was racing, beating painfully hard against her ribs. Her eyes closed as tears welled again.

'Please let me go, Tom,' she whispered as her head spun with dizziness. 'Let *us* go. It's for the best.'

Tom kissed Beth's forehead and gently shook his head. One finger under her chin made her look at him. His eyes had softened and turned to liquid brown. 'I'm never letting you go. Either of you. No matter what, you're stuck with me.' The corners of his lips lifted as he tried to ease the situation and Beth's body from shaking.

Giving him a tight smile, she tried to get up, but he held her to him. His hand was on her thigh, lazily making tiny circles as he crept it higher.

'Don't.' Beth pushed at his hand, and her words irritated his temper again. 'Don't make this any harder than it already is.' She pushed away from him and stood.

Rubbing his hand over his face, he stood and watched her put the lounge chair between them. 'You're not leaving without me. I love you, Beth. I have loved you from the first moment I saw you on that bloody deck across the river. Surely you know that.' His simple declaration held her still. Her heart grabbed painfully.

'You can't, Tom.'

'I can't? Can't love you?' His eyebrows raised, and he tried to walk around the lounge chair to her. Beth moved around the old leather couch, so that it remained a barrier between them.

'Yes. You can't, or he will—' Beth stopped dead. Her eyes rounded. She had been so careful not to mention him. Tom jumped on it instantly and began to stalk her around the lounge chair.

'Who? And *what* will he do, Beth?'

Beth walked backwards towards the kitchen. She gave a quick glance to the laundry door, but it was too late. She heard the lounge chair creak as Tom bounded over it and was upon her before she could run. He stepped her back to the kitchen bench, his body gently pinning hers from her thighs to her stomach. His temper started to rise quickly. She could see it as his eyes turned darker and colder again.

'Who, Beth?' he demanded.

'It doesn't matter, Tom.'

'For God's sake, tell me who the hell it was and what the threat was.'

He wasn't going to let her go now until he found out. Was it worth it anymore? Was it worth trying to push him away when she now knew he loved her and she loved him? Was it worth running again and living through the pain of him not being with her and Emily?

Beth made her decision.

'Your father.'

Two simple words devastated and swamped Tom. He fought to stay conscious as the wave of her words crashed over him, dragging him down a very dark and almost death-like hole.

'What did he say?' It was a demand, not a question, stated through gritted teeth and held dangerously together within his body. Beth could feel Tom's total control locking every muscle in his body as he spoke.

'It doesn't mat—'

'Yes!' Tom quietened a little. 'Yes, it does. Now please, tell me everything.'

Shaking at the memory, and Tom's distant, cold, glazed-over eyes, Beth swallowed the lump in her throat and let the tears fall silently down her cheeks. Her mind replayed that horrible day, and what Mathew O'Loughlin had done to her. Taking a deep breath, and using Tom's body pressed up against her, to remain standing, Beth finally told Tom the truth.

'He said that if I didn't leave you heartbroken and leave town straight away, he would ensure my parents business would fail, and they would lose everything they had ever worked so hard to try and rebuild for themselves.' She felt Tom stiffen even more. 'He tried to give me an envelope of money, to pay me for helping you "sew your wild oats", but I refused and he got upset, stating that if I was to ever contact you or tell you what he said, he would make sure my parents would suffer.' She broke, the truth finally setting her free. Beth crumbled against Tom in a senseless babble of words about how sorry she was, how she couldn't let his father do that to them, how she needed to protect Emily, and how she never wanted to hurt him or anyone. Tom held her and let her cry as he stared blindly out of her mother's kitchen window White-hot anger took over him along with a deadly calmness he had never felt before. His jaw locked and he knew what he had to do.

'Did he ever force you in any other way?' Vileness filled his mouth as the words came out. He had to know the full extent of his father's threats to Beth and how he forced such fear into her.

'It was *implied*.' She barely whispered as the memory of Mathew touching her made her feel sick.

Tom swore under his breath as he held Beth to him, his thinly stretched control over his temper only holding together because she was in his arms. She was his and he was hers. Now, knowing his next step, Tom took another steadying breath and breathed her in.

Holding Beth's head between his hands, he made her look at him. Made her stare into his eyes. 'Pack your and Emily's things in your car and once Emily is given the all-clear from the doctor, you're to go to my ... sorry, *our* home and stay there. You are not to leave this town and run.' Tom searched Beth's eyes, willing her to do as he asked. 'Promise me you won't run.' He kissed her on the nose then on the lips, until she melted against him.

'He will follow through with his threats and ruin my mum's business if I do, Tom. I can't do what you're asking.' She was shaking uncontrollably again with fear of his own father.

'Yes, you can. He could try to follow through with his threats, but he wouldn't succeed in ruining your mum's business. He's not as powerful as he thinks. And besides, we have something he doesn't want to come out.'

'What's that?' Beth's eyes filled with hope that maybe they did have a future together.

'The truth.' His smirk was one of triumph and cunningness, like he finally had succeeded in a war that no one thought he could win.

Beth couldn't believe what she was hearing.

'Don't you hate me for keeping Emily a secret from you?' It was one question she had not wanted to ask. To know that he could hate her even a little bit would have broken her heart that was now finally ready to love him openly and fully. She didn't want hatred or distrust between them now that she had told him everything. She wanted their future to be happy and filled with honesty and trust.

'I could never hate you, Beth. I tried to on the way over here after I pieced it together about Emily, but I couldn't. I love you too much for that. Besides ...' He kissed her quickly, '... I am more in love with you now that I know the truth than I thought possible. You did everything because you loved me. I could never hate you for that.' She smiled and hugged him.

'Don't run, Beth. Please? Promise me you won't run.' He was willing her to do as he asked. She nodded.

'I will be back as soon as I can, but I have to sort this out once and for all.' Tom stepped away and kissed Beth's hand before leaving her standing there in her mother's kitchen, a smile on her face and her body tingling with the excitement of knowing that Tom was hers and she was his.

Chapter 19

The dirt road Tom had driven along so many times in his life, raced beneath his tyres. The hum of the treads and the wind blowing in his window went unnoticed as finally the full story of that summer fell into place like a giant missing puzzle piece in his mind.

He let the memories roll and fit into place—Megan's and the girls' treatment of Beth had been nastier than usual, and his father's behaviour at Megan's and Jeff's low-key engagement party was even more sexually aggressive than his father usually was. And then there was Jeff's attack. His father's then kindness to Beth the day of the summer party had always been something that had not fully sat with him. He had tried to tell himself his father had finally accepted his feelings for Beth for what they were and not some summertime fling. He had known that something had occurred there, but his father had adamantly denied it to his face, telling him repeatedly that Beth had just been unwell. He had even told Tom he had offered Beth a place to stay while she had studied. How she could have used one of their apartments in the city, but had turned it down. Tom had believed it all.

As his temper simmered, Tom remembered it all and as he did, he realised his father had manipulated the whole thing so he and Beth could never be together. To his father, Beth was a real threat for his plans for Tom and the family's properties and fortune. She was a threat to the very image his father had so carefully constructed over the years to show everyone they were the perfect happy family and a constant good in the area in which they had farms. Image was everything to his father—for his political career—and Tom and Beth's relationship didn't suit the look of what Mathew had manufactured. Beth's biggest threat against Mathew, wasn't her love for Tom; it was that she couldn't be trusted to follow his father's rules.

She had encouraged Tom to follow his dreams of working with horses to help rehabilitate people who had suffered unthinkable trauma and PTS, even to train some for film and TV if he so desired. Beth was a threat to Mathew O'Loughlin's future, and she had needed to be removed. And as cunning as his father truly was, Mathew had hit Beth right where it hurt the most. Her weakest spot. Her parents.

She chose them over her own happiness and dreams. Over him and even their daughter to an extent. Beth had sacrificed everything to keep her parents safe. Anger bubbled again, as Tom now understood more. Even after Drake had dragged him back from the city, his father had played the clueless card.

Mathew O'Loughlin had been pissed that Michael and Drake had talked Tom into buying Reggie's and doing his own thing with his horses. But had still played the game so skilfully that until Beth had come back into town, Tom was none the wiser, even blaming himself for driving her away.

His father had let Tom buy Reggie's. He never gave him the money but had signed the papers to release Tom's grandfather's inheritance money earlier so that Tom could buy it outright and have the money to establish it and work it correctly. After all, it was just another purchase of land and equity to the O'Loughlin family fortune. A bitter laugh tore through him as that little bit of understanding now became clear in his mind. Mathew was playing a very skilled game.

Tom still worked for his father on the properties when needed. He did the planting and harvesting, even trying to rebuild a relationship with his father after his father played to his son's heartbreak over Beth. But now Tom understood—he was still under his father's control. But not anymore. Mathew O'Loughlin was about to find out that those days were over. Tom was now his own man.

Driving past the house and following the road to the left, Tom continued down the dirt road. At this time of the morning, and with this heat, his father would be giving his orders to refuel and prepare for an early start to the days heading. The paddocks moved like waves on the ocean as he sped past, leaving dust hanging in the air.

Others would be there, but he didn't care. He didn't care who was going to bear witness to what was about to happen. He never cared what people thought anyway. The green of the large equipment came into view and grew larger as he continued to travel the road. Slowing only to turn into the paddock, he bumped along and pulled up alongside his father's ute.

Not waiting for the dust to settle, Tom found Mathew standing in the shade of one of the headers, a group of men making a semi-circle around him to hear their instructions for the day. They all turned as Tom approached. It must have been the look in his eyes and his stride that told them to part as they did.

Keeping his walk strong and direct as he neared his confused father, he grabbed him by the collar as adrenaline and pure hatred, fuelled with red-hot anger, pumped through his body. Tom lifted the man he had called a father since birth, a few inches off the ground and slammed him into the tractor tyre. Fear flashed through Mathew's eyes at the look on his son's face and his sheer strength to pick him up and move him with such force, making it look easy.

The group of men standing around, watched in shock as the situation unfolded in front of them. They all stood in place as their minds reeled at what was happening before their very eyes.

Mick and Johnny stepped in and grabbed Tom's shoulders to pull him away from his father. 'Back the hell off, boys! If you want to continue to work here, step back and let me and the old man sort it out.' His voice was clear and firm. It was one of a leader who knew that his word would be followed. He had spent too much time with these boys to know they had more respect for him then they did their boss, because one day, *he* would be their boss, and if they wanted to stay employed here, they would back off.

Not once did Tom's eyes waver from Mathew's as he held his father's gaze and watched as his temper and nostrils flared at the humiliation his son was inflicting on him, in front of his own employees. Those beneath the mighty Mathew O'Loughlin.

Tom lowered his voice so only his father could hear, once the boys had stepped back. They didn't step back far enough that they couldn't step in if they needed to back Tom, but enough so they could let this long overdue power struggle finally sort itself out. All the men had borne witness to Mathew's degradation of Tom in front of them. Of his put downs and lectures. They had seen how Mathew drove his son harder than anyone else, expecting him to work like three men on little to no sleep during harvest and planting and then be on show whenever it was time to roll out the perfect family.

They had watched Tom grin and bear it, and they had hoped that one day he would stand his ground. Today was that day. They had never seen him look so angry. His eyes were dark and cold and his strength was unbelievable as he seemed to easily hold his father pinned to the header tyre.

'I know what you did to scare Beth off, and how you kept us apart.' Tom hissed as he spoke. 'If you know what's good for you, you will stay the hell away from her or I might make the mistake of letting it be known to a few of your influential friends in politics, or a few of my friends in the media, looking to advance their careers with such a story about a very wealthy politician bullying and threating the very people he has vowed to represent.'

Tom raised his eyebrows at his father. 'Would make for an excellent story. What do you think, *Dad?*'

Mathew, still pinned to the tyre, sneered, 'I think you're just like me, *Son*. You're not beyond blackmailing me to get what you want.'

'I learned from the best, I guess, but there is one difference.'

'What's that?' Mathew's rasped voice gave Tom pause. Tom's strength began to waver. To keep him there, he was pushing on his father's throat.

Moving closer to whisper in his ear, Tom answered, 'I don't care what people think. But you do!' Tom pulled back to let his father know he spoke the truth. To let him see he wasn't scared of the 'mighty and powerful' Mathew O'Loughlin. When his father didn't say anything, Tom let him go and he dropped heavily to the ground, onto his arse in the dirt of the paddock.

Leaning back against the tyre, Mathew held a hand to his throat as he gasped for breath and struggled to his feet.

'Leave Beth, her mum and that business alone. Got it?'

'Whatever you say, Tommy.' Mathew's eyes narrowed into slits as he spat venom at Tom. Taking a step towards him, standing at his full height, he tried to intimidate his son. Ignoring him, Tom turned to walk away.

'She doesn't love you, you know? She needs a real man to satisfy her. Not you.'

The sound of Mathew O'Loughlin's jaw and Tom's fist connecting echoed around the men with a sickening crack. Mathew stumbled backwards and hit the header's tyre before slumping back to the ground. Tom stood over him, seething, his temper finally finding an outlet.

'You bastard!' he roared at his father, who looked dazed. Mathew looked up at his son and tested the side of his mouth with the back of his hand.

'Is that a *soft* point, Tom?' He spat out blood and sneered up at Tom. It was then that Tom seen the mask slip from his father's eyes. Mathew was scared of him. He was scared of his own son, and was now fully aware of the man that his boy had become. Tom was everything he couldn't be.

Staring at him for a second longer than he wanted, Tom turned and walked back to his ute. Stopping before he climbed in, he looked back at his father, still lying the ground.

'I'm done with this shit. As far as I'm concerned, we are no longer family. I will never forgive you for stealing the first years of my daughter's life from me. You can go and rot in hell as far as I'm concerned.' With that stated, Tom climbed back into his ute and tore off back to his girls.

The wheat rows passed quickly as the ute kicked up dust back down the dirt road towards the main road. Tom was going back to Beth and his daughter. He was a father. It was still strange to think, and he had missed so much already. He had wanted to hate Beth for her betrayal, but he couldn't. It was not her fault. It was because he had known her so well that he couldn't hate her. Deep down, he had known from the day she ran away that something had happened and scared her. He had thought of a million reasons — of all his actions, of all the people they had spoken to that afternoon — but the real knowledge had been there deep inside of him. That it had been something his father had done. But even his darkest thoughts about his father were nowhere near the truth. Tom hadn't wanted to see it, he guessed. He knew his father was a horrible person. He had seen what that man was capable of. What he hadn't realised though, was that his father could do what he had done — to him. His only son. His own flesh and blood.

Now he was free. He would always be an O'Loughlin, but under his own rules, able to live his life as he saw fit with Beth by his side.

Swinging out onto the bitumen road, Tom noticed the blood on his hand. He must have cut his already swollen and broken knuckles open on his father's tooth when he had sent him sprawling to the ground. It had felt so good to watch his head reel back and see the 'mighty' Mathew O'Loughlin's eyes roll back into his head. And the level from which he now needed to pick himself up from in front of his men, was payback. Word would get out from the boys about their confrontation, but Tom would bet his life that the boys would not say a word about the reason it had happened. They would respect Tom and Beth but give the glorious details about Mathew getting his lights punched out.

Blood trickled down Tom's wrist and he wiped it on his jeans. But it flowed more. Reaching over and opening the glove box, he found an old rag and pulled it out.

A little black box fell to the floor. For a moment, Tom looked at it before quickly grabbing it, swerving as he did. It was the promise ring he had bought for Beth three years ago. He had wanted to surprise her with his plans after his father's summertime party, but she had become sick. Her reason now made his stomach churn with regret for not protecting her more. He had planned to give her the ring and tell her he had decided to leave with her when she left for the city.

He had been in contact with the charity that had helped him give Splatter to Kaylee and had decided to follow his heart and start to train horses to help people with PTSD—mainly children. He had already started to make plans and even talked with his father about it.

The thought hit home harder and winded him. His father knew of his plans and thought Beth was behind them. Rubbing an agitated hand over his face at the stupidity of his actions, he growled out loud into the passing wind. Slipping the ring into his shirt pocket and wiping the back of his hand on the rag, Tom smiled to himself and focused on the road ahead, which now led to Beth.

The blur from the right—Tom didn't see it, until it was too late …

Their bags were packed. Excitement and nerves fluttered in Beth's stomach. Emily's things were already in the car as Beth took her own clothes off the clothesline.

A rush of nausea and heat swept through her so quickly, she suddenly felt dizzy, and her world spun in a sickening rotation. Sitting on the grass, she leaned back against the clothesline pole. Thoughts about the emotions over the last couple of days were finally catching up with her. She took some steadying breaths.

Beth had fought for so long to keep everyone safe, and now that the truth had come out and Tom had stood by her and understood, her emotions seemed to have suddenly let go. He had declared his love for her, and she had told him she had always loved him. Now they were going home to his place as a family. Emily would get to know, and have, her father, just like Beth always wanted.

Beth would have Tom and not have to hide her love for him. A happiness she had never felt bubbled deep inside her as she thought about him. He would have spoken to his father by now. There would have been yelling and anger but seeing the man standing in front of her this morning, she knew that Mathew O'Loughlin now knew where his relationship with her, Emily and Tom now stood. Beth knew, with unwavering trust, that Tom, as much as he possibly could, would protect them both from the scandal this would all bring. But once word got out about Emily and why Beth had run, it would be the hottest gossip around town—and the area—for the next few years.

It didn't matter. She didn't care what anyone said anymore. They would be together, and nothing would pull them apart. Looking at her watch, Beth carefully stood and tested her balance. Grabbing the last of her clothes, her dizziness was gone, but her hands still shook. Taking a few steadying, deep, calming breaths, telling herself she had nothing to worry about, Beth smiled to herself at the true happiness she felt. A happiness that filled her mind, body and soul. But she needed breakfast before she headed back to the hospital, or she may faint and risk not being at Tom's when he returned.

The knock on the door sounded as Beth drained the last of her coffee from her cup. She frowned and shook her head at his antics of now knocking on her parents' front door. Tom was such a regular to her parents' home, that he usually just entered without knocking. That he did now, made her laugh as she walked through the loungeroom and looked out the screen door. 'Tom. Why would you−?'

Michael stood on the other side of the aluminium-screened frame. He was dressed in his police uniform, his hat in his hands. He wiped his jaw roughly when he saw Beth, then took a deep breath. Opening the door for her, he stepped to the side to allow her to slowly exit out onto the verandah. Braydon stood at the bottom of the steps, fidgeting with his cap in his hands as he made eye contact with her. She saw he had watery eyes.

Beth's heart stopped and her legs began to shake. They looked at her as the reality of them being there began to dawn on her. Putting her fist in her mouth, she shook her head and tried not to scream. Michael grabbed her hand and wrapped his other arm around her shoulders, leading her to the day bed.

'Beth, just sit. He's alive.' Michael squatted down in front of her as Braydon moved to sit on the day bed beside her.

'Wh−. What happened? His father?' Beth looked directly into Michael's eyes, looking for any sign he might not be telling her the truth. That Tom's father had done something to his son out of anger.

Michael shook his head with a little frown. 'No. He hit a roo and rolled his ute.'

Beth sucked in a breath and started to cry. This was not happening. 'No, NO, NO, NO, NO!!' she repeated as her hands shook. Tears flowed.

'Listen to me.' It was Braydon who was speaking, but her eyes remained locked onto Michael's as she began to rock back and forth, hunched over and in pain with the shock. 'He was talking and asking for you when I found him. The ute's a write off, but I got him out. He's been flown out already by the O'Loughlin plane. Mathew is with him along with the paramedics.'

'How bad is he?' Beth's voice was shaking as she tried to make herself breathe and focus on what they were telling her.

'It looks like a dislocated shoulder and some minor concussion. He was complaining about abdominal pain and a severe headache, so his father insisted on him being flown out immediately.' Michael tried to smile to reassure her, but her tears continued to fall, a wave of panic washing over her.

'I need to get to him.' She tried to stand but a wave of nausea swept over her and she fell back against the day bed.

'Whoa, whoa, whoa. Just take it easy for a moment. Where's Emily?' Michael asked softly.

'In the hospital. My mum is with her.'

Both Michael and Braydon's eyes widened as they both asked at the same time, 'Why? What happened?'

'She got really sick last night, and they admitted her. I was about to go back there now ... but—' How was she to go to Tom *and* be with Emily? 'I have to get to Tom. I need to stay with Emily.' She looked between the both of them. What was she to do? Confused and dazed, she started to breathe rapidly. Shock was taking over.

'I will go and speak with your mum about what has happened and see if Emily can be discharged. I'm sure your mum won't mind driving Emily to you and Tom.' Michael stood and helped Beth stand, his arm remaining around her waist until he was sure she was able to stand by herself. Braydon stood also.

'Tom told me that I had to come and stay with you until he got back. I have to help you and Emily move out to his place.'

Braydon's smile widened. 'He is a very proud dad.' He bumped her shoulder in a playful way. 'You kept that one a good secret from us all. Never seen Tommy light up as much as he did when he told us about little miss Emily being his.'

Both Braydon and Michael's smiles were wide and happy for her and Tom. It was meant to help her relax and not worry as much, but she did. However, having them both here for her and Tom, meant more than she could express.

'Always knew you pair would get it sorted. You're the real romantic and love thing you girls all fuss about.' Beth smiled at Braydon through her tears, his big, beefy arm wrapping around her shoulders. He hugged her tightly, even surprising her with a kiss to the top of her head. 'I will drive you down to him, so you pair of love birds can be together. What do you need?'

Michael left to see Beth's mum, and Braydon and Beth left for the long, four-hour drive to the hospital to which Tom had been flown.

The drive was mentally and emotionally painful. Beth's mind would not stop racing with negative thoughts of Tom's condition being worse than Michael and Braydon had said. She had continuously asked Braydon whether he had told her the truth about Tom's injuries. He would just smile and nod his head, telling her that there was no way Tom would let anything bad happen to himself now he had her and Emily to look after. It had made Beth smile, but it wasn't until she saw Tom in the hospital and had flung herself into his arms, kissing him hard and checking for herself that he was okay, that she felt the panic and sickness start to leave her body a little.

Tom had groaned in pain with her accidental force, but he was very grateful to be holding her. His head felt like it was splitting in half, and his shoulder had been popped back into its socket and was slung up tightly to his chest.

The mind blur from the green whistle gas had passed as well as the illness that came from it. After an ultrasound and x-rays,

Tom was given the all-clear from the doctors to go home the following day and rest for a few weeks while his shoulder, bruised ribs and other injuries healed. He was going to be stiff and sore for days, thanks to the bloody big buck roo.

After seeing the damage to the ute as he was lifted into the plane, even he had to admit that he was very lucky to escape with only the injuries he had sustained, and nothing more serious. He was going to be able to go home. Home with Beth and his daughter. Home with his own little family and the girl who had stolen his heart.

With a look over Beth's shoulder, and a nod to Braydon, who took the hint and quietly left the room—unnoticed by Beth, who was still carefully cuddling into Tom's most undamaged side—Tom kissed her head and held her until his own emotions were settled enough to speak. If he had hit the roo any differently, he may never have been able to hold her like this again.

'Beth?' She sat up and wiped her tears from her face with her shaking hand.

Tom sat up, hiding the pain in was in, and reached around Beth with a grunt, to the little table near the side of the bed. He fumbled around in a little plastic bag, his face screwing up with the pain he could no longer hide as he did so.

'Here, let me.'

'No. You just wait there.' Tom's hand engulfed the little box as he spoke. 'It's not how I wanted this to be—and definitely not with this. I wanted to take you out to a little deck I have built for you at home, just like my grandfather did at Silverleigh, and after the sun had set, I wanted to take you into my arms and ask you—and I promise I will do it more formally—but I want to leave here knowing that you will be mine forever.' He sat up straighter, ignoring all the pain the movement caused him, and held out the little box for her.

Beth's eyes widened and filled with tears. She hesitated and didn't touch it as she looked into his eyes. They were the same eyes that had met hers across the river so long ago and had changed her life forever. They were the same eyes that made her heart skip beats and race with passion and need whenever he was around. And they were the same eyes she wanted to spend the rest of her life looking into.

'Elizabeth Grace Kennedy ...' Tom's hoarsely whispered words filled her with happy tears, '... from the moment I looked across that river and saw your smile, heard your voice and watched you laugh, I knew my world would never be the same again. Everything about you makes my heart beat faster. And you drive me to be a better man each day. I never want to live a day without you by my side or know that I have hurt you in any way. My life is yours. From this day forward, I will forever be yours. You're the one I want to spend the rest of my life with. Will you marry me?' Tom's voice was strong but raspy, full of emotion and conviction of this moment and the potential promise of what lay ahead. Beth smiled and flung herself into him. He cried out in pain as his arm wrapped around her, and they both laughed though their tears. His of pain and hers of joy.

'So, will you?'

'Yes. Yes, of course I will.' Beth planted a kiss on Tom and pulled back to look into his eyes. They looked back at hers. Slowly, she leaned in and kissed him again, this time stirring the embers of their desire and enduring love for one another. Beth was Tom's, and Tom was Beth's.

Loved Book 2? Why not check out book 1

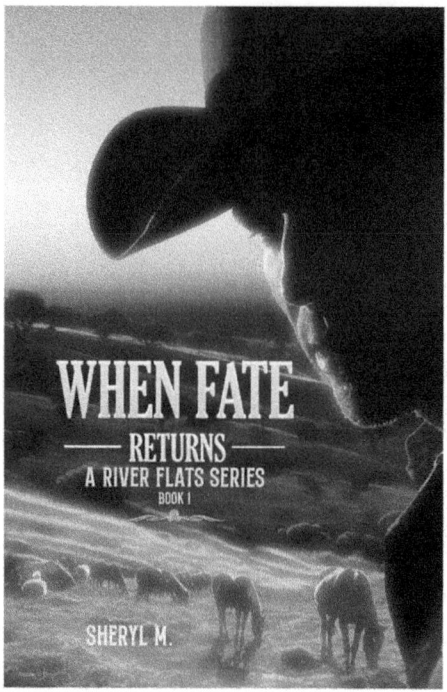

Kathryn's heart shattered when Drake, th
of her life, vanished without a word, and
years later, he stood before her under
dazzling lights of the big city.
Drake loved Kathryn with all his heart, bι
he dare reconnect with the woman he
forced to leave all those years ago, prayir
his haunting past wouldn't resurface to d
their fragile reunion?

In her darkest hour, Kathryn must place
trust in the man who once abandoned he
hope their tangled pasts don't catch up
them. From the bustling cityscape to t
tranquil Australian countryside, Drake
Kathryn embark on an emotional rollercc
filled with tears, laughter, and electrify
suspense.

Will they summon the courage to risk ever
and trust each other again, battling their s
passion and relentless demons? Or will
shadows of the past tear them apart for
Sheryl M masterfully weaves a tale of lι
betrayal and redemption that will keep
riveted until the very last page.

Order your copy today www.sherylm-author.com